Praise for

IF YOU'LL HAVE ME

"I loved everything about *If You'll Have Me*—the warmth, the charm, the Austen-esque romance and circumstance. It was a joy to read."

—AMY HARMON,
New York Times best-selling author

"There are few books that secure a coveted spot on my keeper shelf—very few. *If You'll Have Me* has earned one of those spots. I smirked at the snappy dialogue, swooned at the tender love story, and raged at the horrendous Lord Murphy. The pacing never falters, the characters leap off the page, and the setting sparkles with authenticity. This is the kind of story you finish with a smile . . . and then immediately long to read again. I can only hope there will be a sequel!"

—MICHELLE GRIEP,
Christy Award–winning author
of *Of Silver and Secrets*

"Delightfully funny and charmingly romantic, Esther Hatch is a fantastic voice in the historical genre. An author not to be missed!"

—JOANNA BARKER,
author of *A Love Most Daring*

If You'll Have Me

OTHER BOOKS
BY ESTHER HATCH

A Proper Scandal

A Proper Charade

A Proper Scoundrel

A Proper Façade

The Roses of Feldstone

All Hearts Come Home for Christmas

The Holly and the Ivy

PROPER ROMANCE

IF YOU'LL HAVE ME

ESTHER HATCH

SHADOW
MOUNTAIN
PUBLISHING

Visit us at ShadowMountain.com

Library of Congress Cataloging-in-Publication Data

Names: Hatch, Esther author

Title: If you'll have me / Esther Hatch.

Description: [Salt Lake City] : Shadow Mountain Publishing, 2026. | Series: Proper romance | Summary: "Anna Atwood returns to Breckenridge hoping to escape her past and the persistent suitor Mr. Green. When she reunites with David Tate, now a successful man, their renewed friendship leads to an unexpected proposal. Bound by necessity, their marriage becomes a battleground of passion and duty as they face the threats of Mr. Green and Breckenridge's overseer Lord Murphy, risking everything to protect their newfound love"—Provided by publisher.

Identifiers: LCCN 2025026950 (print) | LCCN 2025026951 (ebook) | ISBN 9781639934560 trade paperback | ISBN 9781649334756 ebook

Subjects: BISAC: FICTION / Romance / Historical / Regency | FICTION / Romance / Clean & Wholesome | LCGFT: Romance fiction | Historical fiction | Fiction | Novels

Classification: LCC PS3608.A86157 I3 2026 (print) | LCC PS3608.A86157 (ebook) | DDC 813/.6—dc23/eng/20250609

LC record available at https://lccn.loc.gov/2025026950

LC ebook record available at https://lccn.loc.gov/2025026951

Printed in the United States of America

Publishers Printing

10 9 8 7 6 5 4 3 2 1

To Samantha Millburn, Amy Parker, and Ashley Gebert.

Thank you, not only for editing and marketing my books but for believing in them as well.

"What we call our despair is often
only the painful eagerness of unfed hope."

—George Eliot, *Middlemarch*

Chapter 1

"If my father has taught me anything, it is this: When you are surrounded by people who love you, you never suffer alone."
—David Tate, 1846, Age 19

It wasn't every day I found myself alone, dangling precariously from a tree and feeling a thousand times a fool. The fool part had become a regular occurrence, unfortunately, but the tree? I hadn't climbed one since I was much younger, and suddenly, it became very clear why. I wasn't prepared for the drop it would take to get me back onto solid ground. I tightened my grip on the branch above me and glanced down around my swaying skirts to the path below. This limb couldn't have been this high eight and a half years ago, for I'd dropped from it dozens of times when I was seventeen. Exactly how many inches had this tree grown in the years I'd been away?

More than I had, that was for certain.

I gritted my teeth and threw my weight, willing my hands with all my might to slide forward and catch a better hold on the thick branch above my head.

Why in the world had I decided I needed to relive my youth?

Alone.

Far enough away from Mr. Preston's cottage that Mama would never hear me, even if I yelled.

The wool of my gloves snagged on the rough bark of the limb above me, but my hands weren't so fortunate and started to slip out of them.

When Mama and I arrived the day before, I'd had high hopes that Breckenridge would afford us the same safety and comfort it had when Papa had been alive, but things hadn't turned out that way at all. Papa's dear friends the Prestons were kind but couldn't help us as much as I'd hoped, and when I'd tried to visit my good friends the Mortensens, I'd found their home empty and so very changed on the outside that I wasn't even certain they lived there anymore.

If I broke my leg falling from this tree, we would not only soon have no place to live, but I would also no longer be able to look for work. All of Mama's fears about coming here would come true. We would be left destitute and alone.

I let out a puff of air in frustration. If I did break my leg and it set oddly, would Mr. Green give up on marrying me? Perhaps we could return to Silverfork. A broken leg would be a small price to pay to rid myself of Mr. Green's controlling ways.

My arms were starting to shake, and my fingers started slipping out of my gloves. I swung my feet up and used the momentum to lift my hands, catching the limb in a better hold once again, but my new handhold would last only so long. Whether I wanted to make the leap or not, I was going to crash to the ground. I closed my eyes and took a deep breath. It wasn't that far. Only six or seven feet. I'd survive. I might not even break anything.

A distinct crunch sounded below me, somewhere to the left. I tightened my grip once more and carefully opened one eye. Through the late-morning fog, a gentleman, with a spring in his step, too young and spry to be Mr. Preston, walked along the path leading directly to me.

I was about to have a witness to my foolishness. As much as I'd hoped for help earlier, suddenly, it was the last thing I wanted now that it was possible. What kind of twenty-five-year-old woman got stuck in trees? I held my breath. I could hold on a few more moments, couldn't I? Breaking a leg was one thing, but breaking it in front of a gentleman?

Mortifying.

I closed my eyes, praying he would pass me by without noticing and I would be able to fall gracefully to the ground after he left.

The steady crunching stopped, and I grimaced and cracked open my eyes.

He was at least ten feet from me, wearing a wool coat with a fur-lined collar, and there was no doubt he'd seen me. Our eyes met. His were a brilliant blue, made clear by how widely they stared in my direction. He was young. Younger than I'd first thought. A man for certain but only recently. The way he eyed me as if I were a strange woodland creature probably made him look younger than his true age.

He tipped his head to one side. "Are you real?" he asked with a strange sort of wonder in his voice.

I shook my head. "No," I replied. "I'm not. Please go about your business."

His mouth closed, and his fists went to each hip. An amazing smile blossomed on his lips, lighting up his whole face. The shock of it made me almost lose my grip again. If I'd been on the cusp of adulthood like he was instead of well past it and world-weary, I would have been flustered by his good looks and charming smile.

He narrowed one of his brilliant eyes at me, and something about the deep half-moons that formed strong lines on either side of his mouth and the way the skin under his eyes lifted as he smiled seemed almost familiar.

"You *are* real," he breathed.

My arms were shaking badly enough for his eyes to catch the motion, and if I lost another inch of branch, I'd be dropping to the ground. "Perhaps you could help?" My voice came out as an undignified squeak.

His look of disbelief was instantly replaced by action. He threw off his top hat, revealing thick dark hair that contrasted sharply against his pale skin and eyes. He left it disregarded on the ground behind him as he ran in my direction. In only a few steps he would be directly under me. I looked down at my skirts, and a sickening tightness coiled in my stomach. Under my overcoat, I wore a second woolen coat, my muslin gown, and several petticoats to keep warm. Multiple layers but perhaps not enough to allow a strikingly good-looking young man to stand directly beneath me without getting a view of my drawers.

"Stop." The word sputtered from my mouth. "Don't come any closer."

He stumbled as he immediately halted and looked up, one corner of his mouth lifted and his eyebrows furrowed. He must be thinking he'd stumbled upon a madwoman. I hated to be particular about the kind of fortuitous help I'd been granted, but would it have been too much to ask for the man to be at least a little less handsome? Or old? Perhaps blind? An old, blind man would have been the perfect person to catch me. But no, I was graced with a man, perhaps twenty, who would cause a stir if he entered a ballroom.

His light eyes sparkled, and he lifted one dark eyebrow in a way that again seemed to spark a memory. "I can't help you from here."

"Wonderful." I tried to smile, but it probably came out more like a grimace. "I've changed my mind. I don't need your help. It isn't far, just a few feet."

"It is more than a few feet. Your toes wouldn't reach my head."

"I do this all the time." The shaking in my arms was a direct contradiction to my words. Every muscle in my fingers begged for relief.

He crossed his arms over his chest. "I highly doubt that, Anna. Or I would have found you here sooner."

My eyes flew to his face again. He knew my name? Who was he? Not a Preston—Mrs. and Mr. Preston's children were all several years my senior. And none of the Mortensen boys could be this well dressed. I'd spent my summer with poor tenants and members of the Preston family. Who else would even remember me? Perhaps someone I'd met at church a time or two, but if that were the case, I had no recollection of him. "How do you know me?"

"Never mind that," he said, walking toward me once again. "I'm going to catch you."

His legs made short work of the few feet left between us.

I sucked in a sharp breath of air. "Just don't look up!"

"Don't look up?" he repeated and then stopped his forward progress for a moment. "How am I going to catch you if I don't look up?"

"If you must look up, close your eyes, at least."

He chuckled, and the deep way it resonated in his throat had me questioning my earlier assessment of his age. A man of twenty didn't sound like that, did they? "Close my eyes?" he asked, incredulity clearly written on his face.

Was this man going to stand there and repeat every word I said? I might not be so fortunate as to have stumbled upon a blind man, but perhaps he had trouble with his memory. He could help me, go on his way, and forget I'd ever been foolish enough to climb this tree.

Of course, the fact that he somehow recognized me from my summer of living in the Prestons' cottage over eight years ago dashed the hope that his brain might be addled. His memory was better than mine.

My right hand finally slipped, and I fell from the tree with a scream.

He jumped forward to catch me, and without his feet steady beneath him, we both tumbled to the ground.

We landed in a flurry of skirts and muffled curses, made mostly by me, before the world settled and became suddenly quiet. I was facedown and definitely resting on top of someone. I kept my eyes closed tightly as I tested my lungs, making certain I could still breathe. Then I tried moving my fingers and toes. They all worked, and my only pain was my sore hands.

A deep rumble under my chest was the first reminder of whom exactly I had to thank for my safe, if not gracious, landing.

The rumble turned into a laugh, and I opened my eyes to find myself face-to-face with my rescuer, his back on the ground. His eyes shined with mirth, and his broad grin didn't even try to contain his merriment. His dark hair was disheveled, but it did nothing to diminish his appearance; if anything, it enhanced it. He closed his eyes and took a deep breath, the action of it reminding me of our indelicate situation. I hurriedly rolled off his chest and sat up, but he stayed there, lying on the ground with his arms splayed out.

Laughing.

"Thank you," I managed to squeak out.

More laughing.

"I'll be more careful from now on."

This made him laugh even harder, and he brought a hand to his eye to wipe away a tear. He sat up in a graceful movement and lifted one knee so he could wrap his arms around it. "Welcome back to Breckenridge. It is uncommonly good to see you again."

A strange feeling bubbled into my chest at his words—feelings directly associated with being memorable to a very handsome young gentleman and the way his eyes found mine, as if we had a long history together. Why couldn't I place him? His cheekbones were high, and his form lithe and wiry but strong. And his eyes? Surely I'd seen them before. He raised one eyebrow and quirked his head to the side. He was expressing questions with his face, and somehow, I could hear them. And just like that, I knew exactly who he was. I'd been trying to picture a man, but when I'd left eight years ago, he'd still been a child.

I pointed at him. "You're that boy, David!"

At the sound of me calling him a boy, he threw his chest back, and with the same athletic movement from before, he swept onto his feet. The last time I'd been here, I'd been at least three or four inches taller than he, but just like the tree I'd fallen from, the pace of his growth had outmatched my own.

I had to look up to meet his eyes—not far, I was above average in height, and he was under average for a man, but still, it was a strange thing to have our positions so drastically altered.

"No one has called me a boy for at least four years."

Memories came rushing back. How old had he been? I might have guessed twelve. He'd been a slight fellow with stick-like arms, but the man in front of me had to be older than twenty if he hadn't been called a boy for over four years. My chest warmed at the thought of how well he'd turned out. It was good to know that for some, life improved with time. Everything I saw in him now seemed to point to the fact that his path had made a turn for the better. His clothing, his health, the way he so readily laughed now. I smiled. Seeing him grown into this man of distinction left me feeling lighter than I had for a long time.

One very strong memory of him came rushing back. I pointed at him again. This was becoming a very bad habit. "You proposed to me!" I sputtered out. He grimaced and ran a hand through his thick hair and then rested it at the back of his neck. "You proposed to me the night before I left."

He shrugged his shoulders and turned away from me slightly.

I laughed and brushed off my dress. "What would have possessed a twelve-year-old boy to do that? Was it a dare?"

He turned around sharply, and I could imagine that gangly boy better now. He'd been so shy. He had spent days lurking around me as I'd delivered baskets before I was able to draw him in with interesting rocks and some foolish games we could play while we walked. Even when he had proposed, he'd had to do it twice because I hadn't heard him the first time.

"I was nearly fifteen." He said, straightening his back as though the addition of a few years would have made his proposal any less absurd.

"So you were fourteen?" I sighed in mock relief. "That's infinitely better than twelve." I hoped he noticed my sarcasm. I was fairly certain he did. Even when we were younger, once he started talking, we'd had no problems understanding each other.

He shrugged. "I just wanted to be the first one to do it. Of course I knew you wouldn't accept."

"Still . . ." I sneaked another glance at him. The last eight years had been very kind to David. "It was rather awkward, wasn't it?"

"Trust me." He coughed out a laugh. I'd heard him laugh more in one afternoon than I had for weeks when I'd first met him. It was like that boy had been some dirty, forgotten egg everyone had given up on hatching, but when it had, he'd emerged as a mighty falcon. "It was much more awkward for me than it was for you."

"I can imagine—I had to turn you down." Without discussing it, we both headed in the direction of the cottage, our feet moving in unison, like two people who walked together every day. David had known where I lived, but I had never figured out exactly where he'd come from. He used to show up at random times but often enough that I'd grown to expect him.

We walked several feet in silence, and I was certain he must be reliving those moments of our summer the same as I was. But I wouldn't look like a falcon to him. Nothing about me had flourished in the past eight years.

He kicked a stone along the path in front of us, and the motion solidified the boy David and this man into one in my mind. When he turned to look at me, I should have been flustered to be caught staring at him, but this was David. We'd spent hours together that summer and often in comfortable silence. I couldn't help but smile at him. He was so changed, clean-cut and grown, and, yet, somehow the same.

He placed both hands behind his back, but instead of returning my smile, he raised an eyebrow. "So, was I?" he asked.

I blinked. "Were you what?"

"The first man who—"

I cleared my throat loudly. He definitely hadn't been a man. My grin broadened, and I narrowed one eye to question his wording. He sighed and gave me that expressive half grin that told me he understood my unspoken protest. "The first *person* to ask you to marry him?"

I laughed softly. "Yes, yes you were. Thank you. I believe I may not have told you at the time, but it was quite flattering."

He nodded and then got quiet. "And was I the last?"

I thought of Mr. Green, and my stomach twisted. "No." I shook my head. "You were not."

"Ah." He nodded again, and his lips made a hard line. He stopped suddenly, and I turned toward him. With an apologetic look, he lifted a finger for me to wait. "Pardon me for a moment," he said, then swiftly turned around and walked back the way we'd come.

I stared hard at his retreating form and the question he'd first asked me came into my mind: *Are you real?* It had surprised me, but now it made sense. Seeing David again, in the same places and on the same paths we'd haunted years ago, but with our circumstances and ages so altered, felt as though I'd stepped into another world, one where everything had twisted to the point of becoming unbelievable.

"Mr.—" I stumbled over what to call him as he walked away. Had I ever known his surname? I couldn't call him David now that he was a grown man.

He waved back at me but didn't turn around to look. "I left my hat," he called. His march turned into a jog, his arms pumping while his fur-lined coat trailed out behind him.

My cheeks warmed, and a sneaky bit of pleasure rose in my throat. My life was currently a disaster, but once upon a time, I'd been proposed to by this man. His boyhood proposal had been clumsy and mortifying for both of us, but looking at him now, I couldn't help but wish Mama could see him and know her daughter wasn't a complete disappointment.

Chapter 2

"I sneaked out today and saw a girl who sings as she walks even though she isn't good at it. I don't understand her. And I wish I had the kind of life where confidence and joy made sense to me."

—David Tate, 1841, Age 14

David bent over, picked up his hat, and dusted it off with his fist. He stamped his feet once before turning around and striding back toward me. When he arrived, his smile was back on his face, but his eyes were a duller blue than they had been when we'd first tumbled to the ground together.

"So, Mrs. . . ." He started, then paused, turning his statement into a question, his voice businesslike and formal.

I laughed softly at his assumption. "I am still Miss Atwood."

His head snapped to the side, and the clear-cut lines of his cheekbones, so angular a moment before, seemed to soften with his surprise. "But you said you were proposed to." He shook his head. "You've been of a marriageable age for . . ." He caught himself, wisely stopping that line of speaking. "I didn't think—How is it possible?"

"Thank you for the reminder of how long I have been out in Society," I said. He grimaced, and I smiled to reassure him that I took no offense at the mention of my age. “If I had to marry any man who proposed to me, I would have been married at seventeen. To you.”

He coughed and rubbed one hand behind his neck, just like he had a moment ago and as he used to when he was a boy and was extremely uncomfortable. I couldn’t blame him. I most likely bore little resemblance to the energetic young woman he’d known during my summer in Breckenridge.

He kicked the toes of one boot against the ground. “It’s not as though I was planning on marrying at fourteen. I was naive but not quite that naive.”

“So you were teasing me? Or you knew I would say no?”

“I don’t think I knew what teasing was when I was fourteen. I *was* in earnest. But I knew you would say no.” He lifted one side of his mouth before squeezing his lips together, as if to restrain himself. He motioned with one hand down the path, and we both started walking. “I suppose I *had* kept myself up all night the night before, wondering if there was any chance you might say yes.” His eyes were sparkling again now, both hands behind his back as he strode assertively toward the cottage. He remembered the path. I wondered if he’d ever had cause to go there over the course of the past eight years. “I had a plan, you see. We would keep it a secret for at least three years.”

“A three-year engagement!” I threw my hands to my throat, determined to keep the conversation light. The thought of being married to this version of David was very different from being married to the awkward boy he’d been. “How would we have borne it?”

He chuckled, which brought back the memory of his chest rumbling underneath my own. I needed to remove that thought from my brain. David may have been strangely infatuated with me when I was seventeen, but I was changed enough from that young woman that it was a surprise David had recognized me at all.

"That was just how long the secret part would last," he said with conspiratorial grin. "We would have to have had at least a six-month engagement after everyone found out."

My cheeks warmed even though this was nothing more than a funny story we were telling each other about our childhoods. "Three years of secrecy. Such a long time." I gave a small chuckle.

"I can be very patient when I need to be." The seriousness in his gaze was disconcerting. He was not helping me keep the moment light. Not even in the smallest of ways.

My lips formed a pout as I tried my best impression of a coquette. It was probably ridiculous, especially at my age. "You wouldn't have come to visit me in London?"

He scowled. "If visiting you in London had been at all possible, I would have tried to find you when I turned seventeen."

It was my turn to be chastised. Earlier, he'd brought up my age, and now I'd reminded him of the lowly circumstances of his youth.

I cleared my throat. "Why when you turned seventeen?"

"It was the first time a woman called me handsome. But don't worry, I'm not so brash or foolish anymore. Perhaps we should speak of something else."

"Yes, of course. Mr. . . . I'm sorry, I don't seem to recall your surname."

His shoulders slumped slightly as he looked into the distance and narrowed his eyes. "It's Tate."

"Tate?" I definitely would have remembered had I known it. "No relation to Lord Murphy?" I left off the words *I hope*, but with our connection, I was certain he felt them. I'd only seen Lord Murphy once. He was a large man, both tall and broad, and even though I was on the other side of the street from him in Breckenridge, the scowl on his face would have been visible from a much more significant distance. The Mortensens had told me enough stories of his iron rule over them and his other tenants that I shouldn't have been surprised by his behavior, but when he raised his voice and took the handle of his horse whip to one of his footmen, the sight had left me physically ill.

"We're related." David's voice was flat and emotionless. He didn't seem interested in speaking of Lord Murphy, and I felt the same. "But not close."

I let out a tense breath. Of course he wasn't closely related to the man—he was nothing like him. Not in size or character. Lord Murphy's influence affected most of the village and its surroundings. He was even worse for this community than Mr. Green was for Silverfork. Perhaps David was a nephew or even more distantly related. No close relation to the viscount would have roamed the countryside dressed the way David had when he'd been younger.

David nodded and coughed lightly into his hand, and when he spoke next, I knew it wouldn't be about Lord Murphy. "What brings you to Breckenridge? And how long will we have the honor of your presence?" he asked.

"I brought Mama and me here." Only a change in subject from Lord Murphy could make me want to talk about the direction my life had taken since we'd last met.

"And your father?"

"He passed away a year after we left Breckenridge."

"Oh," he said softly. "I'm sorry."

I could see he was, but also, I'd never excelled at comforting others when the subject of my sorrows came up. "We've managed. But I'm afraid coming here was a terrible mistake."

"You aren't the type to make mistakes, and I hate to have you thinking that returning to Breckenridge was one."

I laughed at the absurdness of his assertion. "I don't *like* to. I'm not certain anyone does. But I do make them, and I'm afraid I have made very many, especially lately. I thought Mama and I would be able to live in the cottage long-term, at least for the next year and a half." When I turned twenty-seven, I would receive Papa's inheritance whether I was married or not, and it would be enough for us to afford a residence and most of our basic needs. "But the cottage will only be empty until the first of March. In two weeks, we will have nowhere to go. So, no, I cannot count coming here as a wise decision." Mama was probably still crying at home as she had been when I'd left her. Too many problems at once overwhelmed her to the point of making her ill. And I'd caused that by making us come here with no more of a plan than begging Mr. Preston for help.

"I'd heard Mr. and Mrs. Preston had planned to let their home as well as the cottage." David took a deep breath. "Perhaps it wasn't the wisest course of action, but surely not a mistake. You have friends here, and the Prestons are good people. They will be advocates for you, as will I. But why a year and a half? Do you have other plans after that?"

"That is when I turn twenty-seven," I answered, ignoring the heat on my face at the mention of my age. "Atwood Manor went to my uncle, of course, but Papa left me an inheritance large enough for us to live on. I can access it when I turn twenty-seven. Then we won't need to depend on anyone's generosity."

David's steps slowed, though he took several before he spoke next. "Is there no other way to access your inheritance? Have you spoken with a solicitor?"

I shook my head. "The only other way to receive it is if I marry."

He pursed his lips together. "And yet you have continually rejected marriage proposals."

"It isn't as though anyone remotely suitable has asked me," I said with a huff. I'd been offered marriage by a boy and a man twice my age. Never by someone appropriate.

"I see," he said with a slight edge to his voice. "Well, at least you are among friends here. I'm certain the Prestons will be able to sort something out for you. I would be happy to help you as well. I cannot count coming here as a mistake, so unless you have any others to confess to me, I will have to assume you do not make them."

The way he casually spoke of the Prestons and himself helping us gave me the first spark of hope I'd had in days. In Silverfork, no one had ever offered to help us, except Mr. Green, and Mr. Green's help always came at a price.

I glanced up at my old friend and raised my eyebrows. "You will make me report them all to you? How much time do you have?"

That disarming smile of his returned along with the deep lines between his mouth and his cheeks. "I will take any moment you will spare me. Especially if you are here for only a few weeks."

I could feel a flush on my cheeks, and I was grateful David took that moment to look down at the path. It had been years since a healthy young man had paid me a compliment. I straightened my back and raised my chin. Perhaps there was something of that vibrant young lady left deep inside me. "All right, we will start with the most obvious. I shouldn't have climbed that tree. That was a mistake. And as long as I was climbing, I shouldn't have thought the best way to dismount was to drop from such a high branch."

I could practically see his mind spinning, trying to come up with some reason that my folly could be seen as anything but a blunder.

He finally turned to me, eyes sparkling with amusement. "That *may* have been a mistake." A small chuckle escaped his lips. "But I was able to fulfill some very potent youthful dreams by holding you in my arms at last." His smile was so all-encompassing it made his eyes crinkle half closed. "Eight years was a terribly long time to wait."

I shook my head slightly to clear it. He was being improper, surely. Even if we had been childhood friends, a gentleman wouldn't mention the indelicate position we had just been in.

I ignored the draw of his smile and forced myself to feel affronted instead of anything else at his impertinence. I scoffed. "I wouldn't say I was in your arms."

David's hands unclasped from behind his back and dropped to his sides. "You wouldn't? Are you still trying to prove you make mistakes? Because that is certainly one."

My spine stiffened. "I wasn't in your arms."

"Where were you, then?"

"On top of—" I stopped. Perhaps in his arms *was* the better description. I coughed lightly and searched my mind for any better explanation of what had happened. There simply wasn't a delicate way to put it. "I suppose I might have been mistaken after all."

Those lines on each side of his smile deepened.

The frost-covered window panes of the cottage came into view through the trees in front of us. The lightness of my encounter with David seemed to melt away into hopelessness. Mama must be well out of bed by now, and it would be time to discuss our future again. But no matter how much we spoke of plans, we had nowhere to go. The cottage had been our last hope. What in heaven's name would we do now?

My feet grew heavy, and I fell behind David. He glanced at me before turning and catching sight of the cottage. In unison, our steps slowed to a crawl.

"Why didn't you keep in contact?" The question was soft and low, and his expressive face seemed to turn into unresponsive granite.

I sighed. How did one explain years of desperation? "After Papa died, I suppose Mama didn't feel as comfortable asking for help from his friends as she did her own family. Perhaps if she would have, things could have been different."

"Perhaps they would have," he agreed. We reached the small garden that ran alongside the cottage. "If you had even informed Mr. Preston of your new location . . ."

I waited for him to continue his train of thought, but he didn't. "How do you know we didn't inform him?"

One of his feet scuffed the ground, and he rubbed the back of his neck. Once again, I caught a snippet of the quiet young boy instead of the dashing man before me.

"Did you ask after us?"

After a pause, he nodded. "I did, just after a visit to London."

"When? I thought you said you couldn't go to London."

"Four years ago?" He said it like a question. As if he couldn't remember for certain when he had gone, but I suspected he knew exactly when it was. "My circumstances had changed, and I found myself free to travel to London after all. While there, I thought I would find you on my own. It was only after the disappointment of that trip that I asked Mr. Preston about your family. He had no idea where you were either."

"Why were you looking for me?"

He glanced at me out of the corner of his eye and sheepishly put a hand to his heart. "Not for another proposal, truly. I had grown up enough by then to know that was an impossibility. I suppose I just wanted to see you again. I don't know if I would have even had the courage to speak with you."

We reached the door to the cottage and both stopped. I didn't know how to respond to the fact that he had tried to reach me in London a full four years after I had left here. I heaved a sigh. "I had better go in."

"Yes."

"Mama is waiting." I didn't want to return and listen to more crying. Especially when that crying was completely my fault.

"When will I see you again?" David asked. He tipped his head with a smirk. "I would rather not wait another eight and a half years."

I returned his smirk with a smile. Spending time with David would be a pleasure. "The Prestons have invited us to dine with them in the main house several nights a week until they leave. We will be there the day after next. If you are friends with their family, I suppose you could beg an invitation."

"No sooner?"

I furrowed my eyebrows and chuckled. "Than the day after tomorrow?"

He shook his head, and his sudden laughter enveloped me with a rich sound that warmed me, despite the cold. "It is good to have you back, Miss Atwood." He bowed. "I look forward to seeing you at the Prestons. I believe they will allow me a visit."

Chapter 3

"Ever since she found me holding Charlotte, she keeps trying to make me talk to her. I finally did. But only because she showed me an interesting rock. Her name is Anna."

—David Tate, 1841, Age 14

The morning of our dinner with the Prestons, Mama was out of her bed and dressed by the time I stopped by her room on my way down to breakfast. I hadn't been able to convince Mama to ready herself in the morning since we'd arrived, and I took her recovery as a good omen. Perhaps our engagement with the Prestons was brightening her mood. My step was light as I bounded down the stairs. If Mama could start feeling better, then I was certain I was going to be able to find us another place to stay within the two weeks we had remaining. The Prestons were eager to help us and had been looking for new accommodations even in the midst of their preparations to leave the county.

Something else *would* become available. It had to. I was tired of being poor and helpless. I was tired of feeling pity from others. I was tired of being tempted to marry someone twenty years my senior, if only to be able to help others like we used to.

Mama sliced a piece of bread off the loaf Mrs. Preston had sent to the cottage from the main house when we'd arrived. With no cook and the only help a maid Mrs. Preston sent each morning and sporadically during the day, dinner this evening was going to be a very welcome change to the cold fare we'd eaten the last two days. No wonder Mama was feeling better.

I came up behind her and wrapped my arms around her shoulders, embracing her. "Good morning, Mama," I said, a smile in my voice that hadn't been there for days—perhaps years.

She jumped, put a hand over one of mine, and then turned around. I don't know what I'd been expecting. Perhaps a warm greeting? A return embrace? A newfound understanding of why I'd made us leave Silverfork and Mr. Green's grasp? But there was none of that. Her tears were gone, but the lines on her face exposed the exhaustion of the past seven years without Papa.

She wasn't meant to live a life of poverty, and not for the first time, I cursed Uncle Atwood for bringing this upon her. Papa had placed too much trust in his younger brother. Trust that had been shattered within a year of Papa's death, when he'd told us Atwood Manor was no longer our home and it was time to look to Mama's family to care for us.

Mama gave me a nod, then sat at the table and numbly chewed her bread. I cut myself a slice and joined her.

"We should have a lovely dinner this evening with the Prestons," I said.

Mama nodded again.

"I know coming here didn't turn out the way we hoped, but at least we got away from Silverfork, and no one there knows about the summer we spent here. We'll have a new start, at the very least, out of the grasp of those who would take advantage of us there."

Mama rubbed a hand down her face. "I'm not sure what advantage could be taken of women in our position, Anna."

I set down my bread. It was a few days old and starting to taste stale and dry. I'd be better off waiting to eat at the Prestons'. "Our position isn't great now, but after my twenty-seventh birthday, it will be. Papa made certain of that."

"And what will we do until then?"

"I don't know, but we've survived seven years alone. We can figure something out."

"By the end of the month?"

We'd gone over this every day since arriving. "Yes."

Mama's eyes shifted out the window. "We might have to reconsider our options."

"As of now, I'm trying to find options. And I will."

"Mr. Green has a home with fourteen rooms."

"Yes . . ." I said warily.

"And he owns most of the shops in town. We could have nice things again."

These were all the reasons I'd almost considered marrying him just before we'd left. I rose from the table, not wanting to talk about Mr. Green. If she liked his house and his influence so much, she should have tried to marry him. I sighed. For all I knew, she had, but Mr. Green was *not* the type of man who was interested in marrying a woman near his age. "I'm going to go for a walk."

Mama didn't answer.

I strode out of the room and threw on my heaviest coat—a dark-green woolen one Mama had accepted from Mr. Green on my behalf. Even here, his influence permeated the air around me. When would I ever be free of it? But it was better to be in Mr. Green's coat than in his bed, and as soon as I had my inheritance, the coat would be the first thing to go.

Once outside the cottage, I stopped, uncertain of which direction I wanted to walk. I could try visiting with the Mortensens again, but if I followed the left path, would David find me again? He'd often found me on that path when I'd delivered baskets to Lord Murphy's tenants. He'd never come into the ramshackle hovels while I'd visited with the families within, but he'd always been waiting behind a tree or down the lane. He'd been quiet, never speaking above a whisper, and always preferring to be out of sight of anyone else who might have been walking that day.

I turned right. I wasn't certain I could handle one more reminder of how far I'd fallen from the optimistic young woman I'd been when I'd first come to Breckenridge.

Besides, if I knocked at the Prestons' door, perhaps Mr. Preston would lend me his most recent papers from London, and I could spend the afternoon looking for work.

I found Mr. Preston in his study, where he was busy but more than happy to give me his old papers. He handed me a stack of them. "Did you hear we are to have two more guests at dinner tonight?" he asked.

"Mr. Tate and . . ."

"His older sister, Miss Julia Tate. We see Mr. Tate often enough nowadays. He helped put new thatch on the cottage a few years back, and since then, we've become good friends. But I've rarely had the chance to speak to his sister. She's a bit skittish."

"Oh," I said. This was the first I'd heard anything about David's family other than the fact that he was somehow related to Lord Murphy. Had David become a thatcher? If he was a master at the craft, that could perhaps explain his improved clothing.

Mr. Preston eyed me shrewdly. "You don't know why the sudden interest in dining with us, do you?"

I shrugged a shoulder. "I suppose your guess would be as good as mine. I've never even met Miss Tate."

Mr. Preston didn't look convinced, and I wished I knew exactly what David had said when asking for his invitation.

After arriving home, I spent more than an hour penning several letters and responding to governess advertisements. By the time I returned with Mama to the Prestons' home for dinner, my stomach was nigh unto growling.

We arrived after David and his sister and just in time to be ushered into the dining room directly after introductions. David's older sister was beautiful in a reserved sort of way, and she looked to be about my age. Mr. Preston's description of her being skittish fit her well. Her dark hair was similar to David's, but her eyes were a cloudy gray, and they darted about the room instead of focusing on the people in it. David used to have that same look of wariness about him.

My eyes went from David to his sister, comparing them once again. What had happened to change him so drastically?

"How are you enjoying your visit, Miss Atwood?" David asked from across the table.

"It's lovely to be back again," I lied. Other than our conversation the day before yesterday, the past three days had been excruciating.

Mama looked up in surprise at my cheerful answer. "I am certain we are sorely missed in Silverfork."

"Silverfork?" David asked, setting his spoon into his soup. "That is in Derbyshire, is it not? What brought you there?"

"I have a cousin who lives there," Mama said, leaving out the part of the story where we had been able to stay with her for only a few weeks before her husband had declared we needed to find a new place. "And of course, after six years, we now have other friends there as well."

Which friends did Mama mean? Mr. Green had monopolized most of our time, making it clear to others around us that he was to be our only real acquaintance. I hardly thought of him as a friend.

"Ah," David said rubbing the back of his neck in that nervous way of his. He looked as though he wanted to ask more questions but wasn't certain he should pry.

"We are glad you came to Breckenridge," Miss Tate said quietly. They were the first words I'd heard from her since she'd greeted us during introductions. It seemed she would speak only in order to bring comfort to her brother. "We need more friends here."

Mr. Preston looked at his knife and rubbed his finger along the dull edge. Mother cleared her throat, and David's hand hadn't left his neck. Miss Tate must not have known we would be forced to leave in two short weeks, but by the way she dropped her eyes, she must have known she had said something wrong.

"It was very kind of the Prestons to take us in," I said. "And with absolutely no notice. We'll be staying here only until the end of the month though. Mama and I are looking forward to finding a place of our own."

"Yes, it will be nice to be settled," Mama said. I looked at her out of the corner of my eye. As much as I didn't love the despondent attitude of our first two days here, this confidence disarmed me. Where was it coming from? Had she made a plan without informing me? If so, there was no telling what it could be.

"Have you been looking for a different place to stay in Breckenridge?" David asked.

"We have no other acquaintances here but the Prestons," Mama replied. "My guess is we will be going back to Derbyshire."

I narrowed my eyes at Mama. Derbyshire was one county I would rather never return to. Mr. Green had too much influence there. Mama couldn't mean for us to return to Silverfork, could she? After all I'd done to remove us from that situation?

I set my spoon down next to the bowl. I'd been starving when we arrived, but the food wasn't sitting well. "Why do you think we will be returning to Derbyshire, Mama?" I tried to keep my voice neutral.

Mama met my eyes. "It's our home, Anna."

"Mama." My voice was hard. The small noises that so often accompanied dinner stopped. Not a fork or a glass moved. All eyes turned to the two of us. "Mama, you didn't."

Mother glanced nervously at the men and women around her. She couldn't tell them what terrible straits we were in, but I could tell she wanted to. Perhaps this jury could exonerate her.

"Mama . . ."

"We can talk about it later, Anna. For now, let's enjoy our dinner."

Mr. and Mrs. Preston seemed to understand Mama's meaning and pointedly returned to the food on their plates, but David's eyes remained on us until the butler entered the room and whispered something in Mr. Preston's ear. Mr. Preston's face pulled back in surprise before he finally whispered something back to the butler.

After the butler left, Mr. Preston turned to Mama. "It seems we are to have another guest at dinner. A friend of yours, Mrs. and Miss Atwood."

"A friend of ours?" An icy fear twisted at my heart. I clamped a fistful of my dress into my hand and turned toward Mama. She wouldn't look me in the eye. She fiddled with her napkin in her lap, then started straightening her perfectly placed fork and knife.

"What have you done?" What little soup I'd eaten seemed to rise in my throat. I had a sudden desire to run out of the room, but even that desire was overshadowed by the stabbing pain of deceit. How could my own mother have done this?

She didn't respond.

Two servants hurriedly placed another set of dishes in front of a vacant chair. I concentrated on my breathing. I could be wrong. *Please let me be wrong.*

"Mr. Green," the Butler announced, and I crunched the napkin in my lap into a small ball. What could have possessed her?

"Mother!" I whispered harshly under my breath.

She leaned over and placed her mouth near my ear. "I didn't think he would come so soon. I only wrote to him yesterday. I told him to wait another week, when we would be desperate." She sighed heavily. "But be reasonable. What would one more week have gotten us? We have nowhere else to go."

My mouth opened to form a sharp retort, but nothing came.

Had I actually thought I could find us a place to live rent-free for a year and a half? Or that I would be able to find a governess position that would allow Mama to live in the family's home with me? I'd gained some confidence in my plans when Mama's mood had improved, but that had not been because she'd trusted in my abilities; it had been because she'd written to Mr. Green.

Mr. Green walked into the room with an air of owning it, his head held high and proud despite the lack of hair on top of it. His mustard-brown eyes found mine, and he immediately walked in my direction, not bothering to introduce himself to the hosts.

"Miss Atwood." He bowed low from behind my chair, and I instinctively pushed my torso into the table to get as far away from him as possible. "It is so wonderful to see you again."

I barely managed a nod while keeping my face turned away from him. I couldn't look at him. Not yet. Not knowing that this time, if I gave him any encouragement at all, he would become my husband.

"Mr. Green?" Mr. Preston asked politely, standing from his chair.

Mr. Green took one step away from me and toward the head of the table. "Ah, you must be Mr. Preston. What a pleasure. Thank you for allowing me to join you for dinner at such late notice."

"Yes, well, I was quite surprised at your arrival, but of course, we couldn't allow you to wait in the drawing room while we ate."

Mr. Green grinned. "I believe before the night is over, I will have repaid your hospitality with some exciting news." He bowed in my direction.

"Who, exactly, are you?" David said with a voice more like the warning growl of a dog than one for polite conversation. His grip on his fork was forceful enough to make the veins in his hand stand out.

"Didn't Mrs. Atwood mention me? I am Mr. Green. I have been this young lady's neighbor and friend for the past six years."

If by *friend* he meant unfortunate admirer, he was right. He'd claimed to have an attachment to me almost as soon as we'd moved from Atwood Manor to Cousin Agatha's home. If I'd tried to meet or even converse with anyone else in town, he'd always been there, hovering, showing with looks and words that he felt I was his.

I'd thought I was finally free of him. And the sight of him brought back all the reasons we'd left. The man made me feel trapped and isolated, and even looking at him had me retreating into myself.

When I didn't respond to his bow, Mr. Green found his seat and proceeded to dish up copious mounds of food on his plate. I barely spoke for the rest of dinner, but I didn't need to. Mr. Green spoke enough for everyone. And when he proudly mentioned his fifteen hundred pounds a year, I thought I heard a huff from David's direction.

David didn't speak though. Even in the dim dining room, I could see red spots of color forming along his cheekbones. He chewed his food so quickly the muscles in his jaw contracted distractingly with every bite.

When the door was finally opened to the adjoining drawing room, I dashed for it as if I were a prisoner escaping Newgate.

"I will forgo smoking this evening," Mr. Green said quickly as the other ladies rose from their seats, "and head directly to socializing with the women, if you don't mind."

"Oh," Mr. Preston said, surprised. I froze, waiting for his response. Surely he wouldn't allow Mr. Green to be alone with us. But he nodded. "That is a fine idea. Why don't all the men join you, seeing as Mr. Tate doesn't smoke, and I do so rarely."

I silently blessed Mr. Preston. Mr. Green looked defeated, but that didn't stop him from quickly reaching me where I'd stopped halfway to the drawing room. He put out his arm, and just as with every other aspect of our relationship, I felt as though I had no other option than to take it. David rose from his seat and offered his hand to his sister, then walked around the table and proffered an arm to Mama as well, leaving Mr. Preston free to escort Mrs. Preston in.

As soon as we crossed the threshold into the drawing room, I pulled my arm away from Mr. Green and made my way to the bookshelf. I fully planned on ignoring everyone and pretending to read a book. I couldn't believe Mama had done this. Leaving Mr. Green's society was one of the most freeing things I had ever done. He'd known about Uncle Atwood and anyone we may have visited in London, but Breckenridge? I'd chosen it as the one place he'd never know about. And now Mama had ruined everything by telling him where we were.

He followed me to the bookshelf, watching as I chose a book of poetry, then stayed on my heels as I sat on a club chair. Mr. Green looked for a place to sit nearby, but I had chosen the one seat far from any other.

"Mrs. Atwood." Mr. Green didn't look away from me as he spoke. "I would like to ask your permission to speak to your daughter alone."

"No," I said and was surprised to hear my answer echoed by David and Mr. Preston.

I looked across the room at them with surprise. David was standing between my mother and his sister with his arms folded across his chest and legs shoulder-width apart. Mr. Preston had a similar stance, and I could see in his eyes a firmness that implied he wanted to help. Mr. Preston's answer made sense. He felt some responsibility for Mama and me since we were relying on his hospitality.

But David? What reason could he have for answering for my mother?

"I beg your pardon?" Mr. Green gave the two men a look of disbelief. He wasn't used to people standing up for me. *I* wasn't used to people standing up for me. "I believe I asked her mother."

"I beg *your* pardon." David's eyes were hard, and he spoke before Mr. Preston had the chance. "But an answer from Miss Atwood should be answer enough."

Mr. Green took a step toward David. "I don't believe I caught your name."

"That is because you didn't ask it." David's mouth twisted, and he did not extend a hand to Mr. Green. "Mr. David Tate."

Mr. Preston stepped forward but David waved him off. There was no reason Mr. Preston should have listened to David. Other than Lord Murphy, the Prestons were the most influential family in the county. But Mr. Preston did.

"Well, Mr. Tate." Mr. Green cleared his throat and sucked in his paunchy stomach. "I do believe this is none of your concern." Mr. Green was not used to being denied anything. In Silverfork, he owned the butchers and the haberdashery, which also gave him an enormous amount of power with those who worked at the bank. Everyone had to keep on his good side.

For six years, I'd avoided him when I could, given him polite answers to his forward questions, and rejected his proposals, and yet this time, I didn't know what to do. Our short respite away from him hadn't been much of a respite at all.

The truth was, we had nowhere to go. Could I be happy knowing I had provided a home for myself and my mother, even if it meant succumbing to the man who everyone in Silverfork had succumbed to? At least no one would be surprised by the union. Everyone had expected him to win me over much sooner than this.

Mama was getting older. She deserved to be comfortable after these past few years. If we were careful in the writing of the marriage contract about my inheritance, perhaps a marriage to Mr. Green wouldn't be the worst thing in the world. I could find some good to do with Papa's money.

I stood. "I'll speak to him." My stomach felt sick, and my hands had started shaking, but what other option did I have? Moving here had been a mistake, but I had made Mama do it even though she'd expressed her concerns about coming unannounced. She'd been right. There wasn't a place for us here. There wasn't a place for us anywhere.

Mama's face brightened in surprise at my answer, but next to her, David's face turned dark. He unfolded his arms and put them on his waist. "You will do nothing of the sort."

"Pardon?" I asked, once again surprised by David's interference.

"You have nothing to do with this." Mr. Green's voice rose by an octave, and the veins in his neck bulged.

David glanced at me, his face softening in a way I was certain he meant for me to understand. But I didn't. There was a heat in his lingering gaze that belied how little we knew each other. In all our time together, he'd never looked at me like that. Indeed, as a fourteen-year-old, he wouldn't have been capable of it.

"My dear," David's voice was tender as he strode toward me. I looked to each side, thinking perhaps I'd misunderstood that look of his and his term of endearment. But of course, there was no one else but me on this side of the room, unless he was referring to Mr. Green. I sneaked a quick glance at the odious man, but he looked just as confused as I. "I believe we owe your family and friends an explanation about why you came back to Breckenridge."

Oh no.

I closed my eyes tight. Blast the man, he was going to try to protect me. He crossed the room and reached for my hand. It was still shaking, but I allowed him to take it. His look of concern deepened when he noticed the tremors. I forced myself to take a long, slow breath. I needed to be in control.

He leaned forward and, with his breath warm near my ear, whispered, "That man doesn't deserve to breathe the same air as you. I cannot watch him annoy you any further. Let me help. Please."

He squeezed my hand softly and then straightened, his eyes on my face, awaiting an answer. A moment ago, my own mother had practically thrown me at Mr. Green. But now, this man, who had once been a boy I'd spent only a short summer with, was offering an escape.

We'd both removed our gloves for dinner and hadn't had time to replace them. His hand was warm and slightly rough, most likely from thatching roofs. They were the kind of hands a woman could trust. I hadn't had a man's hand wrapped around my own since Papa had passed away, at least no well-meaning one, and something about the familiarity of the motion made me want to lean into him and, more than that, allow him to help me. Especially if it meant I didn't have to go into a room alone with Mr. Green.

I nodded, feeling my chin quiver slightly.

"Miss Atwood"—David's smile projected pure happiness, and Mr. Green's scowl deepened—"Anna"—he corrected softly, and my eyes went to Mr. Green. His face was beginning to match his name—"has no reason to speak with you alone, not when she has come to Breckenridge with the express intent of accepting my proposal of marriage."

I nodded in agreement and then paused. *Marriage?* My eyes widened, and I whipped my head back to David. Had he just said *marriage*? I kept my smile plastered to my face out of self-preservation, but certainly, I'd misheard him. What in heaven's name?

Mama's hands flew to her throat, and her mouth dropped open. Miss Tate's face went pale, and her eyes flashed back and forth between me and David. Only Mr. and Mrs. Preston seemed happy about the announcement. Mrs. Preston clapped her hands in excitement while Mr. Preston smiled and nudged her with his elbow.

"That is preposterous," Mr. Green blurted out. "Miss Atwood has lived for the past six years in Derbyshire. She's never told anyone she was engaged."

"I proposed to her eight years ago." David showed no signs of deceit. He stood firm and steady as a mountain in a storm. "Didn't I, Anna?" His mouth curled to a soft smile that almost made *me* believe he was in earnest. The man hardly knew me. But for whatever reason, he was helping me, and I wasn't going to sabotage him.

"It's true," I said, trying to match his confident smile.

"Why didn't you tell me?" Mama said from the other side of the room.

David's smile dropped, and he looked at Mama as if she'd scolded him. "She knew I wanted to keep it a secret. I was young and needed to prove myself. I'm sorry, madam, if my need for secrecy has caused your family pain."

"You expect us to believe she's been engaged for eight years? To you?" Mr. Green asked, his lips pursed together and eyes narrowed. "You barely look of marriageable age now. You would have been a child."

David straightened, and even though he wasn't a large man, his presence seemed to take up the room. "Matters of the heart are not bound by the years we've lived on the earth. As you must know, seeing as you've pursued a woman half your age."

Mr. Green sputtered, and I pressed my lips together to hold back a sudden laugh. No one ever spoke to him like that.

"How old were you?" Mr. Green asked again, his voice laced with fury.

"Let's see," Mr. Preston said cheerfully. "Miss Atwood's first visit was eight years ago in the summer. Mr. Tate is twenty and three now, which would have made him fifteen." He paused for a moment. "No! Fourteen, as he wouldn't have had his birthday yet." He walked over to David and slapped him on his back. "Knew what you wanted early, didn't you?"

David's eyes met mine, and with the same intense expression he had used eight years ago when he had asked me to marry him, he answered, "Yes."

Mr. Green's eyes bulged and skirted about the room as if he were the only sane man in it. "A man engaged at fourteen. I've never heard of such a thing."

"Is this true, Anna?" Mama asked. "Did he really propose to you that summer?"

I looked between the two men. David stood waiting to protect me. I had no idea what he planned to do after Mr. Green left, but it hardly mattered. Mr. Green was pulling at his cravat, his anger showing in every inch of his body. I couldn't go with him. Mr. Preston would help us once I explained the need. He felt terrible about not having a place for us to stay. There had to be a better answer than marrying Mr. Green, and David had given me a simple way to be rid of him once and for all. I turned to Mama. "He's telling the truth. He came to the cottage the night before we left and asked me to marry him."

"And you accepted him?" Mama asked. "A fourteen-year-old boy? I don't even remember seeing him that summer. When did you have a chance to meet?"

I ignored her first question, grateful she'd asked a second. "He often came to help me on my visits to Lord Murphy's tenant farmers. He would carry the basket." Thank heavens, Mama hadn't seen him then. Some boys looked like full-grown men at fourteen, but David hadn't been one of them.

David stepped forward and took Mama's hand. "Your daughter was a ray of light in an otherwise very dark childhood." He looked at his sister. She bowed her head and looked away from everyone. "I couldn't allow that light to leave without at least asking for her to become a permanent part of my future. I knew I was too young to marry. But now I no longer am, and so she has returned. Do you think she would have come here otherwise? Without even speaking with Mr. Preston about how long you would be able to stay?"

David was quite convincing. His sister watched him intently, her light eyes narrowing at his explanation. When she looked at me next, it was to take my measure. Everyone else in the room had seemed to take a side, either in excitement for what was happening or, as in the case of Mr. Green, all-encompassing aggravation. But Miss Tate was uniquely undecided. Of course she was. David wasn't in need of protection, his announcement did nothing to help him, and Miss Tate didn't care a whit for me; we'd only just met. She had eyes only for her brother. If anything, she should be as unhappy as Mr. Green.

Mrs. Preston strode over to David and patted his cheek. "Congratulations, Mr. Tate. I remember Miss Atwood and how delightful she was that summer. You did well to ask her when you did; otherwise someone else would have snatched her up. I guess now we all understand how she managed to stay unattached so long."

"That's why you haven't accepted anyone?" Mama sputtered. "You were engaged this whole time, and you never told me? Do you know how much I've worried?"

Mr. Green kicked the back of the chair I had been sitting on until recently. "I cannot believe the way this woman has misled me for years. It's disgraceful."

"Mr. Green." David's voice was icy. "I'm going to tell you this once kindly, and if I need to say it again, I will not be so kind. Have a care for how you speak of Anna. Or of any woman, for that matter. I highly doubt she bestowed any special favors upon you over the past years. It is your own folly if you looked upon common human decency and saw it as encouragement."

One of the veins in Mr. Green's neck looked as though it might burst. But he sized up David's arms and general youth and must have thought better of aggravating him further. Instead, he turned to me, his eyes stopping briefly at the point where David's and my hands touched. When his eyes met mine they were furious. "I hope you never set foot in Derbyshire again, for you won't receive any sort of welcome from me or the rest of the county."

"I am aware of that, Mr. Green." I smiled at him and tightened my hold on David's hand, which he immediately returned with a squeeze of his own. This was going to be a mess to sort out once Mr. Green left, but it was worth it to hear him say he was finally done pursuing me. My chest felt light enough that I could fly out the window.

David ran his thumb quickly over the top of my hand before dropping it and striding to the door. He opened it and looked at Mr. Green expectantly. Mr. Green narrowed his eyes and, seeing no support, even from Mama, stomped out of the drawing room. A moment later, the front door slammed.

I waited for David to tell everyone it was all an act, but it didn't happen. We stood there looking at each other. My heart swelled with gratitude for this man and what he had done, but he must be panicking. It was up to me to tell everyone the truth so no harm could be done to his name.

"Mama . . ." How would I start? She looked up at me expectantly, and although I could tell she was put out not to have been privy to this pretend engagement, I also knew she was scared enough to have asked Mr. Green here. But there was nothing to be done about it. I couldn't entrap David. He had too much of his life ahead of him. He might even already have someone in mind whom he would like to marry. "None of this—"

"Mr. Preston," David interrupted. "I haven't actually had time to hear Miss Atwood's reply to my proposal. I wonder if I could borrow a private room for a moment of her time. Assuming Mrs. Atwood and Anna are willing?"

My heart sped up at his words, but not in the way it had when Mr. Green had asked the same thing. Alone, with David?

"Of course," Mr. Preston said. "You may use the library for a few minutes. Would that be agreeable, Mrs. Atwood?"

Mama looked to be in shock. Her eyes widened when her name was called and then seemed to process what had been said. "Yes, I suppose that would be all right." She glanced at David. "But afterward, I would also like to speak with you."

I shook my head. "That won't be necessary, Mama."

Mama's hands flitted about, and she walked up to me and leaned in. "I know us being here means you must have already made up your mind to marry him, but I know next to nothing about the man. I think it is only proper that he speak to me as well."

"Certainly," David said. "I will speak with you directly after I have a word with Anna, that is." He held out his arm, solid and so very different from Mr. Green's. Mr. Green's arm had been a way to claim me. David's was an invitation. "If Anna will join me."

Anna. That was me. I wasn't certain what we needed to talk about in private, but I had no objections to being alone with him in the library. I took his arm. My hand wasn't shaking, at least. That was something.

He gave Mr. Preston a short bow, then led me out of the dining room. He walked directly down a corridor and to the library. I suppose as a neighbor, he knew the house well enough to find it. Opening the door, he motioned for me to step inside the unlit room.

I did.

And then he closed the door behind us.

Chapter 4

"She likes to help those in need, and if she knew my family's name, she might think I don't need her. But I need her more than anyone."
David Tate, 1841, Age 14

The silence in the room was deafening and intimate. We hadn't thought to bring a lamp, and the room was dim, with only the soft moonlight from the window illuminating the walls of books and bathing the man in front of me in silken shadows.

"Mr. Tate," I said.

"David," he corrected, motioning to the door with a tip of his head and a flash of his eyes. His message was clear. Someone could be listening there, and he wasn't wrong. Unless Mr. Preston had physically restrained Mama, she was certain to have pressed her ear against the barrier between us. He leaned forward, and as he was at most two inches taller than I, it brought his face level with mine. "You should call me David. And not only because of what just happened. Mr. Tate feels wrong coming from you."

I sighed because he was right. I'd tried and failed to think of him as Mr. Tate ever since learning his surname; our past made it a nearly impossible task. He was David, the young boy who'd followed me around for a summer.

I grabbed his hand as I might have when we'd been young and pulled him to the tall windows on the other side of the room, where our voices would be less likely to carry into the corridor and more light would get the romantic idea of an actual engagement out of my head. Once there, I took two steps away from him.

"David." His Christian name flowed much easier. His lips turned up at the corners, and his shoulders seemed to relax at my use of it. "You shouldn't have done that. You were less impulsive at fourteen."

"If you recall," his voice was barely above a whisper, "I was just as impulsive at fourteen." His eyes flashed in the moonlight. Having more of it wasn't actually helping, and the way his eyes raked over me wasn't either.

"We don't need to be so quiet," I said, not matching his tone. "We will be explaining ourselves to everyone within minutes. Mama and I are in unfortunate circumstances, but I will find a way out of it."

He dropped his hands to his side and glanced at the door, his jaw tightening. "Would your way include a union with that man?"

I shuddered. "No."

His eyes darted to mine, then slid to the window. "Because it seemed as though you were considering it."

I shook my head hard, even though at the moment, David wasn't looking at me. I placed a hand on his arm. "I faltered. Mama has been so distraught. But that won't happen again. Even if Mama ran after him, he wouldn't have me now, not after that scene." At least any self-respecting man shouldn't.

His eyes narrowed. "He would have you." His voice was gravelly, as if he'd spent the past eight years swallowing rocks instead of kicking them along the roadside. "He would have you no matter what it took."

My face heated, and my hand on his arm went from feeling like a friendly gesture to something I should be careful of. I loosened my grip until I couldn't feel the planes of his arm under his jacket anymore. David spoke about me in a way that made me feel valuable and desirable and anyone would be an imbecile not to think the same way. No one had ever treated or looked at me that way. Not even Mr. Green.

Since Papa had died, I'd obviously been lacking in good company.

"Even so . . ." Why wasn't my voice stronger? I sounded like I'd only just awoken and my throat was not used to the idea of talking yet. I forced more air into my next words. "I cannot hold you to what you said in the drawing room."

"You actually could."

"But I wouldn't."

He smiled. "You aren't even considering it?"

"Why would I consider it? You saw that I needed help, and you gave it, but now that Mr. Green is gone, we can stop pretending."

"Can't you let me be the hero for a change and remain engaged to me? We would keep it temporary, of course, only until you received your inheritance or found a suitable place to live."

I dropped my hand from his arm. I wouldn't receive my inheritance for a year and a half. "David, we aren't getting engaged. There is no reason for it."

"You don't have a place to live; there is every reason for it."

I gritted my teeth. There were quite a few options better than this preposterous plan of his. It wasn't even a plan. Neither of us had thought anything through. He'd simply jumped in to save me, and I would have latched on to anything in order to get Mr. Green to leave. "How would being engaged to you help me find a home?"

"My friend James is a doctor in town. He would happily put me up while you stayed with Julia in my home. Julia could use the company so you would actually be helping me. It is a brilliant plan."

"I'm not going to send you out of your home."

"If my mother were alive, perhaps we could all live together, but with just my sister and me . . ." He paused. "It could damage your reputation."

I scoffed. Did he think there were people worried about my reputation? At my age? No one would think anything of us staying with him. "I'm hardly someone people would be concerned about staying with you. I'm probably your older sister's age, and my mother is with me."

David rubbed his jaw and grimaced. "That might have been true this morning, but I just told a roomful of people I proposed to you."

I put both of my hands on my hips and raised my eyebrows at him. The two of us seemed to have a talent for making a mess of things. "That can be remedied quickly with one conversation. You owe us nothing."

He dropped his hand from his face. "If you truly believe that, you are mistaken."

His eyes caught mine, his gaze intense. I swallowed. I should have spent more time around handsome young men and less time around Mr. Green. I should be able to look David in the eyes without feeling like something noteworthy was happening. He hadn't offered an actual engagement, only a false one to provide me with protection.

"Julia could use a friend," he said softly. "She's been isolated. She had two Seasons in London but didn't do well, and I don't think she will return."

David or his family must have done very well in the past few years if they were able to afford two Seasons in London for Miss Tate. "She is a beautiful woman. I'm surprised she was not in demand."

David grimaced. "Does my sister look like someone who would want to be in demand?"

I shook my head. "No."

"It will be good for her to have someone besides me and our tutor, Mr. Allen, for company. If you could be a friend to her, like you were to me . . ." He paused. "She hasn't yet learned how to live."

I blinked, trying to follow exactly what David wanted from me. Did he truly think me capable of helping his sister? I didn't even understand exactly what their situation was. Why did David and his sister have a tutor at their ages? Did it have something to do with his sudden ascension to wealth?

Still, knowing he wanted something from me in exchange for his protection from Mr. Green calmed some of my worries. If he needed me somehow, that made this agreement of ours better, didn't it? "And you think I could show her how?"

"You showed me."

I laughed. "I'm not certain I could have done that. I didn't even know what life was at seventeen."

He inched closer. A hint of lemon from the bakewell pudding we'd eaten earlier invaded my senses, and for some reason, it made my heart rate increase. I wasn't scared of David, even alone in a room, but he was so different from the boy he had been—now so strong and self-assured—that it was disconcerting. Disconcerting enough to confuse my senses. His eyes traveled my face. "I've never met anyone more alive than you. Do not underestimate how much your brilliant light affected me back then. I want that back in my life, not just for me but for Julia as well."

I swallowed. No one had ever said anything like that to me. Not in my one Season in London and definitely not in Silverfork. I closed my eyes, willing my heart not to be confused. David didn't even know who I was anymore. I shook my head and forced my eyes open. "You mean the young lady I *was*. Mr. Tate, I've changed over the past eight years. Quite drastically. Perhaps more than you have, and unlike you, I can't say that my changes have improved me."

A smile curled his lips, and he took a half step closer, standing as close as he could without touching my skirts. "You think I've improved?"

My face grew warm. He *must* know he had. One side of his mouth lifted higher than the other, and his absolute delight at my discomfort made his eyes brighten in a way that would make anyone want to join his amusement. He was most certainly improved. "Do I need to answer that?"

"You don't need to, but seeing as how I was so cruelly rejected in my youth, it would be kind of you to assuage my hurt pride."

I gave into his smile and grinned up at him. "You've improved and are very different from when you were fourteen." I lifted a finger. "You're taller." Lifted another finger. "More confident." Lifted a third finger. "Better dressed, and"—I pushed my three fingers into his chest softly—"slightly better at proposing."

His lashes lowered as he inspected my three fingers on his chest. When he lifted his eyes back to mine, something in them had changed. "I haven't proposed to you yet."

"I suppose that's true, but you were quite gallant nonetheless."

His smile deepened. "I am relieved to hear that. All of it. You, on the other hand, haven't changed at all. I should have known that when I finally saw you again, it would be in that tree, looking more beautiful and as wild as you ever were at seventeen."

I pulled my hand away from him. We were too close, this room was too dark, and David was too much a man to be saying those kinds of words to me. More beautiful? That was a bold-faced lie. He was trying to charm me. David Tate had turned into a charmer, and he was playing with a fire he didn't know was dangerous. He didn't know how lonely I'd become or what words like that would do to a woman who had been looked over by everyone but a controlling man twice her age. I clenched one hand at my side. Perhaps I could help Julia, and some time in my company would probably do David good. A younger version of myself held some fascination over him, and the sooner he realized that young lady no longer existed, the better. "I will befriend your sister. It's the least I can do. But as far as teaching her how to live? I'll need to relearn that particular skill before I can be a teacher of it."

A broad smile broke out on David's face. "Deal."

Wait. What had I just agreed to? "I mean, I'll help your sister. I don't think I need to be your fiancée for that to happen."

"But it would be much easier for you if you were and much harder for you if everyone thinks you spurned me."

I laughed. "No one is going to believe you actually *wanted* to marry me. If we leave this room as friends only, everyone will think I came here unprovoked by you to force you into renewing an attachment that was made when you were far too young."

His eyes searched mine. "You don't think anyone would believe I could be in love with you?"

I snorted. It was unladylike but better than letting his words take root in baseless ways. This was all a farce, no matter how intense his gaze when he spoke. "We barely know each other. We haven't even seen each other since you were a child, for heaven's sake. This"—I waved a hand between us—"isn't what an engagement looks like."

"Then please tell me what an engagement looks like."

I sighed. "There should have been flowers or messages sent to me at some point *before* the engagement. We should have had morning walks together, duets on the pianoforte, dancing at balls, a few stolen kisses in a garden. A real relationship takes time to build. No one will think we are . . ." Heavens. Are what? In love? You didn't have to be in love to get engaged. But David had certainly implied ours was a love match. Yet I couldn't say something like that out loud. "No one will believe we've been harboring feelings for each other, not like this."

David didn't move. He breathed but so slowly that I barely caught the movement. "I think," he said, "you underestimate how little it would take to convince everyone of my strong feelings. Already, the length of this conversation, behind closed doors, will have them thinking I've missed you very much." His eyes flashed to my mouth, and his meaning became clear. I grimaced, but he only nodded his head toward the door, untroubled by what he was insinuating.

As if on cue, there was a knock at the door. "Mr. Tate." Mr. Preston's voice came out strong from beyond the door. "I believe that is as much time as I can allow. Mrs. Atwood is waiting to speak with you."

"We'll be out in a moment," David called out, then turned his soft voice on me. "What should we do?"

I hesitated. Could we do this?

He lifted his hand until it was just inches from the side of my face and brought his thumb slowly toward my cheek, as if he wanted to caress my face but was fearful of touching me. "Let me be the one to do something for your sake this time. Give me a chance to return a small portion of what you gave me. I promise it won't be unfair to me."

For some reason, tears pricked my eyes. He made it sound so easy. All I needed to do was say yes to him, and he would help me for as long as it took for Mama and me to find a new place to live. Who would have thought David would grow up to be a person I could lean on, someone who would have the ability to take care of me when I needed it most? His chest was solid in front of me, his hand still waiting less than an inch from my cheek, and I wanted nothing more than to fall into him and let all my burdens slide off me. Not onto him—there was still too much of that young boy who I wanted to protect in him—but onto the floor, away from both of us.

The sound of the doorknob turning caught both of our ears, and David's hand finally moved. He didn't stroke my cheek with his thumb as I thought he'd wanted to; instead, he lifted my chin so I would look at him. "Anna?"

I needed to rest. I needed time to breathe, even if it was for only a few weeks. My name on David's lips held such care. I wanted to trust him. I nodded slowly, not daring to meet his eyes, focusing instead on his sharp jawline.

"Is that a yes?" he asked.

"Yes."

He gave me a terse nod in return. "That door is going to open, and I'm going to start on your list of what an engagement should look like. Trust me, it is going to be very easy to make our friends and family believe I want to marry you."

The sound of the library door opening caught my ears, and before I could change my mind or step away, he cupped my cheek in his hand and slid his fingertips into my hair. With his free hand, he caught me at my waist and pulled me into him.

And then David Tate, with eyes burning like a man very much in love with the woman in front of him, angled his head to claim me with a kiss.

Chapter 5

"I proposed to Anna today. She said no, just as I knew she would. But I wanted to propose to someone once, and I wanted it to be her."

—David Tate, 1841, Age 14

His lips stopped a breath away from mine, drifting just above the corner of my mouth. It wasn't a kiss, but it might as well have been for how my heart reacted to his hands in my hair and the way he'd pulled me into a position where everyone from the door would see the two of us exactly as he wanted.

As a newly engaged couple, and a happy one at that.

I lifted my eyes from his mouth to find him searching my face, very much in control of every movement. He knew exactly how close he could hold me without our lips meeting, and he held us at that point without flinching. My lips parted, though I don't know why. It wasn't as though I could speak to him when we were supposed to be kissing.

I pressed my lips closed again, and the way David's eyes followed my movements sent a wave of heat up my neck. How had the boy I'd kicked rocks with and worried about where he would get his next meal turn into a man whose strong fingers cradled my head so protectively?

A throat cleared, and David stiffened and pulled away, feigning surprise. Somehow, in the years we'd been apart, he'd become a master of pretense.

He slid one hand casually down my arm, interlaced his fingers with mine. "She said yes." He grinned like he'd just won a title from the Queen.

Mama clapped and smiled larger than I'd seen her smile in years.

Mr. Preston put his hands on his hips and raised his eyebrows. "I should hope so," he said with a chuckle.

Only David's sister seemed the slightest bit uncertain how to react. Her eyes sought her brother's, but David looked everywhere other than in her direction.

This idea of helping his sister might have worked better had he simply befriended me. If this day could have been relived with some warning on both our parts, we would have come up with a much better plan than this one.

Engaged.

Even if it was temporary, how had I let this happen?

"And now, if you will excuse me, Anna"—David gave my elbow a squeeze, as if it were the most natural thing in the world—"I'd better speak to your mother." He gave Mama the kind of open and trustworthy smile that would have any matchmaking mother pushing her daughters in his direction.

Mama was not unaffected. "Yes, indeed. I can't believe Anna has kept you all to herself." She gave me a scathing look, but there was no fire behind it. This was a side of Mama I'd almost forgotten had existed. A playful side. "I don't even know anything about your family or background."

"His background?" Mrs. Preston's words burst out of her, and she grabbed Mama's hand.

David's fingers tightened on my elbow. I turned to look at him, but he wouldn't meet my eye. The false happiness he'd exuded only a moment ago had melted away as quickly as fistfuls of snow thrown into a fireplace. His gaze was fixed on a point somewhere beyond the doorway.

"You don't know who Mr. Tate is?" Mrs. Preston laughed. "Your daughter just landed herself the second son of a viscount. He's Lord Murphy's youngest child. He may not have the title, but he is the more dependable of the two brothers."

There must have been something wrong with Mr. Preston's library, for the moonlight had confused me the moment I'd stepped into it, and now the room seemed to be spinning. How could David have kept that from me, especially when I'd asked him? A broken engagement with an arbitrary man from Breckenridge was one thing, but having a father who was nobility was quite another. We wouldn't simply be able to break off the engagement. Not without all of the county and most of London finding out about it.

Miss Tate watched the two of us carefully, and then her eyes widened and flickered with understanding. She knew. She knew not only that our engagement wasn't real but also that I hadn't even known to whom I had become engaged.

Mama's eyes filled with tears, and she rushed over to me, pulling me away from David. His hand flopped down to his side. "Anna, how could you have kept this from me? I never would have written to Mr. Green, and I wouldn't have worried about, well, anything."

Mama clearly didn't remember the stories of Lord Murphy like I did, or she wouldn't be this excited. What could I say to her? I couldn't say I hadn't known who he was either.

David looked as though he wished he'd never come this evening. I couldn't blame him. It wasn't every day a man showed up to dinner a bachelor and left engaged to a woman he'd only seen once in the past eight years.

But I didn't think the engagement made him stiffen. He knew what I thought of his father. I'd spoken of him terribly that whole summer, and I'd even made my thoughts known when I'd seen David two days ago. David wasn't worried about the two of us—he was worried about my reaction to whom he'd been raised by. He should have told me, yet after all he'd done for me, I couldn't let him worry about that.

"I suppose I don't think about David's father when I think about David," I said. "They are two very different people."

David's shoulders relaxed, and his head turned slowly toward me. I could see he wanted to say something to me, but we couldn't talk, not with the Prestons and Mama here. Instead, he turned to Mama. "My father is almost never in Breckenridge anymore. I'm not even certain you will have to meet him."

The two of us were talking in code, and the only person in the room who seemed to be following it was David's sister.

"And your brother?" Mama asked. At least one of us had the foresight to learn a bit more about David's family.

"Garrett lives in London. Both he and my father have left the everyday handling of Tate Hall in my care for the time being."

"But they will be at the wedding," Mama said with a smile. "We will meet them then, if not before." David gave a terse nod, and my suspicions about how he felt about his father were more than confirmed. But he needed to get that scowl off his face if we were going to convince anyone of our happiness.

I stepped away from Mama and back to his side. With a deep breath, I pulled his hand into my own and smiled large enough for both of us.

It might be ridiculous, but we had to at least pretend to be happy, and if he couldn't do it at the moment, the least I could do was try to make up for his momentary stumble.

His hand was warm, his calloused fingers a deeper puzzle now that I knew he was the son of a viscount. He didn't look at me, but he closed his hand over mine tighter than I'd expected, as if he were floating out to sea and I was the only one keeping him grounded on the shore.

But Mama soon tore our connection apart. She hadn't forgotten it was her turn to speak with David alone. My face heated. She was going to be only too happy to tell him of my dowry and inheritance, both quite a bit more than would be assumed given our current state of affairs.

Based on the way David had scoffed at Mr. Green's income, perhaps those things wouldn't impress him though.

Mr. and Mrs. Preston did most of the talking while Mama and David were gone. I tried to engage Miss Tate in conversation, but she kept her eyes on the door to the library, looking worried. Did she think Mama would be negotiating a marriage contract that would favor only us?

It wasn't the most promising beginning to the friendship I'd promised David I'd work on.

Finally, the door opened, and Mr. and Mrs. Preston rushed toward Mama and David.

During the excitement, Miss Tate grabbed my wrist. I turned to her, and she spoke low. "Two days ago, David came home whistling. He threw himself on the sofa next to me and said two words." Her eyes flashed to her brother and then back to me. "Do you know what those words were?"

"No." Two days ago would have been when we'd met each other at the oak tree.

"She's back."

"Oh."

"That's all he said, but I knew. I knew from his grin and the bounce in his step. I knew from the reverent and euphoric way those words slid from his tongue that he was talking about you. And so help me, if you hurt my brother, Anna Atwood, God may have mercy on you, but I never will."

Every early impression I'd had of Miss Tate evaporated at her threat. Her stormy eyes fixed on mine with a fierce, uncowering steadiness. She was quiet, yes, and perhaps even wary of people, but she was not timid, nor was she weak, at least not where her brother was concerned.

I blinked. "I don't want to hurt him."

"I'm sure you don't, but I'm not certain that means you won't. And David has been hurt enough for three lifetimes."

Before I could say anything else—not that I had any idea what to say—everyone was back in the drawing room, and Miss Tate was looking forward as if she hadn't said anything. What kind of precarious position had I put myself in? It was getting more complicated by the minute.

David had made it seem so simple when I'd agreed to the engagement, but Miss Tate's reaction had me wondering if he'd brushed aside concerns we should have considered. I wasn't worried he would be hurt because he would fall for me. He might have some fondness for the person I'd been at seventeen, but it would be easy work for him to discover I was no longer that bright and hopeful young lady. Was she worried I would hold him to an engagement and hurt him in that manner? Or ruin his chances with other eligible and younger women in the future? He had a reputation to uphold—he was the son of Lord Murphy, for heaven's sake.

Mr. Preston pushed David down into a seat opposite me. Mine and David's eyes locked, but there was nothing we could say with everyone present. Conversation got loud, thanks to Mama and the Prestons, but neither of us seemed to be following what they were talking about.

David and I needed to speak with one another. Desperately. We'd only just been allowed a private conversation, but we needed another one. Ours was not a love match or even a match at all, but I couldn't imagine there had ever been two people who'd only just become engaged who longed for time alone together more than we did.

It was already dark outside when Mama and I took our leave, but the path to the cottage was short, so we declined Mr. Preston's escort. David looked with longing at the path leading toward the cottage, but he had his sister to attend to.

And if he was willing to become engaged to me in order to help Miss Tate, he wasn't about to leave her alone with the Prestons while he saw Mama and me home.

Instead of offering his services, he lowered his mouth to my ear in farewell. "I'm sorry, Anna. I promise you, you will never have to see him." He didn't have to explain whom *he* meant. And then before David pulled away, he sealed his promise by pressing a soft kiss high on my cheekbone.

A real kiss.

His lips barely touched my cheek, but the brush of his mouth and the slight puff of his breath sent an unexplained rush of raised flesh on the back of my neck. What was wrong with me? The man was simply trying to apologize while also demonstrating his supposed devotion to me, but my body betrayed me. I closed my eyes and inhaled slowly, but that was a mistake. His earthy scent certainly didn't help calm the sensations along my skin.

The sooner I found a position and a home for Mama and me, the better. Even if my mind understood David was just being kind and our agreement was extremely temporary, I could not allow myself to become accustomed to having someone care for me like this. Becoming attached to David would be a huge mistake. If I gave him even the slightest hint that I would like to remain engaged, he would be too blasted grateful for that bright, cheerful woman I'd been at seventeen to do anything else but marry me.

Chapter 6

"Mama can't stop him, no matter how much she cries.
And so now I am quiet when Father lights his cigars."
—David Tate, 1835, Age 8

He is such a fine young man," Mama said for the second time the following morning. We had just sat down for breakfast, and I was certain I would hear it a few more times before the meal was over. Mama had either not noticed the pain Lord Murphy had caused almost everyone under his power the last time we had been here or she had forgotten, so of course she was ecstatic about the match. Not to mention, the scrawny David had grown into a very charming and persuasive man. I wasn't sure how I'd agreed to this whole hoax, nor did I know how difficult it would be for us to end it. "I don't know why you didn't just tell me about him sooner. I have been so worried for us, and for nothing."

Because the boy who'd followed me around that summer had become a distant memory, and even if he hadn't, I would never have come here assuming that invitation to marry him would be binding. "We hadn't seen each other for years. I thought it prudent to spend some time with him before informing you of the attachment. What if he no longer cared for me?"

"I'm quite certain we all saw how much he cares for you yesterday." Mother hid her smile behind her napkin, but it was of no use, as I could see it in the crinkle of her eyes. It was good to see her so relaxed and happy, but it didn't change the fact that I didn't know where we would be living come March.

Mary, the maid whom Mrs. Preston sent to help us at times, also tried to hide her smile. It wasn't just the company whom we needed to worry about spreading rumors but the help as well. Word must have already spread from the large house to the cottage. Who knew who else knew of the engagement?

There was a knock at the door, and Mary gave a short bow and left to open it. It was early for a morning visit. I pinched my cheeks for color, even though I knew no one would be coming through the door.

Sure enough, Mary returned alone but holding a bouquet of delicate lilies of the valley. She was grinning from ear to ear. "These just arrived for you, miss." She handed them to me. "I will run and fetch a vase."

Flowers. I hadn't received flowers from a man since we'd been in London. And the lilies were perfect. I touched one of the small white bells dropping from the stem. Did Lord Murphy own a hot house? If not, where had Mr. Tate been required to travel to find these blooms? Tucked deep into the flowers was an envelope. I set the flowers on the table and opened the envelope, my fingers quivering slightly.

Anna,

I would be honored if you and your mother would accompany my sister and me on an afternoon walk. The skies are clear, and although it may be quite cold for such an excursion, I have been told engaged couples enjoy walks together. Your mother should wear a thick coat and hat, for I can promise to help keep you warm, but I cannot do the same for her.

Yours,

David

"What does it say?" Mother reached for the note, but I pulled it away.

"It is from David." My heart pounded, and my face was aflame. His comment about keeping me warm must have been written for Mama's sake, but surely, he'd taken his role too seriously. She was already quite happily convinced we liked each other. I folded the letter back up. "He's invited us for a walk this afternoon."

"A walk?" She looked out the window and shrugged. "I suppose it looks as though the weather will hold, but it is hardly the time of year for it."

"Yes, he did mention we should wear warm coats." I tucked the note quickly into my apron pocket.

"Well, you must send a reply."

Mary returned with a vase and took the flowers from the table. "The man at the door said he would wait."

I stood up quickly and strode to the little writing table in the corner. Before thinking better of it, I scratched off a reply, leaving out anything remotely flirtatious. If anyone else read it, let them think I was shy. I was not quite as good at pretense as David was. Returning to the dining room, I handed the note to Mary.

"Well," Mama said. "Will we be joining him?"

"Yes, Mama."

She nodded with a smile. "Good. I wrote to Cousin Agatha before breakfast this morning. She is going to wish she'd let us stay longer now that we are going to have a viscount in the family."

I shook my head. "Mama! Please do not send letters boasting about my fiancé's position in life." Cousin Agatha would be certain to spread the news in Silverfork. It was going to be a hard thing keeping track of everyone I would need to inform when we called off the engagement if Mama kept writing to acquaintances about it.

"I don't see it as boasting. It's not as though he is the heir; he's the second son."

Mama was definitely boasting, and we both knew it.

"Still, please don't tell anyone else. The engagement is very new."

"Are you worried he will reconsider? If so, he should have waited longer to hear your answer."

He should have. But it was too late now, and Agatha's knowing would actually be helpful in convincing Mr. Green that our engagement was real. But how many others would she tell?

I prayed not many.

The hours seemed to drag along until it was nearly time for David and his sister to arrive. Mrs. Preston had instructed Mary to stay longer and to aid in dressing over the next few weeks. Apparently, being engaged meant we would need her services more often. I left Mama with Mary so they could prepare and went to my bedroom to gather what I needed by myself. I put on an extra petticoat, then reached for the coat Mr. Green had given me. David's mention of keeping me warm was an obvious jest, but I still wouldn't be caught shivering.

As embarrassed as I would be if Mama read his note, it had made me smirk periodically throughout the morning. Ours was a ridiculous predicament.

I worked my way up the buttons on my coat. David's flowers and invitation to walk were an obvious reaction to what I'd said yesterday about what a true engagement should look like. He was putting forth the effort to make this engagement seem real. What were the other things I'd mentioned engaged couples would do? I'd mentioned dancing, but that was not likely to happen in winter here in the country. Anyone looking for entertainment like that would be in London for the Season. Stolen kisses? My face heated again. I needed to stop that. I was beginning to feel like a young schoolgirl.

Even so, he'd written to me *and* had engaged himself to me. Perhaps a few blushes weren't completely out of turn, even for someone as long out of the schoolroom as I was.

I left my bedroom and went down to the hall only to find Mother still in her apron. "Mama! David will be here any minute."

"I know, but I have never enjoyed winter walks. I'm afraid my coming will only shorten your time out of doors with Mr. Tate. You have waited so long to have this time together. I don't want to spoil it. His sister will be there, so you wouldn't be walking alone."

I shook my head. I barely knew David, and I didn't know Miss Tate at all. I was not prepared to spend the whole afternoon alone with them, not yet. Sometimes, a woman needed her mother. "Oh no, I am not going on this walk with only the two of them. If it is short, so be it."

"But . . ." Mama began, then eyed Mary and waited until she walked out of earshot. Mama leaned forward. "Don't you think your time would be better spent if I weren't there to dampen any of Mr. Tate's—" She checked once more to make certain Mary was still in the other room before leaning toward me. "Ardor?"

"Mama!" I said, shocked. But before I could rebuke her, there was a knock at the front door. We both jumped. "If you don't come," I hissed, "I'm calling off the engagement." I was going to have to anyway. This would just expedite the plan. Mr. Green must already be on his way to Silverfork, so the engagement had accomplished its main task.

"Don't be ridiculous. Mr. Tate is the best thing to happen to us since your father died."

I lifted my chin. "Don't test me. David and I haven't seen each other for eight years, and while yesterday, he was the obvious choice over Mr. Green, today, we have to deal with the reality of reacquainting ourselves. Besides, if your goal is to allow David and me time together alone, that will be better accomplished by joining us. You can be there to entertain Miss Tate."

Mama muttered something under her breath about my stubbornness coming from Papa and dashed out of the room. I followed her, and she managed to get up the stairs and into her bedroom just before Mary opened the front door.

I smiled at the thought of Mama adding her own petticoats in a rush before turning to see David and his sister striding into the small receiving area of the cottage. David wore the same coat as when he'd happened upon my embarrassing tree-climbing incident. The thickness of the wool made his lithe frame look larger, and the fur at the collar gave him a commanding air. His square jaw and high cheekbones showed an elegant strength, even though his face remained smooth and youthful.

Blast. Why did the sunlight have to shine through the doorway, lighting him up from behind as though he were some young lord dashing in to save a damsel in distress? Moonlight and sunlight—they were going to be the death of me.

Miss Tate stood slightly behind him on his right in a dark-blue coat and matching bonnet. She glanced between us, not smiling but not frowning either, simply assessing the way we greeted each other. Perhaps I should have found some way to make my approval of his appearance less obvious, but his eyes seemed to be doing the same thing to me, and we *were* supposed to be engaged. Two engaged people could let their eyes roam over each other when they met, couldn't they?

My lips lifted in a hesitant smile. He narrowed one eye and then gave me a broad and charming smile back.

Mary closed the door behind them and excused herself to help Mama.

"Good afternoon, Anna." David's smile curved up at the corners when he used my Christian name. If he'd been anyone else, I would think it was because he was devilishly happy to have bypassed weeks of courting in order to use it. But this was David. He'd been calling me Anna ever since we'd met.

"Good afternoon, David." His smile broadened at my use of his name, and I struggled not to express a nervous laugh. What a strange thing a pretend engagement was.

"Is your mother at home?" he asked.

I opened my mouth to tell him she would be here any moment, but before I could, Mama reached the top of the stairs. She had removed her apron and tidied a few strands of hair, but she was obviously not ready for a walk in the frigid March air.

"I just need Mary to fetch my coat," Mama said, smiling at David as though he were her own personal rescuer. Which, in fact, he was. She descended. "I was so pleased to be invited on a walk. Some people complain of the cold in the winter, but I have always found it refreshing."

David's charming smile fell upon Mama, and the color in her cheeks heightened. "I'm happy to hear that. I don't know many people who share your love of winter air, but Anna mentioned a detailed list of things she expected me to do now that we are engaged, and walking was first on it." His eyes found mine. "I look forward to obliging her every wish."

I was suddenly roasting in all my winter clothing. Exactly how thorough did he plan to be with that list? And when would he execute it? Was he considering kissing me because of what I'd said? I hadn't actually asked for those things—only said they were what engaged couples would be expected to do. Mother made a noise—a half laugh and half squeal—reminiscent of a six-year-old girl opening a Christmas present. I shook my head and gave David a stern look, forcing myself not to think about what it would be like to be held in his arms again. Mama was going to be heartbroken when she found out this wasn't real, and his teasing wasn't helping.

Mary brought Mama's coat, and David helped her put it on. I kept my eyes off them. I couldn't take any more of Mama's ecstatic looks. Instead, I smiled at Miss Tate. Her eyes were wary, but she gifted me a smile in return. Perhaps the two of us could become friends. Her words yesterday had been said to protect David, a feeling I could definitely understand. I still very much wanted to get to know her. I hoped David's plan could somehow miraculously work.

David opened the door of the cottage and motioned for Mama and his sister to take the lead. After they passed through the door, he held an arm out toward me. "Shall we?" I took it. His warmth immediately permeated the sleeve of my coat, even with the chilling breeze cooling my face. If all he did was compliment me and walk arm in arm with me, he would be fulfilling the promise from his note.

"Where will we be walking?" Mama asked. "It has been too long since I have explored this area. I hardly know what is nearby."

"I was thinking of showing Julia in what manner I found Anna a few days ago," David said, his mischievous smile lines showing how pleased he was to be torturing me at my expense.

I stopped walking, which brought everyone else to a standstill. "We won't be doing that."

"We won't?" He was all innocence and boyish charm. "I hate to disappoint Julia."

"I don't mind," came Miss Tate's firm yet quiet reply. "We should do what Miss Anna prefers."

All three of them looked expectantly at me. The oak tree was my most typical walk, other than making the trek to the Mortensens' small home, but I didn't think we would make it all the way to the Tates' lands with Mama in tow.

I let out a large breath. "All right, we may go to the tree. There is a nice hill nearby as well, with a lookout. You can see for miles."

"Can you see Tate Hall from there?" Mama asked.

"I don't believe so," David replied. He sounded uncertain, but we both knew we couldn't. I loved that vista, and if I had been able to see Lord Murphy's estate, it would have tainted it. "Anna and I will lead, seeing as we know the way." We walked around the pair of them and strode down the path leading to the oak tree.

I tipped my head toward David once I was fairly certain we were far enough ahead that we wouldn't be heard. "Surely you won't tell them in what condition you found me."

He pulled his head back in mock incredulity. "I won't?"

"No," I hissed. "It wouldn't be gentlemanly of you."

"And you think I'm a gentleman?"

"I truly hope you are since you hold my reputation in your hands."

His hold tightened on my arm, and from the corner of my eye, I caught his smile fading into a line. He swallowed and turned to me. "I do. And I've tossed and turned, wondering if I made the right decision. That I overstepped my place is certain, and I can live with that if it helps you, but if this agreement causes you any harm, I would not forgive myself."

"I didn't know Lord Murphy was your father when I agreed to it. I don't know how you expect to keep this quiet. As soon as one person knows of your engagement, everyone will know of it."

"You overestimate my position. My father has never included me in his social circle, and I haven't seen him in years. My older brother, Garrett, is the only one he spends time with anymore. True, people here in Breckenridge will hear of it, but I hope to contain the information to this little corner of the world. Almost no one travels outside of it, and no one keeps correspondence with my father."

"Except your family, I presume. Won't Miss Tate write of it?"

"My sister writes to Garrett but never to Father. And Garrett will not tell him. The three of us are the least likely to send information to our father. If news reaches him, it won't be from his family."

"And if it reaches him in some other way?"

David's lips pressed together in thought, but he didn't answer.

"You must not feel obligated to me. I will not force you into . . ." What was I trying to say? Or rather, I knew what I was *trying* to say. I simply couldn't say it. This conversation was more uncomfortable than having tea with Mr. Green. I gritted my teeth and sighed. "In your position, your family must hope for a much better match for you."

His smile came back, but it was a grim sort of thing, barely comparable to his earlier smile. "I wouldn't feel obligated—quite the opposite. If he ever found out, we would end the engagement immediately." He kept his eyes forward. "I saw your reaction when you heard who my father is. And even if I hadn't, I wouldn't allow him anywhere near you."

"Was he very terrible to you when you were a child?" I asked, knowing that at a minimum, Lord Murphy hadn't bothered to clothe David properly.

The cords in David's neck tightened. "He was."

Chasms of unspoken words filled that short sentence. How much prying would a temporary fiancée be allowed?

"Was he the same with your sister?"

He shook his head. "Not the same. But—" He paused. "He wasn't kind to any of us."

"From what little I know of him, it sounds as though he's never been kind to anyone."

"I think he believes he is kind to Julia and Garrett. Or at least, he believes he has acted without reproach toward them." He looked back toward his sister. "But I don't think you'll find she agrees with him."

"I'm sorry."

He placed his hand over mine. "You are the last person who should feel the need to say that to me. From the first moment we met, you helped me."

That summer blurred into a stream of memories with him, and I couldn't remember which of my memories were the first ones. "When did we first meet?"

"You don't remember?"

I shook my head.

"It isn't a happy story. You found me with a young hound."

Oh, that story. I *did* remember. It was near the beginning of my visit. I had happened upon David—not this confident young man in his prime but the poor child with ragged clothes and words that only left his mouth if dragged—holding a dying pup. It was the first time I'd learned to hate Lord Murphy. The poor thing had been injured past the point of recovery, and it hadn't been an accident. "That poor little thing."

His voice was soft. "So, you do remember."

"I do. I forgot that was the first time we met."

"Do you remember what song you sang to her?"

My face grew unbearably hot. "I sang? I have the most unfortunate voice. I must have been too young to realize it then."

The corner of his mouth lifted. "I'm fairly certain you knew it. But you sang anyway. I even remember the song. Well, the gist of it. Something about being poor and needy and yet the child of a king."

"'The Child of a King.' Our congregation in London would sing it at times. I couldn't believe Lord Murphy would treat his own hound that way." David looked down, and I sucked in my breath wishing I could return the words to my mouth. Lord Murphy was his father, even if he had disparaged him, I should be more careful with my words.

In a few more steps we reached the oak tree, and my eyes immediately went to the branch I had been dangling from. It didn't look as high from here.

David glanced behind him at his sister and then back at me. "You really won't allow me to tell the story of how I found you?"

"Not if you want to be engaged for more than a day," I said. His eyes narrowed, and he pressed his lips together. For whatever reason, it seemed like he was bound and determined to continue with the engagement.

A crunch of boots behind us announced the arrival of Mama and Miss Tate.

"This is it?" Mother asked. "I don't see anything spectacular about this tree. Although it looks like one Anna would have wanted to climb when she was a child."

David's eyes sparked at her comment, and I narrowed my eyes at him. I could see how badly he wanted to tell them what he had found me doing, but I couldn't allow it. Not if he wanted me to look anything but a fool to his sister.

He took a moment to swallow down what must have been a laugh. "She climbed trees?" he asked, eyes wide and innocent.

Mama shook her head. "So often I threatened to take away her pin money. She continued the practice long after it was appropriate."

If she only knew I'd been in this very tree a few short days ago. "Mama, please," I said. "Mr. Tate doesn't need to be informed of all my wild ways." He would enjoy it far too much.

Mama paused, looked back and forth between David and me, and nodded her head. "Quite right."

Miss Tate's eyes were on the oak, her eyes roaming the possible routes to the top. I did the same. It truly was a wonderful tree for climbing. A bit more treacherous than it had been eight years ago, but it still had some relatively low and thick branches that made it easy to scramble up.

I jutted out my chin and found David's eyes. I could see what he was thinking. He wanted his sister to have some enjoyment in life, and he thought the story of me helplessly dangling from this tree might bring her some.

You sang anyway. His words seemed to vibrate between us, a reminder of the young lady I'd once been. The young lady who'd so intrigued him that he'd proposed to her before she'd left.

Me.

Blast him. Giving in to David was starting to become a habit. I took a deep breath and turned to Mama. "Actually, Mama . . ." I began, and David raised an eyebrow. "I was climbing this very tree when Mr. Tate found me a few days ago. So I suppose you can tell him all you want."

"Anna!" Mama's hand flew to her chest. "You weren't!"

"I was. And Miss Tate, if you are looking for the best place to begin a climb, it is on the other side of the tree. There is a knob just fat enough to be a foothold."

Miss Tate shook her head. "I wasn't."

I dropped David's arm, marched over, and took hers. "Here, let me show you. I can't believe you have lived your whole life near Breckenridge and never climbed this tree. It's the perfect specimen."

I pulled Miss Tate to the other side of the tree. At first, she seemed hesitant, but then a slow smile grew on her face.

David jogged up behind us. "Let me help."

I gave him a withering glance. "Oh, no you don't. We won't be going very high and have no need of you. Please stand away. Far away. Why don't you climb the hill we were telling Mother about?" The last thing I wanted to worry about was my underthings while he stood beneath me again.

"I'll just lift you to the first branch and then be on my way." He reached for my waist, and before I had a chance to protest, he lifted me a foot into the air from behind. I yelped, but he ignored my cry and marched me toward the knot I'd told Miss Tate about.

As soon as we arrived at the tree, my hands flew to the first branches they could reach, and I pulled myself into the tree, my foot finding purchase, just as I'd told Miss Tate it would. David's hands remained on my waist, even though I was now perfectly situated to start a climb. He was close enough for me to feel his warmth through the back of my coat. He continued to hold me in place, as if I stood on the edge of a dangerous precipice and not at the base of a very sturdy tree.

"That pup . . ." His voice was a whisper at my shoulder, soft words meant only for me. "Was not one of Lord Murphy's hounds." He didn't call him his father. "Charlotte was mine." His hands tightened at my waist before he let me go. I turned and looked at him. He hadn't lifted me far, so his face was only about a foot below mine, and his eyes burned with a fierce sort of light. "Your kindness to both her and to me has never been forgotten. Thank you, Anna."

He turned away and grabbed his sister by the waist, raising her up to a higher branch than my precarious knot. Even though Miss Tate had just witnessed me go through a very similar process, a surprised breathless laugh escaped her at the sudden movement. The sound of it made the morning even more beautiful.

David's laugh lines appeared, and he chuckled with his sister. "We should climb more trees."

"It is a little late to start now, isn't it?" Miss Tate asked with a hint of laughter in her voice.

"No, it's not." He pulled at one dark ringlet that had escaped Miss Tate's bonnet. "Are you certain you two don't need any more help?"

I shook my head, hard. "No. We can manage being indecent on our own, thank you very much."

With a look of mock hurt, he waved a farewell and stalked off toward Mama.

He held his arm out to Mama, and she took it with a nervous glance in my direction. She didn't know what to think of Miss Tate and me climbing trees, and I could tell it was on the tip of her tongue to rebuke me, but David's smile must have trumped her desire to scold me. "Come, madam, and I will show you the view."

Mama's indecision left, and with a smile of her own, she took David's proffered arm. I turned to see Miss Tate looking up at the branches above her. Her pale skin no longer looked iridescent. Instead, she had two spots of rose on each cheek. A gentle wind blew the curl David had played with. This was certainly a young lady who could use some enjoyment in life. And if that was the only thing David asked of me, I would do my best to give it to her.

Even if my life had been sadly lacking enjoyment from the moment Papa had died.

By silent agreement, we both started to climb. I lost my grip once, and she managed to get her slipper stuck in between two branches. Instead of frustration at our mistakes, we smiled, and soon our laughter rose from the treetop faster than we did. I looked over to see David pointing out something on the horizon to Mama, and my life didn't feel quite so dull after all.

Maybe it was this place. Or maybe it was the woman beside me, reaching up for a branch to pull her to higher heights than she'd ever seen before. In my heart, I knew it was neither of those things.

Somehow, a tattered boy who'd followed me for a summer had grown into a strong and capable man who still looked at me like I held the answers to life's most important questions.

His faith in me made me feel as though I might.

David's back was toward me, so I took time to examine the way the fine cut of his coat accentuated his lean and powerful body. I was drawn to him—this man who had been unkempt and waiflike.

I'd been given a respite from my most pressing issues, thanks to him. I could feel my spirit warming and eking back to life.

Whatever gratitude he had for me as a child couldn't compare to the warmth filling my chest now. I leaned back against a sturdy branch and turned to his sister. With another broad smile, I held my hands out to the side, and let the breeze whip through them. Closing my eyes, I took slow and steady breaths, then opened my eyes and nodded for her to do the same.

She hesitated only a moment. Then, leaning back on a similar branch to mine, she allowed herself to let go of her handholds and throw her arms to the wind. When she closed her eyes, I could almost see some of the tension rolling off her. She raised her hands higher and let the brisk winter air rustle through her hair.

What had it been like, being raised by a man like Lord Murphy? David had somehow managed to break free from whatever hold his father had had on him, but Miss Tate must not have been able to do the same.

When she opened her eyes, she turned to me. "I'm much too old to be climbing trees."

"So am I," I said with a grin. "May I call you Julia?" The words flew out of my mouth as soon as I'd thought them. "Now that we've climbed a tree together, it feels strange to continue on with such formality."

Miss Tate caught my eyes. Hers were bright with the energy I felt. "Only if I may call you Anna."

"I would love that."

"I still think you are going to hurt him," she said. She was smiling this time as she looked over the land below us. I didn't know how to take her words. "But some things are probably worth hurting for."

I raised an eyebrow, not certain I should be one of those things for David. He was doing brilliantly, and I didn't want to disrupt his progress. "I would much rather *not* hurt him."

"It is already too late for that. But I'm sorry I threatened you before. You see, if I were to fall from this branch right now—"

I grabbed her arm. "Please don't. David would be extremely disappointed in me if I allowed that."

"But if it *were* to happen—"

I tightened my hold. "It won't."

She narrowed one eye at me as if she simply wanted to finish her sentence. "The point is, I wouldn't be sad for the climb, even if I fell. Even if I were in pain for days afterward."

Now *that* I understood. I'd climbed and fell from enough trees to agree with her. And if it meant a few days of pain for David after I left, well, that was part of the human experience, wasn't it? I would miss him and Julia when we had to part ways as well.

I released her arm, gave her a salute, and grinned. "Here's to the climb, then."

The breeze kicked up again, making Julia's curls dance. I spread my arms wide once more and let a whoop of joy leave my lips.

Miss Tate's eyes flew open, and I hollered a second time. Our eyes met, and on my third cry, she joined me. Her voice was lovely, even lifted in a strange warbling exclamation of freedom. In a fit of defiance, I unbuttoned my coat and let it fall to the ground. Mama would be furious if I became ill, but I needed to be unshackled by the past six years, and dropping Mr. Green's coat seemed fitting.

Julia stopped her whooping and looked at me in puzzlement. Then, with a shrug, she unbuttoned her own coat.

"No." I leaned forward to stop her. David wouldn't appreciate my terrible influence on his sister, and even though he'd said she was healthy, her pallor begged to differ.

But she shook her head and pulled away from me. After only a moment, her coat was at the base of the tree, the skin on her arms riddled with gooseflesh.

"Your brother is going to flay me alive," I said.

"He would never," Julia quipped, lifting her bare arms into the wind. Just before I joined her, my eye caught hold of a small, circular red mark, only partially visible under her short sleeve as it lifted. It wasn't raised like a rash, thank goodness. I would have felt terrible if she was sick and I was making her climb this tree. It must be a birthmark, so high on her underarm it was most likely never visible.

Not until some wild woman had her raising her arms up in a tree, at any rate.

Julia shouted again, and I pulled my eyes away from her arm, shook my head with a laugh, and joined her.

Only after we'd laughed and howled and finished expressing our freedom did I dare look out at David again.

He was turned this way. Of course he was. We hadn't exactly been quiet. He was too far away for me to catch the expression on his face, but his head was lifted, and I think, perhaps, he was looking at me as if I'd done something good.

My arm was once again wrapped around David's as we made our way back to the cottage. It had been less than an hour since we'd first walked arm in arm, yet I was much more comfortable with him already.

Getting to know his sister would be a pleasure. It had been too long since I'd had a friend close to my age. Just knowing I was on the path to accomplishing the one task he'd asked of me made my spine relax and put a spring in my step that hadn't been there when we'd left that morning.

David seemed more at ease as well. There was a nearly permanent crinkle to his eyes. We walked at a leisurely pace, in no hurry to return to the cottage. Soon, we fell behind Mama and Julia, pausing every once in a while to point out birds in the bushes or a rock that caught David's eye. He'd done that as a boy as well, always noticed the small things in life.

He bent over to pick up a white stone with a dark slash of black running through it and handed it to me. I held it tightly in my fist, secretly grateful that he gave me something besides the flowers. Those lilies would wither and die, but this stone I'd be able to keep long after Mama and I left Breckenridge.

His lips shifted to one side, and he nudged my shoulder with his own as if we were children. Having friends like him and Julia was something I could get used to.

Even if I shouldn't.

He nudged me again, this time softer. "I'm glad you're here, Anna Atwood. Now I don't have to spend another year wondering where you are and if you're well. And thanks to our engagement, I have an excuse to see you every day for the short time you're in Breckenridge."

I pressed my shoulder against his. "I'm glad too." Even if my decision to come to Breckenridge had started out as a terrible one. David had given me a chance to regroup and make better plans. "I think your sister and I will become good friends."

He chuckled. "I can't remember the last time I saw her so unfettered. Thank you." He kicked another stone, and it skidded along the path in front of us. "Some of Father's tenants still ask about you, especially the Mortensens. I'll finally be able to give them an update. You are going to make most of Breckenridge very happy just by being here. There will be a revolt when you leave."

For some reason, moisture pricked my eyes. The Mortensens hadn't moved as I'd thought, and I would get a chance to see them. Mama and I should have been living in a place like this rather than in Silverfork. We'd been fading away there, and it hadn't been until I was once again surrounded by people who saw me as a person of worth that I realized how drab I'd become.

Leaving Breckenridge wasn't going to be easy for me. Nowhere else would I have friends like these. But there wouldn't be work for me here. No one would hire David's former fiancée.

"I've missed the Mortensens. I tried to visit when we first arrived here, but they weren't home. It's going to be harder to leave here than it was to leave Silverfork."

David's toe dragged against the dirt in the path, but he nodded. "We'll find you a much better place to go. I've already started looking into a couple of options. If you would like to come to Tate Hall tomorrow, we can look over them."

"That would be a good idea," I said, even though I'd much rather spend time with him on walks than thinking of the future. But perhaps if we found a place for Mama and me, I could enjoy our time in Breckenridge more because I wouldn't have to worry about the future any longer. We walked in a more subdued fashion for a few yards, no shoulders bumped, no rocks uprooted from their resting place.

I glanced over at David. "If we are discussing those plans, I shouldn't bring Mama."

"Julia would be there. She knows the truth and can act as chaperone, if your mother agrees."

Julia wouldn't have been a proper chaperone if we were in Town, or if I were overly concerned about my reputation, but I was fairly certain Mama wouldn't object to my visiting.

The cottage came into view, and David stopped. My arm was remained entwined in his, so I was pulled to a stop as well. "Shall I send a carriage for you tomorrow?" he asked.

I shook my head. "No. I'd like to walk and visit with the Mortensens on my way."

"And you don't want me following behind you and waiting just around the bend while you speak with them?"

I laughed softly. It would be a strange thing for David to do now. I couldn't even imagine it. "No, if you follow behind me, I will make you come inside." David seemed to weigh the decision. But I would not have my first visit with the Mortensens overshadowed by a pretend engagement. "Please don't. I haven't seen them in years and—"

"You don't want me making things awkward?" he guessed.

I squeezed one eye shut and raised a shoulder. "Is that very terrible of me?"

David laughed. The sound of it was rich and rolled over me like a warm blanket after the fires had been put out. "I will not encroach upon your time with them. I want you to be happy while you are here."

"I'm certain I will be. Thanks to you."

"Thus far, I only remain more in your debt." David nodded toward Julia, who was standing outside the cottage door, smiling at Mama. Julia's dark hair lifted in the wind around her bonnet, and her cheeks were dotted with color. We joined them at the door, and I untangled my arm from David's.

"I will see you tomorrow," I said and then reached for Mama's arm because mine felt suddenly bereft. I lifted my hand and showed him the stone before clenching it tightly in my fist. "Thank you for the gift."

David smiled and then wrapped Julia's arm around his and gave both Mama and me a short bow. "Until tomorrow."

And when he led Julia to their carriage and helped her inside, I couldn't help but wonder if he was looking forward to our time together as much as I was. Losing him and Julia in a few short weeks was going to hurt more than I cared to admit. I hoped Julia was right, that this would be one of those times the climb was worth the fall.

Chapter 7

"I don't think Garrett and Julia believe me. They think I've made Anna up, and I don't blame them. Sometimes I'm not even certain she is real."

—David Tate, 1841, Age 14

How long had it been since I'd woken up excited for my day? How long had it been since someone had mentioned the word *tomorrow* to me and I'd spent the rest of the evening looking forward to what tomorrow would bring?

At least six years.

Mama was very much in favor of me visiting with the Tate family and was happy to avoid the two-mile walk to the estate. I'd told her David would be certain to send the carriage the next time we visited, but I'd wanted the walk.

After finishing breakfast with Mama, I threw on my coat, boots, and gloves and dashed out the door. My first stop would be the Mortensens' home. Mrs. Mortensen had been my favorite tenant to visit. She had six children and always welcomed a second hand to help in holding the smallest of them. In the past, I would have brought a basket, but our pantry was no longer full to excess. I knew Mrs.

Mortensen well enough to know she would be happy to see me with or without a basket.

I took the path that led to their home and, after a brisk walk, was once again surprised by how many improvements had been made over the past eight years.

Mrs. Mortensen had always done her best to keep the house tidy, but this was more than tidiness—the new thatch and plaster made the whole structure appear new. I knocked on the door, and after a few excited yelps behind it, the door swung open to reveal a young lady of about eighteen with blonde hair falling over her shoulders. I quickly did the math in my head.

"Maren?" I asked.

Her eyes went wide. "Do I know you, miss?" Maren asked, her words clear, though I could pick up the slightest Danish accent. Maren had been only ten the last time I'd seen her. She might not even remember me.

Mrs. Mortensen stepped out of the kitchen, wiping her hands on her apron and shooing two young boys away from her side. When she saw me, she pulled her hands from the apron and threw them up in the air. "Is that Miss Atwood? As I live and breathe, I didn't think we would ever see you again."

Maren's eyebrows rose, and she pulled the door open wider. "Miss Atwood?" she asked, smoothing down her hair. "You used to bring us apples."

I laughed. "Yes, I did. I'm afraid I don't have any apples with me today."

Mrs. Mortensen brushed her hand on her apron again and pulled me into her arms. "You don't need to bring apples or anything else. Come in." Her accent was stronger than Maren's, and the sound of it soothed me. She practically pushed me into the rocking chair in the corner of the room, and I sank into it with a contented smile. How often had I rocked little Samuel on this chair?

Besides Maren, two boys followed Mrs. Mortensen around. The older of the two looked to be about eight or nine.

"Is that Samuel?" I asked, and the boy's eyes darted to his mother and back to me. Mrs. Mortensen nodded, and he relaxed. "I used to rock you here in this very chair while your mother made dinner. But you were much too young to remember." I smiled, and he held on tighter to Mrs. Mortensen's side. "And you—" I turned to the younger of the two boys. "I don't think I've met you."

"This is Jacob." Mrs. Mortensen said, patting the boy's dark-brown hair. "My youngest. He'll be turning five next month."

I grinned at him. "Next month?" He nodded shyly. I wished I could promise him I would bring him something delicious on his birthday, but there was a good chance I would be gone by then. A lump settled in my throat. Nowhere else would feel like home after living in Breckenridge. "Happy Birthday," I said. He smiled softly and relaxed enough to allow some space between him and Mrs. Mortensen. "Where are the other children?" I asked, forcing myself away from the melancholy.

Mrs. Mortensen grinned. "They are at the school. Maren stayed home today to help bake bread, but she attends sometimes too—when the schoolmaster doesn't send her home because of her saucy nature."

"I'm not saucy. I simply like to help out by making a few jests now and again." Maren tipped her head and lifted one corner of her mouth in a grin that would be hard to describe as anything but *saucy.* "The students learn better when class is more exciting."

"You *are* one of those students, Maren." Her mother huffed. "You're fortunate not to have been expelled yet."

"There is a school?" I'd been here in the summer when the children were typically busy working outside, but I'd never even heard them speak about a school. I didn't think there had been one to attend back then.

Mrs. Mortensen brought her focus back to me. "Yes. Three times a week, Mr. Allen teaches reading and arithmetic to whichever children can make time to go to the school. It has been a great blessing every winter."

"We eat lunch there too," Maren said.

A male teacher in a small community such as this? Who was paying him—the vicarage? "How long has that been happening?"

"Since not long after Mr. David hired Mr. Allen to be his tutor. Apparently, Mr. David didn't feel the need to be tutored as often as Mr. Allen was willing to tutor, so together they came up with this plan. Despite Maren's flippant attitude, she's one of the more accomplished students. She has a quick mind for learning."

Maren shrugged, tucking a strand of her hair behind her ear. "Books and numbers make a lot more sense than people half the time."

Maren had grown to be a beautiful young woman, and her mother's compliment brought a spot of color to her cheeks that suited her well. I hadn't been certain in what condition I would find the Mortensen family. When I left all those years ago, their home had had holes in the roof, and the thatch had begun to rot. A few of the children had already taken ill, and I'd been worried I wouldn't find all of them here when I finally set foot in the home again. And I didn't, but it was because David had set up a school for them.

David.

The boy who would stand outside trying to be unnoticed whenever I entered a tenant's home. I thought he'd been unwilling to reach out to them or had been uncomfortable for some other reason, but in the end, he'd been able to do a lot more for the Mortensen family than I ever could have with baskets and willingness to hold babies.

"It is wonderful to see you doing so well," I said.

Mrs. Mortensen smiled. "Even that is thanks to you. You don't think I missed seeing young Mr. Tate following you around that summer? As soon as his father left him in charge of the estate, the first thing he did was hire a thatcher to fix our roof. He joined in the repairs too. I've never seen a young man so interested in something as he was thatching. Before long, he was repairing the tenants' roofs on his own using funds he got from selling one of his father's carriages."

So David *had* become a thatcher, just not as an occupation. But it certainly wasn't fair for Mrs. Mortensen to think I'd had a role in that. I shook my head. "You give me too much credit. Mr. Tate would have seen your need." I couldn't call him David in front of Mrs. Mortensen. It would be too humiliating for her to find out we were engaged only to have it called off in a few weeks.

With a shrug, Mrs. Mortensen sat in one of the other two chairs set up in the room. "Perhaps, but he did ask about you every year or so, wondering if you'd ever reached out to us."

I should have. I'd been too focused on my own problems to keep up on correspondence, and I regretted it now. "I'm sorry I didn't."

"Oh, it is no problem. We all have our own lives to live, and I'm certain a bright young lady like yourself has scores of friends to keep track of. And perhaps a husband and some children of your own by now?" she asked.

Even though her assumption about my family status wasn't correct, her comment about me being a bright young lady had me wanting to tuck a strand of my own hair behind my ear. I hadn't been called a bright young lady in a long time. "No, I'm not married. But that is nice of you to say."

Mrs. Mortensen raised an eyebrow. "Have you been to see the young master? He will be most happy to hear you've returned."

"I've seen him. We met by happenstance on one of my walks."

"Good," Mrs. Mortensen said as if that news had made everything right in the world. "No man deserves to have a bit of happiness more than Mr. David. And seeing you would bring him more than a bit of happiness, I should think."

If Mrs. Mortensen knew I'd seen him three times already and on the second occasion, he'd felt compelled to become my fiancé, would she have different words for me? Or maybe she wouldn't. She seemed a little too eager for the two of us to meet again.

"It was very good to see him," I said noncommittally. "I was very impressed with the man he's become."

Mrs. Mortensen's smile made her eyes twinkle. "As you should be. I'm certain you turned his head as well."

I waved my hands while shaking my head. "Oh, no. Don't go getting any ideas. I'm much too old and much too poor for a man in David's position."

Mrs. Mortensen's lips quirked at my use of David's Christian name. I needed to be more careful. "I think the two of us have very different ideas of being poor, Miss Atwood. Your family seemed quite well off to me."

"We've come upon some hard times since my father passed away."

Mrs. Mortensen's cheerfulness melted away. "Oh, my dear, I'm so sorry to hear that."

"We will be all right. I will be coming into some funds in just over a year, but I don't think Mr. Tate"—I made certain to use his formal address this time— "would consider me interesting at all, in the way you were implying."

Mrs. Mortensen shrugged. "If you say so. He hasn't forgotten about you, that's for certain."

The morning passed away quickly as we visited. I asked about several other tenant farmers I'd known when I was here last, and all of them had either moved away not long after I'd left or were faring much better.

Thanks to David.

The oldest of Mrs. Mortensen's children had married and moved to a farm two counties away. He'd been fifteen when I left—not much older than David, though he'd looked several years older than David at the time. They rarely saw him, but they were happy that he'd settled.

When I stood to leave, Mrs. Mortensen asked if I wanted Maren to walk me back to the cottage.

"I'm actually on my way to Tate Hall to visit with Miss Tate."

"Oh," Mrs. Mortensen replied, her face so still it must have been steadied on purpose.

I didn't know why I was comfortable with Mama and the Prestons thinking I was engaged to David, but for some reason, I couldn't bear the thought of the Mortensen family believing it as well. They had known both of us when we were young and had far too high an opinion of me. It was one thing to break off an engagement to a man people thought I didn't deserve, but it would be quite a different story if word got back to Mrs. Mortensen. She saw no disparity in our stations or age and, if anything, saw something positive in our temperaments.

It would break her heart for all the right reasons when the two of us went our separate ways. I was much more prepared to deal with Mama's frustrations, which would be more about security and our position in life, both of which David and I would hopefully have an answer for when the time came.

I wrapped Mrs. Mortensen in an embrace to avoid any more confusion on my part. I'd spent the better part of two days reminding myself my relationship with David was not a real relationship. No one except Mr. Green had wanted to pursue me in the past six years, and that hadn't changed overnight simply because I'd managed to get engaged. I didn't need Mrs. Mortensen's kind opinion of me putting false hopes in my head. Especially not moments before I had a mile of walking and thinking to do on my way to David's home.

Chapter 8

"Anna has returned. I feel like any sentence that brings this much joy should be written again: Anna has returned."
—David Tate, 1850, Age 23

When we'd lived at the cottage before, my walks and visits to some of Lord Murphy's tenant farmers had brought me in view of Tate Hall, with its massive columns and gray stone blocks, but I'd never been inside. I'd never even been down the long lane leading to it. Eight years ago, this house represented pain and suffering and a disinterest in helping those in need.

Now that I stood waiting in front of the oversized and intricately carved wooden door, I didn't know what to think. I rubbed my hand down the green wool fabric of my coat.

When an efficient butler opened the door, I was ushered into the house and shown only slight curiosity on his part. He led me through the large entry hall at a brisk pace, not giving me a chance to gawk at the pillars in each corner or the blond-colored marble on the floor. He opened the door to a drawing room, and I immediately paused to take it in. The room was almost as big as the whole of the first floor of the Prestons' cottage, and instead of being rectangular or square, it was octagonal, with floor-to-ceiling windows on the opposite walls that perfectly framed the green lawn and flowering trees of the back gardens. Pink velvet papers with delicate floral designs covered the rest of the walls.

Julia sat on an ornate cream-and-gold sofa in front of the middle two windows when she saw me enter, she stood to greet me with a smile. Before I reached her, the door opened again behind me, and David strode in.

He had a bundle of papers in his left hand, and he caught up to me with long strides. "Welcome to our home," he said, taking my hand and placing a soft kiss at my knuckles. "It is a pleasure to have you here."

His gallantry felt out of place, and I pushed down a blush. When he acted this way, the boy David seemed a distant memory, someone so different from this charismatic and well-dressed man welcoming me into the grandest estate in the county.

"Thank you for having me."

He grinned at my words; anyone looking at him now would think becoming engaged to a woman he barely knew was a fortuitous happenstance. "I hope you've been well since we last saw one another."

"I have. In fact, I visited with the Mortensens this morning."

That made his smile grow even broader. "I trust that was pleasant."

"It was very pleasant. They spoke highly of my new fiancé."

"They tend to do that. Pay them no heed."

"They spoke highly of me as well."

"Ah." He pulled me toward the windows and Julia. "Now, that you should listen to."

"They said you thatched their roof."

He shook his head. "No, I didn't know how to thatch roofs then. I simply ran about giving supplies to the thatcher while he worked. But that is when I developed a passion for it."

His movements were precise and decisive as he motioned for Julia and me to sit.

After we obeyed, he unceremoniously handed Julia a portion of the pages he'd brought with him. "I've managed to gather several different papers and have brought in the advertisements." He handed me a stack equal in size to Julia's. "If we work together, we should be able to look through all of them and find some positions worth applying for."

The papers he'd handed me were well organized, and some advertisements had been underlined already. Apparently our time for reminiscing was over. All the ones underlined were positions for women, and a few had a double line under them. Those, I soon discovered, included room and board. I glanced through a few of the pages and found two advertisements that were triple underlined.

"What do these three lines mean?" I asked him.

David glanced over at my paper. "Oh, those are within a half day's carriage ride of Breckenridge."

Why would it matter if I was near Breckenridge? I'd spent the last eight years away. I would like to visit with the Mortensens and the Prestons, but once I entered the working class, I wouldn't have many days free for such things. I read the one I'd stopped on. It was a seamstress position in a town not far from here.

"A seamstress?" I nearly laughed. "Have you seen my stitches?"

David shook his head. "No, but it was nearby, so I wanted you to look at it, at least." He glanced back down at his papers again, turning the page over on the one he had in his right hand.

I scanned some of the advertisements he hadn't noted. One, I'd already written to a few days ago. I pointed to it. "What is wrong with this one?" I asked.

David leaned toward my paper, his shoulder touching mine, then he shook his head. "They want someone who can start right away. You don't need to rush to leave Breckenridge."

"I only have a week and a half. That seems fairly immediate." I underlined the posting.

David lifted an eyebrow and looked at it again. "It is in London."

"Many of the positions are."

"Do you want to live in London?"

No. Even being there when we'd had the funds to live a life of ease in London, I hadn't enjoyed it as much as I did the country. "I don't think I have the luxury of being particular."

"You should definitely be particular. This engagement should give you a few more weeks here in Breckenridge if you need it. No one will question us if I move into my friend James's home while you and your mother stay here. We can set a wedding date for a long way off, and you would be able to stay for months if necessary."

Beside me, Julia nodded. "Don't settle for something if you know you won't be happy doing it. David would become such a mope if he knew you were miserable."

David scowled at his sister. "I try not to mope, as a general rule." But then he tipped his head to one side. "However, in this case, you may be correct. I wouldn't want my noble sacrifice to be in vain."

I took a deep breath, the deepest I'd managed in years, it seemed. To have over a month to decide my future with Mama, all while under the protection of an engagement to David, would be a respite I'd never counted on. My eyes traveled around the beautiful drawing room. Mama would be delighted to live here. But if we did, she would be even more heartbroken when I cried off from the engagement. "It already is not in vain. Mr. Green is gone, isn't he? And although I appreciate the offer of allowing me to live here, I think we need to try to find a location for us as soon as possible."

David turned toward me and took the papers out of my hands. "I agree, and I promise I will continue to use whatever resources I have to find such a place. But I hope you will also be able to enjoy your time back in Breckenridge. There are many people here who love you, many more tenants besides the Mortensens who continue to speak of you, and I think the best plan would be for us to look for a position for you but not dwell so much on how this engagement will be ending. Simply enjoy it. I've never been engaged before, and thus far, I think having a fiancée suits me."

"Simply enjoy our engagement?" What exactly did he mean by that?

"Yes." His eyes were bright with the kind of light only a youth with his whole life ahead of him could muster.

I leaned toward him, not certain I was someone who could live my life that way. Not anymore. "Without any thought of how it will end?"

He took my free hand in his. "Yes."

I shrugged, trying not to notice how right my hand felt in his. I had no idea what he meant by "enjoy our engagement," but I trusted the man before me more than I'd trusted anyone in a long time. "As long as we are both looking for a long-term solution for me and Mama, I see no concern with that."

"Wonderful." David squeezed my hand. "Sometime this week, we shall pack some baskets and visit the Walkers and the Smiths. They have both asked after you over the years."

Eight years later and those families still remembered me too? I'd spent enough time with the Mortensens to know they would, but I'd gone to these other homes only a couple of times. "They asked about me?"

David's eyes found mine. "Of course they did. You were only here for a summer, but you left quite an impression on every life you touched."

It was an exaggeration, of course. There were plenty of families I'd met at church or who had dined with us who wouldn't even remember my name. But it was a sweet exaggeration.

We spent the rest of the afternoon circling and underlining possible listings, and in the end, I wrote to only three. David and Julia crossed off several I wouldn't have because of location or the work being too dull.

"Would you like to stay for dinner?" Julia asked after we set down our work.

I shook my head. "I should return home and eat with Mama."

David leaned forward to say something, but then he must have thought better of it and stood instead. "I'll call for the carriage to be readied."

I thought about resisting, but if I did, David would most likely offer to accompany me on my walk home, and he'd already spent the whole afternoon working on my tasks. He must have other duties he needed to attend to. So instead, I smiled up at him. "Thank you."

Twenty minutes later, my arm was linked with David's as he walked with me to the carriage.

"What should we do tomorrow?" he asked.

"Tomorrow?" My feet slowed in surprise. How many more nights would I be falling asleep with that word, spoken in his melodic tones, floating around me in my bedchamber? "Will we be spending every day together now that we are engaged?"

He turned his head toward me, his light-blue gaze dancing with mirth. "Do you have more pressing matters to attend to?"

"No, but I assume you do."

"I will manage my work in the hours we aren't together, or perhaps drag you along with me to some of it."

"What kind of work would you need to drag me to?"

"The Walkers' roof has been overgrown with some moss and lichen. I told them I would bring my thatching tools so we can clean it up. I know they would also like to see you."

The Walkers were another family who lived on Lord Murphy's land. I hadn't visited them as often as the Mortensens, but we had grown close. "I would like to see them as well—no need to drag me."

"Wonderful. As soon as we have a day of sunshine, I shall *invite* you to accompany me."

We reached the carriage, and he held my elbow protectively as I climbed in and sat. When I turned to thank him, the sun, now low in the sky, shone through the carriage windows, lighting his face, making his eyes match the color of the fading sky behind him. My gratitude was caught on my lips, and before I knew it, he'd slowly closed the door and motioned for his driver to take me back to the cottage.

Chapter 9

"Sometimes I wonder how one person could have made such a change in me. But then, I remember the way she treated me. She asked my opinions, enjoyed my gifts no matter how paltry, and always braved ahead, unafraid of consequences. I think, perhaps, one person like that could make anyone's world shine."

—David Tate, 1845, Age 18

Over the course of the next few days, either David came to our cottage to visit with Mama and me, or he sent the carriage so we could visit him. I wasn't certain engaged couples typically spent so much time together, but ours wasn't a typical engagement.

Mama was beside herself with excitement about the attention David gave me. Indeed, her excitement was the only thing that gave me pause. David had asked me to simply enjoy being engaged to him, and I did. But even though he'd asked me not to think about when or how it was going to end, I couldn't help it when I saw Mama smiling softly whenever he put his hand on my back to lead me somewhere or when she would catch us laughing about an old memory.

Neither of us would relish returning to the life we'd been living up until David's proposal.

We'd been engaged a week when David finally deemed the weather clear enough to spend an afternoon working on the Walkers' roof. We went alone. Julia wanted to study, and it promised to be too long of a day for Mama to enjoy it. And so I found myself with my arm linked in his, walking the same paths we had eight years ago.

The paths were the same, but gone were the days when a silent David would often trail behind me. Instead, he talked and laughed and held a brush and a long wooden paddle with grooves that he'd called a leggett over his left shoulder. I liked seeing him like this—his clothing rough and well worn, his tools of trade effortlessly a part of him. I could almost forget his father was a member of the House of Lords and instead remember that David and I were friends and perhaps even equals.

When we got to the Walkers', however, I stopped. He turned and looked at me, puzzled.

"Do you not think it will be odd? Me accompanying you as you work on the roof?" I asked.

David raised an eyebrow. "I thought that was the entire purpose of this visit."

"But if we go in together . . ." I trailed off.

"Then we seem exactly what we are—two old friends who've come to visit."

Two old friends. The words settled somewhere deep inside me. A smile formed on my lips, and I cursed my eyes for wanting to tear up at the most inopportune times. "You don't think they will think something is amiss?"

"Because I managed to convince the most beautiful woman in the county to come with me? They might. But I don't mind them being impressed with me."

I bumped his shoulder with mine. "No, not because of that."

"Are you nervous to see the Walkers?" he asked, dropping my arm and stepping away from me so he could look carefully at my face. I didn't answer him, but he must have seen my answer in my face. He tsk-tsked his tongue and held his hand out for me to take. "You know they will be delighted to see you."

How many times had I tried to coax him into a home just as he was doing to me now? Many, many times. Now it was my turn to decide whether we would go into this home together. I raised my hand to his and grasped it tightly.

Somehow, David and I had become a team, so I followed him into the small home, and when Mrs. Walker opened the door, her delight at seeing me again made all my worries melt away.

After twenty minutes of catching up, David and Mr. Walker brought the ladder and David's tools up against the outside of the small house. I averted my eyes while David removed his jacket and waistcoat.

Mr. Walker held to the bottom of the ladder, and David made quick work of climbing to the very top, to the roof line. Once there, he grounded his feet firmly on the ladder and swung the leggett with a powerful blow. Dried moss flew up around him, but he didn't seem to notice. His linen shirt billowed around him in the soft breeze. David pounded his way down the roof in a steady, well-practiced rhythm.

When the ladder needed to be moved, he balanced on the edge of the house, distributing his weight between his hands and feet so as not to put too much pressure on the thatch. Mr. Walker slid the ladder a few feet to the right, and David climbed back up to the top and started the process over again.

Every so often, he would glance down at me, and when he caught my smile, he gave a short nod and got back to work.

Together Mr. Walker and David moved quickly. After about half an hour, they had finished one side of the house, and Mrs. Walker turned to me. "I would invite you inside for a drink, but I'm afraid those two are making too much of a ruckus."

"I don't mind staying outside." My eyes flicked to David again—he was working his way up the ladder again, his shirt no longer billowing in the wind but clinging to his arms and torso.

Mrs. Walker followed my gaze, and a smile quirked at her lips. "I don't mind either," she said in an appreciative manner.

"Mrs. Walker," I hissed in surprise. She had to be nearing fifty. "Your husband is right there."

"Yes, he is, and I don't mind watching him work as well." Her eyes flicked to her husband holding both sides of the ladder steady while David worked. "There is something satisfying about watching men perform physical labor, isn't there?"

My face heated. I had no idea how to answer her. I certainly couldn't agree with her, even if she had seen me looking quite impressed with David.

Mrs. Walker laughed good-naturedly at my discomfort, and I couldn't help the little smirk that formed on my lips in response. Yes, yes, I had enjoyed watching David work so expertly on her roof, but my smile was the only affirmation she was going to receive from me about it.

David turned just at that moment to check on me again. His hair was damp from exertion, and several locks had fallen forward, the tips beginning to curl. Even more heat rushed to my cheeks, but I managed to meet his eyes. He raised one dark eyebrow in question, and I gave my head a quick shake, hoping he understood it to mean I didn't need anything from him—I was doing well. Perhaps too well. I broadened my grin into a full-blown smile and waved him back to work.

David took one last glance between the Mrs. Walker and me and then resumed breaking the moss off the thatch.

I quickly turned the topic of conversation to Mrs. Walker's four grown children, and fortunately, that was a subject she was more than willing to speak about at length. We didn't follow the men when they went to the other side of the house. Instead, I offered to help clear out the Walkers' garden patch to ready it for planting. Mrs. Walker was more than happy to accept my help.

Less than an hour later, the men came out the front door. David had his jacket back on, but he hadn't bothered with his waistcoat. They must have finished and walked through the house to rejoin us.

I started to stand from where I'd been kneeling when David offered me a hand. I took it, and he pulled me up, then forgot to release me.

"Finished?" I asked, the warmth from my earlier conversation with Mrs. Walker returning to my face.

Mr. Walker shook his head. "We still have to go over the roof and sweep it. David thought you might want to help with that though."

"With the sweeping?" I furrowed my eyebrows. I'd climbed my fair share of trees in my lifetime, but never a roof. "I think that might be better left to the professionals."

David gave my hand a squeeze. "I'll help you. Have you ever been on top of a house before?"

"That isn't something generally recommended."

He raised his eyebrows. "I didn't ask if it was recommended, I asked if you have done it."

"No," I said with a puff of air, for some reason feeling disappointed in myself.

He squeezed my hand. "You are going to love it."

I scoffed, but the way his eyes sparked made me reconsider my laugh. He was serious—not only about me helping but also about his truly thinking I would like standing on a ladder leading to the top of the Walkers' home. I glanced up at the roof. The ladder was on the other side, but I'd climbed at least that high before. A slight breeze caught David's damp hair, teasing it, and the thought of standing near the top of the home, with the wind rustling my hair, made me think he was probably right. I would love it.

David must have seen the shift in my thoughts because he pulled me toward the house. "Don't worry, I'll keep you steady while you sweep, and Mr. Walker will hold on to the ladder like he did for me."

I stumbled—what did David mean he was going to hold me steady? On the ladder? He was going to be on the ladder with me? For a man who had spent over an hour doing physical labor, he had a lot of energy. We were practically running through the Walkers' home, and I couldn't get out a protest.

He brought me to the base of the ladder and motioned for me to start climbing. Then he bent down, grabbed the brush he'd brought with him, and waited behind me.

"You are going to follow me?" This was like the oak tree all over again.

"Yes. I'll be right behind you."

I flushed. That was becoming a problem. "But my skirts . . ."

"I can keep your skirts against the ladder. We will be perfectly respectable."

"Somehow, I doubt my mother would think climbing a ladder to do labor is respectable."

"What do you think?" His eyes met mine again, and this time, it wasn't simply the joy of doing this work that made them spark. There was something else—something deeper. He wanted to share this love of his with me. He wanted me to see this side of him, the side he'd discovered and made for himself.

I swallowed. "I don't actually care what Mama would think. I would like to see the world from the top of a roof you've thatched."

The corners of his mouth lifted, and the world faded away behind that smile. My breath caught, but I don't think he noticed the effect he had on me, because he simply put both of his hands at my waist, turned me around, and, with a bit of a push, said, "Up you go, then."

David was true to his word and followed directly behind me, his free hand holding on to the side of the ladder at my waist and sliding up each time I took another step.

Mrs. Walker was going to absolutely love watching us.

"All the way to the top," David said, his mouth near my shoulder. "And we will brush the debris down."

I nodded and kept climbing, enjoying the feel of David's body keeping me pressed safely into the ladder. When we reached the top, I stopped, unsure of what to do next. David had the brush, and I didn't dare turn around to look at him. My only view was the top of the ladder and an up-close inspection of the roof's thatch.

"Now what should I do?" I asked.

David took one more step so he was only one rung behind me, his chest warm against my back. "Here," he said, handing me the brush. "It's like sweeping. We have to clean up the mess I made earlier."

It took some getting used to, but eventually, I relaxed enough to lift my chest away from the ladder in order to swing the brush up and then sweep it downward.

"Good," David said, his words at the back of my exposed neck and a rush of heat flooding down my spine. I brushed faster. This was a terrible idea. My thoughts were misbehaving along the same lines that Mrs. Walker's had earlier.

We reached the bottom of the roofline, and I stopped. "Thank you for letting me help," I said. My voice sounded a bit too breathless for my liking, but that could be attributed to the work I'd just done. "It might be best if you finish the rest of the sweeping yourself."

"You haven't even had the chance to look out yet. Do one more pass, and then I can finish, if you want me to."

I sighed because he was right. I did want to look out while on top of the roof. "I should have paid more attention to how you stayed on the roof while Mr. Walker moved the ladder."

He chuckled. "We won't be doing that. It would be a bit complicated and not as safe as I'd like with two of us. We'll simply climb the rest of the way down and then back up again."

David started down, and I matched his pace. He helped Mr. Walker move the ladder, and then we climbed up again in the same manner.

This time, when we reached the top, David hooked the brush into some of the thatch. He then wrapped one arm around my waist in a manner no other man would have dared and anchored us onto the ladder with his other hand. "I have you—turn around."

I took a deep breath, which, rather than settle me, served as a reminder of David's arm holding me fast. I blinked hard once, determined not to let my eyes betray any of my thoughts if David caught a glance at them, and then turned around.

The view was magnificent. I'd climbed at least this high before, but something about not having any branches to grab onto or obstruct the scene made it feel like a completely different experience. Mr. and Mrs. Walker stood at the base of the ladder, and the path David and I had walked stretched out before us. The trees were only just starting to bud, and the fields were still brown, but I could imagine what the view would look like once the leaves covered the trees and the fields turned green.

"Oh, David," I said with a soft exhale.

"I like the world best when I get to see it from the tops of houses," David replied. "I like it even better when I can share it with you."

I swallowed hard, reminding myself that our engagement was only a temporary thing. For all I knew, David had brought dozens of women to rooftops.

We breathed in unison for several minutes while the wind whipped around us. I wasn't ready to return to solid ground.

"I suppose a few more passes with the brush wouldn't do me any harm," I said.

"Perfect," he said, pulling me tighter against him so I could safely turn back around.

In the end, we finished the whole of the roof together.

Chapter 10

"Garrett has made a deal with the devil. I don't want to be grateful for it, but I am."
—David Tate, 1846, Age 19

The next morning, long after breakfast had ended and Mary had returned to the Prestons' home, a knock sounded at the cottage door. I jumped up from the drawing room sofa before Mama had the chance to react. She stayed seated while I tried to keep myself from running to reveal the visitor. I mostly managed but had to take a calming breath before pulling open the door.

It was David.

I let my eyes wander over him and gave my heart a moment to rejoice. Happiness had been scarce over the past few years, and knowing that in David, I at last had a dear friend who cared deeply about my welfare made me happy indeed.

The sun shone behind him, accenting hints of red in his dark-brown hair and making it appear as if he wore a blasted crown. His eyes were as bright as the sunlight behind him, and his lip quirked up in a half-smile. He'd traded in his rough work clothing for his clean, crisp coat and hat, and if I hadn't spent the morning remembering his skill on the Walkers' roof, I would think the gentleman standing in front of me had lived a life filled only with gentlemanly pursuits. Both versions of David were fascinating.

In his uplifted hand, he held a note.

I reached out to take the note from him, and my finger brushed his gloved hand. He wouldn't have noticed the contact, but I did.

"Good morning," I said, wishing I could have thought of something witty to say.

"Good morning," he replied easily. "I'm here acting as a footman today. Will you see to it that this note makes it to the ladies of the home?"

"Does that mean you won't be coming in?"

He looked behind me as if he were tempted but then shook his head. "My tutor will be arriving at my home at any moment, and I don't want Julia to have to entertain him until I arrive."

"Mr. Allen?" I asked.

He raised an eyebrow. "Yes. Have you met?"

I shook my head. "No, but the Mortensens mentioned him. They said he also runs a school."

David nodded. "I never had a formal education, so in the last few years, I've supplemented my reading by hiring him. We are fortunate that he also had the time to open the neighborhood school." David never seemed comfortable when I complimented him, but I very much wanted to tell him how thoughtful he was, not just to the boys and girls in the community but to me as well. "I must admit, lately, his lessons seem to interest Julia far more than they do me. Even so, I should return. Once I receive your reply, that is."

"My reply?"

"To my note."

"Oh, of course." Somehow, I'd forgotten the small slip of paper, even though it was in my hands. I turned over the card and read his invitation.

Mrs. and Miss Atwood,

My sister and I would be delighted if you would join us for an afternoon of music at Tate Hall today. If that is agreeable, we will send a carriage to collect you at 4pm.

Yours,

David

"An afternoon of music?" I asked, confused. I'd assumed we would either spend more time looking for work for me or enjoy another walk. Mama and I were down to days left at the cottage, and we needed to decide what our next plan was. "You don't think we should be deciding on where Mama and I will go?"

"I haven't yet fulfilled all my duties as fiancé."

"What duties?" I asked and then grimaced. My list of what I'd thought engaged couples should do had included playing duets. Why had I said that?

I was terrible on the pianoforte. I had a rudimentary knowledge and knew how to play a few pieces badly, but if David thought he was going to be able to open a sheet of music to a complicated piece and have me play it with any sort of talent, it was going to be a disaster.

"My invitation disappoints you?" David was leaning forward, hand on the doorframe of the cottage as though that were the only thing stopping him from coming in and staying for tea.

"No, it sounds lovely. I'm only concerned about how little time we have left in the Prestons' cottage."

"I've already told you I plan to move into James's home, and you and your mother will stay with Julia."

We'd discussed this plan several times before, but I'd hoped we wouldn't actually have to send him into Breckenridge to live with his good friend the doctor there. As far as I knew, he hadn't even talked to his friend about it.

He narrowed one eye. "The face you made as you read my note didn't seem to be the face of someone who thought the invitation was lovely."

"No, but it is. We would love to come. Thank you for sending the carriage. Mama will be very pleased."

"Will my fiancée also be pleased?"

I gave him a smile. "I will, I promise. After all you have done for my family, nothing you could do would displease me." My reassurances didn't seem to reassure him at all. If anything, he seemed dissatisfied.

"All right, then. As soon as I receive my answer, I'll take my leave."

"I gave you my answer."

"You forget, I'm only the footman. Would you like to write a note for me to deliver to . . ."

He paused, obviously unsure of who exactly he would be delivering a note to. "Yourself?" I asked.

He shrugged, leaning against the doorframe and folding his arms. "I'll wait."

I gave a soft groan and grabbed him by his arms, pulling him into the cottage. "Wait inside. You're letting in far too much cold air."

He stumbled forward in surprise. I tightened my grip on his arms until he was steady, then quickly shut the door. The cottage foyer was small, with barely enough room to greet guests and servants who arrived there. David's lean form and vibrant energy seemed to fill the space around us. Only a day ago, his arms had been around me as we had worked on the Walkers' roof together, and having him this near again brought back the memory of him holding me. Not that the memory had ever been far from my mind.

"I'll be back presently," I said with a quick puff of air, turning and escaping to the small drawing room. As soon as the drawing room door shut behind me, I sucked in a long breath.

"Who was at the door? Mary?"

I jumped at the sound of Mama's voice. What had gotten into me? "No, a note was delivered from David." I didn't mention it was delivered by David himself. He was just on the other side of the door. If Mama knew, she would likely accost him and make him stay, and he'd already said he couldn't. I didn't trust him to say no to Mama. He'd proved himself much too willing to put his needs aside for others in the past week and a half.

Mama stood up quickly from her seat and held out her hand. Grateful he hadn't written anything misleading, or provocative, this time, I handed his note to her.

Mama read it at least twice over, a smile rising on her face the second time. "His handwriting is impeccable, isn't it?"

I nodded my agreement. It was. He wrote in a bold script, clear and unembellished, except for the capital letters at the beginning of each sentence. He'd mentioned he hadn't had a formal education. Was penmanship something he'd learned later in life?

"And he is sending a carriage," Mama continued. "Do you think he has planned a concert for us? Hired musicians?"

"I don't think so, Mama. I think it will be just our family and his enjoying music together."

Mama's eyes widened, and her head jerked up from her third reading. "You don't think he will ask you to play, do you?"

I grimaced. "I think there is a very good chance he will."

"But you can't." Mama wrung her hands together. "I mean, you shouldn't. Does he think you are accomplished musically? How important do you think that will be to him?"

"I've never divulged my lack of talent to him. But don't worry, Mama. It will have no bearing on our engagement."

She held David's note to her chest and started pacing in front of the fireplace. "How can you be certain? Perhaps we should suggest something else."

"I'm certain, Mama." I might be humiliated in front of him and Julia, but our engagement's end would be determined not by how much David was impressed by me but by the two of us finding a safe and sustainable position for Mama and me.

I went to the small table that acted as both writing desk and tea table. "I need to send my reply. I assume you will be joining us."

"Of course. Perhaps if I'm there, I can save you from having to perform."

I nodded, took out a card, and sat down. I left my nib in the ink, dabbing it up and down. What should I write? My reply for our walk had been quick and dry. I'd never had the pleasure of correspondence with a man who wasn't related to me, and if this was going to be a regular occurrence, I wanted to get the tone correct. Mama might read my response, so I couldn't make it too brief or businesslike. David was my fiancé after all.

I started by writing his name.

David.

That alone felt more intimate than saying it. Perhaps because I'd called him by his name when he was younger. But addressing a letter to him? It felt like one more boundary I shouldn't cross with a man who would not always be a part of my life.

Thank you for the invitation. My mother and I gladly accept.

My pen paused over the paper. What else? I'd responded to him, let him know we were grateful, but it was much too stilted to be a note written between fiancés. I dipped the nib back into the ink and took a deep breath. We were pretending. What I wrote next wouldn't mean anything real, and David would know that.

I will count the hours until we can see each other again.

That was good enough, wasn't it? Probably too good. David would most likely tease me mercilessly about it after he read it. But the pen still had ink, and I found myself wanting to add just a bit more.

The time I spend with you has made me the happiest I have been in years. I will be forever grateful we found each other again.

Now that I'd started, I found I had even more I wanted to say. I didn't think I could say such things to him in person. He would most likely laugh them off and remind me again of how much I'd helped him when he'd been a boy. But that excuse of his felt weaker by the day. What had I done for him? Allowed him to follow me around while I'd delivered baskets to tenant farmers? Sung to his dying dog? Anyone could have done those things. But what David was doing for me now? He was putting his reputation at risk, appeasing Mama, and interrupting his studies and his work to spend time with me so people would believe in our engagement.

Thank you for being there to catch me when I was certain to fall. There is no other man I'd rather entrust my safety and my happiness to than David Tate.

There were many more words I could say. But I stopped myself. This wasn't a love letter; it was a response to an invitation. I hastily signed my name, then stood.

Mama came to my side as I walked toward the door and read my note over my shoulder. She gave me a nod and a squeeze of my elbow, but thankfully, she didn't follow me into the foyer.

David was standing in roughly the same position I'd left him. There really wasn't anywhere else he could go. But he'd taken off his gloves, and his hair was slightly disheveled after removing his hat.

I held out the note, praying he wouldn't read it while I was standing there. How rude would it be if I simply handed it to him and ran back into the drawing room?

But thoughts of running fled my mind the moment his hand grasped my little card. Just as my fingers had brushed his glove earlier, his fingers now grazed mine. Only this time, nothing was between us, and the shock of his skin left me bereft of any coherent thought.

I had little experience with men, despite my age. When Papa had been alive, I'd attended a few balls, but I had been young enough to believe I had ample time to find a husband, and I had spent most of my time enjoying dancing and watching the colors of the gowns parade across the room in patterns that matched the lilting music. I'd never shown marked interest in any one man, and no one man had shown marked interest in me.

My years of almost no contact with men of an eligible age had the unfortunate side effect of making a simple touch from David send a shiver up my arm and making my breath catch.

David's eyes met mine. I was not certain what he saw there, but I prayed he couldn't see what I was thinking or feeling. He was young and handsome in the kind of dashing way any woman would have a hard time resisting. He most likely caused reactions like this daily. I didn't want him to pity the spinster who couldn't simply touch his hand without having a visceral response.

I turned my lips into what I hoped was an unaffected grin, released the note, and let my offending hand drop to my side. His eyes followed the movement before lifting to the words I'd written.

My face was already hot from my strange response to his touch, but it warmed further as I realized I was going to have to stay here while he read my note, filled with sentiments that, while true, shouldn't be said out loud.

His thumb traced the corner of the card as he slowly read each word. When he finished, his chest rose and fell once. Our calm camaraderie had fled, suddenly replaced by something far more intimidating.

Something tugged between us, a force of nature like a rising storm but not that exactly—a storm was too temperamental, too impermanent. Our connection was steady and strong and would outlast a storm by decades. It was a constant pull, like gravity.

For the barest of seconds, I thought he might sway forward. Every part of me wanted to be closer to him. We were two people standing feet apart but incapable of keeping our distance.

I fought against it. I was delusional. I had to be. Whatever was pulling me to him couldn't possibly be affecting him. I was simply someone who'd helped him in the past, and now he wanted to repay me. He saw my desperation and wanted to relieve it.

I was just like the tenant farmers he helped—in need of care. That was all.

His eyes drifted back down to my note before he cleared his throat. I thought he would say something, but he didn't. Instead, he tucked the note into his breast pocket, gave me a nod, and, without a word of farewell, strode out the door.

I wasn't certain either of us understood what had just happened.

When I returned to Mama, she ushered me toward the stairs, following directly behind me. "With Mary gone, we will need extra time getting ready this afternoon. You are past the age where youth alone will recommend your beauty."

I sighed but trudged up the stairs, not willing to disagree with her—not even certain I did disagree with her.

For the next half hour, we stood in front of the mirror, me in front and Mama behind me. Mama used the hot iron to curl some of the short hairs around my ears and face, turning them into delicate ringlets instead of disheveled wisps. Her dark eyes were nearly black, just like mine, but managed to almost glow. When she finished with my hair, she grabbed my shoulders and caught my eyes through the mirror. "At first, I wasn't certain about this David of yours. You'd never mentioned him to me. I don't even remember him from our visit here eight years ago. But then again, at that time, your father and I let you roam fairly freely. Seeing you together, however, has eased any fear I had. The two of you are obviously well suited."

Her words struck a chord I'd rather not hear. I brushed off her comment with a laugh. "Better suited than Mr. Green and me, at the very least."

Mama sucked in a breath and laid her head on top of mine. "I'm truly sorry about that. If I had known we were coming here to meet your fiancé, I never would have written to Mr. Green. I just . . ."

I sighed because I knew exactly how she'd felt—helplessness was a feeling that left a mark. "You didn't know what else to do."

She nodded, tears welling in her eyes. She brushed them away and pasted on a wavering smile. "But I should have trusted you. I'm sorry."

An ache settled deep in my stomach. She shouldn't trust me. I hadn't solved any of our problems—only kicked them down the road a little, just as David kicked his pebbles. I straightened my shoulders and set my jaw. But I would solve them. David had given me a window of time to find a solution. Once we had my inheritance, we would be able to survive.

I lifted my hand and placed it atop Mama's. "You were only trying to keep us safe. I understand. I may have even married Mr. Green if it weren't for David. But now, everything is in order, and I don't want you to worry about us anymore."

Mama's hands tightened on my shoulders, and she leaned forward and placed a kiss at my temple. "I know. Thank the heavens for Mr. Tate."

I nodded, a strange bubble of nerves bursting in my middle at the mention of David. I stared myself down in the mirror. Mama had managed to make my straight, dark hair shine where it was pulled up and curl where it was loose. My skin was smooth and my eyes more vibrant than they had been in years. I felt beautiful, even if I wasn't seventeen anymore. Did David think I was? He'd been very clear that our engagement was meant to be enjoyable, but he'd also been very clear that our engagement wouldn't lead to marriage.

"Yes," I agreed, giving myself a stern look in the mirror. I couldn't let girlish fancies sour our friendship or make me wish it could be more. "Thank the heavens indeed."

Chapter 11

"Anna isn't in London. At least, I couldn't find her there."
—David Tate, 1846, Age 19

Tate Hall came into view, and Mama pressed against the window. It was an impressive sight as we came to a stop in front of it.

We left the carriage, and David's footman announced our arrival.

I straightened my gown underneath my coat. It was the nicest gown I owned, white with thick vertical lines of blue flowers running down the matching bodice and skirt. The long sleeves belled out and ended in a gold tassel-like trim. I never would have been able to afford such a dress, but Mr. Green had given Mama a significant discount on it, and as much as I despised Mama's accepting his charity at the time, I was grateful now to have at least one dress that seemed to fit the massive home we were entering. A cheerful maid I'd met once before led us from the grand foyer surrounded by marble columns into a smaller room I'd never seen before. It contained several sofas, a pianoforte, stringed instruments on stands in one corner, and a massive covered harp tucked into an alcove.

David and Julia were already there, Julia at the pianoforte and David standing behind her, pointing at something on the page. They both turned at our arrival.

David's dark jacket and trousers were impeccably pressed, and in his breast pocket a small sprig of lily of the valley bounced from his quick movement. He was wearing the same flowers he'd sent me. And blast, there were those sneaky feelings again: Attraction. Longing. A pull that made me question my ability to correctly gauge any social situation, because there was no doubt David would be highly embarrassed if he knew how much the sight of him pleased me.

Here was a man who remembered me as joyful. And by a strange twist of fate, when I was with him, I *was* joyful.

"Welcome to our home," David said. "It is a pleasure to have you here."

"Thank you," I answered in a soft voice that didn't sound like my own. It sounded too much like a woman who was captivated by the man standing in front of her.

I pulled my gaze away from David. He couldn't want me fawning over him, but he did want me to strengthen my budding friendship with Julia. I strode to the stool where she sat, pulled her to her feet, and wrapped my arms around her in a quick embrace. Her slight gasp made me pull back, but the look on her face was only one of surprise, not distaste at my forwardness. The past week had softened her toward me.

I put my hands on her shoulders and gave her a bright grin. "Are you to be our entertainment this afternoon? The music I heard from the corridor was hauntingly beautiful."

Julia's pale cheeks reddened, from my overly friendly embrace or my praise, I wasn't certain. The wild woman who'd climbed a tree with me last week had hidden back in her den.

"No." Her eyes flitted to David, but he was busy charming Mama. "I don't think so." Her uncertainty made her seem younger. Almost as if David were the older sibling, not her.

David noticed our glances and came back to Julia's side, but when he reached us, it was my hand he grasped. "I thought the two of us could play a duet. It is high time someone besides Julia used this room."

Mama made a stuttering noise and sauntered over to us as quickly as she could without outright galloping. "I could play for you. Anna tends to enjoy listening more than playing."

That was most definitely true. David raised an eyebrow and looked at me. I could see the moment he put the pieces together by his slow, sardonic smile. "That is kind of you, Mrs. Atwood, but I'm afraid Anna promised me a duet."

I ground my teeth but somehow managed a smile. Based on Mama's distraught reaction, it wasn't a beautiful smile, but a smile nonetheless. "I'm fairly certain I promised no such thing."

"Ah—" David lifted a finger in the air. "You're correct. *I* was the one who promised we would perform a duet."

"I have some music, if that would help," Julia offered.

I glanced at the sheets of music already on the pianoforte. Notes ran up and down the scales like raindrops on a cobblestone street in a storm. Her music would not help at all. "If I play, I'm afraid it will have to be from memory."

"But, Anna—"

I waved Mama off. "The sooner David knows of my musical talents, the better," I said with a self-sacrificing air, trudging to the pianoforte and taking a seat on the stool.

I couldn't see David's victorious smile, but I could feel it in the way he practically danced to retrieve a second stool and set it beside me. I shifted mine to allow him more room, and behind us, I could hear Mama's sigh of frustration—or dread—as she and Julia each found a seat on a sofa.

David's arm was warm next to mine as he leaned toward me. "What shall we play?"

"What are you willing to play?" I asked.

David leafed through some of the music Julia had left in front of them. "Julia has a Schubert piece for four hands somewhere."

Schubert? I wouldn't be able to play one hand on a Schubert piece, let alone two. Was David a master at the pianoforte, like his sister? I tried to imagine the young boy I'd known spending hours at the pianoforte, practicing. It was nearly impossible.

"Do you have a piece for three hands?" I asked, my voice more hopeful than it should have been. I'd never even heard of a three-handed duet.

David stopped searching through the music and turned to me. "Three?"

"I'm better with my right."

He placed his hands in his lap. "Why don't you tell me what you *can* play?"

I grimaced. "I think I remember some scales. What about you?"

"Julia showed me the beginning of the C scale this morning."

I laughed. What a pair we were. "Brilliant. I can play that one with both hands."

He grimaced. "I may only be able to manage one."

"Perfect," I whispered, then spun on my stool and stood to announce us. David, ever the gentleman, despite making me play the pianoforte in front of an audience, stood with me. I cleared my throat and, in my most ostentatious voice, announced our duet. "My fiancé and I will play *The Notes of C, for Three Hands*."

With a nod to each other, we turned, sat, and counted off, both with words and a slight bobbing of our heads. The scale might have been simple, but our concentration was intense.

We bounced to the rhythm of each of our notes as we pounded through the first five. David had forgotten to cross his thumb beneath his fingers, so our sixth note ended up coming slightly late and unsynchronized. By the eighth note, we'd found our rhythm again, and with a sideways glance at each other, we started back down the scale together.

We made no mistakes on our way back to C, and when we hit it, we both jumped up heroically and took a bow.

Mama sat stunned, but Julia politely clapped at our performance.

"Should I play more?" I asked after David and I took the opportunity to bow a few more times. "I think I remember most of the notes to 'Polly Put the Kettle On.'"

David gasped and put a hand to his heart. "Most of the notes of 'Polly Put the Kettle On' would be a delight."

I cocked my head to one side and nodded. "Then go sit, and I shall entertain you." I shooed him away, and he obliged me by sitting on one of the empty sofas.

"I'm sorry, Mr. Tate," Mama said from the sofa next to his. "I'm afraid my husband and I were rather indulgent with Anna. She always preferred to be out of doors rather than sitting at the pianoforte."

"Please do not apologize for that," David replied. His voice was soft, whispering to Mama, but loud enough that I knew he wanted me and Julia to overhear. "You must remember I first met your daughter out of doors. And if the cost of her joyful spirit and kindness to others is a lack of musical accomplishment, then it is a price worth paying a thousand times over."

My heart lifted at his words. How did David always manage to say exactly the right thing? When he actually did get engaged, his fiancée would be a very fortunate woman.

I, on the other hand, would enjoy my fortune while I had it.

When my fingers touched the keys, the notes of the melody came back to me. After faltering only twice during the chorus, the only part of the song I could remember, I started again, this time adding my voice.

As unpolished as my pianoforte skills were, my singing was much worse. At least with an instrument, I could simplify my playing to a level where I didn't make many mistakes. But I couldn't get my voice to land on the same notes as the keys, no matter how hard I tried, so I didn't. Instead of hiding my complete lack of musical understanding, I let the words burst out of my mouth in unrestrained song.

Mama gasped once again, and if I wasn't mistaken, a snort came from the general direction of where David sat.

Julia didn't make a sound. At least, not one I could hear over the cacophony of my own racket.

I finished the chorus without missing any words, and even before my song died on my lips, Mama clapped in a frantic beat. But because I was a glutton for punishment, I started the chorus over and sang it once again.

This time, Mama started clapping even before I finished the last line, and I decided to let her out of her misery. I slid off the stool and gave a low and elaborate bow. David stood from his seat and clapped even more enthusiastically than Mama had when she'd been trying to make me stop.

Julia was less exuberant, but her eyes sparked as she looked between David and me.

"Would anyone else like to play?" I asked archly. "Or should I favor you all with 'Hot Cross Buns'?"

Mama jumped up. "I don't mind playing—that is, unless Miss Tate would like to play."

David's eyes sparked with amusement. "I'd happily listen to Anna sing 'Hot Cross Buns.'"

Mama made an odd strangling sound in her throat but gulped it down as quickly as she could. Julia glanced at David, a question in her eyes. He gave her a nod of encouragement.

I walked to where David stood, and his fingers curled around mine as though it were the most natural thing in the world.

I smiled my encouragement to Julia and prayed my voice didn't betray the warm sensation David's hand was causing to climb up my arm. "Don't hesitate on my account. I may not play or sing very well, but I do appreciate beautiful music. And I have no pride in this matter for you to concern yourself with."

Mama didn't miss the easy way David had reached for me, and I could see the way his smile and tender touch calmed her fears. I waited for the warmth of his hand to dissipate. It was a calculated decision on his part, but even knowing he held my hand only in order to show Mama we were happily engaged did nothing to make me enjoy his fingers curled possessively around my own any less.

David tugged on my hand with a quick pull, and I tumbled into his side. Mama looked pointedly away. "Someday, I will hear 'Hot Cross Buns' from your lips." He spoke with more breath than voice, making certain Mama wouldn't hear.

I placed my other hand in the crook of his elbow and rose just enough on my toes to bring my mouth to his ear. "Hot," I said the word slowly. "Cross," I said after a brief pause. "Buns," I finished in a jaunty, whispered fashion I would think any engaged young lady would be proud of.

David closed his eyes, the muscles in his neck pulling tight.

Mama dashed toward Julia at the pianoforte in a movement that made me quite certain she'd been watching the two of us. "Let me help you turn the pages, Miss Tate," she said, standing next to Julia, both of their backs to us.

"It looks as though Mama would like us to have a private moment." I laughed, but my laugh died when I looked back at David.

He wasn't laughing.

His eyes had turned a dark, dusky blue.

Instead of sitting back down, he turned and pulled me with him toward the small alcove where the covered harp sat.

I eyed the instrument with marked civility. "If you think I have any skill with a harp, you'll be sad to know I've never even set a finger to one."

He tucked himself behind the harp and pulled me into him. Our heads would be visible over the instrument but only if Mama and Julia left the pianoforte and took a few steps toward us. The wall of the alcove hid us completely. Something in Mama's earlier glances at David told me she and Julia would remain at the pianoforte for several pieces.

"At least . . ." he said, his hand holding mine against his chest, "that would mean you hadn't learned incorrectly."

Our sudden privacy, made even more roguish by our cramped quarters between the harp and the wall, made me swallow hard. David's face was so close I could make out delicate changes of color on his skin and the pupils of his eyes. Not to mention, my skirts and most of my side were pressed up against him. It would take only a relaxing of my spine and a sagging of my shoulders to curl into his chest completely. I forced that image out of my head as quickly as it had come.

With a deep breath and a smile I hoped conveyed friendship and not the look of a woman who might not mind being engaged, in truth, to the man holding her, I caught David's intense gaze. "Are you saying I've learned the pianoforte incorrectly?"

He smirked, and a dangerous gleam sparked in his eyes. "Well—" he began.

I shook my head and allowed myself to sink into him the slightest amount, such a small amount that he probably wouldn't even notice. "No," I laughed. "Don't answer that question. I'd rather keep what camaraderie we have and not spoil it."

"I see." His voice was low and gravelly, a man's voice to match his hands and face. "After one harsh word from me about your musical prowess, I would no longer be a friend?"

"No, I'm not quite so fickle as that." His chest was warm under my hand. I was too comfortable with him. Perhaps I should have allowed him to disparage me. I pulled my hand away from him and started to step back, but David stopped me by putting a hand on my waist and pulling me closer to him.

My right hand came to his chest again with a soft crash, just under the flowers he'd tucked into his lapel and on top of his front jacket pocket. Something flat and rigid lay inside. He'd been wearing a different jacket this morning, but for some silly reason, I thought it could be my note.

I'd told myself all day he couldn't think of me as anything more than a woman who needed his help, but holding me like this was more than playful, wasn't it? Was there any chance his heart was playing the same tricks on him as mine was on me? Or was he simply young and enjoying himself with no thought of how his glances might be misinterpreted by a woman who hadn't ever had the chance to flirt or be held by a man?

I glanced to my side, trying to catch a glimpse of Mama over the harp, but she remained out of sight. I bit my lip. "Do you think we are enjoying this engagement a bit too much?"

"Oh, no." David brought his face closer to mine, his eyes dropping to my mouth. "I'm enjoying it a lot less than I could be. We only just started on your list."

"It isn't a list. It is simply something I said. I didn't know you were going to attach such meaning to it."

He raised one eyebrow. "I happened to like your list. We are making good progress on it." He lifted his hand from mine and raised one of his fingers. "Flowers. I was able to do that one quite simply, and right away." He lifted another finger. "Walks. We have already had several, and they were all very pleasant. I can see why engaged couples indulge in them." He glanced into the room behind us, Julia's practiced notes floating into the alcove. "And we just finished a very remarkable duet on the pianoforte . . ." He brought his hand back over mine and toyed with my fingers. Then he wrinkled his forehead as if he were trying to solve a difficult math problem. "I feel like there is something missing from what you said in the library. What was the last thing?"

I knew exactly what he was thinking about, but he'd made an error. There was more than one thing left on the list. "Dancing at balls?" I asked.

His hand tightened on mine, and he looked me in the eye. "I think we will be forgiven for not dancing at balls if there are no balls to be had. No, it was something else."

I swallowed. "Stolen kittens?" My voice had a scratchy quality that didn't come from singing.

He snorted. "Definitely not kittens."

I closed my eyes, not in invitation but in defeat. When I opened them again, David was there, holding me in his arms, with his face only inches from my own. "Kisses," I managed to hoarsely whisper. "I believe it was stolen kisses."

His face brightened. "Ah yes, that was it. How could I have forgotten?"

He tugged at my hand, which pulled me away from the harp and out of our little alcove. He must have been bluffing, for if he'd wanted to kiss me, he wouldn't have brought us back into sight of Mama.

But he didn't stop walking, instead leading me past the chairs, his pace hastening with each step until he was practically galloping to the door. With a hurried look at Mama and Julia still at the pianoforte, he turned the knob and pulled me into the corridor.

Where we would be well and truly alone.

My heart quickened. What was this dangerous game David was playing? Did enjoying our engagement while it lasted mean actually enjoying everything that came with an engagement? Would he kiss me while knowing our relationship could be ending in a matter of weeks?

Would I want him to?

I took a deep breath and pressed myself against the door we'd just walked through. "You already kissed me. You crossed that one off the list first. Don't you remember?"

His eyes grew even darker, and he leaned forward, his thumb tracing a path across my knuckles. "I did not kiss you. Trust me, I would remember if I had."

I ignored the line of heat he left in his wake on my fingers and concentrated only on keeping my breathing steady. "The point of that list was to convince everyone around us that you wanted to marry me, and a pretend kiss works just as well as a real one for that."

"I'm not certain I've ever heard a sentiment I disagree with more. But even if I didn't, it doesn't matter since I distinctly remember you saying stolen kiss*es*. As in plural."

My heart was already acting up, and now my head was as well. "You are confusing me. How can a stolen kiss help our cause? If a kiss is stolen, no one will see you steal it; therefore, there is no point in it."

"I wasn't the one who made the list. I'm only trying to complete it." He laughed, a soft rumble from deep inside his chest, and my hand instinctively reached for his lapel, my fingers clenching around it, uncertain whether they should pull him in closer or push him away. "Didn't we agree to enjoy our time together?"

I nodded slowly. "We did."

"Are you telling me you don't think you'd enjoy being kissed by your fiancé? Because I think I could make it enjoyable."

My eyes lowered to his mouth, and I didn't try to hide my gaze. I would enjoy it. I would enjoy it too much. That was the danger in it. We'd been engaged not even two weeks, and already, I was dreading going back to the life of just Mama and me. I liked David, and I liked that our engagement tied the two of us together. But if he kissed me now, or later, or, as he seemed to be implying, often, I would be in danger of falling in love with him. He had to understand that, hadn't he? He had to know how bland my life had become before he'd stepped back into it.

How would I go back to living my life on solid ground after he'd made me feel the heat of the sun and the wind on my face that only came from climbing to the treetops?

My fingers played with the edge of whatever it was in his breast pocket. "I'm not certain what I would think about kissing my fiancé."

He placed his lips near my ear. "There is a very easy way to find out."

I closed my eyes, letting his words glide over my skin. It would be very easy indeed. I pushed myself away from the door and leaned into him but kept my head down, resting it on his shoulder. Mama could leave the pianoforte and come find us at any moment, but I didn't care. We were supposed to be engaged, after all, and I needed a moment to think.

Did it matter? Did it matter if I kissed this man and let my heart believe there was a chance the two of us might fall in love with each other? What would it change? I had no plans to marry. I wasn't going to leave Breckenridge and look for a husband. I was going to find a position and work for the rest of my life. Did it matter if I fell in love first?

David's deep-blue jacket was soft against my cheek. I took a deep breath, inhaling the warm, masculine scent of him. His arms and voice and everything about him made me feel protected and cared for.

And as much as I'd thought my dilemma was a hard one, in his arms, it melted away. Of course it would matter if I fell in love with him. Because if this was my one chance at love, even if it was one-sided and fleeting, I wanted it.

I lifted my face from his chest and put my free arm on his shoulder. His eyes searched mine, and I kept mine focused clearly on his so he would know my decision. He might have been teasing me, but I was going to take his teasing to heart.

I raised an eyebrow. "How many kisses exactly does *stolen kisses* imply?"

David's eyes widened, and his breathing quickened under my hand. He searched my face for a moment, not smiling and not playing off my question with a jest, as I thought he might. Instead, he dropped his gaze to my lips, then back up to my eyes. He swallowed. "At least one more."

I slid my hand from his shoulder to his neck. "And at most?"

His foot slid forward as if he needed to step closer to me, but I was already there, in his arms. He dropped my hand and wrapped both of his arms around my waist. The word *infinite* sang through the air around us as real as the music Julia was playing on the pianoforte. But he didn't say it, and neither did I.

"As many as you'll give me, as long as you are my fiancée."

"That feels very imprecise." A wobble in my voice matched the slight tremor of his hands at my back. "How will you know when to cross it off your list?"

"I'll cross it off when you tell me to and not a moment before."

It wasn't infinite. It wasn't any more than he'd already given me. Our engagement was never supposed to move forward into a marriage. But what if it did? He leaned forward, and suddenly, my plan of being in love once in my life before resigning myself to spinsterhood felt a lot riskier than it had only a moment ago.

"David?"

His head was dipping toward mine. "Yes?"

"Would it be very terrible if I enjoy kissing you too much?"

He paused, even the tremors in his hands stilling. "What do you mean?"

I shook my head, cursing myself for being such a fool. "Nothing. I shouldn't have said anything."

But it was too late. David's fingers no longer flexed into my lower back. He closed his eyes hard and cursed under his breath. A moment later, he released me and stepped away. "I'm sorry. I've been a cad."

"No, you haven't. I shouldn't have said anything."

His eyes hardened. "I *want* you to tell me what you are thinking, so please do not stop telling me. But I believe I got a bit too carried away in our game today, and I owe you an apology. I was very close to taking advantage of our agreement."

No. No. No. He spun on his heel, but I stopped him, fisting my hand into his lapel. He froze, but he didn't turn back around.

"You still owe me at least one kiss while we are engaged. One more was the minimum, remember?"

His chest rose and fell as he turned. His eyes were wary, watching me like I was a wild animal that would pounce on him at any moment, but he stepped forward.

He stopped mere inches away from me and slowly put a hand on my cheek. I forced my breathing to remain as normal as possible. His reaction to my fears had made one point very clear: If he thought I might be affected by his touch, he would run again.

"You're right," he said. "And I think the sooner I kiss you and cross that off our list, the better." His thumb brushed my cheekbone, but he didn't reach for my waist or pull me to him as he'd done before. Instead, his head inched toward mine almost reluctantly.

David Tate might have been interested in me at fourteen, but now that he was a man, he'd outgrown the idea. A few lighthearted kisses in a corridor had been tempting to him, but one word about those kisses meaning something more and now a kiss was only a task to be checked off sooner rather than later.

He seemed unsure of his decision, even when his lips were only a breath away from mine. Any moment, he could step away and throw out his list. But he didn't. With one last burst of decision, he closed the distance between us, and his lips gently landed on mine.

He was so very careful in his touch, but despite that, his kiss washed over me like an ocean wave I hadn't seen coming. A tide of wild emotion, nothing like friendship, crashed into my unsuspecting heart, welling up from that treacherous organ and overflowing to all my extremities. My eyes fluttered closed, and I forced myself to memorize the softness of his mouth and the carefulness of his hand at the side of my cheek. He was motionless, not moving, only allowing our lips to meet as carefully and painlessly as possible.

But that was not at all what I wanted. If he was only going to meet the minimum requirement of kisses, this would be my only one. It might even be my only chance to experience kissing anyone, and while I didn't need passion or love from him, I also didn't want my one and only kiss to be merely perfunctory, not when it felt anything but perfunctory to me.

His hand slid slowly down my cheek, but it wasn't because he was moving it to my neck; this was the beginning of the end, and I wasn't ready. I leaned in to him, then reached up and pressed his hand back to my face, willing him to feel at least a small amount of the wonder that had overcome me.

He stopped pulling away.

He stopped breathing.

I took a step forward, and the movement awakened him. He didn't turn into a savage beast or a man who would take advantage of a woman he'd promised to help. Despite what he'd said earlier, he was no cad. But for the first time since his lips had made contact with mine, he started participating. He awoke like the sun did each morning, with hints of delicate, nearly imperceptible beams promising more light to come. His thumb pressed into my cheek, and he tipped his head first to one side, then the other, as if he were testing my lips for the best angle. Then, as if neither side had come out the victor, he kissed me full on, bringing his other hand to my face and tipping my head this time. Every movement was slow, careful, and soft. Protecting me, even in this.

I melted against him, letting my head fall where he coaxed it.

So, this was kissing.

I *liked* it.

I liked it enough that if I had any sense, I would pull away before I made it extremely obvious to David how much I was relishing his touch.

And I would.

Eventually.

For now, I ran one hand up his fine back and tangled my fingers into the hair at the base of his neck.

He inhaled sharply at my touch, and my other hand clenched his lapel tight enough to permanently ruin his jacket. How had I managed to spend twenty-five years of my life not kissing David? And how was I supposed to spend the rest of it the same way?

I had to stop and pretend that having his mouth on mine had not been life-altering and thank him for being a man of his word, as far as that list of his was concerned. If I didn't soon, we might not be able to remain friends. I wouldn't see him daily, and he might even change his mind about me living in his home.

I forced my grip on his lapel to relax, took a slow, steadying breath, and drew a picture in my mind of what the two of us must look like. I traced the lines of us tucked together in a darkened corridor, his hands on my face, and my lips brushing over his, marking the parts of my gown that pressed against him, putting to memory this stolen moment. I folded the picture and tucked it safely into my soul, a memory to unwrap whenever I wished. Then I pulled away.

I forced my eyes open only to find his were still closed.

His dark lashes were half-moons of shadows. I pressed my hand to my side to stop myself from running my fingertips over his eyes.

He was so still I thought he might be considering kissing me again. But he took a long, steady breath and slowly opened his eyes. He blinked at me once, his gaze taking in my mouth, my hair, and my mouth again. His lips parted then closed, and swallowing hard, he turned away. He didn't open the door and return to the music room;

instead, he strode away to some other part of the house, leaving me alone.

Not a word about crossing an item off his list, nor a funny quip that would set me at ease. He simply left.

I fell back against the door and raised my fingers to my lips, and since David wasn't here to witness it, I allowed my lips to curve into a slow and steady smile.

Whatever happened in the future, kissing David had not been a mistake.

Chapter 12

"No one should become part of the Tate family.
We keep our misery to ourselves."
—David Tate, 1845, Age 18

The next day, I didn't see David at all, and he didn't send a note. Which was understandable, I reminded myself. He shouldn't be expected to spend every waking moment with me. He probably had things he needed to catch up on after all the time we'd already spent together.

It was, after all, only a temporary engagement.

I'd relived our kiss a thousand times in my head, and every time, a sneaking ribbon of pleasure interrupted my worry over what the kiss had done to drive David away.

After another day passed without a word from him, the thrill of remembering his hands on my waist and my fingers in his hair turned more and more into the worry I'd been pushing away. I needed to see him. I lay in bed knowing I couldn't spend one more day in the cottage with only Mama and my own thoughts. If I did, the carpets would be threadbare from my pacing. We were engaged. I could visit his home without an invitation, couldn't I?

The last time I'd talked to David, he'd planned on Mama and me moving into Tate Hall. With only a few days left until the Prestons' tenants arrived, I needed to know if that remained our plan. I would visit with the Mortensens on my way so I wouldn't appear quite so desperate to see him, and then I'd call on Julia. It was perfectly reasonable for me to call on Julia.

In the morning, I dressed, then sat at my dressing table, carefully examining the skin on my face in the mirror. I didn't feel old. If anything, my time in Breckenridge had made me feel younger than I had in a long time. But what did David see? He'd once proposed to a seventeen-year-old woman, and at only twenty-three, a seventeen-year-old might still be what he would fancy.

I frowned, twisted my hair into a simple knot and went to breakfast. I shouldn't be thinking about what David preferred. Young as he was, he most likely preferred no attachment at all.

I greeted Mama and grabbed a hunk of bread and cheese. "I'm going to Tate Hall this morning," I told her when I sat down. "Would you like to join me?"

"Will Mr. Tate be sending the carriage?"

I shook my head. "No, I'm going to walk."

Mama grimaced at the sound of the wind against the window. "I'll stay home, but have a wonderful time, and send both Mr. and Miss Tate my regards."

After my short visit with Mrs. Mortensen restored my spirits and left me feeling as though anything in the world were possible, I arrived at Tate Hall and told the footman I'd come to visit with Julia. If he thought it strange that I'd come to visit her instead of my supposed fiancé, he didn't say anything.

I was shown into the large octagonal drawing room, and I found I could pace here as well I did in the cottage. I'd only asked to see Julia, but if David knew I was here, he would come, wouldn't he?

It took only a few moments for Julia to enter. She came in quietly but with a smile that showed she was happy to see me. I peeked behind her, and she must have caught the motion.

"I'm sorry, David isn't here to visit. He is in Lincolnshire, meeting with a school friend of our brother, Garrett. David thinks he might have a position for you and your mother there."

Any lifted opinions I had of myself after Mrs. Mortensen's praises fled. David hadn't visited because he'd left without telling me, and he'd left on an errand that would hasten our separation. We'd always known I would have to leave the cottage, but he'd never seemed to feel any urgency in finding me anywhere else to stay but Breckenridge. It was hard to believe his sudden fervor in finding us a home didn't have anything to do with the kiss we'd shared.

"In Lincolnshire?"

"Yes, I've heard it is a lovely place. I hope, for your sake, his plans work out and you can live there until you turn twenty-seven."

I blinked, my eyebrows furrowing. "David told you about my inheritance?"

"Yes. I hope you don't mind. I was worried about you."

"Of course I don't mind." I could imagine how that conversation had played out. Julia must have been concerned about how much I enjoyed being engaged to David and wondered if, after all her concern over him, perhaps he was the one who was going to hurt me. David would have reassured her by mentioning all the plans we'd made beyond simply finding me work and a place to live. Plans that, up until our kiss, had seemed reasonable to me.

I pasted a smile on my face, trying to look unconcerned, when, in reality, the large room had started feeling confining. I shouldn't have come. "I'm glad you and David can both let your minds rest as far as I'm concerned."

My smile must not have been very convincing, for Julia wrapped an arm around mine and pulled me to her side. "You must know both David and I will miss you. I was harsh to you the first time we met, and while I don't take back those words, I do regret them. Even in the short time I've come to know you, I can see why David thinks so highly of you."

I nodded, feeling numb. Somewhere over the course of the last few days, I'd gotten used to the idea that I'd be moving into Tate Hall, and now it seemed as though that might not happen. How was I supposed to help Julia when we'd only just begun to know each other?

I felt hollow, as though I were watching our conversation from a position above us. I didn't want to go back to being a lonely spinster living with her widowed mother on less money than we needed. I didn't want to be friendless again.

Julia cleared her throat. "You must be parched and frozen from your walk. Would you like some tea? David rode on horseback, so the carriage will be free to take you home after we visit."

I nodded again, unable to think of a reply. When had Julia become the one out of the two of us to know how to carry on a conversation?

I'd become lost the moment I'd heard David was in Lincolnshire. In Lincolnshire, there was no David, Julia, or the Mortensens. It was bound to be a dreary place.

"Julia—" David's voice rang out from somewhere inside the house. "I'm home."

I closed my eyes to a sudden rush of desire to hear David calling my name in that familiar manner whenever he walked through that door.

It was a ridiculous thought.

The door to the drawing room opened, and David stepped in, disheveled, with his coat half on, and enough stubble on his cheeks to make him look older than his twenty-three years.

He didn't notice me. "I think I've found a place for Anna, and she will be able to move there even sooner than expected."

His voice bounced off the walls without a hint of sadness. His relief and joy at finding me a place far from here left me suddenly bereft. If I could have disappeared through the floorboards, I would have happily done it.

Julia's eyes widened, and she tipped her head toward me.

David's grin disappeared, and with it, so did any hope that he wanted me to stay longer in Breckenridge. Finding me a place to live had been an item on his list, and he was even more anxious to cross that one off than he had been about the stolen kisses.

"Anna . . ." he started, running his hands through his hair. He groaned. "I'm sorry. I didn't realize you were here."

Yes, he'd made that quite clear when he'd enthusiastically declared how eager he was to be rid of me.

I stood, my legs unsteady. My embarrassment of him finding me in a tree was nothing compared to what I was feeling now. "I can go."

"No," both he and Julia said at the same time. David turned to his sister, a strange look of pleading on his face.

Julia took my hand in hers and pulled me back down to the sofa. "You need to have tea first, and it will take some time for the carriage to be prepared; we can't ask you to walk home. Please, stay."

David nodded. "I'll be back shortly." He rubbed a hand down his unshaven face. "Let me make myself more presentable, and then I'd like to tell you what I've found."

David strode out of the room, and Julia pulled me toward the table. "It sounds as though David's trip was a success." She squeezed my hand. "Helping you has made him as happy as I've seen him in years. I'm certain he will be relieved to have a more permanent solution for you and your mother."

"Yes," I said in response, having trouble finding my voice.

A servant brought the tea, and then a few minutes later, David opened the door again, this time clean-shaven and clothes in impeccable order.

He glanced at me but went first to Julia and kissed the top of her head. "It is good to be home."

She smiled up at him. "It is always good to have you home."

I held my breath and waited to see if he would greet me similarly, but he didn't. Of course he didn't. No one here thought we were engaged.

He sat and turned to me. "How have you been, Anna?"

I forced a smile. At least he wasn't calling me Miss Atwood. "I've been well. I visited the Mortensens before coming here."

David's mouth curved into a smile. "They are a great family and an asset to the estate. We are lucky to have them."

Julia nodded in agreement, and I did as well. A lot of agreeing occurred over our tea, but with no mention of David's errand, nor of what he accomplished there.

I took a deep drink of my tea and cleared my throat. "Julia said you went to look into a position for Mama and me . . ."

David rubbed his hand along the edge of the table. "Yes. My brother, Garrett, has a friend from Cambridge by the name of Lord Pippen. He has a cottage sitting empty on his Lincolnshire estate. I went to visit him to see if it would be a suitable place, and I think it will do quite nicely. Lord Pippen was very kind, and he seemed more than happy to have the cottage occupied instead of empty.

"When I told him you would be willing to work to pay for your board, he mentioned some nonsense about my brother saving him from becoming a social pariah. He refused to accept your work. He was certain the cottage would be free for at least two years before he may need to do some repairs on it."

I lifted my chin. "That all sounds lovely."

David's head rose. "Does it?"

"Yes." I raised my hand to set it on his to reassure him but changed my mind and pulled away. His eyes caught my movement, and a flash of pain, or remorse, crossed his features. Our kiss had made me hesitant to touch him, and he knew it. "Thank you. I don't know what I would have done without you."

He shrugged. "Married Mr. Green, I suppose."

I wanted to laugh, but lightheartedness didn't come. "I suppose so."

"I was in jest, Anna. No one should be forced to marry someone not of their choosing."

I attempted another smile. He was talking about Mr. Green, of course, but I couldn't help but feel like perhaps our kiss had made him realize the last thing he wanted was to feel obligated to marry me.

That kiss had sent David to Lincolnshire and cost me weeks of time I could have spent engaged to him. I'd known it was a risk, yet somehow, my foolish heart had garnished hopes over the past few days that perhaps David had enjoyed kissing me enough to want to do it more often.

I took a sip of tea. Although it was no longer scalding, I drank slowly from my cup. Tate Hall didn't feel dark and forbidding like it had eight years ago. It felt more like home than anywhere else I'd set foot in since Atwood Manor.

And just thinking that made me feel ridiculous.

I abandoned my plan of drinking slowly and instead drained the rest of my tea in a few large swallows. I placed my cup on the table and caught Julia's eye. "If you think the carriage is ready, I should return home to Mama and tell her the good news. Or rather . . . I can't quite yet, can I?" I was getting ahead of myself. "I need to break the engagement first."

"Oh." Julia glanced at David and then at the door as though it were an escape. "The carriage might be ready. I'll go check."

"No," David stood. "I will, then I can accompany Anna home so we can discuss how to tell her mother."

He strode out of the room, and Julia and I were left alone. Whatever confidence she'd found earlier was gone, and mine hadn't returned, so we sat in silence. Every once in a while, one of us rearranged our tea things.

David returned a few moments later, wearing his coat. "The carriage is ready."

I grimaced. The only thing worse than sitting here drinking tea with David would be sitting in an enclosed carriage with him. Even as an engaged couple we shouldn't be alone together. Not that I was under the delusion that he had plans to kiss me again. "You don't need to escort me. You only just arrived."

"It isn't far in the carriage. And we need to speak to one another."

We did. However, I wasn't ready to discuss our plans. "Please, stay with Julia. I'm very grateful to you, but I'd like some time to think before we discuss how we are going to tell Mama. Let's talk about it tomorrow."

"Today might be better. You will need to start packing, and I was planning on repairing some fence line with Mr. Walker in the morning."

I shook my head. "We have to pack either way. It won't make a difference if Mama thinks we are preparing to come here to Tate Hall or to Lincolnshire. Come tomorrow afternoon, and we will speak of it then."

David looked as though he were about to protest, but Julia laid a hand on his arm and shook her head softly. He heaved a sigh and nodded. "I'll call on you tomorrow, then."

It turned out that riding in a carriage just after discovering your world would soon be falling apart wasn't the best decision. Covered by the four walls of the carriage, I was completely alone with nothing to distract me, and as soon as the carriage was out of sight of Tate Hall, I slunk down in my seat and covered my face with my hands. All the energy and zest for life David had started to convince me I had slid away. My life was once again ruled only by the thought of surviving until my twenty-seventh birthday. Hot tears formed behind my eyelids. Hope was such a quiet and fleeting thing; I hadn't even noticed it sneaking up on me until it had been snatched away.

Chapter 13

"Julia and Garrett never believed Anna was real. I'm starting to wonder if perhaps they were right."
—David Tate, 1848, Age 21

By the afternoon of the next day, I'd accustomed myself to the idea of leaving Breckenridge. I'd had a few days of seeing what life could have been like if I had been the kind of woman who was given her heart's desires. I'd had a fiancé, a sister, neighbors who cared about me, a place to live, and a mother who hadn't needed to worry about how long we would be welcome in our place of living. And now I didn't, and that was life.

When there was a knock at the door, I was fully prepared not to break down while having one last walk with David to discuss the dissolution of our engagement.

Mary was at the main house, so I motioned for Mama to stay seated and went to the door myself. Smiling what I hoped was a confident and friendly smile, I pulled open the door.

Only to find Mr. Green standing hat in hand, his greased hair slicked down to the side in an effort to cover the balding spots on his head. My stomach lurched at the sight of him.

"Miss Atwood," he said stiffly. "Is your mother at home?"

"I . . ." What was he doing here? And why would he want to speak to Mama? "She is."

He nodded. "Good. I have some papers for her."

I frowned. What kind of papers would Mr. Green have for Mama, and why couldn't he have simply sent them through the post?

Mr. Green cleared his throat, and I grimaced, realizing I'd been standing there staring at him as though he were an apparition. I wanted nothing more than to shut the door in his face, but instead, I opened the door wider, and he stepped in.

He sniffed at our closet-sized foyer, then looked to me for directions. Gritting my teeth, I led him to the drawing room.

"Mama, Mr. Green has come," I announced when we walked in.

Mama's eyes flew to mine and widened in a way meant to convey that this time, she'd had nothing to do with his arrival. She stood from her sewing. "Mr. Green, to what do we owe the pleasure?" Her voice held anything but pleasure in its tone.

"I'm afraid visits of pleasure are no longer possible between our two families," Mr. Green said with an air of superiority. "Today, I've come on business."

The color drained from Mama's face. "What business?"

Mr. Green walked unbidden to a small table and placed a satchel on top of it. He unfastened the strap and pulled out a stack of papers. "I have here a list of items with outstanding debts. Debts I have been overlooking for the past five years, due to our"—he took a sidelong glance at me— "connections. But now that those connections have been severed, I would like to take care of this business in the most expedient manner possible."

He handed Mama the papers, and she rifled through them, her eyebrows furrowing as she glanced quickly down each page. "Almost every one of our purchases are on here," she said. She pulled the last page from the stack. "Going back to 1844."

Mr. Green nodded. "1844 is when you started receiving a discount."

I marched to Mama's side and looked over the papers with her. It was true. Every purchase we'd made at the haberdashery and the butcher shop was there. Most of the totals were small—only a portion of what meager items we bought for ourselves—but a few were larger. One, in particular, caught my eye.

"My coat? You gifted that to me," I said.

He shook his head. "No, I credited it to you."

"This is preposterous, Mr. Green," Mama said. "You never set any expectation that these were credits that would need to be repaid."

"Do you have receipts to prove that?" Mr. Green pressed his thin lips together while waiting for our reply. Of course we didn't have receipts to prove anything, but anyone could look at Mr. Green's accounts and understand what he'd done.

"Why would we keep receipts for five years?" I asked, letting my exasperation show.

"I did." He pointed to the papers calmly. "And I will expect payment within two weeks."

"Two weeks?" Mama gasped.

"Yes, but I'm certain that won't be a problem. After all, your daughter is engaged to a viscount's son. An amount like that should be paltry to his father."

"I don't want to ask David for money," I burst out.

Mr. Green winced at David's name. "That, Miss Atwood, is your concern, not mine. I'll be sending my solicitor to collect the payment in two weeks' time."

With a groan, I stormed out of the room and raced through the foyer toward the kitchen, where my coat hung. I ripped it off the rack and marched back into the drawing room.

"You can take this payment now." I threw the coat at him, and he barely managed to catch it, the top half of it covering his face. "Mama, scratch the coat off the list."

Mr. Green pulled the coat from his face and held it out. "It is not at all in the same condition as when I bought it for you. If I sold it now, it wouldn't be worth half of what I paid for it."

I strode right to him and pointed a finger at his face. "What did you just say?"

"I said the condition is not the same as when I bought it."

I narrowed my eyes. "So, you *bought* it."

His lips disappeared when he pressed them together, realizing his mistake. "For you."

"Which most of the world would consider a gift. I didn't ask you to buy it for me. Scratch it from the list."

Mr. Green narrowed his gaze at Mama. "Reduce it to 25 percent of what I paid for it. That is very generous of me."

"No, Mama, don't mark anything." I blew out a deep breath. Seeing Mr. Green so ostentatiously use the word *generous* made me ill. I couldn't allow him to feel as if he were doing us any favors. "I'll pay for all of it. And he can take the coat as well. We've had enough of your *generosity*, Mr. Green. It is a perversion of the word."

Mr. Green shrugged. "I'll send my solicitor in two weeks."

"You could have sent him today," I said. "Didn't he feel comfortable telling a widow and her daughter you've been secretly putting them in debt for years?"

Mr. Green wouldn't meet my eyes, so I assumed it was so.

"You could always get your own solicitor," he said. "Although with the court systems being what they are, it could be years before this is settled. And let's be honest, it isn't that large of a sum."

I'd seen the sum. It was large for us.

"Please leave." Mama's voice was icy. Mr. Green turned to her in surprise. He'd expected me to be the one to expel him from our home. "And never darken our doorway again."

Mr. Green narrowed his eyes but gave her a very short bow. "I never plan to."

I didn't bother showing him out. It wasn't as though he could get lost in our little cottage. We both heard the door close, and the moment it did, Mama crumpled the top paper in her fist. After taking several deep breaths, she turned to me. "I cannot believe I almost made you marry that man."

"But you didn't."

"When I see the difference between him and Mr. Tate . . ." Mama shivered. "Some things are worth going through hardships for, and a marriage to a man you can trust is one of them. I'd starve before I allowed him anywhere near you again."

My eyes pricked, and I strode over to Mama, dropped to my knees at her feet, and put my head in her lap. Immediately, her hand went to my head. When I'd been younger and had worn my hair down, she used to stroke it while she told me stories or while Papa read to us from the Bible. My hair was pulled up now, but she smoothed what she could.

I'd been dreading going back to living with just Mama, not having anyone else to turn to, but we would be able to do it. We'd been doing it for seven years.

If only we didn't have to pay Mr. Green. The total was 150 pounds, a bill that would have been noticed, but not with alarm, when Papa had been alive. We'd spent triple that amount on my one Season in Town. But Mama's jointure had withered to nearly nothing. What was left was only enough to cover the cost of food and a few items of clothing each year. If I were able to take a position near the cottage David had found for us in Lincolnshire, it would take me years to earn enough to pay Mr. Green back.

"Perhaps we will be able to talk some sense into his solicitor when he comes," I said. "There has to be a way to fight him."

"Tate Hall must have a solicitor."

I squeezed my eyes shut. We had no right to anything Tate Hall had to offer. "As Mr. Green said, even with a solicitor, it could be years before we are done with this."

"Then we can speak to the solicitor about making the payment at a later date. Your inheritance is ten times that amount. We can pay it once you are married."

I settled deeper into Mama's lap, wishing the world could be simple like it had been when I was a child. I wasn't going to marry David, and I doubted Mr. Green would be willing to wait a year and a half for his money.

Mama didn't know it yet, but she was about to get a lot worse news than this bill from Mr. Green. Would it be better to tell her now, while she was already distraught, or wait until I'd formulated some kind of a plan with David? When David and I had parted, it had been clear that I would wait until we'd spoken, but I no longer understood why. This was my mother. And who was David to me? He was practically a stranger, or at least, he would be in a few years. Mama was the person I should be making plans with, not him.

But I wasn't ready to give up this moment of her hand on my head quite yet. I kept my eyes closed and pretended my biggest concern was how I was going to escape my lessons on the pianoforte.

But I wasn't as good at pretending as I used to be. With a deep breath, I lifted my head and met Mama's gaze. She gave me a wobbly smile, but then she must have seen something in the way I looked at her, for her face froze.

"What is it?" she asked.

"Mama," I said, my voice breaking.

She put a hand to my cheek. "Tell me."

"I'm not marrying David." I waited for the relief that would come at admitting the truth to her, but it didn't come. The words broke something inside of me instead. "He is coming today, and we are going to speak. I'm planning on ending the engagement. He isn't in love with me, and he doesn't want to marry me."

Her eyebrows furrowed, but not in anger, in confusion. "Anna, I don't think I've ever seen a man more in love with a woman. Don't think I wasn't aware of what you two were doing when you left the music room the other day. I'm not naive."

"No, even that wasn't real. He simply wanted to help us."

She leaned forward and put her other hand on my cheek as well. "We often want to help the people we love."

I sniffed and shook my head. "He is grateful to me. That is all."

She frowned, the enormity of my words finally sinking in. "Have you asked him?"

"Asked him what? He just returned from Lincolnshire. He's found a different cottage for us to live in, and he is happy about it. I heard him tell Julia, Mama. The relief in his voice . . ." I broke off, not able to continue.

Mama shook her head, her lips pursed in grim determination. "You can't let him go that easily. A person can't pretend *that* well."

The unmistakable clacking of a carriage sounded outside, and unless Mr. Green had returned to add to his long list of money we owed him, it would be David coming to speak to me about how we were going to inform Mama. Little did he know, I'd already done it.

His knock came soon after.

Both of our eyes went to the door. "Do you want me to answer it?" Mama asked.

"Would it be so terrible if neither of us did?"

Mama took a deep breath and squeezed her eyes shut. "If that is what you want, I will stay here with you and ignore him." She wiped the moisture from my cheeks with her thumbs. "But you are going to have to face him someday."

He knocked again, and I nodded. Mama lifted my arms from her legs gently. "I'll open the door and give you a moment to gather yourself."

She pulled me up with her and wrapped her arms around me. "I don't understand what happened, but this time, I will leave the decisions to you. I would have been very happy in Tate Hall, but if we need to remove to Lincolnshire, I shall bear with it better than I would have two weeks ago. Perhaps Mr. Green won't be able to find us there. But please consider what will make you happiest. These past few weeks . . ." Her arms tightened even harder around me. "It is like I had my daughter back after a long time of watching you fade so slowly I didn't even see it. I've been wearing blinders. And I refuse to wear them any longer."

Then she kissed my cheek and left.

I squeezed my eyes shut, willing any redness to leave them, then dashed to the mirror hanging above the mantel. I tucked what hair I could back into place and dusted off my skirts. Before I was prepared, David was there.

He hadn't taken the time to remove his coat, and in his right hand was my old one. Mr. Green must not have wanted to sell it after all.

"What happened?" he asked the moment he laid eyes on me.

"Nothing," I replied, but at the same time, Mama said, "Mr. Green was here."

David strode toward me, his powerful legs making short distance of the space between us. "Did he hurt you?"

"No." I couldn't look David in the eyes, so instead, I focused on the dark-brown fur lining of his coat collar.

"He did something." David's voice sounded dangerous. "Why did I find your coat outside on the steps?"

Mama came up beside him. "Mr. Green must not have wanted it back."

David dropped my coat as if it were made of hot iron. "*He* gave you this coat?"

I laughed dryly. "I suppose that depends on what your definition of *give* is. If by *give* you mean 'gifted it to me and then demanded payment years later,' then yes, he 'gifted' it to me."

David glanced about the room, and his eyes caught hold of the papers Mama let drop to the floor beside the chair she'd been sitting on. One was crumpled, and the others lay scattered about in such a haphazard way that they stood out among the otherwise tidy room.

He marched over to the chair. "What is this?" he asked. When neither Mama nor I answered, he waited a moment to see if we would gather them up or hide them from him. When we did neither, he stooped and picked up a few of them.

His eyes flew down the contents of each page, and his face grew dark. He gathered the remainder of the papers, skimming over the information on each one before turning to me, his eyes brilliant with fury. "Does he expect you to pay this?"

Mama took a deep breath and gathered the papers from David's hands. "I don't think this is something that concerns you." Her voice wasn't unkind, but it lacked the element of care she typically used with David. "Not anymore."

His eyes went to mine.

The sharp fury I'd seen in them shifted into something dull and painful. He knew our facade was over. I'd told her without speaking to him about it first.

Mama set the papers on the table and put her hands on her hips. "You two need to have a discussion. Anna tells me you've found a place for us that you are very excited about. Thank you. It is very kind of you."

A muscle in David's jaw clinched. "I didn't do it to be kind."

"Nevertheless, we are grateful. How were you planning on speaking with Anna?"

"I was going to take her on a carriage ride." David's voice sounded hollow.

Mama nodded. "Then please do so. The sooner we have this matter settled, the better."

I wouldn't meet David's eyes. I had no choice but to speak with him. I should have allowed him to ride with me last night because at least it would have been a carriage ride of short and finite duration. And I would have had a coat I didn't despise wearing.

I gritted my teeth and went to pick up Mr. Green's coat. What was one more humiliation on top of everything else?

But David saw my motion and beat me to it. He grabbed it from the floor and tossed it away from me. "You won't be wearing that."

Something inside me hardened. David had no right to interfere with my life anymore. "I haven't another coat to wear."

He started to unbutton his, but Mama put a hand on his elbow. "She's had enough of coats from men. She can wear mine."

David's hand paused, then he said something so low I couldn't make it out. With gritted teeth, he thanked Mama and turned toward the door. "I'll wait for you in the carriage, Miss Atwood."

A few moments later, David sat across from me as the carriage rolled away. Mama stood in the doorway of the cottage without anything to protect her from the weather, watching us until we turned the bend. Only then did I face David and find him watching me.

He didn't look like a man who wanted to get rid of me. He looked at me as if I were a rare gem or, at the very least, a rock with a rare spiral of color splashed across its surface, sitting on the path in front of him. He looked like the last thing he wanted to do was kick me away.

I closed my eyes. I couldn't look at him. He'd given me a glimpse of something I could never have, and now that I knew for certain I would never have it, I wanted to move on to the part of my life where I could look back on our time together with wistfulness and omit the part where I had to feel all this pain.

"We need to talk." David's voice was low and achingly soft.

"I know."

"I assume you told your mother about our agreement."

I kept my eyes closed and gripped the side of the carriage. "Yes. Do you know when the cottage you found will be ready for us?"

"Lord Pippen said it was available now, but if you need more time, we could wait a week . . . you would, of course, be welcome at Tate Hall."

My eyes flew open. I couldn't be around David another week. Even this carriage ride was excruciating. "No. Let's not wait. That would only mean removing our things twice."

David's shoulders sagged but after only a moment, he nodded stiffly. "Then I suppose our time together is coming to an end."

I nodded in return.

His hand went to the side of the carriage, his finger sliding back and forth on the velvet just below the window. After several passes along the fabric, he dared a glance at me. "Seeing you again—being near you—has been a pleasure. One I wasn't certain I would ever have again."

I sucked in a breath. "I don't think you should say such things to me."

He swallowed hard and pulled his hand away from the window, clenching it at his side. We rode in silence then, neither of us wanting to say the wrong thing.

"I told the driver to take us to Tate Hall and back again. I could tell him to turn around now, if you would prefer."

I shook my head. It would be only a few more minutes before we turned around anyway.

David's clenched hands and jaw slowly softened after we made the turn. I spent most of the time looking out the window, especially when we were in view of Tate Hall. It was probably the last time I would see it. I might come and visit the Mortensens when funds allowed it, but I didn't think I would have the courage to walk anywhere near Tate

Hall. Especially not after David married, which he was certain to do in the future.

We arrived back at the cottage after saying only a few sentences to each other. David alighted the carriage, turned, and held out his hand to me. I took it, and he helped me down. My feet landed on the ground, and we both turned toward the front door. His hand was still warm in mine, and he showed no signs of releasing me. We stared at the door. The moment we crossed into the cottage and sat with Mama, our short charade would be over. Neither of us moved.

From the corner of my eye, I caught a blustering movement. I looked up to see a smattering of snow falling from the sky. A few large flakes drifted to the ground, then a few more. I held out my free hand to catch one, but the second it hit the warmth of my glove, it melted.

So beautiful and so short-lived.

Just like our engagement.

David's grip on my hand tightened, and he pulled me off the path leading to the front door. "You can't go in yet," he said.

"But I must."

"No." He was firm. "At the risk of sounding like Mr. Green, once again—" He glanced at Mama's coat. "You owe me one thing."

If he told me we hadn't met our quota on kissing, I didn't know what I would do. I held firm in the belief that kissing him once hadn't been a mistake, but to do so twice? How would I ever leave him?

"What is it?" I asked, uncertain I could say no if he asked me. Uncertain if I wanted to say no at all.

"A dance." He motioned with his free hand toward the path that led to the rear of the cottage, away from the eyes of the footman and where Mama was unlikely to see us through a window. "The last thing on our list."

"You said we should skip over that one. And Mama already knows we aren't engaged. We don't need to convince anyone of anything anymore."

David's eyes were serious. "I convinced everyone the moment they walked into the drawing room and found you in my arms. That list has never been about anyone else but us, and I want to finish it."

He motioned with his hand again. I sighed and allowed my feet to take a few steps in that direction. He pulled me gently forward until we reached the back garden. With a quick glance, David strode behind a large beech tree, placing it between us and the view of the house before he stopped and turned to me. "Will you dance with me, Anna? Please? One waltz, perhaps two. Then we can officially dissolve our engagement."

I took a steadying breath. Dancing in David's arms was going to be the sweetest pain, second only to kissing him. But I couldn't say no. Mama and I would be isolated again in Lincolnshire. After receiving my inheritance, I could try to find love, but with a broken engagement and not enough funds for a Season, I couldn't count on ever having another chance to be this close to a man. He'd shown me what it was like to be loved by him, and even though none of it had been real, I didn't think I'd ever be satisfied with anything less. No one but David would ever be enough.

I wanted more memories. I was greedy for them. David was my one chance to fill a jar of tender moments, and I wanted his arms around me one last time before I closed the lid. "We don't have any music." My protest was weak—a protest I meant for him to overcome.

His mouth slowly slid into a grin, and he took an unfaltering step toward me. "I've heard the music you make. I think we will manage without it."

I gave him a look of mock indignation. The world shifted, and I found myself back in our comfortable place of jesting and pretending. This dance didn't have to be painful. I wouldn't allow it to be. David had been drawn to me as a boy because, he claimed, I'd been a bright spot in his otherwise unhappy childhood. I would dance with him and be brilliant so when he looked back on this time of ours together, he could feel the same way again. "This from the man who needed reminding of the words to *Polly Put the Kettle On.*"

He lifted my hand toward his shoulder with a question in his eyes. I nodded, and he let my hand fall onto the warmth of his coat. "This from the woman who thanked me multiple times for the rock I gave her but never for the flowers."

An edge of sun broke through the clouds, and snowflakes burst into bright spots of light. David put his hand on my shoulder blade, and even through Mama's thick coat, I was immediately warmer under his touch. "I didn't mean to disparage your voice earlier," he said. "Your voice is what I will miss the most. I would actually love it if you sang for us."

I blinked and saw David as he'd been eight years ago—a scrawny boy holding his dying hound. He hadn't cared then that I couldn't carry a tune, and he wouldn't care now. "I don't know any waltzes with words."

"Then perhaps you could hum?"

I nodded and began humming one of Chopin's waltzes, at least to the best of my abilities. I was stiff in my first few notes, but when David exhaled deeply, as if he'd released all his worries out into the world, I let my worries slide away as well. The hand at my back tugged me closer, and I sank into his arms.

Torture was a strange beast.

I let my years of dancing instruction slip away. David wasn't following the precise movements of a man who had spent his adolescence preparing to lead women out onto a ballroom floor anyway. Whether that was because he hadn't been trained or he was simply throwing his training out the window, I neither knew nor cared. His hand slid lower on my back, and he tightened his hold on me. I closed my eyes, allowing all the air in my lungs to escape, then dropped my head onto his shoulder.

During my one Season, I'd danced polkas and waltzes as well as a few country dances, but no one had ever dared hold me this close. This wasn't a dance; it was an embrace. A farewell. One made only slightly more appropriate by being hidden within a waltz.

As he completed a turn, the weight of his chin settled on my temple, and I missed one of the notes in my song. I couldn't even remember what the next note should be. A steady hum from David's throat picked up where I'd faltered, and the song came rushing back to me. We finished the last few strains together, our voices softening and slowing as we neared the end.

When we ran out of notes, David stopped dancing, but he didn't release me.

With no song to hum and no steps to worry about, my mind went back to the place I had tried so hard to avoid.

This was farewell.

The garden blurred, and I blinked hard, willing myself not to cry. David was my friend. I was a joy to him, and crying wouldn't leave him happy. It would leave him worried that he'd hurt me when, in fact, he'd been one of very few people to understand me and help me through my difficulty.

But my nose betrayed me with a sniff. David pulled back and searched my face.

I could pretend a lot of things, but there was no chance I could convince him I was unaffected by our parting.

He lifted a thumb to my cheek and wiped the smallest bit of moisture from it. "What is wrong?"

I closed my eyes. I couldn't answer him.

"Anna, please."

I wanted to laugh. Wasn't it obvious? When a lady cried right before breaking an engagement and saying farewell to her fiancé, one would think it was obvious that she didn't want to do either of those things.

And I really didn't want to do either of those things.

We hadn't even had two weeks together, so I knew I was being ridiculous, but days spent with David had meant the world to me. Tree climbing, walking together, singing, cleaning thatch, feeling as though someone appreciated me—I wanted all those things, and they were being ripped from me.

By the one person I couldn't open up to about how much this hurt.

Or could I?

Was it so important that he remember me as a flitting brightness that came and went from his life that I couldn't take a chance by telling him I didn't want to end the engagement? If I wasn't going to end up marrying him anyway, did it matter if I told him how much I'd started to dream about staying with him?

Because if there was even the slightest chance David would want me to stay, I wanted to give that chance life.

I met David's eyes. They were filled with concern. I inhaled his scent and forced myself to say words I would never be able to take back. "Do I have to end our engagement?"

David swallowed hard, but he didn't look away. "Do you want to wait a week after all? I thought you said that would be more work."

"No." My hand slid up his arm and grasped at the fur on his collar. "I mean, after carefully considering all the paths my life could take, I strongly prefer the one where this engagement doesn't end at all. Not unless it ends in the more traditional way," I took a deep breath, hoping it would calm the racing of my heart. "With a marriage."

Snow fell around us, but that couldn't account for how frozen David stood. His eyes stopped moving, caught at a point somewhere just below my eyes. His back stiffened, and his fingers tightened at my waist.

It was obvious enough from his reaction what his answer would be, but still, I waited for it. I'd taken a chance—a bad one, it seemed—but I would not leave before hearing his response. He wasn't the only one who could propose marriage at inopportune times.

The first part of him to move was his eyes. They came back into focus and searched mine. "That's not what we agreed upon."

I swallowed and straightened my spine. The tears, which had been threatening to fall only moments ago, had burned away in my determination. "I know. And I'm sorry, but when we made that agreement, I had no idea how much I would love being your fiancée or how quickly I'd come to cherish my relationship with your sister. How could I have known that the young boy I knew would redefine himself as one of the best men I have ever met? You make me feel as though I have myself back, and leaving you is like watching the best parts of me slip away."

David's breathing was coming faster, and I didn't think it was because he was interested in my proposal. He looked as scared as he'd been when he was younger. My feelings about him didn't seem to be helping my cause. They were murky, even to me. Had I fallen in love with him? Or was I only scared of going back to living life on my own? I didn't even know if it mattered what the answer to that question was; everything I'd told him was the truth. I didn't want to break our engagement. I wanted to be David Tate's fiancée. I wanted to be his wife.

But I should probably think of a more practical way to explain myself. "I know I must seem old and unfortunate to you, but because of that, I'm also willing to be humble. I never thought I would beg for anything, except perhaps food for Mama if life got extremely bad. But I'm begging you now, David, if you think there is any chance you could come to love me as a wife, to consider my proposal. Consider me."

"Anna." David's eyebrows furrowed so deeply they created a solid *V* between them, and his voice shook.

Mine shook as well. "I'm sorry I'm not younger or as beautiful as I once was. I'm sorry I have no connections to—"

A hand came over my mouth, and David's eyes hid some deeper turmoil. It was the closest thing to anger I'd seen in them when he was addressing me. "Stop apologizing for things I care nothing about. I don't want that."

I waited patiently for him to remove his hand from my lips, and eventually, he did.

"But do you want me?" I asked, and those blasted tears were suddenly blurring my vision again. Over the past few days, David had made me think he felt as drawn to me as I was to him. His kiss had been so tender, and only a moment ago, he hadn't wanted to let me go without having one more chance to hold me. Our waltz hadn't been about checking the last thing off a list. "Or could you perhaps want me if we had more time together?"

One of David's hands fell from my waist to his side. "Does this have anything to do with Mr. Green and that disgusting bill he gave you?"

I shook my head, my right side missing his warmth. "A marriage would solve that problem because of my inheritance, but I wouldn't ask this of you for only that. Mama and I can find a way to solve it on our own. I asked you because I think I might want to marry you." A sad, soft laugh passed over my lips. "And I'm foolish enough to ask you even though I thought you would say no. We aren't very different after all, are we?"

"I'm afraid we're not." His eyes searched mine. "If you give me a few months, I could have that amount in hand."

A few months wouldn't be fast enough, but that hardly mattered. Based on his responses to my questions, David wouldn't be involved in my life much longer. "And what would our relationship be during those months?" I asked.

David's jaw moved, sliding to one side and then back into place. His arm shook around my waist. "Anna, I don't know. I cannot marry you."

Something deep inside me cracked. I'd put all my cards on the betting table, and I'd lost. I lifted my chin, determined not to show how broken I'd just become. "Then you need to stop trying to take care of me, David. If we are ending our relationship today, you have no right to that responsibility."

David's eyes closed, and he took one staggering step backward, almost as if I'd pushed him away. When he opened his eyes, they were dull, the bright blue shifted into a cloudy gray. He took two slow and heavy steps away from me. "I can't, Anna." He rubbed his face with his hands. "I wish . . . I wish . . ." He stiffened his back, even though the coloring in his cheeks made him look as though he were going to be sick. His eyes fixed on a spot on the cottage behind me, and slowly, the shaking I'd felt when his hand was around my waist stopped. "We need to go into the cottage and tell your mother about our decision." A muscle twitched in his brow. "Now."

I reached a hand out to him and stepped forward. He caught the movement with hard eyes and stepped away from me. My hand dropped.

I had my answer.

If I'd told him I needed to marry him only so I could pay Mr. Green, would he have done it? My heart sank at my foolish pride, yet I couldn't manipulate David into marrying me because of his kindness.

He walked me back to the cottage but kept four feet of space between us.

It felt like an insurmountable distance, but it would be the closest I would ever be to him again.

We entered the cottage together and informed Mama of our intention to end the engagement. Somehow, even Mama's eyes remained dry while we discussed the plans for removing to Lincolnshire. Everything was done in a businesslike fashion, patterned after David's formal stiffness.

After he left, Mama and I spent an hour packing our clothing into trunks. We didn't have much. My hands shook only once, when I pulled the lilies David had given me out of the vase and tossed them in the bin.

They were dead now anyway. My engagement had lasted almost exactly as long as cut hothouse flowers.

"It is over, then?" Mama asked when I started up the stairs to go to sleep.

I stopped, but I didn't turn around to face her. "It is."

I shut myself in my bedroom alone, grateful the Prestons' cottage had enough room for me to have this private space to mourn for what I'd lost, even though I'd only ever had shadows of it in the first place.

Chapter 14

"Sometimes, when everyone else around me thinks the world is being silent, I can hear her singing."

David Tate, 1842, age 15

I awoke with bleary eyes and a headache to the sound of banging on the cottage door. There was only the slightest bit of light coming through the window, so dawn must have arrived only a few minutes ago.

The banging sounded again. It was too early for Mary to have stoked the fires or helped us prepare for the day, so whoever was outside would have to be either ignored or greeted by Mama or me.

I threw on a wrap and crossed the small corridor to Mama's room. I opened her door without knocking and found her sitting in bed with eyes at least as bleary as mine.

"Who is at the door?" she asked with an edge of irritation.

"I don't know. But it seems urgent."

Mama nodded. I grabbed her wrap from her wardrobe and handed it to her. Then we darted down the stairs, Mama mumbling about what she was going to say to whomever was behind the door.

But when Mama pulled it open, David stood there, his fist raised to knock again.

He looked worse than either of us did. His coat was half opened to the bitter wind, and he seemed to be wearing the same clothes he'd worn the day before. The stubble that had adorned his cheeks when he'd returned from Lincolnshire was back again.

He dropped his hand and glanced between us.

"Dav—" I began, but his eyes, fierce and icy, stopped me.

He held out a piece of paper in his left hand. "I've changed my mind," he said with such force that he might have been declaring war on a sovereign nation. "Anna, I've changed my mind. I do want to marry you. If you are willing."

Words caught in my throat. I'd cried more than I cared to admit while falling asleep, and now he was here telling me he'd changed his mind? He'd been so cruelly certain. What could have possibly happened to change his mind in such a short amount of time?

Mama didn't have the same problem talking that I did. "You told her yesterday you didn't want to marry her."

"That is *not* what I said."

"You definitely didn't agree to marry her."

David nodded. "And as I said when you first opened the door, I've changed my mind."

Mama put a hand on her forehead and ran it down her face. Then she backed away from the door, leaving it open, which David took as an invitation to come in. He handed Mama a sheet of paper. She took it absentmindedly, glanced at it, then froze, and glanced at it again. She looked up at David. "This is signed by the archbishop."

David nodded. "He was a friend of my grandfather's."

Mama blinked. "The archbishop of Canterbury?"

David nodded again, his disheveled appearance becoming clear. If he was here, and this wasn't a strange, vivid dream my poor addled brain had concocted, David would have been on trains and horses for most of the night to get that signature.

Mama blinked. "But why a special license?"

"I don't want the banns read, nor do I want to make a spectacle of the event. I'd like us to marry quietly. Today, if possible."

Today?

He'd left me to cry myself to sleep, made me doubt my worth in some of the most excruciating ways possible, and now was here, with a special marriage license, telling me he'd simply *changed his mind*?

Was he mad?

"David, you can't be serious," I said.

"I'm deadly serious."

Mama stumbled toward the drawing room and opened the door. I followed, my own feet unsteady and unbelieving. Mama took a seat near the window, catching the earliest morning rays to read the writing on the special license over again.

A soft touch on my elbow made me turn to face David. He held my arm carefully, as if he were afraid I would run away. Or perhaps to keep himself from running—I wasn't certain. It wasn't long ago when he'd refused me quite decisively. He lowered his head. "May I speak to you alone about this? Please?"

"I . . ." I was going to let him speak to me. I couldn't spend an evening crying over his loss without trying to understand what had changed over the course of one night. But my mind was struggling to come to grips with what was happening. I rubbed my eyes again, not entirely certain my brain wasn't addled. "Of course . . . It is just . . ." The cottage had the drawing room and the kitchen on the ground floor, and it was much too cold to follow him outside with only my wrap. "Mama?" Her head jerked up. "Could David and I speak privately?"

Mama jumped up from the chair and nodded. "Of course, of course. I'll return to my room. But please"—her eyes caught mine—"come and explain everything to me as soon as you're finished."

Mama climbed the stairs with the special license held so tightly in her grip a hurricane wouldn't have been able to loosen it. That paper held the solution to all our problems. Mr. Green, where to live, our finances . . . everything. Perhaps even the broken heart I'd nursed all night.

But I didn't know what had changed his mind.

The moment we heard Mama's bedroom door shut, David started pacing.

I motioned to our all-purpose table. "Would you like to sit?"

He shook his head and ran a hand through his already mussed hair. "No. I don't think I could."

I eyed his attire and his general state of nervous energy. He'd seemed more of a sound mind the night before when he'd rejected me than he did now.

"Have you slept?" I asked.

He shook his head again. "No, I couldn't." He finally stopped his maddening pacing and took a step toward me. "You asked for a favor yesterday, and I refused you."

That was what this was about? His unfounded gratitude toward me? "You had every right to refuse me. It wasn't as though I'd asked to borrow a spare chicken."

His expressive eyebrows furrowed much like the night before, and for the first time since he'd walked in the door, the near crazed look in his eyes dissipated, instead replaced by mild confusion. "No. It wasn't like that at all."

I raised my chin and continued on my wild tangent. As much as I needed him to explain what was happening, I also needed him to look at me with some sense of normalcy. I wouldn't agree to marry him if our marriage made him this agitated. "I'm certain you would have been able to sleep quite soundly if you'd refused a simpler request."

He had turned to resume his pacing, but at my words, he stopped and spun back to me expelling a lungful of air. "I would have given you a chicken, Anna."

"It would have been easy to give me a chicken and easier to refuse. My point is that was *not* what I asked for."

He strode toward me, his eyes imploring. When he stopped, he was close enough for me to reach out and touch him. Suddenly, the drawing room seemed excessively small. "Can we please stop speaking of chickens?"

I was instantly mollified. "Yes, David."

"I want to give you anything you ask for. No. More than *want*, I think I *need* to give you anything you ask for."

A nervous laugh escaped my throat. "Because I was nice to you when you were a child?"

"No." He reached a hand toward my face but then pulled it back. "Not because of that."

I swallowed. My heart was suddenly pounding. "Why, then?"

His chest rose and fell, and he looked at me as if I were a small bird perched and ready to fly off if he were to move too quickly. I felt like a bird ready to fly to him. "Because, my dear Anna, you are the single most important person in my life, save my brother and sister. In truth, it feels as though you are the *only* person in my life, save my siblings. I don't want to lose you. I don't want you to leave, to find a position as a governess or live off the kindness of others. And I definitely don't want you to marry some eager inferior lout because financially you must. I would do anything to help you, Anna. Anything."

"Even marry me when you would rather not?" I asked, my voice cracking.

He sighed heavily, his eyes searching mine for something I didn't know if I had. "As it turns out, because of all the reasons I just listed, *especially* that."

"Oh." My heartbeat, which had somehow managed to increase its pace with each of his words, seemed to stop. He'd just admitted he didn't want to marry me. That hadn't changed. "I can't rob you of a future with someone you want to marry, no matter how dire my circumstances."

He shook his head, and a deep sadness filled his eyes. "You won't be robbing me of anything. I decided years ago I would never marry. You are the only woman who could make me change my mind. But, Anna—" He swallowed and put his hand on the back of his neck. "There will come a time when you will need to leave, and we have to make certain you can. If we marry, it will be so you can pay off Mr. Green and have enough of your inheritance to live off of."

He wanted me to leave? Even after marrying him? "I can't simply marry you, take my money, and leave. The courts would know."

"No, and I selfishly don't want you to. I want you to be my wife and live with you as long as I possibly can. You have to leave the cottage today, and I want you to move into my home not as my fiancée, as we'd originally planned, but as my wife. Today."

There it was again. Today. We'd barely had any time together. What was the rush? Mama and I had to leave the cottage, but David had already initiated a plan for that.

"Why such urgency? And if I marry you, I will not leave you. Why should I? I want to be your wife, David. I thought I made that clear enough last night."

His eyes found mine for a split second, and then he looked away. "Marrying quickly is the best way to keep our marriage quiet. I will not have my father know of it." He took my hand in his and held my gaze. "You must know my life is complicated. You knew me when I was young; you saw how I was treated. I'm doing much better now, but bringing you into my family could tip the very delicate balance we have." David leaned forward until his forehead was pressed into mine. His touch was so intimately familiar that I gasped. He didn't seem to notice. "My father would see you as a pawn. A means to gain the upper hand with his children, and I would *never* expose you or any other woman to that."

"I'm not going to run away because of your father."

David's grip on my fingers tightened, and he pulled away from my forehead to look me in the eyes. "I cannot have him near you. If he finds out about us, I won't hold you to the marriage. I'll find you somewhere to go." His voice was like steel. "I promise."

He was promising all the wrong things.

I swallowed the hurt as I remembered the boy I'd thought had come from a poor tenant family when all along, he'd been the son of a viscount. The way Lord Murphy had injured David's dog Charlotte and how he'd treated his own footman the one time I'd seen him. What exactly had Lord Murphy put David through? Even now, without being here, he was controlling what kind of marriage his son was to have.

"I'm not scared of your father." That wasn't completely true, but it was true enough. I wasn't so scared of him that I would leave David behind if I had to face him.

"Anna. This is my one condition. I will marry you, but I won't tie you to a man like him. Our marriage must be one that can be dissolved at a moment's notice. And that moment will be when he learns about you. Because the second he does, he will come to Tate Hall, and he will torment us." His eyes were firm and his voice like steel. This was something he was not going to retreat from, no matter how much I tried. Which meant I needed to decide whether or not to accept his condition.

"And if this happens years from now? What if we have children? Would you turn them away also?"

"We won't. We can't. I'm not offering you that kind of marriage."

Heat rose to my face. "What are you saying?" David was as confusing as ever, and this was something I refused to be confused about. "Is ours to be . . ."

"We won't be sharing a bed," he said bluntly. If I expected him to blush or be embarrassed by our conversation, I was wrong. He only held my eyes steady. "We can't have any impediments when you leave."

Impediments.

He meant children. I put a hand to my neckline, gripping the hem and willing my breathing to remain steady. So this was what David was offering me: a place to live, a path to pay Mr. Green, and the opportunity to be his wife in name only. The clock on the mantel ticked in a slow, steady rhythm, unaffected by the words David had just said, but everything else around me seemed to fade into a hazy fog.

I should crawl back into bed and pretend Mama and I hadn't opened the door to him.

I should take his generosity and move to Lincolnshire.

I never should have told him I wanted to marry him.

"I cannot allow you to make that kind of sacrifice only so I can pay off my debt to Mr. Green," I said quietly.

"That isn't what this is about," he said, his voice low, matching my own.

"Then I cannot allow myself to agree to such an arrangement. It would only be a shell of what I want from a marriage someday."

David lifted his chin. "An annulment should be possible. You will be able to have that someday. Just not with me."

Was he trying to be noble?

My trunk was half packed upstairs. Where did I want it to go? If I didn't marry David, Mama and I would live alone again, working for years to pay off Mr. Green.

I could try to find a man willing to marry me in truth and pay Mr. Green back in that manner.

But if given the choice between a true marriage with someone I only slightly knew and a marriage in name only to David, my choice was easy—I'd rather be a sister to David than a wife to anyone else.

"All right," I said softly.

He lifted his head away from mine, and his eyes widened. "All right *what*?"

"All right, I will marry you. Today, if you'd like."

He pursed his lips together as though he were trying to hide a smile, but it escaped anyway. "You're certain?"

I nodded. "I am."

He suddenly let out a whoop like a young boy who'd just been given a long-anticipated gift, grabbed my waist, and lifted me in the air. The sound of my shocked laughter burst into the room. Last night, I would have thought it was a sound I wouldn't hear in ages. He spun us around and lowered me down.

Once my feet were back on solid ground he put a hand on the back of his neck and stepped away from me. "Sorry," he said with a sheepish grin.

My head was spinning, and only a small part of that was due to his outburst. I smiled back at him. I didn't understand David at all, and somehow, in a few hours, I was going to be his wife. "Don't be," I said with a laugh. "I'm not certain what is making you so happy, but I suppose I should go look in my wardrobe for a wedding dress. I can't get married in my nightgown."

David's eyes slid down to what I was wearing. His neck reddened slightly. I glanced down to find his energetic spin had left my wrap open, exposing my collar bones and most of my shoulders. I hastily pulled it closed.

He turned his head to the door and cleared his throat. "I won't make a habit of being too familiar with you. Not very often, at least. I promise." Another horrible promise. He looked at me once again, carefully keeping his eyes on my face, even though I'd made myself decent. "I know what kind of marriage we've agreed to and will be careful to respect the boundaries of propriety. I don't ever want to be responsible for making you cry again."

"People make other people cry at times." I shrugged because there was no possible way he'd missed my red-rimmed eyes when he'd first arrived. "I will bear it if it happens."

"I'm not certain I will."

I gave him a smile. What kind of man married a woman in this manner and was happy about it? He was much too kindhearted, and I was taking advantage of him. The room dimmed as if it were the end of the day and the sun was setting instead of just coming up. David was too happy with far too little. Somehow, I needed to find a way to give him more.

"What time shall I tell the vicar to arrive?" he asked.

"Here?"

"I would rather we marry here than at Tate Hall, and if we marry at the church someone from town might see us. That is one of the advantages of the special license. We can marry anywhere."

"Oh." My voice cracked. I'd always thought I would marry in a church. I nodded, not trusting my voice to say another word without displaying too much emotion.

He pulled out a pocket watch. "Will four hours be enough time to prepare?"

I nodded again and pulled my wrap tightly around my neck. The cold had finally managed to seep through me.

"Then I need to go home, tell Julia, and prepare." He turned to leave.

I placed a hand on his arm. "Wait."

His shoulders tightened before he turned hesitantly back toward me.

"What should I tell Mama?"

His expression relaxed. "Whatever you think is best."

I rubbed my face. We'd had only a day of truth between us. Did I dare inform her that David, the man I'd told her I wanted to marry, was willing to marry me but not able to commit to staying married to me? "What are you going to tell Julia and your brother?"

"They will need to know the truth. I don't want them to think I'm taking advantage of your situation. But anyone else will see nothing other than a typical marriage between us." A soft smile formed on his lips. "That is something I never thought I would have."

He still wouldn't. Our marriage would be anything but typical, yet . . . I could feel his longing for it. What kind of monster was Lord Murphy to have broken his son so thoroughly that he couldn't become part of a healthy marriage? Life was terribly unfair at times, and there was little I could do about it.

Or could I? I could do for David what he'd done for me when we'd entered into our engagement. I swallowed down my worries—all my concerns about what to tell Mama and whether or not I would have the strength to leave David when the time came. If we had a finite amount of time together, I wanted to spend it in a way that would make him happy. "And what *does* a typical marriage look like?" I asked with a raised eyebrow.

He understood my intention immediately. I could tell by the look of wonder in his eyes and his long pause before he carefully added the first item on what was to be our marriage list. "Breakfasts together."

I nodded. That would be very simple. "What else?"

"I'd love it if my wife would spend time with my sister."

"And I would love to do it."

His lashes lowered, and he shifted his weight from one foot to the other. "And I think touching you would become ordinary. Something that is a part of my life for every day we have together."

I stepped into him, my nightgown swishing in the small space between us. "And stolen kisses? Should we keep that on our list?" I asked.

He looked up, raising a hand to my face and putting his finger and his thumb under my chin. "No," he said firmly. I blinked down my disappointment. That was probably for the best. He lifted my chin. "Once we are married, there will be no reason to steal them."

The room brightened. "There will be kisses?" I pressed.

He nodded.

Smiling, I leaned into his touch. Perhaps I wasn't to be a sister to him after all. "I think we should begin with that one."

"I'm not your husband yet."

"Then I think you should go fetch the vicar."

He laughed softly and shook his head as if he weren't certain what he was going to do with this new wife of his. "I'm going to keep you safe, Anna. I want that responsibility, and I want you to know I'll take it very seriously. Nothing is more important to me than that."

Then, because suddenly it was the most natural thing in the world, he leaned in and, without touching me anywhere else, pressed an achingly gentle kiss to my mouth. It was brief, but more than a light brush—he lingered just long enough for the warmth of his lips to wash away the most pressing of my fears.

And then he turned and strode away.

Chapter 15

"It has been one year since Anna left. I wanted to do something, so I went empty-handed to the Mortensens'. She'd always brought a basket with her, but they invited me in anyway, even though they knew who I was."

—David Tate, 1842, Age 15

In the end, I couldn't tell Mama our marriage was to be temporary. I wasn't completely convinced we wouldn't eventually find some way to thwart David's father. The man couldn't live forever, could he? I did tell her David was marrying me only to help us, but Mama pushed that thought aside as if it were the most ridiculous thing I'd ever said. Even when I told her we weren't going to have the wedding in the church, all she did was shrug. The only thing that gave her pause was that the marriage was to happen without Lord Murphy being present.

Despite my reassurances that this was what David wanted, it was the first thing she said to him when he and Julia walked in the door a few hours later.

"Are you certain we shouldn't wait for your father?" she asked before he'd even removed his coat.

I glanced behind him. The vicar wasn't with him. He must be arriving separately.

"Yes," David said firmly to her before turning to look at me. I'd chosen to wear the dress I'd worn when he'd pulled me out of the music room and into the corridor to kiss me. It was sentimental. David hadn't said anything to make me think he wanted to be sentimental, but I couldn't help it. If we were going to be married in name only and not even in a church, I wanted at least one thing to be special about this day.

Based on the way his eyes ran down my person and returned to my lips, he remembered exactly which dress this was.

Mama sniffed, unaware of the tension between my soon-to-be spouse and me. "I would be heartbroken if Anna married without me present."

David turned to her. "My father will not be heartbroken. Even if he were, I wouldn't inform him of or invite him to our wedding. We are estranged, and I'd like to keep it that way."

Mama opened her mouth to perhaps ask another question but then must have thought better of it. She hadn't been completely unaware of the kind of man Lord Murphy was on our last visit.

David waited just long enough to be certain she was satisfied and then turned back to me, his eyes once again raking over me. "Hello, Anna."

"Hello." My voice sounded strange in my ears, as if such mundane words didn't have a place on my wedding day. I stepped toward Julia first. "Thank you for coming, Julia." She looked nervous, as always, but a soft, hopeful smile toyed at her lips. I dropped a soft kiss on her cheek before stepping in front of David. "And thank you for coming as well."

David's lips curved up. "To my own wedding? Of course—" His sentence was cut short as I dropped a kiss on his cheek too. He was now clean-shaven, his clothing was impeccable, and even his eyes no longer looked tired. I stepped away, and with quick blink and a short clearing of his throat, he continued, "Of course I would come to my own wedding."

I took his hand and pulled him in to the drawing room. He followed quietly, and I didn't dare look at his face. There was no privacy to be had in the cottage, Mama and Julia would not be far behind us, so I tugged him close when we were far enough away whispers would not be overheard. "I couldn't tell Mama about all the details of our marriage. She knows we are marrying for my sake, but I didn't tell her our marriage is likely to end. I want her to think you are happy to be marrying me."

He pulled back, put a hand on each of my shoulders, and looked me in the eye. "I *am* happy to be marrying you."

Ugh. This man. "You know what I mean," I hissed back at him. "Did you have time to tell Julia?"

"Yes."

"Oh." Julia's smile had looked genuine. Why would she be happy about the wedding if she knew it wasn't going to be a true marriage? She'd warned me about taking advantage of his kindness; wasn't that exactly what I was doing?

"Other than Julia and my brother, no one else will need to know until the time comes for you to leave. We will tell them then."

Until the time comes for you to leave. It was a foregone conclusion in his mind. No matter what I did or how happy we might become, because of his father, he was certain I would either leave him or he would make me leave.

I bit my lip. "Do you think there is any chance that day might never come?" I asked softly.

David sighed heavily. "Even if it doesn't . . ." He shook his head. "I don't want you to think that way. If you tire of a half marriage, you may leave at any point. I will pay whatever it takes to have the marriage annulled, and you can find a man who is free to love you fully. I don't want you to stay with me if you are unhappy."

All my certainty of his devotion to me wavered.

We should have talked more about this. We should have made time for it. But pushing off the wedding now would be rash. The vicar and two families were on their way here to witness it. And for what? David's certainty on the subject wasn't something I was going to be able to change over the course of a conversation, and even if he never changed his mind, marrying him remained my best option.

Another knock sounded at the door, and a few seconds later, Mr. and Mrs. Mortensen came into the drawing room, followed by Mama and Julia. They rushed over to us, hugging us both profusely. David laughed at their exuberance.

Mrs. Mortensen grabbed my hands and pulled me in one more time for a quick embrace. "I knew the two of you would make quite the match. And you were so certain otherwise."

David raised an eyebrow at me, but I ignored it, shrugging my shoulders and returning Mrs. Mortensen's hug. "Thank you for coming."

Over the course of the next few minutes, both the Prestons and the aged vicar arrived, and soon the cottage was filled with the kind of cheer and noise that made it difficult to remember none of this was real. Not in the way everyone but Julia thought it was.

When the vicar asked where the ceremony should be held, Mama suggested in front of the fireplace, and suddenly, the room went quiet.

The vicar ventured past each of the guests and stood in front of the fire before he turned and looked at us, and David took my hand and led me to forward. We stopped in front of the vicar, but David did not let go of my hand.

With a warm smile, the vicar opened his prayer book and began the ceremony. I'd never been to a wedding, so I listened closely, fearful I would find myself in a state of disapproval with God, but nothing he said made me feel like I was lying. Nevertheless, I held my breath when the vicar asked about impediments. Would Julia see our agreement not to remain married because of her father as an impediment?

She must not have, for the cottage remained silent after the vicar's question. David's face was still and serious when the vicar recited David's vows, David repeated them, his words firm. Something caught in my throat, and I blinked. Was this happening? Life had a strange way of throwing me surprises, and David was the most surprising one of all.

When it was my turn to speak, I tried to sound as steadfast as David had, but my voice cracked the moment I opened my mouth. By the end, my words were clear.

And when we both answered, "I will," to the vicar's question, tears filled my eyes. Somehow, our little cottage felt as holy and sanctified as any church.

"Such a beautiful wedding." Mama's eyes were wet when she embraced me after the ceremony. Everyone else had very similar sentiments, including the vicar.

Mrs. Preston embraced me tighter than anyone else and bent to my ear. "I was so very worried about not being able to help you more. I'm so grateful everything turned out so well for you. Mr. Tate is one of the kindest men I know."

After Mama and I served tea to everyone, our guests left with smiles on their faces. The carriage ride to Tate Hall was full of stolen glances between David and me, all while Mama and Julia discussed what rooms had been opened now that the family was expanding.

When we arrived, the servants lined the entry hall, and the second Mama saw them, she gave a quick little gasp and squeezed my hand.

For the size of the estate, there were fewer servants than I would have expected, but to have any help other than borrowed help would be a luxury Mama and I hadn't had since Atwood Manor had fallen into my uncle's hands.

David held my hand throughout the introductions, and afterward, the servants were dismissed, and he pulled me aside. "We will have to hire a maid for you and your mother. I was thinking one of the Miss Mortensens might be taught, if you would be open to a maid who would need training."

I beamed at him. "That would be wonderful." Tate Hall was magnificent, and if Mrs. Mortensen could spare Maren, that would add one more thing to my happiness.

David swallowed and nodded, taking a step away from me.

"Would the two of you like to have dinner alone?" Julia asked.

"No," I quickly responded. I wasn't ready to spend an hour alone in my husband's company. Not so soon after everything we'd vowed to each other during our wedding. It still felt too real. "We are all family now, and you are as important to me as David."

Julia laughed. "I hope that isn't true, but it is very kind of you to say."

I smiled at her and grabbed her hand. "Show me to the dining room."

Julia laughed. "I'm happy to show you to *your* dining room."

I should have walked into the room with David, but instead, he took Mama's arm, and they followed Julia and me. David and I sat next to each other, and every so often, I had to remind my hands to keep to themselves. It would have been so easy to take his hand or brush some nonexistent lint from his shoulder. If I'd been a true wife to him, my fingers would have sought his throughout the meal. Perhaps I should have done all of those things—I was bound and determined to do everything on David's list, including touching him in these kinds of ordinary ways. But I didn't feel ready to start on the list yet.

After finishing the pudding the staff had made to celebrate the wedding, Julia and Mama stood simultaneously.

"It has been a very eventful day," Mama said. "I believe I will retire early."

Julia nodded her agreement. She walked to our side of the table and kissed David on the forehead and me on the cheek. Mama followed her, kissing both of my cheeks and tearing up slightly. Then turning to David, she grabbed both of his cheeks and to my complete mortification, placed a quick kiss on his mouth. David's eyes widened, but thankfully, he laughed.

Mama put a hand on her hip, unrepentant. "I won't be making a practice of that, but I want you to know how happy you have made us. I'm proud to call you my son."

Then they were gone.

David and I were alone, in our shared home, as husband and wife.

He sat back in his chair, reached for my hand, lifted it to his mouth, and kissed it. I inhaled sharply. Mama wasn't here, and despite his kiss this morning, I'd thought such little touches would be saved for when she was near.

"Mrs. Tate," David said, "I hope you found the day agreeable?"

I nodded, not trusting my voice. I was a married woman, and I was married to a vibrant man with the kindness of angels. The fact that only weeks ago, I'd thought I may have to marry someone as unlikeable as Mr. Green was not lost on me. My life had taken a dramatic turn for the better.

Footsteps sounded in the corridor just outside the dining room door. After spending so much time in a small cottage, the vast and nearly empty rooms of Tate Hall seemed to make the noises of the servants' busy work echo around us.

David dropped my hand and smiled a half-smile. He coughed softly and ran a hand through his hair, mussing it in a way that reminded me that despite how much he'd grown, despite his skilled thatching hands, and despite the fact that he now had a wife, he was still young. "Should I show you to your room?"

He was not, as it turned out, so very young as to not make that sentence loom with meaning, even if he hadn't meant it to. I nodded. "Yes, you must be exhausted."

"I suspect I will fall asleep immediately tonight," he said with a small chuckle. "Finding myself a wife cost me a full night of rest."

He kept hold of my hand and pulled me forward. We left the dining room and climbed the stairs to a long corridor. We passed several doors on each side while we walked down it but didn't stop until we arrived at a door that stood at the end of the corridor. David paused with his hand on the doorknob. "This was my mother's room. It hasn't been used for over thirteen years. I didn't give the servants long to prepare it, so if you need anything—anything at all—ring the bell, and they will see that you have it."

He opened the door, and I gasped softly. I'd never seen a more beautiful and unique bedroom. We were directly above the octagonal drawing room and my bedroom was the same shape. Four large windows with rose-colored drapes took up half of the eight sides, making it feel as though if I stood in that part of the room, I'd be practically in the back garden. The bed was large and tall with drapery that matched the curtains on the windows. It took up one of the four remaining walls, and a wardrobe occupied another. The last two walls held doors, the one we were standing in and another one I suspected led to David's room.

"Oh, David, it's lovely."

"It is, by far, my favorite room in the house." His thumb traced my knuckles almost absentmindedly as he inspected the room from the doorway. "And now that it is yours, I think I may love it even more."

We stood unmoving. I wanted to rush in, jump on the bed to test its softness, then throw the drapes completely open and bask in my view, but that would mean parting from David, and I wasn't ready for that. I cleared my throat and took one step over the threshold. "Would you like to come inside?" I asked.

David's mouth quirked. "I'd better not."

I nodded because he was right. "Where is your room?"

He nodded toward the last door we'd passed on the left. "It isn't as beautiful as this one, but it is the closest room besides my father's." He pointed to the adjoining door. "I had the servants move my things into my room last night as well. Your mother now has my old room, next to Julia's at the top of the stairs."

"I thought your father never came here. Why do you need to leave his room free for him?" The question hung in the air. How certain was David that his father wouldn't come? If he did, where would I sleep? For it wouldn't do to have only a door between us. Hadn't David considered that when . . . But then I remembered. If his father knew I was here, I would be on my way somewhere else. There was no chance of us ever being in the same house together, let alone sharing an adjoining room.

"I'll never sleep in that room. Not even after he dies. Garrett may choose to when he visits since I commandeered his room. I'll let him deal with that when he comes."

"And how often does Garrett visit?"

"Very rarely. He and Father have entrusted Julia and me to run the estate, but the price of keeping Father away from here and out of the day-to-day management of the tenants and servants was Garrett's promise to remain in London by Father's side." A heaviness settled on David. "He has been able to visit without Father knowing a few times secretly, but it is much less often than we'd like."

I nodded but didn't press for any more answers, even though it became very clear exactly when the tenants' lives had improved on the Tate lands.

"David?"

"Yes?" His eyes met mine, and they were, in fact, very tired, as if it were all he could do to keep standing.

"Thank you for marrying me."

David inhaled slowly, in a way that seemed to draw him nearer to me. If I didn't know any better, I would think the hooded gaze he gave me was the exact variety a husband should have for his wife on his wedding night. The kind of look that would have him stepping forward, wrapping me in his arms, and covering my mouth with his own.

Instead, he closed his tired eyes and nodded. "Anything for you, Anna."

Then he turned quickly on his heel and marched to his own room, where he would most certainly sleep deeply.

I, on the other hand, would not be able to sleep, knowing the sentence he'd only just spoken to me was a lie, even if he didn't know it. Because the truth was, David wouldn't do *anything* for me. He would only do *almost* anything for me. Otherwise, we would have married in a church a few months from now, and when I'd invited him in on our wedding night, he would have joined me, even if he hadn't slept for days.

Chapter 16

"If anything, I will have more scars because I've learned to be happy. Father can't understand why I've changed, and he doesn't like the things he cannot understand."

—David Tate, 1842, Age 15

The next morning, David was waiting outside my bedchamber when I left it to go down to breakfast.

That was one advantage of having servants. They could act as spies between husband and wife. The maid who'd helped me ready myself must have let him know when to expect me.

He held out an arm. "I thought it would be best if we went down to breakfast together. I was so tired yesterday, I'm afraid I may have neglected my new wife."

My eyes wanted to glance back at my bedroom door, but I forced them to remain on David. He'd been very clear about what our marriage was to be, and I'd chosen it, regardless. I'd been frustrated when I'd gone to bed, but a good night's rest had set me to rights.

I happily took his arm. "You didn't. I had everything I needed in my room, and Julia's maid helped me this morning. I'm settling in splendidly."

"Good." His smile was broad, and I couldn't help but wonder if he felt the same way I did—that any day we were able to spend together was bound to be a good day. "Shall we cross one thing off our marriage list?"

I gave him a mock scowl. "I should be the one completing the items on our marriage list. Just as you were the one to send flowers and plan walks. If you mark off anything by your own merit, I'm going to have to add another item to it."

"But it's *my* list," he said, leading us down the corridor to the stairs. "You don't get to add items."

"Then I'll have to make you add one."

He chuckled. "Somehow, I don't think you are as threatening as you think you are. You think it a punishment for me to add to a list of actions that will make our marriage feel conventional? It isn't." We descended the stairs.

"My goal is not to punish you. I'd like to make you happy."

His eyebrows furrowed, and he shook his head. "Anna, are you in earnest?"

"Of course I am."

With another low chuckle, he turned his head to look at me as if didn't believe me. "You've been making me happy for years."

He led me to a set of double doors I hadn't seen last night, then stopped and turned toward me.

I put a hand on my hip. "You say things like that, but I have no idea what you mean. We only had one summer together."

He grinned, his eyes bright in a way that made me feel young again. "You taught me what happiness was, Anna. Anytime I'm happy, it makes me thankful for you."

"Oh," I said, that sneaky warm feeling encompassing my chest and working its way up to my cheeks. When it became clear that I wasn't going to add anything else to that statement—because how could I?—David pulled the doors open to the breakfast room.

Mama and Julia were seated at a table with plates less than half full of food, and they both jerked their heads toward us in surprise when we walked in.

"Awake already?" Mama asked. "Julia and I were just conspiring as to how to make ourselves scarce for the next few days. I suppose we will have to come to breakfast half an hour earlier tomorrow."

"No, Mama," I said quickly. "There is no reason for that."

Mama ignored my reproach. "Or I suppose we could have breakfast sent to our rooms, couldn't we, Julia?"

Julia glanced at her brother. "If you would like us to, David, I wouldn't mind."

"Don't do anything of the sort on our account," David said as he reached for two rolls from the sideboard and placed them on a plate for me and a plate for him.

"Ah." Mama snapped her fingers. "Better yet, I'll ask the servants to have a breakfast tray sent to the two of you."

Was she trying to embarrass us?

"Mama, we are happy to eat breakfast with you. If David and I want to be alone, this home is quite large enough for us to find a place without anyone in it. Do not feel the need to conspire with Julia over such things."

Mama shrugged an I-was-only-trying-to-help shrug. She had three pieces of fruit and some sliced meat on her plate when David started dishing up our breakfast, but by the time we had gathered our food and sat down, she'd already finished eating and was pulling on the back of Julia's chair.

"Come, we will visit with them more tomorrow, if they insist. Today, let's allow them to take their breakfast in peace."

Julia glanced at David, unsure of what she should do. David gave her a slight nod. She nodded in return and trudged after Mama, leaving behind half a plate of food.

I grimaced and turned to David. "I don't believe I've ever been happier to see my mother leave a room."

David lifted a berry from his plate and threw it into his mouth. "Somehow, I think she knows that, even if it is not for the reason she presumes."

I practically snorted. "I'm certain you're correct. It is a little strange to me that she imagines us so very much in love when I told her you were only marrying me to help us, and we have only spent a few weeks in each other's company."

At that, David raised an eyebrow. "I've told you several times already that she believed it the moment she and the Prestons opened the door and found you in my arms."

I waved away his explanation. "I think in her case, having my happy marriage solve all our problems doesn't hurt." She'd also seen me crying over him, and in general, I wasn't one to cry over trifles. But I didn't want to admit that to David. Not when we were enjoying our first breakfast together, crossing an item off his list.

His memories of me were the kind that brought happiness. He'd as much as said so just before we'd entered the breakfast room, so I would hide my growing longing for him, and I wouldn't melt in the face of the lovely things he said about me. I would be a delightful wife within the bounds he'd set and tuck my yearning deep inside my heart.

"I believe my next duty as your wife is to enjoy some time with Julia. What are her interests?"

"You don't need to march through our whole list in one morning," he said with a chuckle. "I think just having you here will help her immensely."

"This is the one thing you've consistently asked of me while giving me so much. I'm not going to put it off for another day."

He looked as though he might protest but then changed his mind. David might not know all my thoughts, thank goodness, but sometimes I felt as though he understood me better than anyone. I needed something to do to repay him for his kindness as well as to keep busy while living here, and I wanted it to be something that would help his family.

David leaned back in his chair and tapped a finger on the table in thought. "The only thing she has shown interest in is her studies. She plays the pianoforte at times, but she doesn't engross herself in it, not like she does learning. She sits in on my lessons with Mr. Allen, but I'd like her to go outside more, to breathe fresh air and feel the wind in her hair. I'd like to see her taking more enjoyment out of life."

I nodded. A few weeks ago, the task of bringing a young woman back to life had seemed impossible, but being around David *had* changed me. His confidence and trust in my abilities made me feel more capable. Honestly, even having him sit next to me, facing the world in his own surefooted way, made me feel more capable. "We could work on designing and planting a garden. Or perhaps if she is interested in animals—"

David's finger stopped its tapping. "No animals."

I glanced up at his face. It was closed off in a way I had only seen since he'd told me he wouldn't marry me. I gave him a wary smile. Was that because of Charlotte? Had he ever allowed himself to care for any other animals after her? Or did he worry about bringing any living thing into a household where his father might visit? "A garden, then?"

It took a moment, and it looked as though he had to force his features back into their more familiar, relaxed form, but he managed it. "I think a garden project would be ideal."

I raised an eyebrow. "Spring has not yet arrived."

"Prepping for a garden should be done in winter, should it not? Then when spring comes, we can be ready to plant. You wouldn't mind feigning interest in making a part of the estate your own while you are here, enlisting Julia's help, would you?"

My interest in planning a garden for David's home would not have to be feigned. The idea of having the space and capabilities to transform a piece of land into something beautiful was so far removed from who I'd been only a few weeks ago that it was difficult to digest. It would be an indulgence I would never have the chance to pursue without David, even if I wasn't certain to be around to see it when the beauty of spring came. "I would love to do that. I will need a budget."

"I'll look into it this afternoon. I'm fairly certain we could enlist some help from the Mortensens. Their two oldest boys at home would be happy for some extra work."

"Do you have any streams on the estate?"

"Several."

"Ponds?"

"Not near the back garden. Some of the tenant farms have ponds for watering their animals."

"Do you think Walter and Anders Mortensen would be interested in digging us a pond and diverting stream water to fill it?"

David smiled. "I think if you asked them nicely, they would jump at the chance. And while you are asking, you can speak to Mrs. Mortensen and Maren about her training to be a lady's maid. I've become very particular about the servants who live here since my father moved to London permanently, and I think her lack of skill is more than outweighed by her trustworthiness." Maren would be perfect. "But before talking to the boys," David continued, "speak to Julia to see what she thinks of the garden idea. I'll get to work on the budget." He stood from the table and bent to kiss the top of my head before taking his leave.

His touch was so quick and so familiar, the touch of a husband and wife. Not a couple who'd wed only the day before but one who had lived years together in peaceful coexistence.

It robbed me of my breath and made my spine stiffen, but David had turned away from me, and if he noticed my reaction to him, he didn't show it. Did he think doing things like this would make simple contact like that become ordinary? If so, it was only working for him. Nothing about his touch, even when brief and familiar, felt ordinary.

Since my agreeing to marry him, he'd kissed me twice and I him once. True, only one of those kisses had been on the mouth, and all of them had been very brief, but if David didn't mind kissing being a part of our marriage, perhaps I would encourage Mama in her plan to offer us privacy over the next week after all.

Chapter 17

"Mama has been sick for a week. Dr. Clarke hasn't said she could die, but he is frowning a lot. I know the vicar would tell me not to be selfish and to be happy that she would be in heaven and away from all her pain. But instead, I keep praying she can stay."

—David Tate, 1837, Age 10

I found Julia in the library. She had several books laid open in front of her on the table. I stepped into the room, but her eyes didn't lift from the book she was reading, so I knocked softly on the door. Her eyes shot up, and a hand came to her chest. I had startled her.

"Anna," she said in relief, looking behind me.

"I'm alone."

She nodded, and I took that as a welcome to come into the room. An extensive rug covered most of the floor, and my feet sank into it with each step. When I reached her, I inspected the books that had her so enthralled.

Latin.

Julia was studying Latin.

I wasn't certain what I'd been expecting, but not that. "Latin?" I asked her.

Her cheeks reddened slightly. "Yes. Mr. Allen will be coming tomorrow, and I wanted to go over the chapters he will be teaching beforehand."

"Are you almost finished?"

She shut the largest book in front of her. "No, but I have all day."

"I don't want to interrupt."

Julia shook her head. "I want you to feel welcome here. I didn't think any of us would ever marry, least of all me or David. I want your time here to be pleasant."

I was silent, suddenly glad I hadn't told Mama the complete truth of our marriage. Little words like the ones Julia had just spoken, reminding me my time was limited, hurt, even though I had no right to be hurt by them.

I forced a smile onto my face. I was here to bring happiness, I reminded myself. "I spoke to David this morning about a few tasks to keep me occupied while Mama and I live here. In the end, we decided perhaps planning a garden would be a good idea. Would you be willing to help me with it?"

Julia stilled, her only movement a finger sliding back and forth along the edge of the tome she'd just closed. "Do you think that is a good idea?" she asked softly. "Perhaps something less permanent would be better."

"I . . ." I wasn't certain what she meant. "Do you think it will be too expensive? David said he would look into the books."

A corner of her mouth lifted. "I'm certain if you want a garden, David will find a way to pay for it."

My smile faltered. It wasn't for me. David wanted the garden for *her*. "If you don't think I should work on a garden, I can think of another project. I'd like something to occupy my time."

"No." She shook her head. "I like the thought of a garden at Tate Hall."

She hadn't looked like it was a good idea a moment ago.

"Would you help me with it? I've never planned a garden before, and you will be the one who has to live with it if I end up needing to leave."

"Not only me." I'd never heard Julia speak loudly, but her voice was even softer than was typical. "David will as well."

"We will get approval from David. I won't leave you with an elaborate courtyard filled with ceramic monsters and invasive vines."

"I'm not worried about David's approval." Her deep-set eyes found mine. "I'm worried about the reminder of you after you're gone."

I furrowed my brows. Did she think I would make David's life so miserable he wouldn't even want to think of me? Some wives might become embittered in a relationship like ours, but I wouldn't. I was David's spot of brightness. I wasn't about to ruin that, especially when I knew what kind of marriage I'd agreed to. "I don't think I will be such a terrible wife to him that he won't be able to stomach looking at something I've left behind."

"No, I don't think so either." Julia sighed so deeply it sounded as if she'd given up on life ever being good and fair. "I think he will love the garden after you are gone. My worry is he will love it too much."

She looked so solemn. So earnestly concerned for her brother. But why? He was the one who'd said I had to leave. Had David omitted that very large detail when explaining our marriage was to be temporary? Did she think I was the one who didn't want to stay? "Julia, I think you may have misunderstood something about my relationship with your brother. I have no plans to leave him."

She smiled at me like a mother might smile at a willful child. "I know."

I shook my head. "No, I don't think you understand. I *wanted* to marry your brother. True, this marriage does solve my financial problems, which is probably the main reason your brother agreed to it. But I was the first to suggest making our engagement fulfill its natural course and end in a marriage, and it wasn't to solve my problems alone.

I . . ." Humility was a strength, wasn't it? One I should improve upon? And if I wanted to help Julia, she needed to know that David was the one who didn't want this to be a real marriage, not me. I couldn't have her sad for him that I would be leaving when he was the one who'd told me I had to go. "I care for your brother. Very much. If, for any reason, I leave, it will only be because he asks me to do so. Otherwise, I plan on remaining here."

"I know that."

"Then why should it matter if I leave a garden behind me if I go?"

"It shouldn't matter. But it will." Julia glanced up at me. "But I think all will be well. I think it will bring him some joy."

The two of these siblings—so concerned about keeping the other one happy. Were they trying at all to find joy for themselves? David wanted me to make Julia happier, and Julia wanted to make certain I didn't leave David sad. Between the both of them, it looked as though I would have plenty to do in whatever time I was granted in this house.

"What would you like to have in a garden, Julia?"

"I actually think I'd rather have an orchard," she said. "I've always wanted plum trees."

I nodded. "Then let's look into ordering some plum trees. Would you walk in the back garden with me so we can decide where we will start?"

Julia stood. Now that trees had been mentioned, her eyes showed a bright spark of interest. "I'll bring my sketch pad, and we can write down our ideas."

Chapter 18

"I might never be a master at repairing thatch, but I've learned to be a good assistant. When the Mortensens' roof was finally finished, I sat back in wonder at what my hands could do."

—David Tate, 1847, Age 20

Over the next few days, David and I established a routine. He would work most of the day in his study or ride out to see some of the tenants, and I would only see him at dinner or on the occasions where he came out to see the progress Julia and I had made on the orchard.

After dinner, he would spend time with Mama, Julia, and me in the drawing room, and it was there he would be the most affectionate. Not always physically, but his words were laced with an endearing quality that charmed me throughout the evening until he walked me to my bedchamber when it was time to retire.

Outside my door, he would offer the most formal of good nights, and even on the days where he'd plant a kiss on the top of my head in front of Mama, he did no more than offer me a short bow at night. The small part of me that was led to hope in the drawing room died night after night outside my door.

This evening, after we finished dinner, instead of leading me to my room, he asked me to join him in his study. I nodded and followed him into the room I saw him enter and exit multiple times a day but that I'd never seen inside.

The study was lined with deep wood, and an ornate desk sat near the window. Papers were spread about the top of it, and a few books and an inkwell filled the rest of the space. He took my hand, strode over to his desk, and bade me sit.

He pulled out a sheet of paper and placed it in front of me. "I have our marriage documents all in order. It is time to write to your solicitor."

I turned and smiled at him, and he half sat on the desk to see me better.

"Happily," I said and started my letter.

After a moment, he pointed to what I was writing. "Don't you think you should include some details about how dashing and kind your new husband is?"

Dashing and *kind* were excellent descriptors. I put them in.

When I finished, I folded the letter and handed it to him. "You are an excellent husband. I could have written more wonderful things about you, but I didn't want to look suspicious."

"You should have. I would have loved to read them, and I believe brides are forgiven for doting on their new husbands."

Time and time again, he'd proven what an extraordinary husband he would be, to me or any other woman of his choosing, and it grated on me that his father was keeping him from such happiness.

"How old were you when you decided you would never marry?" I asked.

David looked up from the letter in surprise. After my disastrous question on our marriage day, I'd avoided asking anything about the conditions of our marriage.

"I was nineteen."

"Did your father do something terrible that day?"

David shook his head. "No, he was already living in London."

"Then what made you decide such a thing?"

He looked me in the eye, leaned forward, and said the last thing I ever would have expected. "I'm afraid a large part of the decision at that time was vanity and pride."

I furrowed my brows. "Really?"

He put my letter down on his desk and took both of my hands in his before lifting me from his chair. Once I was standing, he dropped his hands to his side and just stood there looking at me. "Remember, I was only nineteen, and vanity and pride were very critical reasons. I wasn't as humble as I am now."

"Humble?" I asked, raising an eyebrow and reaching for the letter I'd given him. "Should I add that to *dashing* and *kind* in my letter?"

He pulled it away from me. "No need. Your letter is lovely as is. Besides"—he groaned softly—"it probably isn't true. I'm afraid those two vices still have a firm grip over me, but in my case, they did serve a good purpose. After I determined to never marry, I saw the wisdom in it, and each year, my resolve grew stronger. By the time I saw you again, I no longer even questioned my reasoning. It was a good plan."

I grimaced. "Until I ruined it?"

He laughed. "No, not ruined. You made it better. With you, I get to see some of what it would be like to have a marriage. It is more than I ever expected to have."

"If you wanted"—I touched the edge of his lapel—"I could become an extremely unpleasant wife and make you feel better about being alone in your old age."

He shook his head, and his laughter deepened. "No, I really don't think you could."

"You only say that because you don't know me very well."

He placed his hand over mine and pressed it firmly against his heart. "We both know that isn't true." The way he looked at me made me feel well known indeed. And even though his answers didn't make sense to me, I could feel the truth in them. Which meant my husband had secrets I didn't know about yet, and they were secrets he would rather not reveal. Someday, I hoped he would share them with me, but I wouldn't drag them from him.

My eyes slid down to his lips. Should I kiss him as my reward for being brave enough to ask about his past? He hadn't minded any kisses thus far, and I was being very good and not pressing him to reveal more than he was willing to share.

I lifted onto my toes and leaned forward. His eyes widened in surprise, but his free hand went to my waist.

And then there was a rap at the door, and Mr. Stoddard, the butler, stepped into the study without waiting for an answer. He immediately reddened at the sight of us. With a stuttered word about the wine stores, he quickly turned and left.

David's arm was still around my waist, but after a few seconds of indecision, he dropped it. Blasted butler. Couldn't he have found some other time to speak to David about the wine?

David cleared his throat. "I have one more thing for you." He strode to the corner of the room, where a large box sat. He picked it up and handed it to me. Despite its size, it wasn't very heavy. "Julia bought you something."

"Julia did? I asked.

"Yes." He put a hand on the back of his neck. Was he nervous? What exactly was in this box? "Or rather, we both did. But it isn't only from me."

I set it down on his desk, untied the thick ribbon wrapped around its middle, and lifted away some tissue paper, bringing an instant grin to my face. Dark-blue wool and black buttons stared back at me.

"Do you think Mama will allow me to accept this? From a man?" I asked.

"I told you it is from me *and* Julia."

I pulled the coat out of the box. "This is a much more suitable color than green."

"I thought so too," he said. "Blue has always brought out the fire in those stormy walnut eyes of yours."

"Did Julia say that?"

"No." He shook his head. "She isn't as poetic as I am. She only said it would look lovely with your dark hair. You'll have to thank her in the morning. I'll walk you to your room."

I nodded, knowing full well I wouldn't get kissed after he made that statement.

Two days after David sent my letter to the solicitor, Julia and I spent the afternoon working on the orchard. We'd picked a naturally wild spot not far from Tate Hall. It had a stream running through it, which we could use to make a pond.

David had ordered plum trees as well as two pear trees and a fig tree. The fig tree had been Mr. Allen's idea, and Julia's eyes had lit up at the idea of it. David claimed he needed to go over accounts and other estate plans every morning, but by afternoon, he often meandered out to us or found us in the library going over our ideas.

Much to my chagrin, we'd decided against flowers. Flowers would have given Julia much more time out of doors than her small orchard would, but flowers hadn't excited her like fruit trees had, and I'd pressed the idea of the pond, which she seemed more in favor of. If she didn't have flowers to keep her outside, perhaps David could make a boat, and a boat would provide more outdoor activities for the two of them.

Walter and Anders were indeed glad to be hired to prepare the land, and since it was too early to plant trees that hadn't even arrived yet, we'd started clearing the ground for the pond.

We'd been working for over an hour when Julia decided to try to pull out one of the larger gorse bushes on her own.

"I've got the Mortensen boys to do that," Mr. Harris, the gardener, said, coming up behind Julia as she struggled. Mr. Harris's advice on location and planning had been invaluable, even if he huffed any time Julia or I put on gloves to help with clearing the land ourselves.

I left the spot of ground where I'd been pulling grasses and came up beside Julia. "Mr. Harris, we will be helping, and we will be getting our aprons dirty. We've gone over this several times before."

Mr. Harris's deep, wrinkled face curved into a frown, but I was the lady of the house now, and even though he'd grumbled at some of my suggestions, he always did as I asked. It was a strange thing to be listened to and respected. I had David to thank for that. All the servants were extremely loyal to him and Julia and, therefore, to me as well.

He huffed. "At least wait until the boys get a bit more digging done around that bush before you start pulling on it. I won't have the young miss straining herself because of their lack of preparation."

"Of course." I waved Walter over. He came jogging up to us, shovel in hand. "Can you loosen the roots of this gorse?" I asked.

Walter nodded and gave me one of his toothy grins, then stuck the shovel into the ground and jumped on it with all his weight. Mr. Harris gave the boy a satisfied nod, then left to help Anders several yards away.

Footsteps sounded on the path behind us. In only a week of waiting to hear David join us every day, I'd become very familiar with the rhythm of his gait. I didn't turn around, instead keeping my eyes trained on Walter. I always needed a moment for the excitement to settle before I met David's gaze. It was a delicate balance we had to keep as husband and wife.

"Let me spell you for a bit, Walter." David's playful, spirited voice made it impossible not to glance at him. His coat and jacket were gone, and he was in his shirt and waistcoat. The waistcoat looked to be an older one, made for warmth instead of style. He wore thick work gloves with his shirtsleeves rolled up just above his wrists.

David had come to work. Images of his powerful arms swinging his leggett on the Walkers' roof flooded my mind. It wasn't gentlemanly to work so deftly with his hands, but his skill at it made me feel sorry for any young wife not fortunate enough to have the pleasure of watching her husband handle tools and work up a sweat.

His hands gripped the shovel as he ruffled Walter's hair and bumped him out of the way. Almost immediately, the shovel hit one of the strong roots that had prevented Julia from removing the gorse earlier.

David lifted the shovel, slammed it into the root, and jumped onto the blade with both feet. What little bit I could see of his arms, just above the top of his gloves, flexed as he pushed the handle of the shovel straight down. The root snapped under his weight, and the shovel sank deep into the earth. I knew I shouldn't spend the afternoon watching David shovel dirt and pull bushes out of the ground—especially after I'd chided Mr. Harris about allowing Julia and me to do our part—but I also couldn't look away.

He worked the shovel from side to side, loosening the earth around the roots in steady increments. The bush groaned and lifted in response. Walter and Anders were only a few years younger than David, but those years had added a strength and power into David's lean frame that the Mortensen boys couldn't match.

Julia turned to me and opened her mouth to speak, but then stopped. She tipped her head to one side and raised an eyebrow.

Immediately, heat rushed to my cheeks. My appreciation of David's vigor must have been written on my face. "What is it?" I whispered in her direction.

She took a step closer to me. "If I mentioned the way your eyes like to devour him while he is working during dinner tonight, I wonder what David would say."

A strangled laugh escaped my lips. "Eyes can't devour someone."

"It seems yours are trying very hard to do just that."

"No, they are trying very hard *not* to. And your brother doesn't need anyone telling him he looks decent while working the land. I'm certain he already knows it."

"He spends most of his time with me, Mr. Allen, and some of the tenant families' sons. He might need someone to tell him."

"Well, it won't be me."

"Would it be so terrible for my brother's wife to find him handsome?"

"Julia." We'd had too many talks about this while working. It was unfair of her to say things like that, and I'd told her so every single time.

"You and David can lie to yourselves if you want to. I never agreed to do the same."

"We aren't lying to ourselves," I hissed. "We are keeping to our agreement."

"And your agreement included not enjoying watching him work?" she asked.

I gritted my teeth and didn't respond. If Julia had noticed the way I couldn't keep my eyes off David, then I might as well enjoy watching him while I could. Because she was right, our agreement hadn't forbidden it. In some ways, it encouraged it, especially when we had an audience. David moved on to another stubborn bush. At the moment, there were no roots to break through—only dirt—but even his less-forceful shovel strokes didn't take away from the fact that his arms flexed with each movement or his hair flopped forward until he blew it away with an exasperated huff or dragged his forearm along his forehead to get it out of his eyes.

His body was compact in a way that spoke of muscles ready to spring and lithe movements waiting just below the surface. When we sat still at dinner or when he wrote letters with us in the drawing room, all that power was buried beneath the surface, but I could always feel it, humming and waiting for him to unleash it with a kick to an unsuspecting rock on our walks or on bushes that refused to give up their place in the ground.

He was achingly attractive.

How in the world had I landed myself such a specimen of a husband?

That answer was obvious, of course. I was destitute, and he was kind.

He glanced up and caught my gaze. I don't know if I was making the same face Julia had teased me about earlier, but the head of the shovel landed in the ground with less force than its earlier blows, he put no force behind it, and gravity alone pulled it to the earth.

He took two heavy breaths—from exertion, certainly—and raised one solitary eyebrow in my direction. "Am I doing this correctly? You look concerned."

Concerned? I looked concerned?

Julia snorted. "I think you know you're doing it right, David. Carry on. Your wife is enjoying the exhibition."

"I'm not . . ." David's neck seemed to flush. "This isn't an exhibition. I'm clearing the land."

Walter straightened from the pile of rubbish he'd been gathering and puffed out his chest. "There is no reason you can't do both," he said with a wink in my direction. "Roll up your sleeves a bit more. I think they are getting dirty."

David's flush went away, and his eyes narrowed at Walter. "I don't think my work will improve by rolling up my sleeves."

"But it wouldn't hurt, would it?" I called out, emboldened by Walter's teasing.

David's face whipped to mine. His mouth pursed, considering his options.

Walter nudged him with his elbow. "Your wife wants you to keep your sleeves clean, Mr. David. I don't know much about wives and things, but I do know everyone in our house is happier when Pa listens to what Ma has to say."

"Why, Walter," I said, "I believe you are wise beyond your years." I smiled broadly at him, and he shifted his feet and sneaked a glance at David.

David scowled. "If my wife's intentions are to keep my sleeves clean, I would do better to leave them down. Touching them with my gloves will sully them more than leaving them in place."

Julia put her hands on her hips. "Are you implying her intentions could be anything besides helping you keep your sleeves clean?"

I pulled off my gloves, lifted my skirt, and made my way over to David. With Walter here, we *had* to play the part of a happily married couple, after all. Having an audience made my decision completely logical—it made it easier to pretend I was doing this for their sake and not my own. "I'll help you. Then your sleeves won't need to get dirty."

David's eyes flashed to Julia's, and for a moment, I saw pure panic in them. I kept walking, but when I reached David, instead of immediately rolling up his sleeves, like I'd planned, I stopped in front of him. "David?" I asked softly enough I hoped neither Walter nor Julia would hear. His eyes met mine, and they were not the confident blue I'd become accustomed to. These were the eyes of young David, scared and unsure. The eyes of the boy he'd been before he'd even dared speak to me. "May I help you roll up your sleeves?"

It felt like a very formal question for a wife to be asking her husband. True, his jacket was off, and I'd been eyeing him, perhaps a little too forcefully, but we'd spent a week together as husband and wife, and he'd never looked at me this way, like he was preparing to run. With a deep sigh, he forced a word through his lips. "Once."

I leaned in toward him, and he stiffened even more. “What do you mean by ‘once’?”

He glanced down at his wrists. “Please just roll them once, no more.”

Had my gaze disturbed him so much he was worried about what I would do if I saw more than two inches of his forearms? I’d been a very obedient wife. I wasn’t going to do anything to disturb our charade outside with Walter and Julia looking on.

“Of course,” I responded, not knowing what else to say. “I wouldn’t do it at all, except Walter might be quite disappointed in us if I didn’t.”

David’s mouth twisted, and his spine finally relaxed. He held out his hand. I could feel his eyes upon me as I slid my thumb underneath his cuff. His skin was warm and smooth. My thumb tarried, investigating the feel of the inside of my husband’s arm. A wife shouldn’t find such a small slip of skin fascinating, but I wasn’t a typical wife. David stiffened again.

He leaned forward and put his lips to my ear. “If you’re trying to put on a show for Walter, I think there are better ways to do that than acting as if you don’t know what to do when your skin touches mine.”

I froze because of course he was right. I gritted my teeth, rolled the sleeve on top of itself in the quickest, if not tidiest fashion I could, and held my hand out for his next arm.

His chuckle was low and soft as I rammed my hand under his cuff this time, my thumb encountering smooth, warm skin once again, which I pointedly ignored. Or at least tried to ignore until my thumbnail caught slightly on the rough edge of a slight bump. If he hadn’t just remarked on my inability to simply roll up his sleeves without being affected by his skin, I would have explored the raised flesh longer, but I’d exercised all my privilege of curiosity on his other arm. I pretended I hadn’t found anything interesting and turned the sleeve over without sparing him another glance.

“There you go,” I said quickly, not daring to look up at him.

He let out a heavy breath and reached for my hand. "Thank you, my dear." He gave my hand a quick tug, and I stumbled forward into him. He placed the barest of kisses on my cheek, a touch so soft it might have been indiscernible if I weren't so aware of the man doing the kissing. When he pulled back, his eyes flashed in the direction of Walter and then to me with a smile.

He was taking advantage of our audience, just as I had.

"You're welcome," I quipped back, and with a broad smile, I returned his soft kiss. In an effort to outdo him, mine landed less than an inch from the corner of his mouth. My lips barely grazed him, but the warmth of his cheek, right at the spot his smile would begin, sent fire into my veins. He'd kissed me several times over the course of our marriage, but it had been a week since I'd been brave enough to take advantage of that aspect of being married. The thrill I got from that small touch was testament to the fact that I probably should not do it again anytime soon. I didn't dare look up at him, didn't dare let him see my eyes, for my heart would certainly be in them, and it wouldn't change anything.

I turned and walked back to Julia before he had the chance to outdo me and kiss me again.

Or, at least, before I gave myself a chance to be disappointed if he didn't.

When I reached Julia and turned back around, David was back with his shovel in hand, Walter lightly elbowing him in his side. I saw him only in profile, but a smile curved David's mouth, and crinkles formed around his eyes as he laughed off Walter's teasing.

David smiled and laughed so often I didn't know how much of that was because of me. But I hoped at least some of it was. If I couldn't make his heart burst into flames like he did to mine, at least I could be playful with him and make certain he kept that smile on his face.

I was his bright spot after all.

ꕤ

It took only a few more days to clear the rest of the area for the orchard and pond, as we'd planned. David came to help once or twice more, but never for long and always with his sleeves already rolled up. Julia's coloring had improved greatly in the days we'd spent out of doors.

"I think gardening suits you," I said to Julia one afternoon, after we'd spent the morning marking where the trees would go with rings of rocks. Her arm was in mine as we made the trek back into Tate Hall to have our baths and prepare for dinner. "Have you really never done it before?"

Julia laughed softly. "I've never had cause to garden before. You are the first person to drag me out of the house for labor purposes."

I raised an eyebrow. "For company purposes, you mean."

"Are you telling me I'm not quite up to snuff in my labors?"

I shook my head. "Of course not. Only that if all I wanted was labor, the boys and Mr. Harris could have done quite well on their own. I don't know what I would have done with myself, sitting inside the house all the time."

Julia glanced up at me. "Has it been terribly hard on you? Being married to David?"

That was a question I had no idea how to answer. In truth, I thought being married to him under the circumstances we were in would have been much harder than it had been. I'd thought David might leave the house or at least skulk about, trying to avoid me, but he'd been just as friendly as ever. "No, it hasn't. I've loved planning the orchard, and David is a perfect model of a husband."

Julia sighed softly at my comment. "I wish he could be more than that for you." Gentle storms brewed behind her soft, gray eyes. "The world can be terribly unfair at times."

I patted her hand. "The world was very kind to me when I quite literally landed on David again. Don't worry about me. I've known for years I was unlikely to marry a man who loved me."

Julia's head turned toward me sharply. "What do you mean by that?"

I laughed. "Exactly what I said. My years for making a love match are long past. I'm simply grateful to have a place to live."

Her steps slowed but didn't stop. Had I offended her? Julia was my age. I should have been more careful with my words.

She inhaled deeply. "I don't think David would like to hear you speaking that way."

That was what she was worried about? Not herself, but David?

I shrugged my shoulders. "It's the truth. And it is fortunate for both of us that I understand it. It frees me to be grateful for the marriage I do have."

"But you must know . . ." Julia started, then shook her head and didn't finish her sentence.

"I must know what?"

"Nothing," she murmured.

We continued on our path until we reached the servants' entrance. I walked in silence, hoping she would give me more insights into my marriage, but she didn't. What did she think I must know? If it was how grateful David was to me for our summer together, he'd made that abundantly clear, and I did know that. But somehow, I thought she meant something more than that.

We always came in through the servants' entrance after working to leave most of the dirt where it would be easiest to clean.

After we removed our muddied boots, I turned to head toward my room, but Julia reached for my hand and turned me around. "I love having you here," she said with firm conviction. "I want you to know that. Any man would be fortunate to have you as a wife, and your predicament with David, well . . . it isn't your fault."

"It isn't David's fault either." His father was squarely to blame, and both Julia and I knew it.

Her eyes sharpened, then slid toward the corridor that held David's study. "No, it isn't his fault either."

I gave her a smile that would make her think the conversation hadn't rattled me. "I'm very grateful to your brother. He's given me much more than I ever could have asked for."

Julia leaned forward as if she wanted to say something more, but then she blinked and must have decided against it. "I'll see you at dinner."

I nodded and dashed down the corridor.

But I never made it to dinner.

Chapter 19

"Having Anna near, and not only near but to be engaged to her? For the first time since Garrett moved to London, I'm feeling sorry for myself, and I can't let anyone see it.

"So I will let them see only how happy I am to be with her again, because that emotion is just as real as my self-pity but much more pleasant."

—David Tate, 1850, Age 23

When I reached the top of the stairs moments after leaving Julia on the main floor, Maren was standing in the corridor, wringing her hands. I stopped. "What is it?"

"It's your mother." She glanced at Mama's door. "She's fallen ill. I was on my way to come find you."

I started toward her bedroom door with a sour taste in my mouth but then stopped. "Does David know?"

She shook her head. "I only just went in to see about helping her dress for dinner. She was in bed, her skin raging with heat."

"Will you tell him for me, please?" I was going to need him. Ever since Papa passed away, even the slightest illness could make me tremble. And based on Maren's concern, Mama's fever wasn't slight.

Maren nodded and ran down the stairs. I dashed to Mama's room and pushed open the door to find her in her nightdress, pale and sallow. She'd eaten breakfast with us, but I hadn't seen her after that. I'd been so busy with the orchard and my plans with Julia that I hadn't even noticed her absence. She'd been careful to give David and me privacy over the past week and a half, and I'd grown accustomed to not seeing her for long portions of time.

My steps slowed once inside her room. "Mama?" I whispered.

She didn't move. I quickened my pace, dropping to my knees and placing a hand on her forehead.

Her skin was indeed raging, just as Maren had said. Not only that, but it felt lax and dry too. I glanced at Mama's bedside table and reached for the glass of water that sat there.

"Mama?" I asked again, this time louder. Her eyelids fluttered open for a moment, but she didn't speak. "I'm going to give you some water."

Her head lifted slightly, and even that small movement gave me some comfort. I put the glass to her lips, and she drank a few small sips, spilling almost as much as made it down her throat.

Footsteps sounded behind me, but I didn't turn. I knew the sound of David's boots. None of the servants were as noisy when they made their way through the house.

He came up beside me and placed a hand on my shoulder. "I've told Maren to send for James."

Right. The friend David had planned to move in with was the town doctor. "Thank you," I said, my voice unsteady. Mama was almost never sick. Over the past few years, I'd found her in bed, overwhelmed with indecision about what to do with our lives, but rarely with anything like this. "I saw her this morning. How . . . ?"

"Sometimes these things come on quickly. James will be here soon. He is an excellent doctor; he will know what to do."

Soon was a relative term, especially when worried about a loved one. While we waited, David quietly stood by my side, asking the servants to bring water and fresh bed linens. By the time the doctor arrived, I'd bathed Mama's head and removed the heavy quilt she'd had over her.

David greeted his friend, who was younger than I would have thought, based on David's recommendation of him. I had a vague memory of David saying James's father had been the town doctor before him, so perhaps James grew up learning by his father's side. James shook David's hand quickly, called him by his Christian name, and came to Mama's bedside.

James met my eyes. "I'm Dr. Clarke, a good friend of the family." His brown eyes were full of kindness, but they gave me only a quick glance before he turned to Mama and opened his bag.

"Thank you for coming, Doctor," I said.

He nodded, removing a stethoscope from his bag. I stood up and stepped back to allow Dr. Clarke to do his work. David took my hand and squeezed it tightly.

Fevers were unforgiving things.

Papa had been hale and hearty one day, then down in his bed the next. He didn't leave his bed alive. My breathing started coming quicker, and David released my hand and put his arm over my shoulders. I turned my face into his neck and struggled in vain to hold back a sob.

His hand stroked my hair, warm and comforting. "She is going to be well, Anna. James and his father have been treating my family for years. You won't find a better man, not even in London."

I nodded into his neck with a sniff, but I couldn't say anything. I was making a fool of myself. We hadn't even heard what the doctor had to say. Perhaps the fever would be a quick one. Perhaps even now, she was starting to recover.

But as much as I wanted to gird myself and be strong, I couldn't. If I lost Mama and David sent me away, I would be alone in the world. Completely alone.

Dr. Clarke cleared his throat softly, and David tugged lightly on my shoulder. I took a deep breath, wiped my eyes, and turned to face the doctor.

His eyes were fixed on David. Even when I turned to fully face him, he didn't glance at me. After a moment, he did look back down at Mama though. "As you have most likely already discovered, your guest has a fever. Her pulse is strong, and the water and bathing should help bring the fever down. I assume Mrs. Ward still has my father's mustard plaster recipe?" David nodded. "Her lungs are clear now, but if she starts having any trouble breathing, have Mrs. Ward make the salve and apply it to her chest."

"Is there anything else we can do?" I asked.

His eyes flicked to mine, then quickly to David's arm draped over me. He shook his head but gave me a kind smile. "Her fever is high, but most fevers pass within a few days. As long as she is able to eat and drink and her breathing remains stable, she should recover. The lady is your mother, I presume?"

David stiffened, and the doctor's reticence to look me in the eye suddenly became clear. In the rush to have Mama examined, no one had introduced us. David had wanted our marriage to remain a secret, and apparently, it had, even from the man he was planning on living with before we'd decided to marry.

"James," David started. "I'm sorry. I've been remiss. The woman you have just treated is Mrs. Atwood. And her daughter"—he tightened his hold upon me— "is my wife, Mrs. Anna Tate."

Dr. Clarke's eyes widened, and his mouth broadened into a smile. He strode forward and clapped David on his shoulder. "I'm happy to hear it." He turned to me, his eyes no longer guarded but shining. "I wish we had met under better circumstances, Mrs. Tate. But I assure you, your mother, though very sick, should come out on the other side of this with no complications."

I forced my lips into a smile. His words were a comfort to me, and his instant joy for David made me like him even more. "Thank you, Doctor."

"Call me James. David always does."

It was a strange thing, to call this man, who was probably only a few years my senior, by either Doctor or James. But I nodded. "Thank you, James."

Dr. Clarke left a few more instructions for the staff, then David pulled him aside, no doubt to ask him not to mention our marriage to anyone in town. Dr. Clarke's eyes flashed to mine just once, but then he nodded in understanding. If he thought it was strange that David would want to keep our marriage a secret, he didn't show it.

David left with the doctor, and I spent the next few hours at Mama's side, listening to her breathing and rewetting the towel on her head. David checked in on us several times, but each time, I quickly sent him away with a task. I wanted to care for Mama as much as I could on my own.

The sun was down, and the room dark, save for one solitary candle, when David returned again. "How is she doing?" he asked, taking in my position, curled up on the floor at the side of her bed.

"Much the same."

"James seemed to think she would be like this for at least few days. Before he left, he made me promise to make certain you slept."

I sighed, not ready to stand. I must look a disaster. My dress was crumpled, and my hair had several pins loose. I felt like I needed to sleep for a week. My knees ached, and I had a dull pain in my skull. "I'll try. I'm sorry Dr. Clarke learned of me."

A cloud covered David's face. "I'm not."

"But . . ."

"James is a close friend. I should have invited him over sooner to meet you. He won't spread any rumors."

"Our marriage isn't a rumor." My headache along with the hours of worrying after Dr. Clarke left made me less careful with my words. I needed sleep and a warm, thick blanket.

David strode to Mama's bedside and knelt. "I know it isn't, but—" His hand settled on mine, and he paused. His eyebrows furrowed, and he took my hand in both of his. "Anna, your skin."

I closed my eyes, letting the pain in my head settle in. "I think I'd better go to bed."

David's arm was immediately around my waist. I tried to push him away. I was definitely going to be ill, but I could walk to my room. His arm only tightened around me while his other arm slid under my legs. He lifted me to his chest as if it took no effort. He was so warm, and I was chilled to the bone from lying on the floor. This was an easy fight to lose. I grabbed the collar of his shirt, and with a deep sigh, I rested my head in the crook of his neck. He strode out of the room.

"Will you make certain Mama is cared for?" I asked.

"Of course." His voice was the most reassuring sound. I hadn't wanted to admit I was starting to feel ill. For so many years, if I'd gotten sick, I wouldn't have had anyone to care for Mama. But once again, David was proving my life was better with him in it.

He strode down the corridor until we reached my door, then he leaned back, tightening his hold on my legs while reaching for the doorknob with his hand at my waist. Once he had me back securely in his arms, he crossed over the threshold, and for the first time since we'd married, he entered my room. He quickly brought me to the bed and deposited me on top of the quilts. His arms slid out from under me, and I immediately missed his warmth. Closing my eyes, I said a quick prayer of gratitude for the quality of the mattress beneath me. It could be days before I left it.

I curled into myself, aware that I should've taken off my shoes but not caring enough to sit up and do the work. My fingers went to the back of my bodice. Breathing was starting to become difficult, and I wanted nothing more than to loosen my corset. I pulled at the knot hidden just above my skirt and managed to get it undone, but I couldn't loosen the cords with my bodice on. There would be a lot more undressing to go before my lungs received any relief.

"I'll fetch Maren," David said with an odd quality in his voice. I glanced up at him, and he lowered himself to one knee so he could look me in the eye. "Can you manage on your own for a moment?"

I dropped my hand from my dress. Had I tried to loosen my corset with David in the room? I pushed a hand into my hair and rubbed my scalp. "Of course. I was helping Mama only a few moments ago."

He nodded but looked uncertain. His eyes flitted to the back of my dress, and I wondered for half a moment if he was considering acting as my lady's maid. He would be even worse than Maren. The man probably didn't know how lacing worked. A soft chuckle escaped my lips, and his eyes flew back to mine, searching them with a concerned look. Should I not be laughing? I probably should not be laughing. He squeezed my hand, then turned and left, leaving the door open behind him.

My clothing was a lost cause without Maren, but I could do something about my hair. I wasn't a complete invalid. Not yet, at any rate. I gritted my teeth against the chill in the air and pulled pin after pin out of my hair. Maren was still new at styling it, and whenever she was in doubt of a lock holding in place, she added another pin. Taking my hair down at the end of each day was always a relief.

Most of the pins were resting beside me on the bed by the time Maren arrived. She put a hand on her hip and made a tsk-tsk sound. Her fear from earlier today must have been assuaged. "You've managed to catch the fever as well, I see."

I nodded weakly. For some reason, her near insolence made tears threaten my eyes.

She walked into the room. "We'd better get you resting, then." She turned to look behind her, and only then did I notice David had followed her back into the room.

Maren turned to David. "At the bottom of the wardrobe, there are extra blankets." Maren pointed to the lower drawers. "Can you add them to the bed while I help her get undressed? Then we can get her tucked in nicely in almost no time."

I was too tired to even look up and see David's reaction. Julia was the only person who knew the truth of our marriage, and aside from improperly asking her employer for help, Maren had no idea she was also asking him to help in a room he'd never set foot inside of before this evening.

His feet shuffled in the corridor. "Shouldn't I fetch Mrs. Ward to help with that?"

"She and Margaret left half an hour ago to replenish some of the supplies Dr. Clarke wanted us to have on hand. I'm afraid you'll have to do. I've seen you put thatch on a roof, Mr. Tate. I'm certain you can manage the bed."

He put a hand on the door molding, his eyes not meeting mine. "Perhaps Julia?"

I shook my head. "No, David. Julia isn't strong. I don't want her in the room."

His eyes met mine then, and they had a very specific question written in them. "But you do want *me* here?" His words were careful and hesitant, hovering somewhere between a statement and a question. He looked torn between wanting to run away and scooping me into his arms and wrapping me in blankets himself.

This whole day had been exhausting. Yes, I wanted him here. I'd wanted him here for over a week. "Please."

He nodded once and took a step inside. Maren raised me to a sitting position on the bed by my elbow. Before starting to undress me, she padded silently to the door David had absentmindedly left open and closed it. When she returned, she undid my shoes first, and I slipped out of them. Then she made quick work of unlacing the bodice of my dress and pulling it up over my head. I sneaked a glance at David, but his eyes were on the blankets he'd removed from the wardrobe. Maren pulled at the laces of my corset, releasing my lungs. I inhaled deeply, but even though my corset was loose, my lungs still felt tight.

Dr. Clarke had said Mama would recover as long as the fever didn't affect her lungs. Were mine already affected? I held on to Maren's shoulders while she pulled me to a standing position. David took that chance to go to the bed and set down the blankets. He was careful to keep himself busy positioning each corner of the blankets just right, keeping his attention on the bed while Maren removed my skirt and petticoats. With only my wide-necked cotton chemise on, the cold air brushed over my bare shoulders and legs, and I started to shiver.

"Sit back down so we can remove your stockings and get you in bed," Maren said in a matronly voice belying her age. "You're trembling."

David had resorted to propping up pillows, but the pillow in his hand dropped to the bed at Maren's words. If I didn't feel so terrible, this whole scene would be extremely comedic. I could practically sense his panic, caught between wanting to be a gentleman and also wanting to appear as a husband in front of Maren.

I was sick enough not to feel overly concerned about his seeing me in this state. He was my husband, and I was past caring about anything but the cold. But for his sake, I invented a task for him. "David, could you fetch my hairbrush?" I asked. If he went about that task slowly enough, it should keep him occupied until Maren had my stockings off and I was finally nestled under the blankets.

His spine relaxed, and he gave us a brief nod, moving quickly away from the bed, then slowing as he reached my dressing table. Maren made quick work of my stockings, and without waiting for any help,

I slid my feet underneath the heavy quilt and linens David had pulled back. Maren put the blankets over me, and I curled into a ball once more. Immediately, I was overcome by shivering.

"I'll fetch a basin of water and a towel and be right back," I heard Maren say, but her voice sounded farther away than it should have been.

"I can fetch them," David said, his voice nearer than Maren's.

"Nonsense. Stay with Mrs. Tate. She'd much rather have you. I'll only be a moment."

The door closed softly, and David made no noise. My face was toward the windows, and turning to look at him would require me to lose what little warmth had started to fill the small space I'd huddled into.

My body would not stop shaking.

"Anna." David's voice was quiet with concern. Something cool pressed against my cheek, and I started. As quickly as it had landed, it was gone. "Sorry," he mumbled. Only then did I realize it had been the palm of his hand.

I clenched my teeth against the cold and forced myself to roll onto my other side so I could look at him. "I'm—so—cold."

David fell to his knees at the side of my bed. "What can I do?" His eyes were pleading, and his hands seemed lost between reaching for me and pulling away. He finally settled on rubbing my shoulder through the thick blankets.

"I don't want you to get sick."

He shook his head. "I never get sick."

My head lifted. Could that be true? Everyone gets sick sometimes. He was probably saying it so I wouldn't ban him from helping me like I'd banned Julia. I sent up a silent prayer that he was telling me the truth and locked my painfully dry eyes on his worried ones. When I was a child, Mama or Papa had stayed in bed with me, their body heat warming the bed and their contact making any pain or discomfort more bearable. The only thing I could think of that might make me feel better was David's arms wrapped around me, his warmth heating the blankets my feet couldn't reach. "Could you . . . hold me?"

David's hand stilled on my back.

His throat worked and lips parted, but no sound passed through them. If I didn't feel quite so miserable, I might have taken the chance to tease him.

I shook my head carefully so it wouldn't hurt worse. "You don't have to. It was . . . it is a terrible idea, no matter how nice it sounds." I was weary and haggard. I hadn't even had time to properly clean myself after spending time in the orchard. If I were in my right mind, I wouldn't want him anywhere near me while I looked and felt like this. "You might catch the fever."

I braved the currents of cold air around my legs and turned back toward the window again. I wouldn't be able to rest with him looking at me. I closed my eyes and wrapped my arms tighter around my middle.

There was a soft clunk behind me, as something fell to the floor. A moment later, a second sound followed, and the bed dipped behind me. I barely had time to register that the sound I'd heard had been David's boots before one of his arms went around my middle, and he pulled me into him. He was on top of the blankets, but his warmth radiated through me. My back settled into his chest, and his legs tucked in behind mine. Almost immediately, my shivering stopped, and my whole body seemed to exhale in the relief of someone cradling me.

His chin rested on top of my head, and when he spoke, it tousled my hair. "I told you." His voice was only just above a whisper. "I never take ill."

I nestled deeper into him. I was sick and chilled, and it was perfectly legitimate of me to want someone—anyone—to hold me. The fact that it was David made no difference. Or rather, it certainly did, but I hoped he didn't think much of it. "But what if you do?"

His arm lifted from my waist, the comforting weight of it gone. I thought perhaps he'd changed his mind, he didn't want to risk being sick, or he felt as though someone else should be caring for me. Instead, his fingers came to the crown of my head, and he gingerly lifted it, sliding his other arm under my cheek like a pillow. When his arm returned to my waist, it felt so much like coming home after a long trip away I almost forgot I was sick.

"If I do," he said, his voice firm, "then I expect you to come into my room and return this favor."

My shoulders shook, but it wasn't a chill. It was a sad attempt at laughter. "That seems like a very bad bargain."

"Perhaps for you," he whispered.

I shook my head. David was ridiculous. He was also very kind. He was, in fact, everything I could have ever wanted in a husband or a friend. I was fortunate to call him both, even if one of those titles would only ever be temporary. With the shaking gone and David and the blankets keeping me warm, the muscles in my body finally calmed.

"Stay with me?" I asked.

"Of course," he replied. I couldn't help but wish he'd said something more permanent. Something to let me know it would always be this way. But that was a promise he wouldn't make, and although I knew a lot of that blame was to be set at his father's feet, I wished I were tempting enough to make him change his mind.

For now, though, I let myself pretend this wasn't the only time David would be in my bed and that whenever I fell sick in the future, he would be the one to comfort me. I let my mind wander to what spending the rest of my life with him might look like. It looked a lot like this moment, stretched into infinite possibilities.

My breathing eased and deepened, and in the comfort of the arms of a man who cared fiercely for me, I sank into a quiet oblivion.

When I awoke later to complete darkness, stifling heat, and night sweats, David was there, his forearm under my neck and his chest pressed up against my back. My hair was damp and cold—David had bathed it sometime during the night—but instead of giving me the chills like it would have hours ago, in the cool night air, it was a relief against the climbing heat spreading throughout my body.

I lifted my head and instantly regretted it. I didn't wake David, but my headache returned fiercely. I rested it back down on David's arm and lifted the blankets away from my chest instead. Cool relief rushed over my skin, but David started at my movement.

The hand at my waist lifted, and I could tell from the way the bed dipped that he'd sat up. I turned on my back and kicked off more of the blankets.

His hand went to my cheek, his fingers probing my temple and brushing aside some of my damp hair. "Your fever's broken," he said.

All I could do was nod. It was too dark for him to see my movements, but with his hands on my face, I knew he could feel it. I swallowed hard as memories of his gentle care came flooding back.

Headache or no, waking up wrapped in the arms of one's husband was an experience I'd not be likely to forget.

He stood. "I'll find you some water."

I put a hand on my neck, taking long, steady breaths, thankful David couldn't see me with my hair completely in tangles, spread out on the pillows, my skin covered in a cold sweat.

I could sense him moving about in the room. He was close enough for me to hear his breathing and sense where he stood. Clinking sounds came from my night table, and I glanced up to where he must be, catching only the slightest silhouette of his form against the softest seam of light coming from underneath the door.

Light flared impossibly bright, and my hands flew to my eyes as I squeezed them shut against the flash. He must have lit a match. I stretched out on the bed, waiting for my eyes to accustom themselves to the idea of opening.

"How are y—" David started, his voice soft, but then he paused. I cracked an eye open to find a blurred David half sitting against my dressing table in his shirtsleeves, as if he'd fallen back on it after lighting the lamp. When he caught my gaze on him, he turned his head, looking instead out of the window.

His shirt was untucked from his breeches, and he wore no cravat. Several of his buttons must have come undone, for under the flickering light of the oil lamp, I could see almost half of his torso. It was covered in strange circular marks.

I blinked, unable to take my eyes off the sight of him. He was still staring at the window. I knew I should pull the linens back over my chemise, but I was incapable of tearing my gaze from the indented white marks on his skin. I'd seen a mark like that before, once. High on Julia's arm.

"David . . ." My voice traveled to him like a puff of smoke, weak and floating, but he turned nonetheless. I couldn't lift my eyes to his and didn't see his expression, but I heard his curse.

He set the lamp down roughly, pulled the edges of his shirt together, and took two long strides toward me, roughly throwing the lightest of the linens back over my body.

I grabbed his hand as it lifted away. I was so weak it would have taken no effort on his part to pull away from me, but he didn't. Instead, he met my eyes.

His were blazing, and not from the lamp. "Anna, I . . ." He moved to stand, but my fingers tightened around his wrist, and he paused again, half bent over my bed. We stared at each other, my eyes searching his, but he didn't offer any explanation to what I'd just seen.

I lifted my fingers one by one off his wrist, and he stayed, hovering over me. Instead of dropping my hand, I slid it up his arm, lifting the cuff of his sleeve as I went. The lifted bump I'd felt just the day before came into view. The beginnings of a small circle, no larger than the pad of my thumb, sat upon his otherwise perfect skin. I slid my fingers higher underneath his shirt. More bumps and indentations rose to meet my fingertips.

David closed his eyes, let go of his shirt, and let it fall open again. "You were never supposed to see me like this," he said, a hard edge to his voice.

I removed my hand from underneath his sleeve and brought a fingertip to a circle sitting just above where his heart lay beneath his ribcage.

The moment my skin touched his, he hissed and sprang away. "Don't touch them."

"Do they hurt?"

His eyebrows furrowed, making shadows of his eyes in the lamplight. "What? No." He shook his head.

"But you don't want me to touch them?"

His face was hard as he pulled his shirt closed. "Never."

"But . . ." But what? Did I think because he'd offered to be my husband in order for me to receive an inheritance, it gave me some right to this part of him? The part he hid from everyone. "Has Dr. Clarke seen them?"

"Yes, and his father has as well."

"Is there nothing that can be done?" I didn't even know what the marks were. I'd seen men pockmarked from disease, but those marks looked nothing like David's.

"Everything that can be done has been done. It was an affliction I suffered as a child, and I'm not a child anymore."

He was definitely not. I made certain to keep my eyes on his face. "Something like smallpox?" I asked.

"No. It wasn't a solitary disease. It was a recurring ailment, but I've outgrown it." He turned and strode away from my bed. "I'll go fetch Mrs. Ward and Maren. I think it might be better if they care for you for the next little while. I'm glad to see you feeling better."

His hand went to the door.

"David?"

He stopped, clenched his fist around the doorknob, and slowly turned around. All the fire from earlier was gone from his eyes. Instead, I saw only sadness, a deep sorrow he'd hidden from me all along.

"How long has it been since . . . ?" I didn't even know how to finish asking that question. Was it an episode he would have? A sickness with blisters or boils? Were those marks part of the reason he'd been so unkempt the summer I'd been here? Had he been ill?

My thoughts went back to our time together then. Usually, he was perfectly capable of keeping up with me. He'd climbed trees even better than I had. But he'd also had days I'd had to slow for him and days he would lift his arms to climb a tree, then wince and change his mind.

He *had* been sick. He'd been terribly sick all along. And for some of those days, at least, I'd managed to help him forget that. We'd found others in need and delivered food to them. We'd climbed trees and left the world below us. I'd laughed with him like I wouldn't laugh again for years—not until I'd met him again and we'd sung so badly together and flirted in ways I had hoped he wouldn't understand were real. He'd been the very last part of my childhood, a memory of what I'd had before I'd been forced to grow up too quickly. And apparently, I'd been the brightest part of his childhood. He'd been trying to tell me all along, and I'd never managed to listen.

David's spine stiffened as if he were trying to convince himself of his own strength. His strength was nothing I needed convincing of. "It's been years."

"Good."

"Please don't worry about me. They don't bother me anymore."

My eyes met his. We both knew he was lying.

If I'd brought light to him in the past, I'd happily do that for him again. And I could see that more than anything, he wanted this conversation to be over. I smiled and sighed, hoping he wouldn't think those marks would haunt me. "That's good, then."

He nodded as if we were agreeing about the prospect of bad weather. His hand went back to the doorknob.

"David?"

He took a deep breath, steeling himself for more questions. "Yes?"

"Thank you," I said softly.

A corner of his mouth lifted, and the deep line between his eyebrows softened. "You're welcome, Anna."

And then he left.

Only after he'd been gone several minutes did I realize it was the first time he'd allowed me to thank him without telling me he was the one in my debt. Even our marriage had been difficult for him to accept thanks for.

But caring for me through the night and showing me those marks had cost him. More even than entering into a marriage for my sake. It had taken enough from him that, perhaps, at last, he could place us on equal footing. For when he looked at me before he left, it wasn't as a man who saw only the girl who'd given of herself, tirelessly, to a broken boy—but as one who had come to see me as a woman, capable of reaching into his soul and taking something as well.

And despite everything we'd already been through together, it felt like a beginning.

Chapter 20

"We keep our misery to ourselves. We keep our misery to ourselves. We keep our misery to ourselves. No one with loved ones ever suffers alone."
—David Tate, 1850, Age 23

The day passed in a haze. True to his word, David kept Julia away from my room and saw to Mama's care, telling me she looked better than I did because he knew I wasn't the kind of wife or daughter who would want to hear anything else. Despite telling me he'd have Mrs. Ward or Maren care for me, he tended to all but my most private needs himself. I was no longer chilled or feverish, but the illness had taken a toll, and my body was weak.

I slept on and off throughout the morning, and sometime in the afternoon, David knocked on the door and brought Dr. Clarke into my room.

The doctor's dark-brown eyes assessed me from the moment he walked in. He strode to the chair David had set next to my bed and sat down. He gave me a stern look that wasn't meant to be threatening, and his eyebrows lay low on his forehead. "I was hoping our next visit would happen because David invited me to dine."

"I'm sorry," I said.

He shook his head and placed a hand on my head. "You don't have to apologize to me. I do, however, hope you will use your influence over your husband and force him to entertain company every once in a while. It would do you and his sister good."

I could see why he was a close friend of the family. Julia and David were naturally closed off—Julia, perhaps, more than David. It would take this kind of gruff assertiveness to break through some of their walls. "We would love to have you come, wouldn't we, David?" I ended David's name with a cough, which shook my body, but it was over quickly enough.

"It isn't company she needs now," David said, his voice heavier than Dr. Clarke's. "She needs a doctor."

Dr. Clarke turned in the chair to send back a retort, but the look on David's face must have stopped him. Even cleaned up as he was, dark circles ringed his eyes, and lines creased his forehead. Had David slept at all the night before? My lips pulled up in a tired smile. Perhaps if I were sick often enough, he would age faster, and my lack of youth wouldn't feel like such a stark contrast between us.

Although being sick often would age me as well.

Dr. Clarke leaned forward and placed a hand on my head. With a nod, he pulled his stethoscope from his bag. "May I?" he asked, pointing to the quilt that covered me up to my neck. I nodded without glancing up at David. He pulled back the quilt and the linen underneath it.

Maren had helped me put a nightdress over my chemise earlier, so my collarbones and shoulders were no longer exposed.

Dr. Clarke placed the cold metal of his stethoscope over the thin material on my chest. "Will you take a deep breath?"

I'd seen him do the same with Mama only the day before, and his mannerisms were no different with me than they had been with her, but my cheeks warmed knowing David watched the exchange. I hoped there was nothing in my heartbeat or rise and fall of my chest that would alert the kind doctor to my embarrassment, as it had nothing to do with him.

After several breaths, he straightened, pulled my covering back over me, and put his stethoscope back in his bag. "I believe the worst of this sickness has already passed. I was fairly certain of that fact the moment I set eyes on you. Otherwise, I wouldn't have been quite so casual in my remarks." He sent those last words to David.

I let my gaze go to my husband. His face was tight, and if he was at all affected by the sight of me in my nightclothes, he didn't show it. Not like he had when I'd surprised him by removing my blankets in the dark.

David nodded at Dr. Clarke, and it seemed that would be his only acknowledgment of the doctor's apology.

Dr. Clarke leaned back in the chair. "You look well, and your color is good. How are you feeling?"

"Much better than yesterday. However, I'm fatigued. I spent the morning sleeping, and now when I try to stand, I feel faint."

Dr. Clarke nodded. "That is most likely an aftereffect of the fever, but if you had any of those troubles before falling ill, it could be a sign of being with child. Have you had any other signs? Have your courses remained normal?"

I shifted uncomfortably in the bed. If I'd thought having David in the room when Dr. Clarke listened to my heart was embarrassing, this was much worse. "Yes."

"Yes, your courses are normal? Or yes, you've had other signs of being with child?"

I couldn't help it. My eyes flashed to David's. His face was unreadable, but his chest was as still as if he'd stopped breathing. I thought he would glance away as he had earlier, but his eyes held mine until I looked back to Dr. Clarke. "We haven't even been married two weeks."

Dr. Clarke raised a shoulder. "For some, that is enough. And . . ." Now it was his turn to glance at David. "Forgive me, David, and even more so, Mrs. Tate. I am asking this only as your doctor. But your marriage *was* quite rushed."

David was stone. I shook my head vigorously, remembering too late the extent of my headache. "We had other reasons. Not . . . I'm not . . ."

"James." David's voice was icy and hard.

Dr. Clarke most definitely felt David's rising indignation, but he shrugged it away. "I'm a doctor, not a priest," he said, unrepentant. "I don't make judgments, but I need information in order to care for your wife. If she was with child, we would want to take extra care with this sickness."

David's dark-blue eyes shifted to a steely gray. "You are a friend who should know me well enough not to feel the need to ask that question."

"I was asking Mrs. Tate," Dr. Clarke said, his voice adopting the icy tone of David's. "Now it might be best if you go downstairs and order some tea for us before you think too hard about *that* statement, because once you do, I have no doubt I'll end up with a broken nose."

David went pale. His eyes found mine, and there was fury behind them. He gripped the doorknob as if it were the only thing stopping him from rushing his friend and laying him flat. "Are you insulting the virtue of my wife?"

"No." Dr. Clarke was motionless. "I'm asking pertinent medical questions of a patient. And I know you well enough to know I *do* need to ask that question. If a woman came to you in trouble, you are just the type of man who would help her, no matter the cost."

David grimaced. "My marriage with Anna has *only* given me joy and has *cost* me nothing. Thus far, it has been the happiest time of my life."

If David were closer, I would reach out and try to calm him, but he was too far from me. If he'd said that a day ago, I wouldn't have believed him. But his past had been a painful one, even if he'd hidden his pain well.

"You do know my husband," I said softly. Dr. Clarke had taken one look at me and our hasty marriage and had known David was hiding something. I'd warned him people wouldn't believe he was in love with me, and my prediction had quickly come true. We'd needed only a true friend to see it. "He is exactly the type of man who would help a woman in need." I caught David's eye and braced myself for the words that were about to leave my lips. They were true, but he wouldn't believe them, which made me braver than I could have ever been otherwise. "It is one of the many reasons I fell in love with him." Some of David's bluster faded at my words, and his eyes slid from Dr. Clarke to me. "But I am as certain as a woman who has only been married a short while can be that I'm not with child. My sickness is only from the fever."

Dr. Clarke nodded as if I'd answered a question as simple as when I'd had my last meal and not one that had caused turmoil in both my and David's hearts. He made a quick note in his journal.

The muscles in David's hand twitched over the doorknob, neither opening the door to leave nor stepping deeper inside the room. His eyes were still stormy. I'd never seen him angry before, but I didn't think the emotion in them was anger. It was something else—something I couldn't understand. I wasn't certain he understood it either. It was a strange thing to be married to a person to whom you were not a true spouse. We both seemed to be feeling that strangeness at the moment.

I curled my lips up in a quick and, I hoped, unaffected smile. "Tea?" I asked, reminding him of Dr. Clarke's suggestion.

David took a deep breath, gave me a curt nod, and left the room.

Dr. Clarke asked me a few more questions about my health, without referencing anything that had just passed, before he closed his journal and placed it back in his bag. "I think you will be feeling much better by tomorrow, Mrs. Tate."

I nodded, still not used to the name. "Thank you, Doctor. May I ask you one question?"

Dr. Clarke stilled. He'd been unflappable while David had been in the room, asking me every sort of question without fear, but I saw the slightest bit of concern edge his eyes now. He would keep my questions secret from David if I asked it of him—I could feel that—but he wouldn't like it. "It is not about my health but about David's."

He visibly relaxed. "I'll answer anything I don't feel would betray his confidence."

"He said you knew about his . . ." I paused. I didn't even know for certain what the marks were. "The circles on his skin."

Dr. Clarke's eye's narrowed, focusing his strong gaze on me. "Yes," he said carefully.

He didn't elaborate, and suddenly, I was at a loss as to what exactly I had the right to ask. David had told me little, other than the fact that they were an affliction he had suffered from as a child. What right did I have to any more information than he'd given me? A wife had a right to know some things, didn't she? I scrambled to come up with a reason, and the most obvious was one Dr. Clarke had already mentioned. My stomach turned at the thought of using my position as wife to glean more information about David, but I also didn't want to bring up the subject with him again if it would cause him pain. "Is his condition hereditary? Will our . . . ?" I struggled not to stumble on the word. ". . . children suffer as he did?"

The stiffness in Dr. Clarke's spine softened, and his eyes grew tender, even as a question seemed to form in his mind. "No. They will not."

"Are you certain?"

"I'm very certain."

"What are they? Those marks?" I asked quietly. It was a question I shouldn't be asking.

"He hasn't told you?"

"No."

Dr. Clarke took my hand in his. "Then I cannot tell you either. I'm sorry."

"Was he very sick?" My voice shook. I couldn't get the image of all those marks on his chest out of my mind.

"Your husband was often in pain as a child. My father helped him as much as he could, but he wished he could do more. Be patient with him. Even a man as kind as David has his pride."

I furrowed my eyebrows, not sure why David's pride was once again being mentioned, nor could I understand how it could have anything to do with a sickness in his youth.

I could see from the sharp edge of Dr. Clarke's jaw that he would rather not continue speaking on the subject, and marriage notwithstanding, I didn't have a real claim to know David's most personal history.

It was only by chance I knew of it at all.

Until David was ready to tell me himself, I needed to put it out of my mind. That sickness I'd felt in my stomach before asking Dr. Clarke had been a warning. Mentioning those marks to anyone else would be a betrayal. I was fortunate Dr. Clarke was a more loyal friend to David than I had been.

Chapter 21

"Anna slept in my arms last night. How am I ever going to let her go?"
—David Tate, 1850, Age 23

The stronger I got, the less I saw of David. He came to my room each day but never in the evenings. Unless I struck ill with a sickness even worse than this one, he would likely never climb in my bed or hold me close again.

That didn't stop me from reliving the memory constantly. What else was a woman to do while passing the time in her bedchamber? At night, I would imagine he was there again, his arm wrapped around me, his body warm against my back. But I wasn't delusional. I knew those moments were dreams and dreams only. In the morning, I awoke, and the room felt cold and empty without him, and I was growing accustomed to the feeling.

It was strange, wasn't it? He'd spent one night in my room. One. I'd slept either by myself or with Mama for the past twenty-five years. If anything, having him in my bed should have been shockingly peculiar instead of something I'd struggle to live without.

Two days after Dr. Clarke's visit, I felt well enough to wash and dress, and although the effort was tiring, I felt much better for it.

Maren was brushing my hair when the soft knock I'd come to recognize as David's rapped at my bedroom door.

"Enter," I said loud enough for him to hear. I'd never barred him or told him to wait when anyone else was around. There would be no reason for a wife to ask her husband to wait until her hair was up to come in.

David strode in. His eyes went to the bed before he turned to find me sitting at the dressing table, my dark, freshly washed hair brushed and falling to my waist. For the past three days, he'd seen me in various stages of undress, usually with a wrap or blanket over me. Seeing my hair out of its long braid shouldn't have caused him pause.

But it did.

His step faltered, and his eyes slipping to my waist, then slowly traveling up to the crown of my head.

Usually, when Maren was in the room, he would immediately come to me and place the slightest kiss upon my forehead—just enough contact to quiet any whispers about the two of us. Sometimes, I allowed myself the luxury of believing he was also checking on my fever, reassuring himself it was indeed gone.

He didn't kiss me this time. He didn't move at all. But something in his face must have caught Maren's attention, for she immediately set down the brush, gave him a short curtsy, and left the room.

It wasn't until the door closed behind her that David turned toward where she'd just been, shaking his head with the word *wait* on his lips.

But he was too late.

We were alone in my bedchamber again, and for some reason, my unbound hair—or, at least, the way David had looked at it—made me feel as exposed as I'd been in my chemise.

I could see the moment David realized he was acting very unhusband-like.

He blinked hard, straightened his spine, and looked toward me without exactly meeting my eyes. "It is good to finally see you dressed and out of bed," he said stiffly.

I closed my lips tightly, but I knew my eyes still widened at his comment. He couldn't have said anything more inappropriate if he'd tried. And based on the way spots of color were rising to his cheeks, he'd definitely not tried.

"I meant—" He squeezed his eyes shut and ran a hand down his face. With a deep breath, he tried again. "What I meant to say was, you look well."

I let my smile blossom on my face. I did feel well. Better, even, than I had a few minutes ago, now that he was in my room, bumbling up our conversation. "Thank you. I knew what you meant. And I feel much better."

He stayed where he was, even though I wished he would come nearer. Having him to myself was a luxury.

"We've had a guest arrive," David stated.

"A guest? Someone I know?"

"No, but he is very anxious to meet you. My brother, Garrett."

I quirked an eyebrow. "And he knows about me and about . . . everything?"

"Yes. He knows."

I nodded. He'd told me he would have to tell his family, and while I understood his desire to be truthful to them, I wondered what his brother would think of me—a woman who had trapped his brother into a marriage when he'd never wanted one. "I suppose that will not make me a favorite in his eyes."

"On the contrary. He has given me no end of exultant grief since arriving and is delighted by our arrangement. If you aren't feeling up to coming down for tea today, I'm more than happy to give your excuses. One of us putting up with his merciless glee is, perhaps, enough."

I reached for the brush Maren had set on the dressing table. It was wicked of me, but I'd seen how he'd looked at my hair. And Maren hadn't finished her task. "I'll be ready. It will do me good to be out of my room and conversing again."

I turned back to the mirror and ran the brush from the top of my head down to the ends of my hair. David finally moved from just inside the doorway to stand behind me, his face almost reverent as he watched the brush glide through my thick, straight tresses.

After a moment, he lifted his eyes and caught mine in the mirror. "I'm glad you are feeling well enough to join us." He lifted a hand, and for a moment, I thought he might reach for my hair, but he dropped it and caught my gaze again. "You gave me quite a scare."

I shrugged my shoulder. "It was a simple fever. Dr. Clarke said as much."

"James didn't see you at your worst."

"Was I so terribly bad?"

"You looked nigh unto death, weak and shivering. I'm so accustomed to seeing you strong." He shook his head slowly at the memory. Apparently, that night had haunted him as well, but for very different reasons.

I put down my brush, reached behind me for his hand, and pulled it up so it rested on my shoulder. My hair had fanned out from brushing it, and some of it caught underneath his palm. I wanted him to touch my hair, and I wished he would stop holding back when I knew he wanted to close the distance between us.

I gave his hand a squeeze. "Thank you for caring for me."

He closed his eyes for a moment, and his thumb moved just enough to trap a lock of hair between it and his forefinger. He tested the strength and softness of the strands, pulling delicately down, letting them slide along the pad of his finger. When he opened his eyes, they looked pained. "I wish I could care for you more."

The flush of excitement I'd reveled in when he'd walked in the room froze and died. Enjoying the sight of me and not wanting me to die was a far cry from loving me enough to let me understand his secrets or face his father, and he continued to make that very clear.

What was it that made hope so tenacious and long-suffering? I should have killed it long ago, but it refused to die.

But I couldn't resent David for it. He'd done nothing wrong and had done more to care for me than anyone else in the past eight years.

I'd seen his childhood desire to help the tenant farmers when he accompanied me to deliver baskets, and I'd heard from the Mortensens of his continued kindness over the past several years. I couldn't fault him for also being uncommonly kind to me when it was my turn to need help.

David cleared his throat. "I'll send for Maren so she can help you with your hair again."

I quirked an eyebrow at him through the mirror. "You don't want me to come down like this?"

He put his hand on my other shoulder and leaned forward so his head was nearly resting on mine. If I didn't know our story, I would think we made the perfect picture of a young, newly married couple. Even after being sick, my face seemed to glow with a healthy light when David was nearby.

"You would give poor Garrett a heart attack. He isn't fortunate enough to have a wife, let alone one so beautiful."

I'd only just told myself to be careful, but his words warmed me again. My poor, foolish heart.

"Do you really think yourself fortunate?"

He slid his fingertips into my hair, and his hands inched their way down through it to my waist. With eyes half closed, he placed a gentle kiss at the crown of my head. "I am mediocre in all things except my choice of a wife, so yes, I consider our marriage fortunate. You've given me the opportunity to best my very clever brother for once."

I tipped my head pretending to be in serious thought, even though what I wanted to do was lean back into him. "So Garrett is clever, older, *and* unmarried?"

David narrowed his eyes, the soft gaze from his kiss gone. In its place was something playful, slightly offended by my praise of his older brother. "Don't be fooled by his age. He hardly acts it. I've always been the more serious brother."

I smiled through the mirror at David. Nothing about him seemed boyish anymore, except, perhaps, his grin. "Is there anything else I should know about him?"

He heaved a deep sigh. "He is a good six inches taller than I am."

I furrowed my eyebrows. "So he does have a flaw."

David laughed, a deep rumble starting low in his chest and grew into a sound that had me dreaming about jumping up from my chair and placing a kiss on his mouth. If I were a proper wife, I would have done so. David stepped away from my chair, his laughter crinkling his eyes. "Please tell him how disappointed you are in his height. It will do him good."

When he reached the door, I turned around in my seat. "David?"

He turned, still smiling. "Yes?"

"I've seen how you work to improve the estate, and the way your mind has navigated my problems and found ways to help me. I haven't met Garrett, but I think you *must* be the clever one. Also"—I let my eyes roam from the top of his head down to his feet and then back up again—"you must know you've aged extremely well. At times, I might wish I were younger, but I don't wish you to be older. And the fact that you are married is one of your nicest features."

He straightened to his full height, just an inch or two taller than I was. "And my height?"

For the briefest of moments, I was back in my bed with my back pressed up against him while I wrestled with a fever. We'd fit together perfectly. I grinned brightly, praying he couldn't hear my thoughts.

"Oh, that is a point well in your favor. It makes the times we are obliged to kiss much simpler."

His eyes went to my mouth, and I thought he might come up with a reason to kiss me right then and there. But he gave me only a jaunty grin. "Glad to be of service."

Not glad enough, or I think he would provide that service more often.

He opened the door, and with a wink, he left.

Maren returned a few moments later, and we quickly did my hair as best she could manage. I was very interested in meeting this brother of David's. Not because he was clever or tall or unmarried but because he'd put a lightness in his brother's step, and I already loved Garrett for it.

I stopped in to see Mama on my way to the drawing room, and she was sitting up in bed.

"How are you feeling?" I asked.

Mama sighed heavily, and I didn't see any difficulty in the movement. "Much better, though not as good as you look." Mama reached a hand out, and I strode over to her and took it. "I'm so glad to see you looking well," she said with a squeeze of my hand.

"I understand the sentiment." I returned her smile and grasped her hand tightly, grateful we'd passed through this sickness unscathed. "David's brother is here."

"Maren mentioned that, but I don't feel ready to meet anyone until I've got a bit more color in my face."

Mama looked pale, but I doubted David's brother would mind. "Are you certain?"

Mama laughed softly. "I am quite certain. And you need more time with your new family. Go. Bewitch that brother of his."

I laughed. "I have no plan of bewitching anyone."

"You never do, but you always manage it."

"Mama, if that were true, it wouldn't have taken me until age twenty-five to marry." Nor would I have had to beg for the marriage.

"We both know Mr. Green discouraged other young men from pursuing you."

"But I had a whole Season in London before that."

"Yes, and I watched you that Season. While you might not have noticed it, several men were very interested in you, but you were indifferent to all of them, and they could feel it. Your father and I didn't think you needed to hurry into a marriage. We thought there would be plenty of time for you to find a man who made you happy. And I'm so glad you finally did. I think you were meant to wait for David."

A lump formed in my throat, because as improbable as it was, I agreed with her. I couldn't imagine living my life with anyone but him. I had no recollection of the men she was speaking of from my Season, but I certainly hadn't met anyone who had interested me. I hadn't realized I'd been so obvious about it.

"Thank you, Mama." I placed a kiss on her cheek and then made my way down the stairs to meet Garrett.

Chapter 22

"Today, I got to hear Anna sing. She is just as horrible as ever. And I kissed her for it. Mother, I've finally lived that moment you promised me long ago. Be at peace."

—David Tate, 1850, Age 23

When I entered the octagonal drawing room that sat just below my bedroom, Julia stayed sitting with a contented smile on her face while both David and his brother stood. David's assessment of his older brother's height was correct. If anything, Garrett might have been more than six inches taller than David. But even more impressive than his height was the breadth of his shoulders. Unlike David and Julia, who seemed more comfortable fading into the background of a room, and had the body compositions to do so, Mr. Garrett Tate would always command attention.

Lord Murphy had commanded attention like that the one time I'd seen him, and the thought made me shy away from confidently striding into the room like I'd planned to do. I met his dark-blue eyes for a moment before finding David's lighter ones.

David stepped forward with his hand outstretched and his eyebrows quirked. He'd definitely noticed my reaction to his brother.

His movement shook me out of my stupor. Garrett may look like Lord Murphy, but that didn't mean he would have his temperament, and I was being incredibly rude. I shored up my courage and met David partway. He took my hand in his and tugged me over to the large table that sat in front of a wall of windows.

"Anna," David said softly. "This is my brother, Mr. Garrett Tate. Garrett, Mrs. Anna Tate." David spoke with obvious pride, like I wasn't a woman who'd hoodwinked him into marriage, and I wondered at his reasoning for acting that way. Both Julia and Garrett knew the truth of our marriage.

I held out my hand, and Garrett took it firmly in his. There was no gallantry or flourish in his grip. With his overpowering looks and position in Society, I wouldn't have been surprised to see him act as a dandy or a flirt. "It is wonderful to finally meet you, Mrs. Tate. I always assumed David had imagined you all those years."

"Garrett," David warned.

"What?" Garrett smiled good-naturedly at his brother. "She sounded too much like one of the women from our paintings in the library willed into life, and you never told us her name or how you came to be acquainted. It was all quite suspicious." He turned to me, his smile so similar to David's that my thoughts of his resemblance to Lord Murphy fled. "I can assure you, I've never been happier to be wrong. And"—he elbowed David in the chest—"his description of you back then didn't do you justice."

So he could flatter after all. A quick glance at David showed him to be less than impressed with his brother's words. He narrowed one eye at Garrett and said in a low voice, "That's because she's grown more beautiful."

My breath hitched at David's words. Was he in earnest? Could he really believe I was more beautiful at twenty-five than I had been at seventeen? Certainly not. But my thoughts ran back to the way he'd slid his hands down my hair a few minutes ago and the way he'd fallen backward when he'd lit the lamp in my bedroom. He'd made me feel beautiful then.

Julia nudged Garrett with her elbow, and Garrett's smile truly blossomed. He gave me another appreciative stare—not in a lecherous way nor even in an honorably interested way—with a smile that hinted at pride and outright joy for his brother.

Still, Garrett acted as if I were doing David a kindness, as if I'd delivered him out of a terrible existence by marrying him, which was exactly the opposite of the truth.

But I hid my thoughts with a jest. "You didn't tell your family who I was?" I asked David in mock affront.

"I'm telling them now."

"After we are married."

If I thought David would be cowed, I was wrong. If anything, my accusation made him stand taller. He leaned toward me and placed his mouth near my ear. "I was very selfish at fourteen. I found you, and I wanted to keep you. You were the buried treasure I happened upon in the sand, and I wasn't about to share you with the world."

David's words curled around me like heat rising from a boiler's vent on the floor, wrapping around me and protecting my poor heart from the uncertainty that was my constant companion. Garrett's flattery was pale in comparison.

Julia watched our exchange with cautious but hopeful eyes. This was her first time seeing us together since I'd been sick, and she studied us. Did she see a change?

David put a hand on my back and led me to my seat. The motion was not lost on his brother, who raised an eyebrow in Julia's direction.

Julia served tea with more joy on her face than I'd ever seen. The color in her cheeks from being outside, along with the return of her brother, made her almost look like a different person from the nervous woman I'd first met at the Prestons' home.

Garrett snagged a biscuit and casually leaned back in his chair. "It has been much too long since I've come to visit. The lack of my presence must have done you good. You both look very well."

Julia carefully poured tea into Garrett's cup. "Anna has me slaving away, planting an orchard."

"An orchard?" Garrett asked, that already familiar smile blossoming on his face. "Is that the mess of earth and debris I saw on my way in?"

Julia pulled the teapot away, even though she'd only half filled the cup. She raised her chin. "We nearly have the land ready for planting, and if you say anything else to disparage it, you won't be allowed to eat any of the plums we harvest."

Garrett clamped his mouth shut with his hand. When he released it, his smile was gone, his expression serious. "What I meant to say earlier was that with your help, the orchard is certain to be a master of horticultural genius."

"Thank you," Julia said primly, setting down the teapot. "I agree." Then she held her hands out to her elder brother. "But look at my hands. I'm developing calluses."

Garrett pulled her hands closer to inspect them, and Julia's sleeve hitched up slightly. It reminded me of the day we'd climbed the oak tree and her short sleeves had risen, exposing a partial view of a mark very similar to David's. If the condition wasn't hereditary, why did Julia have a mark as well? And how many others were hidden beneath her clothing? If David rolled up his sleeves, would I see more than the one I had felt that day in the orchard?

Garrett turned Julia's hands one way, then the other, sliding his fingertips on each surface before dropping them. "I see nothing wrong with your hands, Julia. Are you making your poor, newlywed sister-in-law do all the work?"

Julia pulled her hands back to her with quick force. "No, I do not make Anna do all the work. We work together." She bent lower over her hand and pointed to one of her fingers. "There is one, see?"

Garrett narrowed his eyes. David and I did the same, trying to make out the callus Julia was so very proud of. Finally, Garrett rubbed a finger over the spot and raised his eyebrows. "I stand corrected. That is a very impressive callus. Well done." Garrett turned toward me. "Do you manage to get your husband to work with you? Or has he become idle now that he has a wife to work the land?"

For a man who knew David's and my marriage was temporary, he certainly liked to draw attention to the fact that I was David's wife.

"Julia and I have worked longer hours than David. He seems to think he has work to do in his study instead."

Garrett eyed David suspiciously.

David shook his head and lifted his hands in defense. "I *do* have work to do in my study."

"Well," Garrett said, "tomorrow you shall not be allowed in your study. We will all work on the orchard, and I will see for myself who is pulling the most weight."

"You aren't afraid of calluses?" I asked Garrett, the playful banter of the gathering making me bold.

He held out his hand. He had calluses on most of his fingers, and his knuckles were thick and heavy—nothing like the hands of a gentleman. "Too late for that, I'm afraid."

Both David and Julia frowned at Garrett's hands. Those calluses must have come from his time in London. Did everyone in this family have secrets?

"How do you explain those to Father?" David asked. "You won't get hands like that at brothels and gambling halls."

Garrett grunted. "I also don't go around holding Father's hands. There is a limit to what I will do to stay in his good graces."

David's spine stiffened. "Your limit is, perhaps, too high already."

"I saw the Mortensens' new roof on my way in," Garrett quipped back. "I think they might disagree."

Julia could see I was struggling to follow the conversation. "Garrett has quite the reputation in London, and according to Father's accounts, he spends an exorbitant amount on riotous living."

"And Lord Murphy doesn't mind that?" I asked.

"Mind it?" Garrett laughed. "He sees it as an established way to control me. As long as I'm living well above my means, I'll always need to toe the line with him."

I looked at his hands again. "What are you doing while you are supposed to be in those places?"

Garrett's face flattened. "Don't think too highly of your new brother, Mrs. Tate. A lot of the time, I *am* in them. He would know if I wasn't. And the times I'm not?" He shrugged. "I find other ways to keep myself busy." Garrett didn't seem to want to talk about his life in London anymore.

I took a deep breath, resigned to my role as one who was always bright and airy about anything that came her way. "I suppose, if your hands will not be on our conscience, we have no choice but to allow you to do our manual labor for us."

Garrett laughed, and his eyes went to David. "I think your childhood instincts were right about this one. You *should* keep her."

His words, light as they were, hit like daggers. He *knew* of our agreement. He knew David never would. David didn't look at me, but I wondered if his brother's words had hit him as hard as they had me.

After tea, the four of us played whist for the rest of the afternoon. David must have already started his ban from the study, for he showed no signs of leaving now that Garrett was here.

David and I were always on a team and played well together. David seemed to know exactly what I was thinking and could play the correct card based on how long I stared at him.

How did I know a slight flick of his eyebrow meant I should lay down a spade? I didn't—not for certain—but I'd been right seven out of ten times, which was enough for us to trounce Julia and Garrett.

When I looked up at the clock after what had seemed at most an hour, I blinked. "It's five o'clock already?"

"It can't be." David turned to the clock and seemed as surprised as I had been. Julia and Garrett nodded as if their inferior play at cards was, at least, trumped by their more accurate ability to guess at the passage of time. "I hate to leave when we are so terribly ahead at cards, but I'm afraid Anna and I will have to excuse ourselves to dress for dinner."

"I have no doubt it pains you very much," Garrett said wryly. "Tomorrow, we shall have to separate the two of you. Together you have too much of an advantage."

"I'm never good at cards." David said. "The credit goes to Anna."

"Perfect," Garrett said with his dazzling smile. Where did these Tate men get such perfect smiles, with their fine teeth and just enough spark in their eyes to make one think they were hiding something? "She will play with me."

I put a hand to my chest. "I cannot guarantee a repeat performance. I've never played better than I did tonight."

Garrett shrugged. "As long as David plays worse, we should fare well enough."

David stood, took my hand, and lifted it. I gave a parting smile to both Julia and Garrett as I stood from the table. "I will see you at dinner."

Once again, David put a hand on the small of my back as he led me away from the table. "Do you have time to stop in my study? Something came for you while you were sick, and Garrett's arrival made it slip my mind."

"Something came for me?" Almost no one knew I was here.

David nodded.

"A good something?"

"A very good something."

Chapter 23

"Anna asked me to marry her. I told her no. I told her no. I'm sick, and I need to sleep, but I can't, and I don't know what she is going to do, and I don't know what I'm going to do, and I don't feel like I can live knowing I could help her, but I won't. Because how could I? It isn't as though I could marry her and protect her fr . . ."

—David Tate, 1850, Age 23

We left the drawing room and crossed the foyer to David's study. He pulled the door open and ushered me in with his hand on my back once again. It was such a small motion, such a light touch. It shouldn't have made me want to lean into him or feel as though I belonged to him when I knew I didn't. Not permanently, at any rate. But it did.

When his hand left me so he could step over to his desk, I immediately missed the warmth and weight of him.

He pulled a thick envelope from his desk. "Your solicitor brought this to me."

"My solicitor?" I raised my eyebrows and dashed to the desk, pulling the envelope from his hands. There was only one thing my solicitor would have brought. "My inheritance?"

He nodded. "Yes. As your husband, I signed for it."

I pulled out the paper; it was a note from the National Provincial Bank with an amount of available funds listed under my name. I gasped when I saw the number. I'd known, of course, how much was coming, but it felt different now that I had it. With this, Mama and I would be able to pay Mr. Green and be done with him.

To my abject horror, my eyes were suddenly moist.

David did not seem bothered by my emotion. Instead, he folded his arms over his chest and grinned. "I should write a book on how to make one's wife happy. It is so very simple."

"It is?" I asked, trying but failing to keep my voice from wavering from the relief this money brought.

"Definitely. You need only one thing."

"What is that?"

He motioned to the paper in my hands with his chin. "Ill-gotten gains."

I burst into a grin and jaunted over to his side of the desk. "You should surely write that book." I put a hand on his elbow and placed a brief but very firm kiss on his mouth. I didn't know what had come over me, but I was so grateful for this man. My whole life had improved the moment he'd stepped back into it, and I couldn't help myself. "Thank you, David, for everything."

His eyes flared, and he took a step backward. He unfolded his arms and folded them again. "Please don't thank me. You know I'm happy to help."

"I do know that about you. I don't think I've met anyone more helpful."

"Mostly toward you."

"And Julia and your father's tenants. I'm very fortunate I was the first woman in your vicinity to need a husband, or I would have been too late."

"Are you so certain you were? Perhaps I make a habit of marrying women only to have the marriage annulled. After all, I started asking women to marry me at age fourteen."

I snorted. "I don't think so. I don't think Garrett would have been quite so pleased to torture you about me if it were so."

"What did you think of my brother?"

I shrugged my shoulders. "He seemed nice enough, but he has his flaws."

David narrowed his eyes. "What flaws?"

"He was, as predicted, much too tall."

His eyes darkened again, and his eyes went to my mouth. "Really?"

I nodded, thinking back to our conversation in my bedroom. "And too old."

"He is only a few years your senior."

"Don't remind me. I am also, perhaps, too old."

"You aren't."

I was finally starting to believe him when he said things like that. The appreciative look in his eye made it hard not to. I should have been brave for a few minutes longer and lengthened that kiss. "Don't flatter me, David. I'm not certain I can manage myself if you do."

He pointed to his mouth. "You think that kiss was *managing* yourself?"

Had he not noticed how short it was? "Very much so."

His eyes lowered, the smallest crease forming at the corners of his lips. Not quite a smile, but it was gone almost as soon as I'd noticed it. When he met my eyes again, he looked like a sailor facing a hurricane—wary but settled, one hand bracing himself on the chair tucked into his desk. "Tell me what other flaws you find in my brother."

"I don't think he would marry a woman simply to help her."

He shook his head. "I'm not certain that is a flaw."

"His hair is too dark, by a shade."

David swallowed, his hand clenching tighter on the chair.

"He's never held me while I was sick."

His eyelids closed slowly enough for me to watch their descent.

"And he resembles your father."

David stiffened, and whatever he'd been steeling himself against disappeared. My comment had taken him by surprise. His eyes flew open. "He isn't anything like my father." His voice wasn't angry, but it was firm.

"I mean in appearance. It's unsettling."

David nodded once. "I think on that point, Garrett would agree."

I thought perhaps he would ask me to point out more things Garrett lacked, but he didn't. Our chance of quiet flirtation had disappeared the moment I'd mentioned his father.

"I suppose we should dress for dinner," I said.

His eyes searched my face. "Only if you aren't too tired. If you need to rest, I can make your excuses."

"Are you worried about me hearing any more disparaging remarks your brother might make about your work ethic?"

"Of course not. We both know he is grasping at straws to get a rise out of me."

I smiled. "I feel well enough. And I like having a guest. I hope he will visit more often." The words were out before I realized my mistake. Even if he did visit more often, I might not be here the next time he came.

"Garrett tends to stay in London with my father."

"I don't understand Garrett's relationship to him. Do they live together there?"

David hadn't had a positive word to say about his father, and I'd assumed, based on a few things he'd said, Garrett and Julia had similar feelings toward him.

"My father keeps him close, but two years ago, Garrett managed to move into some rented rooms of his own." David looked down at his desk and moved a few papers around. "Now," he said, making it clear he had no desire to keep speaking of his father, "If I'm going to ignore my duties for the next few days while Garrett is here, I have a few things I need to look over before I dress for dinner."

It was a dismissal. Not a harsh one but a dismissal nonetheless. I nodded, holding my inheritance to my chest. "Thank you again, David."

He gave me a quick smile. "I wish I could do more."

There it was again—his feeling that he was in my debt. I didn't understand this man, yet somehow, I did. I just wished I knew what I could do to be more than someone he was grateful to for things I'd done for him so long ago.

Before dressing, I checked in on Mama again, but she was resting, and I decided not to wake her. When I got to my room, exhaustion overtook me. Rather than ring for Maren to help me dress, I lay down on my bed, fully clothed. Light shone through my four windows, but I closed my eyes and managed to doze off anyway.

I woke to noises coming from the adjoining room—a trunk being dropped and feet shuffling around. It seemed as though Garrett would indeed be sleeping in his father's room. A strange arrangement with me in the adjoining one. I would have to ask David about the keys to the door. Did I have the only one? David trusted Garrett completely, but I'd met him only a few hours ago. I double-checked the door and made certain it was locked before glancing at the clock on the mantel.

I was over half an hour late for dinner.

Chapter 24

"Father saw me come in after I spent the afternoon with Anna. I paid for it. But memories of her make the pain fade, so I cannot regret it. And I will continue to sneak out as often as I can."

—David Tate, 1841, Age 14

I looked in the mirror quickly and eyed my wardrobe, considering the few evening gowns I had there, but shrugged. Garrett and Julia wouldn't mind if I came to dinner in a day dress, especially since I'd been so recently ill.

I padded down the silent halls unnoticed. As I neared the dining room, I heard laughter and paused. Garrett's arrival had done something to this home. He'd brought a cheer with him I hadn't known was possible here. Even Julia seemed to be on the verge of laughter more often than not. It was a beautiful thing. I crept forward with feet even quieter, not wanting to disturb the three siblings. The door was closed when I got to it, but I didn't open it. Not yet. This house needed more laughter in it. My life needed more laughter in it. And I'd finally found it, thanks to the three people on the other side of this door. I'd never had siblings before, and David had gifted me with two.

How was I ever going to leave this place? I wanted to taste the fruit of that orchard ten years from now, when the trees were large and bearing massive crops. I wanted to hear laughter spilling out from the dining room on a regular basis or, even better, to be a part of that laughter. I wanted it all, and on paper, it should be mine.

But it never would be.

I took a steadying breath, placed my hand on the door to push it open, but paused when Garrett's voice lifted above the laughter.

"You know she is in love with you."

Had they been speaking of me? I did love David, and apparently, I hadn't been able to hide that during the afternoon, but would they laugh about that? David's poor wife, who was in love with him? My hand froze. I couldn't enter the room now. But I also couldn't make myself walk away.

David must have said something in return, but he mumbled, and I couldn't make it out. No one had laughed at Garrett's declaration, at least.

"That is a good thing, man," Garrett said in response to David's unintelligible response. "To have a wife who loves you."

"No, Garrett, it isn't." David finally spoke loud enough for me to hear. "And she doesn't. I mean . . ." He made another sound like a groan. "She isn't supposed to."

"Why not?"

I should go in or leave. At any moment, a footman would arrive to bring in more food or clear away plates, and he would find me standing at the door listening.

"You know why not." David's voice was firm now. "She can't stay here. Every day she is here is a risk. And even if it weren't, I refuse to taint what is so lovely in her with the darkness in me."

"There is no darkness in you." Julia's voice was soft, but she spoke clearly enough for me to hear.

The room was eerily silent after her words until Garrett echoed his sister's statement. "Julia's right. There is no darkness in you."

"It would be a darkness for her." This was spoken so softly I barely made out the words. And I knew—whatever they'd been laughing about earlier wasn't because they'd been mocking me. There had been no laughter throughout this conversation. All three of them had been deadly serious.

A noise sounded behind me, and I jumped back from the door. What kind of mistress listened at the doors of her own home?

"Well, what are you waiting for?" A deep and frustrated voice said behind me. "Open the door." I turned to see which footman would talk to me so brusquely only to step back and gasp.

Lord Murphy stood behind me, frowning with such vehemence. I checked his hand for a horse whip. Thank the heavens his hands were empty. I slid back against the wall. He was older now, with more gray hair than the dark brown he'd had eight years ago, but there was no mistaking him. He was an older version of Garrett, tall and powerful and much too good-looking for the snarl currently occupying his face.

"You must be new here, but I assure you, I am the master of this house. Not David. You will do as I say, and you will do it quickly."

My breathing hitched, and the light from the oil lamps seemed to darken. Lord Murphy was here. He was here, in Tate Manor, and that meant one very permanent and terrible thing: My marriage to David was about to be over. "I'm—"

"I will not hear excuses." He interrupted. "David has been lax in the training of his staff. If I were here, things would be very different. Now, open the door." I bit my lip and reached for the door handle. He came up close behind me, and with a sharpness I'd never heard from any of his children, he practically spat his next words at me. "Change your dress before you return. Patterns should not be worn by servants."

"I'm not—"

He turned to me, a fire of rage in his eyes, and one of his hands fisted at his side. I opened the door without making another sound.

Lord Murphy strode into the dining room, and all three siblings' faces dropped. David's eyes found mine almost immediately, and I could see a frantic question in them. I shook my head softly, not sure if he was wondering whether his father knew who I was or if his father had caused me any harm. Either way, the answer was the same.

"Garrett?" Lord Murphy stated with a hint of surprise. "I thought you were at a house party in Kent."

Garrett's face was the most serious of all, a frown etched into his face where only smiles had been earlier. "I will be joining the house party late."

"This is hardly on the way."

Garrett didn't say anything to that, but he kept his face and back straight, revealing nothing.

Lord Murphy marched toward the table like a soldier facing an enemy in battle rather than a father joining his children for a meal. "It seems you've violated your agreement, Garrett. You haven't been meeting with Chartists, have you?"

Garrett waved a hand in dismissal. "I gave up that cause long ago. Did you have me followed?"

"No. I came for a different reason."

"Then it seems you are in violation of *our* agreement." Garrett's voice was as hard as steel.

Lord Murphy snorted. "Do you think I *want* to be here? I'd rather forget this place exists. But while visiting the archbishop last night, he happened to congratulate me on adding a daughter to the family. Although I wouldn't be so pathetic as to ask the man to which of my sons he was referring, it was fairly easy to deduce it must have been David. So, David, where is this wife of yours?"

David's eyebrows furrowed, and both Garrett's and Julia's eyes flashed toward me in confusion. The motion wasn't lost on Lord

Murphy. He turned toward me. "Are you still here? I thought I told you to change your clothes."

My face heated. I had no desire to impress Lord Murphy. I wished him far away from here. His presence had killed all the laughter. But his insistence that I was part of the staff was a humiliation hard to ignore.

Julia lifted her chin. "She is the mistress of this house and has been ill. If she doesn't feel well enough to dress for dinner, that is her prerogative." Her voice was steady and flat, like Garrett's had been.

While I hadn't been able to eke out a long enough sentence to explain to him I wasn't a servant, Julia was able to confront him openly. This was a new side to Julia. She was stronger than I knew.

"There is no mistress of this house. There won't be until Garrett marries." Lord Murphy barked, then he turned and looked at me again, this time actually taking the time to examine me. "*That* is your wife, David?" Lord Murphy smiled for the first time since I'd seen him. A laugh that was more like a cackle came out of his mouth. "I thought she was a maid. Couldn't you convince a younger woman to marry you?" Lord Murphy looked David up and down. "I suppose not."

I had no idea how to respond. David and I hadn't ever spoken of what I should do if I were to meet his father. I'd thought, foolishly, that perhaps I would never have to. Based on the rage forming behind David's eyes, it looked as though he'd had the same assumption.

"Get out," David growled.

"This is my house, David, or have you forgotten?"

David gripped the table in front of him. "Leave this home this instant. You will not spend the night here. You will not spend the evening here. You will leave."

Lord Murphy tsk-tsked. "I don't think so. I've already had *my* servants move my belongings into my room."

That was the noise I'd heard earlier? Lord Murphy's belongings being brought into the adjoining room? I swallowed down bile as it rose in my throat. He'd most likely dressed in the room while I was still there.

Garrett stood. "I won't be returning to London with you. Not if you so blatantly ignore our agreement. I've been wanting to visit the Americas. I've heard the women there find men with titles extremely fascinating." He forced the words through his teeth.

"Now, now, enough of such talk." Lord Murphy smiled. "I'd like to formally be introduced to my daughter-in-law—" His eyes grazed over me again. "Now that I know she isn't a maid."

"No," David said.

"You won't tell me her name? Is her family so lowly you are embarrassed to admit it? You didn't marry one of the tenant girls, did you? I've heard how much time you are spending with them."

I stepped forward. I didn't understand half of what was going on, but I was part of this family, even if only temporarily. If Julia could speak boldly to this man, so could I. "My name is Anna Atwood. My father was a gentleman, and our family estate was a fine one. I know David thanks to the mutual acquaintance of Mr. and Mrs. Preston."

Lord Murphy raised an eyebrow at me. "I assume, by your word choice, your father is dead."

I lifted my chin, unwilling to let him know he'd hit a painful mark. "Yes, but that makes him no less a gentleman."

He tipped his head causally to the side as if he might argue that point, but the sound of David's chair scraping the floor stopped him.

David strode toward me. "I'll have your dinner sent up to my room, Anna. You need to rest."

Lord Murphy's sharp eyes turned toward me—this time, perhaps, noticing my pallor—then back to David. "Did she fall pregnant?" That low laugh left his mouth again, sickening and blackhearted. "No wonder you needed a special license from the archbishop. Are you even certain the child is yours?"

I didn't even see David move. He was standing in front of me one moment and was halfway to his father before I had a chance to react. As fast as his legs moved, his fist was faster, flying through the air and landing with resounding force on his father's jaw.

Lord Murphy stumbled back, and one foot caught on the rug, toppling him into a sitting position on the floor. For seconds afterward, the only movement in the room was the rise and fall of David's chest from his heavy breathing.

Then Lord Murphy interrupted the silence with cold laughter. "Do you know what the punishment is for striking a member of the House of Lords?"

"Report me," David said, turning and striding back toward me. His face was cold, so unlike the David I knew. Gone was his gentleness and kindness, replaced by a hardness that made him nearly unrecognizable.

"Wait." Lord Murphy's voice had changed, transforming into a plea.

David stiffened but then turned.

Lord Murphy took a large cigar out of the breast pocket of his jacket. "Before you go, could you fetch me a candle? I'd like to smoke."

Julia hissed, Garrett swore under his breath, and David grabbed my arm and propelled me out of the room. We marched down the corridor at a speed nigh unto running. When we reached the stairs, he didn't slow but took them two at a time. My breath started coming in gasps. My foot slid off the edge of one step, and I would have fallen if he hadn't held my arm.

He whipped his head around, his face dark and thunderous, but when he caught sight of me struggling to right myself, the hard ridges and planes of his face melted away, shifting into the softness I was used to. But this time, the softness was clouded with regret. "Anna," he said, his voice soft enough to crumble into dust around us, "I'm so sorry."

"No, I'm well. Of course I'm well."

"No, you aren't. You were confined to your bed just yesterday, and I'm dragging you up the stairs."

"I've caught my breath. We can continue."

But he shook his head, swept me up in his arms, and marched us up the stairs. Instead of turning into my room at the end of the corridor, he turned the handle on his own door and kicked it open. Without a word, he placed me gently on his bed, then returned to the door and locked it. "You can't stay in your room as long as he is in the house, and you won't be left alone." He pulled a bell for service. "I'll have Maren and Julia stay with your mother until we have your things packed."

"Packed?" I asked.

"Yes. Garrett's friend in Lincolnshire said the cottage will be available whenever you need it."

He was sending me away.

This evening.

"Will you be coming with us?"

I knew the answer before he gave it. "No, Anna. We always knew this arrangement would be temporary. It has accomplished everything it needed to do. We've found a safe place for you, and you also have your money. There is no need for the farce to continue."

The farce. Our engagement, our marriage, and everything that had happened between us over the past weeks reduced to one very malignant but accurate word.

David winced, and I knew he could see the hurt that word had caused, but he didn't apologize. Instead, he paced at the foot of the bed until a knock sounded at the door.

He carefully unlocked it and cracked the door open. Then he slammed it shut again, turning the key and swearing under his breath. "My father has replaced the servants." He ran a hand down his face.

"He's what?" Why would the man replace the servants?

David waited a moment, then listened at the door before opening it. He pulled me into the corridor. If he wanted to avoid the servant, he'd led us out too early, as the man was at the top of the stairs. David grabbed my hand and led me across the corridor into my room.

As soon as we were inside, my eyes flew to the adjoining door. "I can't stay here," I whispered.

"You won't." He closed the door loudly and locked it. "Grab a few essentials—only what you can carry in your hands now." He refilled the oil lamp sitting next to my bed and lit it while I grabbed my most utilitarian dress, an extra pair of stockings, and a few personal items. He nodded at my small bundle, his eye catching on the rock with the black stripe.

He left the lamp on my bedside table, and listened once again at the door. When he opened it this time, the servant was gone. He took the key from inside the door, then shut it and locked it from the outside.

"We left the lamp burning," I said.

David nodded. "I'd rather he think we are in your room tonight."

We padded back into his room. "Does he always send away your servants when he visits?"

"Because of his agreement with Garrett, he hasn't visited for years, but he knows the servants here are faithful to me and Julia. It is for the best, even though this does make planning more difficult. He'd fire any servant that helped us, and as much as I like to pretend this house and estate are mine, they aren't. He's only allowed me to manage it for a couple of years."

"What exactly did Garrett agree to?" I asked.

David locked the door and turned, resting the back of his head against it. "Until about five years ago, Garrett did everything Father asked of him. He spent his days trying to be exactly the kind of son and heir my father wanted him to be. But no matter how perfect he was, Father managed to find fault in the smallest things and punish us. Then one day, Garrett must have decided he'd had enough. He embarked on a wild year of willful rebelling. He was rarely home, he befriended men of far lower station, and he even found ways to contribute to their causes. He actively campaigned for members of the Chartist movement, when Father had voted and vehemently opposed universal voting rights. It was a hellish year, even by our family's standards.

"One day he came back and told my father he was going to marry the daughter of a working-class man. He didn't love her, but he was determined to live his life in direct opposition of my father.

"After my father threatened the woman and she stopped contacting Garrett, my father and Garrett finally came to an agreement. Garrett would live life as my father saw fit in London. He wouldn't marry anyone my father didn't approve of, and in return Garrett made him promise to leave Tate Hall for Julia and me to live in and care for. Father only agreed to it if Garrett promised to do the same."

"Why would your father keep you apart?"

"He wants to mold Garrett, to make him become his heir in every sense of the word. And he sees country life and me in particular as bad influences."

"He gave up the life he wanted to free you and Julia from your father's grasp?"

"Yes. And even though the world might think of Garrett as an exact replica of my father, he isn't. He is the kindest man I know, and any of my accomplishments came only because of what he is doing for me and Julia every day in London. Julia and I can plant orchards and help families like the Mortensens because he has to live daily with that . . . that . . . monster who calls himself a parent."

My comment about Garrett being like his father rang dissonantly in my ears. It was the absolute worst thing I could have said about his brother.

"You admire your brother a great deal, don't you?"

He furrowed his brows. "Of course I do."

"Is that why you are sending me away? So you can be like him and take the brunt of life's burdens on you while I go live in safety?"

He pushed himself off the door and put his hands on my cheeks as gently as if I were a skittish foal. "They aren't your burdens, Anna." His thumb traced a line from my nose to my ear. "They are mine. I never should have married you when I have them to carry. I simply couldn't say no to you. I thought we would have more time together, but this marriage was always going to end. It had to. I won't let you make that man downstairs a relative."

"If I have to leave, then come with me."

"And leave Julia?" His voice was husky.

"Bring Julia."

He closed his eyes as if he were tempted. "I don't think I can do that to Garrett."

"Have you asked him?"

He shook his head. "No, because he would let me do it."

"He is already sacrificing for you."

"If I left, he would have to live here and care for the estate. Father is always worse in the country. In London, at least there are appearances to keep up."

"He could hire a steward. Mr. Mortensen would be an excellent one."

"My father would murder half the county before he allowed a tenant farmer to be his steward."

"Then definitely not Mr. Mortensen. But someone." My voice was shaking, but I didn't care. My world was falling apart, and I had to find a way to fight for it. "Someone else could do it."

He dropped his hands and started to pace. "I don't think you understand what you are asking. If we were to leave, I would have nothing. Your situation wouldn't become better; it would become worse. You wouldn't only have your mother to worry about, but you would have me as well. I hired my own tutor with funds Garrett was able to present as ongoing gambling debts to my father. I was never sent to school; I can thatch a roof, but you should be married to a gentleman, not a laborer. And if I ever secured a position worthy of you, my father would hear of it and find us. We would have to live in hiding."

Without his hands holding me up, I let my legs collapse under me, and I sat on his bed. "Why?" I asked. "I know your father is a terrible person, I've seen him treat his servants in the most despicable manner, but you are his son. Certainly we could find a way to live most of our lives away from him and bear his monstrous personality during the few times a year we must see him."

"No, Anna. It wouldn't be like that. For Garrett and Julia, perhaps, they could work out an arrangement like that someday, but not me. Father has always punished me the most, and he will not hesitate to hurt me by hurting you. He would be relentless, and I simply will not let you live your life like that."

"I don't want to live my life without you. Not if you love me. Each day we spend in each other's company, I'm more and more convinced you do. I'm fine living in hiding from him if that is the only path you will accept. I'm not afraid of being poor. I'm only afraid of losing you."

David took in a slow, shaky breath, walked back to the door, and rested his forehead on it. "This is torture."

I pushed myself off the bed and came up behind him, placing a hand on his shoulder. "Then make it stop."

He heaved a deep sigh and turned around to face me. "That's what I'm trying to do. Living with you has been excruciating. My wife sleeps across the corridor from me every night. I can hear you when you walk past my room. You've kissed me exactly twice since we've been married, and I held you once through the night. All three of those moments repeat in my mind whenever I'm not forcing myself to keep busy. You've laughed with Julia and built something beautiful here, in the wreck of a home I despised growing up. You are everything I've ever wanted and the one thing I can never have." His voice hitched, and I could see the pain written all over his face. "At some point, the torture has to stop, doesn't it? I can't be tortured forever. Not if I want to remain sane."

"If I actually am everything you've ever wanted, why can we not remain married, and married truly? Your father made you unhappy enough during your childhood. Let's not allow him to take away the joys of the rest of your life as well. I'm in love with you, David. I want to be your wife."

Something changed in his eyes at my words. Desperation was sucked away into a type of hope—a desperate, unlikely hope. Ice bursting into flames. He took a half step forward and stopped.

I grabbed his lapels and moved my face only inches away from his. "Stop keeping your distance, husband. It is torture for both of us."

"I cannot."

"Well, I can." I threw my arms around his neck and tucked my head to the side of his. He didn't resist my embrace or pull away. Instead, he exhaled a deep, ragged breath and let his head drop to my shoulder. His arms, which had been stiff at his side, wrapped around my waist, and he pulled me closer, inhaling deeply into my hair. I held him while we came together in this desperate moment, breathing each other in softly. Whatever happened next, I wanted it to happen together.

I pulled back slightly and pressed my mouth against his cheek, just below his ear. "I love you. I don't know exactly when it happened, but I do." I kissed him again, this time lower, along his jawbone. "My kisses shouldn't be numbered as if you are keeping track of them until they are gone. Please don't make me leave you and call it a kindness. It would be too cruel."

His fingers dug into my back, like a drowning man needing something to cling on to. "You've been my hope for a better world for so long," he murmured, his mouth hovering over mine. "But I've never thought I could turn that hope into a reality. There are so many obstacles in our way that I cannot see a clear path."

"Darling." I kissed his mouth gently. His lips were so soft, so giving; they sent a wave of belonging rushing over me. Poor, wealthy, hidden, or living out in the open—it didn't matter to me as long as we were together. I pulled away and pressed my forehead onto his, needing a moment to breathe and wanting him to hear my words clearly. "We don't have to see our future to believe in it. That is exactly what hope is—not knowing but believing anyway."

I could see the moment David let go of his panic and despair and started questioning his determination to force me away. He nodded, the motion making my head shake with his, two people so utterly connected no one should have the power to tear us apart.

He lifted his hands to my face again and studied my eyes, my nose, the curve of my mouth. He traced the lines of my jaw with his thumbs. "These last few weeks have been miraculous. I didn't think I would ever be happy, and I can't help but feel like if we try to make this work, I will be the most selfish man on earth."

"It isn't selfish of you," I told him. Hesitant shadows creeped around his eyes. "Our happiness will forever be entwined. In gaining your own happiness, you would also be granting mine."

I watched the thought settle on him, the certainty of my happiness being dependent on his own. Whatever torturous devices he'd used to keep me at arm's length finally seemed to fall away.

"Anna." He whispered it as reverently as a prayer. I held his gaze, encouraging him silently. "Anna," he said my name again, this time firmly, as if in that one word our worlds would unite. His fingers slid into my hair, and he pulled my lips back to his with an urgency I'd never felt in him before. His mouth covered mine, drinking me in, the fingers of one hand slid up my back and behind my head while his other hand pulled at my waist.

My breath hitched at his sudden fervor, the tension of the last hour fading away. I basked in the feel of David relinquishing the last of his doubts and reveled in the spots of light that seemed to burst forth wherever his fingers and mouth touched me.

And when I thought I could bear no more of only being kissed and not kissing in return, I pressed forward until he was against the door, and I held him there with my arms, my mouth, my body, with everything I had. I would not let him go, and I would not allow him to send me away either. That was my promise, and I told it to him in every way I could imagine.

He answered accordingly.

I trailed kisses down his cheek, under his chin, and released his back with one of my hands, lifting it to the cravat at his neck. I tugged at the knot, needing more of him to kiss.

His hand came over mine, stilling it, even as his mouth captured mine again, distracting me from my target. But it only took his mouth leaving mine to press a kiss to my temple for me to remember my goal. I tried once again to loosen the knot at his neck.

He shook his head. "I can't . . ."

Images of him pulling away when I'd rolled up his sleeve and of his shirt hanging open when I'd been sick came back to me. He always pulled away, never wanting to show them to me. "I know about your condition. I don't care."

He stilled even further. "My condition?"

"Those marks on your skin. I don't care about them. Dr. Clarke said they aren't hereditary. They won't affect our children." I'd asked about those children in a very different way when speaking with Dr. Clarke. At the time, I'd thought that would never be a possibility for us. To talk of them now, after declaring war against anyone or anything that would pull us apart, made the room seem brighter. Our future family could be one of laughter and hope.

"You spoke to Dr. Clarke about my skin?"

"Yes." I took a deep breath. How long had it been since I'd taken a full one? "I'm sorry if that was a breach of your trust. You said he was your doctor as well, and after I saw the same spot on Julia's arm, I thought perhaps they were the reason we couldn't . . ." My voice trailed off.

David's eyes had gone cold, his body rigid.

"What?" I asked. I placed my fingertips on his cheeks, but he didn't even notice my touch.

"You saw a mark on Julia?"

I nodded. Surely he knew about it.

But the look on his face contradicted my assumption. David's jaw clenched, and it looked as though he might be ill. He took hold of my hand, unlocked the door, and, with a quick glance for servants or his father, pulled us into the corridor and toward Julia's room.

Chapter 25

"He hates me, and he makes everyone in the family pay for it. It is even worse now that Mother is gone."
—David Tate, 1839, Age 12

David knocked on Julia's door the instant we reached it.

"Who is it?" Garrett's voice answered low and protective.

"David," David replied. "Is Julia in there with you?"

The latch from the door slid free, and Garrett opened the door wide. "Yes," he said, motioning for us to come in. Julia was sitting on her bed, eyes dry but not focused on anything. She didn't even look up when we entered the room.

David dropped my hand as soon as we were safely in the room, then strode to Julia and knelt in front of her. "Show me your arm."

Julia's eyes came into focus. She searched David's face and shook her head. "No."

"What is this about?" Garrett asked. When the two of them wouldn't answer, he turned to me.

"I'm not exactly certain." It was the truth.

"When did he hurt you?" David's voice was dangerous. My stomach twisted at his words; pieces of a puzzle I should have put together sooner clicked into place. David didn't have a skin condition. He never had.

Julia shook her head again. "He didn't. He's never hurt me. Not in that way."

"Then why did Anna see a scar on your arm?"

"What?" Garrett's face went pale.

A scar. Those marks were scars. Scars made by someone intentionally hurting the person who bore them. I stumbled backward until my back pressed against the door. David didn't have just one or two of those scars. I'd seen dozens of them, and I'd only seen a very small portion of his skin. There was only one *he* David could mean. What had Lord Murphy done to his children?

Julia straightened, all her strength from dinner returned. She met David's gaze without flinching. "Father didn't hurt me. I did it to myself."

Did what to herself? What exactly had Lord Murphy done to them? Suddenly, David's resistance to bringing me into his family made a lot more sense. He was protecting me, not from a terrible person but from a fiend.

"You did it?" David's voice was a hoarse whisper, almost a plea. If he asked the question softly enough, maybe her answer would change.

Julia's eyes filled with tears, and she swallowed hard. "Do you know how many times I had to watch him burn you? Do you?"

Burn. Bile rose to my throat at the word.

David reached out his hand. "I know very well how many times. I can count them."

She shook her head violently. "No, you can't. There are a multitude on your back that you cannot see. But I can. I see them whenever I close my eyes. I can see them happening, over and over. I feel them, and I . . ."

David pulled her into his arms. "No, Julia, no. I don't want this."

Julia collapsed into him. "None of us wanted this. But it was what we were given, and I needed to know—" Her voice caught, and part of her hard exterior collapsed. "I needed to know what it was like, not just the burning but also the scar."

She carefully extricated herself from David's arms and lifted her short sleeve to show the mark I'd noticed in the oak tree. "It's barely there. I couldn't—" She broke again. "I lit the cigar, made myself smell its stench, and then pressed it on my arm, but I couldn't hold it there. It was too painful, and I was too weak."

"You are *not* weak." David shook his head. "I cannot understand why you would do it." His voice held a sob.

Instead of answering, Julia glanced up at Garrett. Their eyes met, and an understanding passed between them. "Tell him."

Garrett held his sister's eyes for a long second, then undid several buttons on his shirt, pulling it open to expose a perfectly formed circle, deep and rough at the edges, just above his heart.

"You both did it? Together?" David's voice gained strength with his anger. "How could you let Julia do such a thing?"

Garrett shook his head. "I didn't know she had."

"But you told her you did?"

"No." His answer was quiet.

"Then how did she know?"

Garrett ran a hand angrily through his hair. "Because we both lived through it. Watched or, at a minimum, had to listen to your screams. And most of the time"—Garrett's spine stiffened, and his hands fisted—"it was for stupid things *I* had done."

David shook his head, falling from his knees into a sitting position on the floor. "They were excuses, Garrett. Those stupid things were excuses. Do you think he cared about mud on your boots or not eating your dinner quietly enough? He *wanted* to hurt me, and he was always going to find a way to place blame on someone—me or you or Julia for not getting her piano pieces perfectly right. He wanted to pit us against each other."

What kind of sick man . . . ? I held my stomach and concentrated on keeping my breath steady, but it was a lost cause. Lord Murphy had tortured David and made his other children watch. That was the boy I'd met all those years ago. The days he'd seemed sickly or tired but had tried to smile anyway, he'd been burned by his father recently.

And if muddied boots or not eating food according to their father's demands had warranted those scars, then being caught spending time with me would have definitely come at a cost.

And still, he had come. Almost every day I had been there that summer, he had come. I sank to the floor and put my head between my knees.

David was there in a heartbeat, his arms around me, his hand smoothing my hair. I sobbed against him, my world breaking apart. I'd thought I'd known what hardships were. I'd thought losing my father had been excruciating, but having a father like mine—even if I'd had to lose him—had made my life a paradise compared to David's.

David was whispering something, consoling me, his mouth on my cheek, his hand stroking my back. His words were soft, with a rhythm-like chant. "It was a long time ago. I was young. Garrett found a way to control him. He lost interest in hurting me once I was large enough to hurt him in return. Not long after you left, he gave up on the sport."

At the word *sport*, my stomach rebelled. I covered my mouth with my hand, but to no avail. Julia had the washbasin in front of me before I had the chance to move. She'd known. She'd known I was going to be sick.

Because she'd lived through this, only much, much worse.

And I'd tried to fix that with an orchard.

"She didn't know?" Garrett asked.

"I was about to tell her when . . ."

"She told you about my arm." Julia finished.

David nodded.

I lifted my head from the bowl and found David's eyes. I was wretched, my hair a tangled mess, my mouth foul. I didn't care. I was like an animal in that moment. "How could he do this to you? To his own children?" My voice shook. "He is the kind of man who shouldn't be allowed to live."

"He's a viscount," Julia said in a hollow voice. "Anyone who lays a hand on him will go to prison, and if someone were to kill him, they would hang."

Lord Murphy's words after David had floored him echoed in my ears. He'd taunted him about that fact. That he was untouchable. And judging from the flat way Julia had said the words, it wasn't the first time he'd made that point.

Then he'd pulled out a cigar and asked for help lighting it.

I was sick again, even though there was nothing left in my stomach. When I finished, I looked back up at the three of them. "I'm sorry," I said, feeling lightheaded and unsure about what I was apologizing for.

"Don't be." David's voice was soft, his hands brushing away the tears that streaked my face.

Garrett walked to Julia's table, wetted a cloth, and gave it to me. "Don't worry," Garrett said while I scrubbed at my face and hands, trying to wash away the images of that younger version of David in pain. "None of us are going to hang because of him. He's done enough damage already."

Julia handed me a ginger candy, and I sucked hard on it. The sharp taste did nothing to distract me from everything I'd just learned. I couldn't look at any of them, not without leading to a rise of more tears.

"Why did he do it?" I asked, looking down at the floor, knowing there would never be an answer that made any sense.

Garrett sighed deeply. "Our father was always a violent man, but when I was very young, he managed to hide it quite well. I'd seen him injure servants, but he was always so certain it was the right way to train his employees that I didn't question him." Garrett jammed his hands into his pockets. "Sometimes I worry about what kind of man I would have grown into if it weren't for our mother."

The only thing I knew about David's mother was that she'd died a few years before I'd come to visit Breckenridge.

Garrett took a deep breath before continuing. "He hid that part of him from her, but one day, about a year before David was born, she saw him beat a servant savagely, and she never looked at him the same after that. He tried to explain his reasoning to her as he had to me, but Mother wasn't a child—she knew depravity when she saw it. And after a few months of trying to convince her he wasn't that kind of man, he gave up and no longer felt the need to control himself."

"I was born at a time when my father knew our mother didn't love him anymore." David continued Garrett's story, his voice soft and careful. He knew how close I was to breaking. "He always questioned my birth. At first, he would talk about it as if he wasn't certain he was my father, but as the years progressed, he became more and more convinced I wasn't. And because of that, I became a tool to discipline the children he knew were his."

"Do you actually think . . . ?" I couldn't ask the question, David's anger at Dr. Clarke's questioning my virtue making a lot more sense.

"No." Garrett's voice was firm. "Our mother was heartbroken about who our father ended up being, but she had almost no contact with anyone outside of our family, and she didn't have the heart of a deceiver."

"Besides," David said firmly. "She would have told me if it were true. I wished for a different father and begged her to tell me I had some other man's blood running through my veins. But she couldn't. Lord Murphy is my father, but nothing I can do will ever make him believe it. He's built his whole life around that hurt in order to excuse his actions."

I forced my head up, and just as I feared, tears coursed down my face when I caught David's eyes, so tender, so loving, and so full of a hurt he'd hidden for the whole of his life. I wrapped my arms around his neck and pulled myself to him. Needing to hold him, needing to let him know I saw his worth, his pain, and his heart, needing him to know I loved him. Not in spite of those things, and not because of them. I simply loved *him*.

His hands went around my waist, and we sat on the floor, my arms not letting go of him and his gathering me into his lap. The room was silent, save for our breathing, for several minutes before Garrett eventually coughed softly.

"We need to arrange a way to get you away from the house," Garrett said. David loosened his hold on me but only slightly. I glanced up to see Garrett giving us an extremely apologetic look. "One of your servants, a Miss Mortensen, who I assume must be one of Obadiah's daughters, was able to catch me on the stairs to let me know she was taking Mrs. Atwood to her house."

I nodded. Bless Maren for seeing a need and immediately taking action. It couldn't have been easy to convince Mama to go.

"Yes, she is one of Obadiah's daughters," David said.

I was trying to catch my breath and make sense of everything around me. Meanwhile, the three of them were already moving forward with plans, making me appreciate the businesslike tone in which their family communicated when faced with Lord Murphy.

Garrett nodded. "That's good. Father wouldn't set foot in a tenant's home." Garret caught my eye. "As far as I know, our father doesn't even know your mother was ever in the house."

"Thank you," I said.

"You will have to thank Miss Mortensen when you see her next," Garrett said. "It was all her doing and quite brilliant of her. Now we just need to find a way to get the three of you away from here without him knowing."

"All of us?" David asked in surprise. "You don't think Anna should go and I should stay here?"

Garrett looked at his brother like he was an idiot. "She's your wife. If she leaves, you need to go with her."

"But I told you—"

Garrett brushed a hand through the air. "That was hours ago, before I saw the two of you together and long before you walked in here disheveled after obviously showing her some of your scars."

In a different world, I might have been embarrassed by Garrett's comment. David hadn't actually shown me his scars; he'd stopped me from opening his shirt. Embarrassment simply felt like too weak of an emotion after everything we'd just been through.

David slid a hand down my hair. "Do you still want me to come with you?" he asked, looking around the room to remind me of what had just transpired.

"Yes," I answered as firmly as I could. "Of course I do."

"It is decided, then," Garrett said.

"What will Father do when he wakes in the morning to find us all gone?" Julia asked. "And what of our servants?"

Garrett's mouth was a flat line. "I can handle Father. I've managed him quite well over the past few years. And if you give me the names of everyone who works here, I will write to them. It might be a few weeks until I can offer them work again, but Father will need his servants in London. Their positions will remain secure. As long as you have somewhere safe—farther away from here than the Mortensens' home—to go."

David wrapped his hand around mine. The familiar warmth of his fingers settled some of my nerves. "We do."

"Lincolnshire?" Garrett asked.

David nodded.

Garrett put a hand on David's shoulder. "Do not write to me. When I feel it is safe, I'll contact Mr. Mortensen, and we can communicate through him." Garrett reached into his interior pocket, pulling out several bills and a coin purse. "Take this." Julia's eyes widened. There must have been over a hundred pounds in his hand. "Apparently, I was particularly bad at gambling this month."

David grabbed the bag and embraced his brother. "Someday, Father is going to discover you aren't a wastrel."

Garrett returned David's embrace, a flash of pain crossing his eyes that I'm not certain anyone else saw. "Let's pray that day is a long way off."

Chapter 26

"I'm sitting at my desk, watching Anna and Julia plant an orchard through my window. It is moments like these that make me think perhaps there is hope for us. It is moments like these I dream of making Anna my wife, even though on paper, she already is."

—David Tate, 1850, Age 23

The four of us spent another half an hour planning our escape, and by the time David and I walked back to his room, the sun had fully set. The corridor, which was typically lit, was dark. David had closed his door but hadn't locked it when we left, and now it stood open. He looked inside. There was just enough light from the moon through the windows for us to see his bed and the other items in his room. He motioned for me to stay near the door while he searched the room for intruders. When he was satisfied no one was inside, he pulled me into the room and had me stand against the wall behind his open door.

"I'll be back in a moment," he said in a whisper, putting a finger to his lips for me to remain quiet. He removed his shoes and dashed into the corridor. I watched him through the crack between the door and the wall as he put his ear to his father's door and listened. After a few moments, he must have been satisfied with what he heard since he carefully stepped over to the door of my empty bedchamber.

Once there, he bent low and rolled something under the door and into my locked bedroom. The metallic clinking sound of something rolling across the floorboards broke the silence, and then he was next to me, both of us hidden behind his open door and holding each other in the dark.

Muffled cursing sounded from inside Lord Murphy's room, followed by banging. Not from the corridor; he was still inside his room, but he was pounding on the door that stood between his and mine.

"Let me in, David. I didn't even get a chance to introduce myself to your wife." Another bang sounded as he pounded his fist once again.

I shivered, and David drew me in closer, his lips in my hair quieting me without making a sound.

The pounding happened again, but this time, it was softer, and lacking strength. More words sounded, but this time, they were too slurred to understand. The rattling noise David had caused in my room must have roused his father from sleep or from drink, because already, he didn't sound completely in control of his senses.

After a moment of silence, David slowly pushed his door closed. He pulled a key from his pocket and locked it. "It sounds as though he has been drinking," he said with relief.

The plan we'd devised in Julia's bedroom was twofold. First, we needed to incapacitate Lord Murphy, and then we had to escape without his servants being alerted to our departure. Years ago, and unbeknownst to Lord Murphy, David had replaced his father's scotch with a specially made batch that was much stronger than what he was used to drinking every night before bed in London. We were counting on it being enough to dull his senses and deepen his sleep.

"Should we go tell Garrett and Julia?" I whispered near his ear.

He shook his head. "Not yet. If I know my father, he had another glass after I disturbed him. In another hour, he should be even more incapacitated by it."

"Until then, we wait?"

He nodded. "Quietly."

The room was dark, save for the scant bits of moonlight, and there was no chance he would light a candle. Nor did I want him to.

My arms went around him, and I held him tightly. Now that the planning was done, I allowed myself to start processing everything I'd learned. When one of my breaths made a strange racking noise, David pulled away and studied my face in the shadows.

He put a thumb to the corner of my mouth. "You aren't feeling sorry for me, are you? Because that doesn't make a husband feel good about himself."

I shook my head. "No," I managed to eke out, but my voice was too weak to be believable.

He pulled me back into his arms, and I breathed him in. "Julia and I have done very well the past few years. We've been happy, and now we are going to leave. We'll be even happier with you."

I sniffed. "And Garrett?"

"You heard him." He leaned back so he could look me in the eye. "He handles Father well. At least, that is what he tells us. He lives two lives in London. He has friends there who know who he truly is, and with them, I believe he can be happy too."

"And the rest of London?"

A slow smile spread on his lips, and he smoothed my hair on the sides of my head. "He says he doesn't care about the rest of London."

I drew in a shaky breath. "Well then, will you allow me to feel sorry for the younger David? The one I didn't know was hurting?"

"No." David wrapped his arms back around me. "Not for him either. Because he found you."

I shook, my throat trying but not succeeding in holding back a strangled sob, and even though I tried so hard to keep them at bay, tears slid from my eyes. "I don't think that makes up for all those scars."

He pressed a soft kiss to my temple. "On that point, we will have to disagree."

I nodded into his collarbone, even though he was being completely ridiculous. It wasn't as though I could ignore the pain I'd just witnessed. No one could see that and not be hurt by it. "I can't be bright and happy right now. I can't. I've tried so hard to remain that cheerful young lady you met when I was seventeen, but this . . ." I had no choice but to feel his hurt as deeply as my heart was capable.

"Do you think you were always happy that summer?"

I sniffed. Isn't that what he'd said? "I don't know. I thought that was how you remembered me. I've been trying so hard to live up to who I was then, but I simply can't do it. Not right now."

"No. Anna, no." He placed a kiss just below each of my eyes, letting my tears stain his lips. "You brought light into my life because you were braver than anyone I'd ever met. You left songs in your wake, even though everyone who heard them knew you couldn't sing." His thumb finished the job of drying my cheeks. "You had the audacity to knock on the doors of some of the gruffest of my father's tenants, leaving them baskets filled with foods like fairy cakes and berries. You held Charlotte as she panted her last breaths. You taught me to live when all I'd been doing up until that point was hiding. I'm in awe that a woman who lived her life like that could love *me*. And I'm grateful." His voice faltered for the briefest moment before he continued. "I'm so overwhelmingly grateful you do because I don't think anyone else would be brave enough to see my world and then plead to be let in it."

I opened my mouth, but I didn't have any words to say. Not a single one.

David looked at me in concern, led me to the bed, and made me sit. "You're still recovering from your fever." He bent at the waist and dropped another kiss on my forehead. "You should rest."

I reached for his arm, not willing to let him move away from me after everything he'd just said. My mind was reeling, and I wanted nothing more than to touch him, hold him, and show him how deeply his words had seared my soul. Before he had the chance to stand up straight, I placed a hand on his forehead, still feeling as though I needed an excuse to touch him. And he thought I was brave? "You haven't felt sick?" I asked.

He let out a shaky laugh. "Unfortunately not."

I tried to imagine our mad dash into the night with a very sick David. "Unfortunately?"

He nodded. "I recall some very specific promises were made about how you would care for me if I did fall ill."

"Ah." I closed my eyes, remembering the feel of his weight settling onto my bed, his chest warm upon my back. I slid my hand from his forehead to his cheek. "On second thought, you do feel rather warm."

David leaned closer to me, tipping his head so it rested in my hand. "I *have* been feeling under the weather, now that you mention it."

"You should rest," I said, motioning to the empty space on the bed next to where I sat.

He nodded. The bed dipped beneath him, and he turned to face me. He looked the same, his eyes still a soft blue, his skin clear and smooth over the planes of his face, just as it had been before, but I saw him differently. We'd been dancing around issues for weeks, and even though I'd thought I knew him and even thought I'd loved him before, what I felt now was deeper. My love earlier had been selfish. I'd wanted David in my life for the happiness he brought me. Now, more than anything, I wanted to fill his world with joy.

I reached for one of his hands and cupped it in both of mine, tracing the base of his palm and wrist with my fingertips. I could feel his eyes on me, watching my every movement in the dim light.

With a reminder to myself that I was the brave young lady he'd once known, I found the button on his cuff and undid it. Lifting his sleeve slowly, I pulled it past his elbow and found the first scar I'd touched. It was nearer to his elbow than his wrist, and the skin was lighter than the rest of his arm. I slid a finger softly over it. The skin was surprisingly soft. David flinched, but he didn't pull away.

"I'm not sure I can bear you touching them."

I pulled my hand away from his arm and placed it on the perfect skin of his cheek. "David, I saw your chest. At least some of it. They're everywhere. If you don't want me to touch them, I'll understand. But I'm telling you as your wife, I think you should reconsider." He swallowed, and slowly, the sorrow in his face shifted, sloughing away some of his pain until I saw young David again. Not young, as he'd been when we'd first met, but young as I'd first seen him a month ago, striding toward me in the oak tree, dashing and handsome with curiosity and wonder in his eyes.

I cradled his hand once again and lowered my head to the crook of his bare arm until my mouth hovered over that first scar. I looked up at him through my lashes, and after three long, slow breaths, he nodded. I pressed my lips to the spot, and in my hopeful, pathetic way, I prayed my touch might heal a part of him.

At first, every muscle in his arm was tight, but after a moment, the tightness softened. With a slow, steadying breath, he placed a hand on my cheek, then dropped it and lifted his sleeve as high as it would go, letting me into a part of his world he'd shown no one else.

There were three more marks on his inner arm, and when I turned to inspect the outside, I found several more. Some were so faint I could barely make them out, and others left recesses in their wake.

"Oh, David." I couldn't help the strangled use of his name at the sight of them.

I traced each mark with my fingers first, then lowered my mouth to them one by one. His arm trembled at times under my touch, but he never pulled away. When I was certain I'd tended to all of them, I dared a glance up at him.

His eyes were soft and full of wonder. "Are you real?" he asked, echoing those first words he'd murmured to me on the path to the cottage.

I laughed softly. "I think so."

He lifted his other arm expectantly toward me, and with a smile, I undid the buttons on that cuff as well. I resumed my ministrations by first tracing his scars with my fingers.

I pressed my thumb against one and raised his arm to my lips. David put his hand on my shoulder, and I immediately stopped. Had I gone too far? Patience wasn't my best virtue. But if it took months for him to allow me to see all his scars, I would wait for him. He'd waited eight years for me.

When I looked up at him, it wasn't fear or pain I saw in his eyes. It was something else entirely, something that made me think I would not be waiting months to see the rest of his scars. Slowly, his hand went from my shoulder to the cravat I'd tried to loosen earlier.

"Four years ago, I decided I would never marry," his voice had the timbre of a man starting a long story. With a few deft pulls, he slid his cravat from his neck, and the top of his shirt fell open. There were no circles exposed in the perfect v of skin that came into view. His father must have been careful to hide his burns in places no one but the servants would see. "Up until that point, I'd always known it would be incredibly selfish of me to bring a woman I cared for into this family, but for some reason, I held on to hope that a miracle would make it possible." His hand moved to his buttons, and he undid one, then another, never taking his eyes off mine as his scars came into view. There were multitudes, some of them blending into each other and warping the skin around them.

"When I told you vanity and pride were the reasons I never wanted to share my life with a woman, that was true. I didn't want to show anyone what my father had done to me." He undid another button. "I don't think it is a coincidence my father scarred me so severely. There are other ways to cause pain. But this," he touched one of the deeper scars, "would keep me from ever opening myself up to love, would stop me from bearing children who would carry his name, even long after he was gone."

The rage I'd felt in Julia's room reared its ugly head again, threatening to overcome me, but I pushed it down. David wasn't telling me this story to solidify my disgust for his father. He was telling me something else entirely. I reached for a scar that sat just above his heart and rested my hand on it. Beneath all the damage his father had inflicted upon him beat a heart, strong and steady.

David lifted my hand and pressed a kiss to my wrist. "His plan might have worked if I hadn't fallen in love with you before I knew what vanity was."

"You were too young to know what love was then," I said. Because if I didn't, I might always wonder.

"No, I wasn't. As real as my feelings are now, they were real then. I was just at an age where love doesn't usually last. Men tend to fall out of love or in love with someone else in time. I never did. And it wasn't because I was isolated here. I've been to London. I know some of the daughters of other gentlemen in the county. No one has ever touched my heart like you did then, and no one has ever come close to owning it like you do now. If you'll have me, Anna, I will always be yours."

My eyes slid from where he was tenderly holding my wrist back up to his face. He'd asked me only a moment ago if I was real, and I was starting to wonder it myself. David loved me. He always had. All the pain in the world couldn't burrow a hole in the happiness those words seared into my soul.

"I'm going to kiss every single one of them," I said. "His plan will be thwarted, easily and with all my heart."

He placed his hand below my jaw and drew my mouth to his for a kiss so deep I lost myself in it. When he lifted his lips away from mine, I still felt the pull of him, as if my body could not be separated from his and live.

He slid his mouth to my ear. "For the first time ever"—his voice was a rumble in the dim light of the room—"I don't mind how many scars I have." He slid a finger down my cheek, then grabbed the bottom hem of his shirt and pulled it up over his head.

White marks covered his chest and stomach, but I barely noticed them. Not when David was looking at me like he was. He lifted my chin between his thumb and forefinger and held my gaze. "You may get tired of hearing this over the course of our long and illustrious marriage, but you were right."

I was still adjusting to the fact that David was mere inches away from me while his shirt now lay on the floor. "I was?" I struggled to know exactly why he was talking, let alone what on earth I could have been right about.

He nodded. "You asked me to reconsider, and I have." I blinked hard, willing my brain to follow his train of thought. My eyes went to his, and I finally understood. His smile was deep but not filled with hints of laughter—it was filled with promises of something else altogether. "Touch them all."

I swallowed shakily, and then, with his permission completely granted, I put both of my hands on his chest. I took my time, sliding my fingers down his torso, around his waist and up his back. None of his skin was smooth, but the way he shivered under my touch was flawless.

I chose a scar just below his collarbone to kiss first, loving the way his skin trembled under my touch. I worked in a slow and organized pattern, knowing I needed to keep my promise. I had to be careful in the dim light, using not only my eyes but my fingers and mouth to make certain I discovered each one and tended to them with utmost care.

David wasn't as concerned about my precision or my plan, however, because the moment I reached a spot in the middle of his chest, he interrupted me by bending from his sitting position, putting an arm underneath my knees, and lifting me onto his legs. His arms wrapped around my waist and tightened. He mumbled something low that might have been my name, but it was so muffled against my cheek I wasn't certain. And then his mouth was on mine again, kissing me, hungry and deep.

I was lost, my careful considerations scattered like stars across the sky. I fell into him, saving my exactness for another day.

Chapter 27

"She gives me her time and her song and the hope that the world is a better place than I ever thought possible. And I give her interesting rocks. From her face, you would think it was a fair trade."

—David Tate, 1841, Age 14

An hour later, hand in hand, we softly made our way down the corridor. David had tied my possessions and a few of his own inside a shirt and wrapped the sleeves around his neck. It wasn't the most auspicious beginning to our new life together, but it was ours, and I would choose it over and over again, even if I had the opportunity to live a thousand lives.

When we got to Julia's room, Garrett was there, looking appropriately disheveled. The smell of liquor hung heavy in the room.

Garrett was to be our distraction. Despite looking the picture of a very drunk man, his eyes were sharp.

"While wandering the house under the pretense of finding Father's best wines," he said by way of greeting, "I discovered he's set sentries at each of the doors as well as at the stables. When I leave, I should be able to distract those at the front door and in the stables. I'll make enough noise for you to know when I'm leaving. That will be your chance to exit through the library windows."

We nodded. It wasn't a perfect plan, but with Lord Murphy asleep upstairs, it was our best option. Garrett held some sway over his father's men, and without Lord Murphy to contradict him, he should be able to keep one side of the house clear for us to escape.

Garrett embraced Julia first and then David, holding each of them for a long while.

Then he turned to me and placed his hands on my shoulders, pulling me in for a brotherly hug. "It looks as though you are to stay my sister after all, Mrs. Tate."

"I am," I whispered back.

"We are a strange lot, but welcome to the family." Then he was gone, landing a soft blow on David's shoulder as he passed him. The moment he stepped into the corridor, his posture shifted, one shoulder slumping as his step faltered. A low sailor's song drifted from his lips in an uneven cadence, and even after David closed the door, we could hear Garrett's progress down the corridor.

David dropped to the ground, watching under the door for any sign that his father had heard Garrett and followed.

When Garrett's song faded, the house was silent for several minutes. I opened Julia's window and dropped her parcel as well as David's and mine from the window. If we were caught on the way to the library, at least it wouldn't be obvious we were trying to leave.

The clock on the mantel ticked in the quiet until, finally, we heard Garrett demanding someone get his carriage ready. There were several back-and-forth comments, ending with Garrett's slurred, "There is no one of import in this backwater town. I'm continuing to Kent."

David threw open Julia's door, checked for anyone in the corridor, then motioned for us to follow him.

I fought every instinct to hunch over and walk silently on my toes. David reached for my hand, and I grasped his, forcing myself to look calm. We were simply heading to the library in our own home.

We made it down the stairs and into the library without encountering anyone. Garrett had demanded the attention of most of the staff.

Once the library door was closed behind us, we divided, everyone searching the room to make certain we were alone before following David to a large window facing the side garden.

Garrett made another large ruckus, demanding to go to the stables himself and help the groomsmen ready the carriage. We used his disturbance to cover the sounds of the library windows opening. David jumped the few feet to the ground, before helping Julia and me scramble down. Our one tree-climbing incident together had proved useful after all. David then climbed back up and quietly closed the window while we waited in the bushes.

When the rattling of Garrett's carriage and Garrett's loud, slurred yelling covered any noise we would make, we left the darkness of the bushes and started walking toward the Mortensens'.

We didn't speak. David held my hand, and I held Julia's. I looked back to see the beauty that had been my home for weeks. We would never come back. Not as long as Lord Murphy was alive.

David never looked back, and when Julia did, I noticed her eyes only searched for the little plot of land we'd decided to make into an orchard.

We reached the first fork in the walking path. One way led toward town, and the other led to the Mortensens'. Even if Lord Murphy or his servants discovered we'd gone, they would assume we would walk into Breckenridge. Once we turned toward the Mortensens' home, the most pressing part of our escape would be behind us.

I squeezed David's hand, my breath finally coming a bit easier, when we heard a sinister laugh from the trees that lined the path toward town.

I narrowed my eyes, looking for any movement in the dim light when a large body, familiar in the breadth of his shoulders and his significant height, stepped away from a dark tree trunk.

Lord Murphy folded his arms in front of his chest, his legs spread wide. It was too dark to see his face at this distance, but I was certain if I could, it would be set in a sneer.

"Did you think I wouldn't notice the strength of that scotch?"

David's hand tightened over my own, but other than that, he didn't move.

Lord Murphy jerked his head, and two other men stepped out from behind the trees. "Julia, I'm quite disappointed to see you leaving. I thought you, at least, would stay with your dear old father."

Julia didn't say a word.

"The first thing I did after you three so tastelessly left me in the dining room was check which windows had been adjusted to be opened. Once I knew you would leave by way of the library, this was the only path you could have taken without being seen. Everything about your foolhardy plan was extremely simple to deduce. Only one thing has surprised me."

"What is that?" David asked tersely.

"That makeshift bag of yours. You don't even have anything decent to put your wife's things in. I'm sorry, my dear Mrs. Tate. David never was one to care about appearances."

As tightly as David held my hand, I clung to his harder. Why hadn't we thought to pack a pistol? Or a knife? Or anything that could have been used as a weapon.

"We are leaving," David said, a hand on my arm, steadying me.

"Oh, David." Lord Murphy tsk-tsked. "If you could leave by simply informing me of that fact, you would have left this evening after dinner. If you manage to get away from me, I'll raze all those homes you helped improve. The poor tenants—where would they go?"

David's face turned to stone. "If you have no tenants, there will be no one to work the land. You won't be able to keep this place profitable."

Lord Murphy scoffed. "I don't need it to be profitable. The tenants barely make a pittance now, with the new Corn Laws. This property is for status only. I have allowed you and your sister to pretend to run it, but you don't. You never have."

He was trying to get a rise out of David, but David didn't take the bait. I hated the man who'd conditioned my husband to lock away his hurt and bite his tongue.

I, on the other hand, had been raised by a father who hadn't minded my raising my voice on the rare occasion that called for it. "If you don't need someone to run the estate, why do you care if we leave?" I ground out through my teeth.

Lord Murphy closed the distance from twenty feet to fifteen. "That depends."

"On what?" I asked.

"Are you carrying his child?"

I narrowed my eyes at him. "*That* is none of your business."

He smiled, and now that he was closer, I could see it. A dark smile, with his eyes nearly glowing in the moonlight. "I'm afraid it is, you see. Until Garrett finishes sowing his wild oats and settles down, any male child of David's will be considered my heir. And I can't have my heir, whether actually my blood or not, running around the countryside without me there to help raise him. Can I?"

I swallowed hard. There was no chance he was going to go anywhere near any of our children. "I'm not," I said forcefully.

Lord Murphy shrugged his shoulders. "Well then, I don't care what you do so long as you stay away from David. But I would have to keep you in London for several months to be certain. I've learned from experience I can't often trust a woman's word."

My stomach turned at the thought of living with Lord Murphy. That wasn't going to happen. He had no rights over me.

David closed his eyes. "You will not touch my wife, nor will you take her from me. Nothing about my blood is questionable, and you insult our mother every time you insinuate that."

Lord Murphy sneered. "That is wishful thinking on your part."

"No, Father, it's not. No one would wish to be your son."

Lord Murphy's face went dark, his mouth twisted with rage. "She hated me by the time you were born."

David was slowly trying to put me behind him as he spoke. "That doesn't mean I'm another man's child."

Lord Murphy spat on the ground. "Have you looked in a mirror? You're half a foot shorter than either me or your brother."

Julia dropped my hand and stepped forward. "You didn't give him enough food." Her voice was low and steady, and something about its quality made me think, perhaps, she was the most dangerous person on this path. "And you were spouting off just as much nonsense about his birth before he ever reached his final height. Your mind distorts everything, but that doesn't make it true," she sneered. "You can't slowly murder someone and then wonder why they are dying."

Lord Murphy's hands fisted, his eyes flashing. "You never would have talked to me like that if David hadn't come along and spoiled everything. You were my treasure, my darling girl, and he has gone and ruined that by making you choose sides. I should have beaten your mother badly enough that he wouldn't have been born. I shouldn't have allowed her to give birth when I didn't trust her." His eyes slid to me. "It is a mistake I won't make twice. Johnny, Bert, grab my children and take them back to Tate Hall. I'll take care of the bride."

Lord Murphy strode forward like a man possessed. David thrust me behind him in one swift movement. Instead of discouraging Lord

Murphy, a strange light flared on the viscount's face, cold and furious as he turned on his son.

He reached into his coat and drew a knife, the blade flashing in the moonlight. "You won't let me take her?" he hissed. "Well then, it is never too late to rid the world of a problem that never should have been allowed to live in the first place." His face was an inhuman snarl. With a growl, he lunged forward.

A gunshot shattered the night.

One of Lord Murphy's legs snapped backward, and his body pitched sideways to the ground as he released a bellowing curse.

I grabbed my ringing ear and turned to see Julia standing tall and unshaken, an American revolver in her hand. She lifted the gun from Lord Murphy to aim at the two stunned men standing behind him.

She narrowed her eyes at them, ignoring her father's moans. "As my father likes to say, this is a family matter. You needn't get involved." Both men held still, arms slowly lifting in the air. "If he lives, he will kill you. He wouldn't want a story spread about how his daughter shot him."

"I would not kill you, you idiots." Lord Murphy's words were punctuated by pain as he held his leg in his hands. "Don't listen to her. She doesn't have the nerve to shoot you. Grab her gun."

But the look on Julia's face and the fact that she *had* just shot someone must have made the men falter.

"I don't want to shoot you," Julia said, her voice steady. "But I will. If you know anything about our family, you would be idiots not to believe me. Leave now, and I will let you go. That is more than you will get from my father."

The man on the left took a step toward Tate Hall first, shifting backward as he kept his eyes on Julia and the revolver. The other followed his lead almost immediately, most likely not wanting to be the easier target.

Lord Murphy cursed loudly again, pressing hard against the wound in his thigh. "Wait . . ." Lord Murphy called from the ground. "If you fetch the doctor, I won't hunt you down."

It was a much better order than he'd given them earlier, and the two men nodded, seemingly happy to take the chance to leave the unfolding drama.

"No," David said, and the men stopped again. "Don't fetch the doctor."

Lord Murphy hissed. "I'm the one paying them, you ingrate."

"We all know you won't be paying them anymore." He turned to Julia. "Put the gun back on them," David said. Julia nodded and trained the gun on them once again. "We will let those men go and fetch James once we've reached an agreement. The first one is this: You are never to speak to my wife again."

"Or me," Julia added.

Lord Murphy pressed down on his wound, blood seeping through his pant leg and onto the ground. "I've never hurt you, Julia."

"You never burned me, but you hurt me. You hurt me enough that I'm not certain I won't shoot you again. This time with better aim. It would be a mercy to our family to have you gone." Julia's voice was like granite.

Lord Murphy gritted his teeth, his eyes dulling after Julia's words. Had he really thought he could retain her love after all he had done? The man was sick.

With a groan that seemed to imply he felt he was being treated unfairly, Lord Murphy tore his eyes from his daughter and focused on David. "I'll promise never to see the two of you again if you promise you won't have children. I can't have tainted blood in line for my title."

"No," David said. "You will not dictate when or how many children we have. If we do have children, we don't want them anywhere near you. If you try to find us, we will bring them to London and set them as heirs. We will make certain everyone knows exactly who they are. But if you leave us alone, we will change our name and disappear."

Lord Murphy pushed harder on his wound, a dark pool was starting to form under his leg. "And if I don't agree to this plan?"

"I suppose you will have to hope that bleeding stops on its own, because we are leaving one way or another." David motioned to the two men Julia had her revolver trained on. "Those two men are your only chance at getting James here to treat you, and we are happy to keep them here, delaying the doctor, until you do finally agree."

Lord Murphy swore loudly, banged his fist on the ground, and then quieted. Silence fell over the path. Finally, he nodded. "I'd rather never look upon you again anyway. We have an agreement. Thank the heavens, I have one child who has not squandered the life I've given him."

Julia lowered her gun, and the men waited until she nodded to leave. The sound of their boots pounding down the path grew softer until all we could hear was Lord Murphy's groaning. Julia still held the gun, and she was the first of the three of us to move. She strode forward, never taking her eyes off Lord Murphy. It took David and me several seconds to realize exactly what she was planning, but when it dawned on us, David dashed forward, while I sank to the ground. As Julia had said, this was a family matter.

If Julia wanted to shoot her father again, I wasn't going to stop her. Not after what he'd done to David and what he'd threatened to do to our future children.

David reached Julia just as she put a foot on her father's chest and pushed him flat onto the ground, the revolver pointed directly at his heart.

David put a hand on her arm but didn't push it away from its target. "Don't do it, Julia," he said softly.

For the first time since the gun had come out, a crack formed in Julia's cold countenance, and her hand trembled. "I should. I think it's the right thing to do."

David shook his head. "No, it isn't."

Julia whipped her face toward him. "You think he deserves to live?"

David's shoulders slumped, and he moved his hand from her arm. "I don't have an answer for that, but I know you don't deserve to have him take one more thing from you."

Lord Murphy spat up at David. "You're so weak. Even now. I tried to make you tougher, but—" Julia pressed her foot down harder on his chest, his grunt of pain cutting off his sentence.

"Those words do not make me want to shoot you less," she said with an edge of madness in her tone.

The sound of pounding hooves came from the house, but when we glanced up, the horses were headed away from Tate Hall. It looked as though Lord Murphy's men were leaving.

"Let's go." David motioned not to the house but to our original route.

Lord Murphy groaned. "You're going to leave me here? Bleeding?"

David's face had gone as cold as Julia's. "I assume your friends will be clear in their directions to James. He can help you back to the house."

"One man?" Lord Murphy looked small curled on the ground, his eyes measuring the distance to Tate Hall.

David nodded. "He won't be able to carry you, so you may have to walk. A bit of pain will toughen you up."

David came back to me and brushed the hair away from my face. "Are you well enough to continue on?"

I nodded, and David put his arm around me, helping me stand. Julia came up behind him, her gun finally lowered.

She was the only one with enough foresight to bring a weapon, and I dashed to her side and threw my arms around her. "Thank you, Julia."

Julia bit her lip and looked as if she were about to cry. She held back for a moment before a soft laugh escaped her throat. "For shooting my father?"

Her laughter, slight as it was, brought a strange kind of relief, and one burst of laughter escaped my mouth. "For bringing the gun. I wish I would have thought of it."

"Oh, no. No one but a member of the Tate family should be allowed to shoot him."

"But I am a member of the Tate family."

This time when Julia laughed, it was deep, from her gut. "So you are. Next time, I'll let you shoot him."

David shook his head and took our hands. "No one else is shooting him. We need to go."

But as we walked away, Lord Murphy slumped to the side in a faint. We all paused.

"Is he acting?" I asked.

David blew out a frustrated puff of air. "I wouldn't put it past him."

I glanced at Lord Murphy for any signs of pretense, but I couldn't tell. "Should we check?"

Julia shook her head. "I'm not going near him, not unless David changes his mind and wants me to kill him."

In the end, we found a place to sit and listened for the sound of hooves. Ten minutes later, we could hear them galloping up the drive and turning down the path.

Dr. Clarke pulled his horse to a stop roughly five feet away from us. He jumped down and surveyed the scene. Lord Murphy looked as good as dead on the ground, and we all sat away from him, Julia with a gun in her hand.

Dr. Clarke watched Lord Murphy for several seconds, most likely doing the same thing we'd done over and over during the passing minutes. Watching for the rise and fall of his chest. After he found it, he ignored him and stepped toward us.

He pasted a smile on his face as if this were a social call. "I would have been here sooner, but I heard it was Lord Murphy who'd been shot."

David snorted, and Julia let out a quiet sob of relief.

Dr. Clarke walked gently toward her and held out his hand for the revolver. "May I?" he asked.

Julia practically tossed it to him, handle first, at least, with the barrel pointing down.

Dr. Clarke pulled the bullets out of the gun and placed them in his pocket. He returned to his horse and took his doctor's kit out of a bag on his saddle. With a march slow enough to mark him as a man in no hurry to treat Lord Murphy, he stepped over to the man's prone form and tied a tourniquet just below Lord Murphy's hip. Then he started prodding the wound to assess the damage.

Lord Murphy stirred, swatting at Dr. Clarke's hands and cursing.

"Lord Murphy," Dr. Clarke barked at him. "It looks as though you've been in a hunting accident. We need to get you back to Tate Hall."

Lord Murphy cursed louder. "A hunting accident?" His breath was ragged, but he drew some kind of strength from his anger at Dr. Clarke. "What kind of idiotic doctor are you? It's the middle of the night."

"I don't pretend to understand the things the nobility do to pass the time, sir. I only treat wounds. And I cannot think of any other explanation for a bullet to be in your thigh, except a hunting accident."

Lord Murphy spat on the ground and looked at Julia, his thin lips set in a straight line. "We are a strange lot."

Julia made a noise at the back of her throat, almost as if she were going to start laughing, but Dr. Clarke whipped his head in her direction and gave her a look of ferocious censure. She closed her eyes and stopped whatever emotion had been hurtling to the surface.

Dr. Clarke turned to David. "Will you help me get him on my horse?"

"We were just leaving," David said. Somewhere over the past few minutes, we had all become very comfortable with the idea of never being anywhere near Lord Murphy again.

Dr. Clarke understood and didn't press David further. He took a deep breath and put an arm under Lord Murphy's back. Lord Murphy let out a long string of curses, and Dr. Clarke returned nearly as many, challenging him to rise to the occasion.

With a sigh, David pushed himself to his feet and joined his friend, grabbing the other side of his father's back, hefting him to his feet. They slowly made their way to Dr. Clarke's horse.

"You couldn't have brought your horse any closer?" Lord Murphy said through gritted teeth.

Through sheer force, they managed to get Lord Murphy into Dr. Clarke's saddle. "Get me away from here," Lord Murphy growled.

"I will," Dr. Clarke said. "But now that you are settled, I need to look over everyone else to make certain there are no other injuries. If you can't wait for me, you can take my horse to Tate Hall on your own."

"There are no other injuries," Lord Murphy said with another curse, but Dr. Clarke silenced him with a glance that was nigh unto murderous. Lord Murphy's cursing stopped. Apparently, knowing his life would be in Dr. Clarke's hands made him capable of listening.

Lord Murphy gave each of his children a withering glance and turned the horse toward the house.

David and Dr. Clarke returned to Julia and me. Julia's eyes were downcast, her hands were starting to shake. Her laughter from earlier had fled.

Dr. Clarke knelt in front of her, put a hand under her chin, and lifted her face. He studied her eyes, then took off his gloves and put a hand on her wrist, feeling her pulse.

"You may be in shock," he said softly.

"No." She shook her head. "I am well."

Dr. Clarke turned to David. "Are you certain you want to leave tonight?"

"We aren't going far," David answered. "At least, not tonight."

"Will you tell me where you are going?"

David shook his head. "No."

Dr. Clarke stood, put his arms around David, and held him close for a moment. Then he slapped one hand hard on David's back. "Good," he said. "It is unfortunate for me to lose a friend, of course. But I'm very happy for you."

Dr. Clarke turned to me, took my hand, and kissed my knuckles. "Mrs. Tate, I wish you a long and happy life." He held my gaze for a moment before turning to Julia. "And, Julia." He dropped my hand and took hers in a firm grip. "Get in a bed and sleep as soon as you can."

Julia nodded.

Dr. Clarke hit his hands on the side of his legs, cleared his throat and started his walk back to Tate Hall.

This time, Julia and David both took their time looking over the house, the lands, and the man walking slowly away from them before turning around and walking away from it all.

David took my hand in his, and I dropped my head onto his shoulder. He put his other arm around Julia, and the three of us walked away, bedraggled and tired. David kicked a stone, and it rolled down the path, bouncing and jumping as it hit bumps and divots. I sighed softly, and then David's voice, low and melodic, broke the quiet of the evening with the first words to the hymn "Rock of Ages."

I basked in the sound of it for several bars and then lifted my voice to join him.

By the time Julia joined in, David and I had left our soft voices behind, and we belted the song into the night.

When we finally reached the Mortensens' home, Maren swung open the door, took one look at us, and put her hands on her hips.

"I could hear the three of you for the past five minutes coming down the path. It takes a lot of nerve singing out like that this late at night."

David laughed. "Nerve is all we have left, Maren. Let us have it."

"Did I hear a shot earlier?" she asked as we walked in the door.

I nodded. "Lord Murphy was in a hunting accident."

Maren's eyes widened, and she looked at the path behind us. "Is he . . . dead?" she asked.

Julia shook her head. "No, David wouldn't let me kill him."

Maren blinked and looked back and forth between the two siblings. "Will he be coming here tonight? Is my family safe?"

"He won't be coming," David responded. "He is in no condition to look for us tonight, and we will be long gone before he is."

Maren visibly relaxed and then motioned for us to sit in the chairs by the fire. She'd laid out four beds on the floor, but Mama wasn't in any of them.

"My mother is here, isn't she?" I asked.

"Yes," Maren said quietly, not wanting to wake anyone. She looked down at the four beds. "Mr. Garrett won't be joining you?"

"No," David said. "He's gone to Kent."

"What are you going to do?" she asked.

David took my hand in his and kissed it, his gaze steady and full of promise. "We are going to be happy," he said.

We didn't know what the path ahead looked like, but we would make it a good one. When problems arose, whether they came from Lord Murphy or any other source, we would solve them together.

And if there was a problem we couldn't solve, well then, I suppose I would just have to get Julia to shoot it.

Epilogue

"To David,

Now that you are old enough to write, I wanted you to have this. Everyone should have a secret place to write out their dreams and their fears. Keep it hidden. You are the brightest part of my day—a joy to behold—and someday we will find a way to make your life so sweet the bitter will be washed away.

With all the love of my heart,

Mother"

—Celeste Tate, 1836, Age 29

David leaned forward against the back of the sofa, where I sat in our Lincolnshire cottage. His arms were draped around my shoulders, his shirtsleeves rolled up to his elbows. Several of his scars showed, but neither of us worried about anyone seeing them anymore. I lifted each page of the newspaper, searching the headlines for the story David wanted me to find.

"Could you give me a clue, at least?" I begged. "Which section of the newspaper should I be looking in?"

"Hmm . . ." David rubbed his cheek against mine, the soft stubble making me tuck my chin into my shoulder with a shiver. It was such a distraction, having a husband. "But I'm so enjoying the anticipation."

"Mama and Julia will be back from their shopping trip in less than an hour. Don't you think there are better ways we could be making use of our time than having me read the entire paper?"

David huffed and nipped softly at my ear. "You always know exactly how to get what you want." He swatted my hands away from the paper and quickly pulled down the pages until he found the one he wanted.

"The financial section?" I asked. What would be of interest to me in the financial section?

"There is a business for sale that might interest you."

A business? David and I were happy here in Lincolnshire, going by the names of Mr. and Mrs. Ford. We'd made a life here quicker than I'd ever thought possible. Did he want a change already? If he did, I would follow him.

"Do you want to buy a business? I thought you enjoyed working as a steward for Lord Pippen."

"I do enjoy working for Lord Pippen, and I don't have any desire to buy this business, but if *you* want us to buy it, I would take some perverse pleasure in it."

I turned my neck to get a better look at him. That sounded very unlike my husband. He sighed and came around to sit next to me on the sofa, pointing to the exact article he wanted me to read.

Only it wasn't an article. It was a notice.

HABERDASHERY AND BUTCHERY FOR SALE
CONTACT BRADLY GOODWIN
SILVERFORK, DERBYSHIRE

"Bradly Goodwin? Who is he? He doesn't own those stores. Mr. Green does."

"Ah." David tapped the side of his nose. "But Bradly Goodwin is his solicitor. Someone recently had reason to look into Mr. Green's books, and it turns out your bills were not the only ones he manipulated."

I turned to him. "Mr. Rawlings?"

He nodded.

I let my head fall back and rest on the sofa. I hadn't bothered to think about Mr. Green for the six months we'd lived in Lincolnshire. That part of my life seemed so far away. But if he was taking advantage of the people of Silverfork, I was extremely grateful my father's solicitor had asked questions instead of simply paying Mr. Green's bill when I'd sent it to him.

"He's going to be ruined," I said more to myself than anyone else.

David nodded.

I turned to David with a smile tugging at my lips. "So it's a good thing I didn't marry him after all." I heaved a sigh. "What a relief."

His smile dropped. "Pardon me?" he said, his head tipping dangerously toward me.

I shrugged my shoulders. "I could have married him, you know. A woman often wonders if she made the right choice." I pointed to the paper. "Now I know. Thank you for showing me this. You've set my mind at ease."

A growl rumbled up from David's chest. He put his hands on my hips and pulled me toward him. I squeaked in protest as my head dropped to the seat of the sofa. David hovered over me, walking his hands up the cushion until he paused with his arms at my sides. His face loomed over me, and in his eyes was a challenge. "How long did you say it would be before your mother and Julia return?"

"Probably about forty minutes," I said, sinking deeper into the cushions and running a hand up David's arm. "Why do you ask?"

He narrowed his eyes at me. "Because I want to know precisely how much time I have to prove to you that you ended up with the right husband."

I pulled my lower lip into my mouth, trying to hide a smile, then cocked my head to the side. "That sounds like a daunting task. Will forty minutes be enough time?"

"No," he replied. "But it will be a start."

"I'm a very busy woman." I furrowed my eyebrows in mock concern. "Exactly how much more will you need?"

David brought his mouth next to my ear, and I shivered as his weight settled over me. "All of it," he replied.

I smiled, wrapped my arms around him, and caught his mouth with my own, because that was precisely the amount of my time I wanted to give him.

Sometimes in life, you need one person who sees you better than you see yourself. One person to hold you up. One person to love you. One fervent light in an otherwise dark world by which you can find your way. And that one person, for me, was David.

Acknowledgments

Every book with my name on it owes its nuance, clean timelines, and polish to so many others who have helped me over the course of making it the best it can be. I'm very grateful to the women who took time out of their very busy schedules to read this book in its earlier form, and every single one of them made this book better. Thank you, Anneka Walker, Heidi Kimball, Kasey Stockton, Lisa Kendrick, McKenzie Ray, Mandy Biesinger, Adrienne Everitt, and Kim Dubios! All of you are amazing and insightful, and I'm grateful to also call you friends.

From the cover to the editing to the marketing, there is a whole team at Shadow Mountain who have brought this book from a manuscript to the beautiful novel it is today. Thank you, Samantha Millburn, Amy Parker, Troy Butcher, Nikki Sue Larkin, Haley Haskins, Tasha Bradford, Lehi Quiroz, Brianna Cornell, Breanna Anderl, Halle Ballingham, Callie Hansen, Heidi Taylor Gordon, Brooke Groneman, Amy Nielson, and Alison Nelson.

Thank you to my family. Writing a book is a huge undertaking, and they not only support me but are also excited for me, and that kind of love is what I hope all my characters find.

And none of my books would have ever made it to the shelves without the encouragement and love of my Heavenly Father. Thank you for leading me down this path. I hope to walk it with grace and humility.

Discussion Questions

1. **Childhood Bonds**: How did Anna's and David's shared childhood influence their relationship as adults? Did their age difference affect how they viewed each other then versus now?

2. **Shifting Power Dynamics**: In what ways do the roles of protector and protected shift between Anna and David throughout the story?

3. **Depiction of Trauma**: How does David's childhood abuse affect his sense of self and his ability to form close relationships?

4. **Anna's Growth Arc**: At the beginning of the novel, Anna feels as if she is "on the shelf" because of her age and her situation. How does she evolve by the end?

5. **David's Internal Conflict**: What do you think is the real reason David hesitates to make the marriage permanent? Is it truly fear of his father or something deeper?

6. **The Father's Shadow**: Even though David's father doesn't appear frequently, his presence is felt throughout the book. How does this unseen character drive the plot?

7. **Julia's Trauma**: How does Julia's trauma manifest differently than David's? Do you think the siblings have found peace, or are they still in survival mode?

8. **Anna's Inheritance**: How does the inheritance timeline create tension in the story? What does it say about women's legal and financial agency during this era?

9. **Parental Expectations and Control**: How are parents depicted in the novel? How do they shape Anna's and David's lives, both in support and in harm?

10. **Romantic Tropes**: This book features a fake-engagement trope. How does it compare to other stories you've read with the same setup? What makes this one unique?

11. **Setting as Character**: How does the setting of 1840s England contribute to the story? Could this story be told in another time period?

12. **Themes of Protection**: Several characters attempt to protect others (David protecting Anna, Garrett protecting David and Julia, Dr. Clarke protecting the Tate siblings). How is protection shown as both noble and problematic?

13. **Healing Through Love**: Do you believe David and Anna genuinely help each other heal? If so, how?

14. **Emotional Honesty**: What scenes stood out to you as emotionally raw or truthful? Did any moments surprise you?

15. **The Power of Memory**: David idealizes Anna because of her brightness in his dark childhood. How do our memories of others shape our adult relationships?

16. **Social Pressure**: How does societal pressure around marriage, status, and age shape the choices of the characters?

17. **Exploring Theme**: What central themes did you notice throughout the novel, and how were they developed through the characters' journeys and choices? Which theme resonated with you most, and why?

Ready to find your next romance?

Let us help.

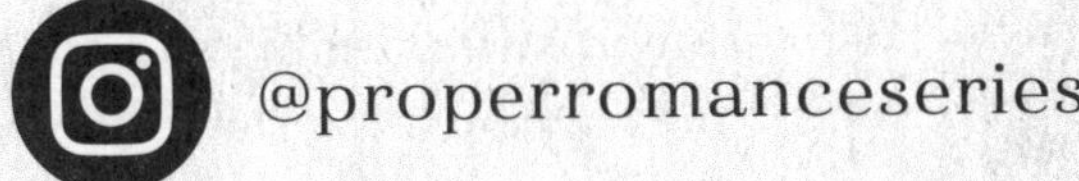

The Proper Romance series is a collection of sweet romance novels from award-winning authors, with strong heroines and handsome heroes.

About the Author

Photo by Evelyn Hornbarger

ESTHER HATCH grew up on a cherry orchard in rural Utah. After high school, she alternated living in Russia to teach children English and attending Brigham Young University to earn a degree in archaeology. She began writing when one of her favorite authors invited her to join a critique group. The only catch was she had to be a writer. Not one to be left out of an opportunity to socialize and try something new, Esther started on her first novel that week.

Learn more about Esther at estherhatch.com and follow her on social media.

Facebook: Author Esther Hatch

Instagram: @AuthorEstherHatch